P9-DXK-073

PRAISE FOR
PATRICIA RICE

Impossible Dreams
"Hours of reading delight."
—*Romantic Times*

Blue Clouds
"Totally engrossing . . . Fast moving, great characters, suspense and love—a must read!"
—*The Literary Times*

"Snares the reader right from the start."
—*Library Journal*

Garden of Dreams
"Ms. Rice's debut into contemporary is a huge success with this magnificent novel. Her characters are charming, and the reader will fall in love with every one of them. The plot is refreshingly delightful and she throws in a few curves that add to the fun. A definite joy to read."
—*Rendezvous*

Also by Patricia Rice

IMPOSSIBLE DREAMS
NOBODY'S ANGEL
VOLCANO
GARDEN OF DREAMS
BLUE CLOUDS

Books published by The Ballantine Publishing Group
are available at quantity discounts on bulk purchases
for premium, educational, fund-raising, and special
sales use. For details, please call 1-800-733-3000.

ALMOST PERFECT

Patricia Rice

IVY BOOKS • NEW YORK

Sale of this book without a cover may be unauthorized. If this book is coverless, it may have been reported to the publisher as "unsold or destroyed" and neither the author nor the publisher may have received payment for it.

This book contains an excerpt from the forthcoming paperback edition of *Must Be Magic* by Patricia Rice. This excerpt has been set for this edition only and may not reflect the final content of the forthcoming edition.

An Ivy Book
Published by The Ballantine Publishing Group
Copyright © 2002 by Patricia Rice
Excerpt from *Must Be Magic* © 2002 by Patricia Rice.

All rights reserved under International and Pan-American Copyright Conventions. Published in the United States by The Ballantine Publishing Group, a division of Random House, Inc., New York, and simultaneously in Canada by Random House of Canada Limited, Toronto.

Ivy is a registered trademark and the Ivy colophon is a trademark of Random House, Inc.

www.ballantinebooks.com

ISBN 0-449-00603-4

Manufactured in the United States of America

First Edition: March 2002

OPM   10   9   8   7   6   5   4   3   2   1

To Varney,
the obnoxious class clown who didn't *inspire this story.*
May your soul find laughter wherever you are.

ACKNOWLEDGMENTS

Thanks to Roberta Tepper of the Mecklenburg DA's office for explaining the ins and outs of jail terms, federal supervision, and parole, and for keeping me from making major errors. Any that I do make are not her fault and could be entirely intentional on my part!

Kudos also to Katherine Bernardi and her obsessive-compulsiveness. I'll never look another "that" in the face again.

And to my brainstorming group—where would I be without your peacocks and logic?

Last, but very definitely not least, my undying gratitude to Mary Jo Putney for telling me I definitely have a book here!

⁂ ONE ⁂

I am a rotten person.

Biting her lip, Cleo Alyssum painstakingly printed this fact into her journal. She thought the whole idea of a journal of emotions about as silly as it got, but if the counselor wanted honesty, that's what he would get.

She would do anything to transform herself into the kind of mother Matty needed. *Anything.*

Of course, that's how she'd got into this situation in the first place. Sitting back in her desk chair, she gazed out the sagging windowpanes of the old house she was restoring. She missed Matty so desperately, her teeth ached, but the court had set December as the deadline for his return—provided she danced to the steps the counselor called.

Matty needed security and stability, they said, and her sister provided it.

She'd tried suburban life with Maya, but she just couldn't hack it. Trouble found her too easily in crowds. Out here on the island she could get her head together without too many people in her face. She was far less apt to jeopardize Matty's return if she stayed away from people.

These last few years she'd learned to restore old buildings, turning decrepit dumps into useful, viable businesses and homes, and she loved the satisfaction of

1

seeing the visible results of her hard work. Too bad the difference she was supposed to be making in herself wasn't as obvious.

The opportunity to buy a small-town hardware store had opened up just as she'd run out of buildings to restore, and at the time, it had seemed ideal. She knew the business inside and out, loved the isolation of the South Carolina coast, and when she'd found this run-down island farmhouse for a steal, she'd known she'd found a home. The beach cottage down by the shore might be beyond hope, but she hadn't given up on it yet. Maya and the kids might visit more often if she could fix it up. In the meantime, she was diligently turning the main house into the home she'd never known. She hoped.

If she could only convince her federal supervisor she was a fine, upstanding citizen, she'd be free and clear soon, and almost in a normal world for the first time in her life.

Having a job she could do without hassles from any boss, and a home where she could lock the doors against the world, she thought she finally had a chance of living a civilized life. She wasn't doing this for the feds, though. Matty deserved a sane mother, and she was doing her best, if the process didn't kill her first. At least now when he visited on weekends, she could give him her entire attention, and he seemed to be blossoming into a new kid with the change. Even Maya had noted how much happier he was.

Cleo ran her fingers through her stubby hair and returned to staring at the almost empty page of the notebook. She didn't think she was capable of verbalizing all her conflicting emotions about her sister. Maya could have written an entire essay on how Cleo felt about her. Cleo would rather hammer nails.

If she compared her mothering skills to Perfect Maya's, she was destined for failure.

The muffled noise of a car engine diverted her attention. A fresh breeze off the ocean blew through the windows in the back of the house, but the only things coming through the floor-to-ceiling front windows were flies. Thickets of spindly pines, palmettos, and wax myrtle prevented her from seeing the driveway entrance or the rough shell road beyond.

She didn't encourage visitors and wasn't expecting anyone. A lost tourist would turn around soon enough.

She returned to the blank page of her journal and printed: *People are pains in the a . . .* She struck out the "a" and substituted "butt."

She crinkled her nose at the result. One word probably wasn't any more polite than the other.

The smooth hum of the car's powerful engine hesitated, and Cleo waited for the music of it backing up and turning around. Someone took good care of their machine. She couldn't hear a single piston out of sync.

She rolled her eyes as the obtuse visitor gunned the engine and roared past the four-foot blinking NO TRESPASSING sign. One would think a message that large would be taken seriously, but tourists determined to reach a secluded beach were nearly unstoppable.

"Nearly" was the operative word here.

Biting her bottom lip again, Cleo reread her two-line entry. She had to go into town and open the store shortly. She didn't have time for detailed expositions, if that's what the shrink wanted. It looked to her like a few good strong sentences ought to be sufficient.

Adding *Men are the root of all evil* struck her as funny, but she supposed a male counselor wouldn't appreciate it. She left it there anyway. The counselor had said he wanted honesty. Of course, she was probably sabotaging all her efforts. She'd had enough therapy to acknowledge her self-destructive tendencies. Now, if she'd only *apply* that knowledge . . .

She lifted her pen and waited for the car engine to reach the next turn in the half-mile-long lane. The sound of waves crashing in the distance almost drowned out the wicked screech of her mechanical witch. Still, she heard the car tires squeal as they braked. The battery-operated strobe light was particularly effective at keeping teenagers from turning this into a lovers' lane at night. During the day, well . . .

She shrugged and capped the pen. That was enough introspection for one day. The counselor ought to know she was a mucked-up mess. She shouldn't have to lay it out in terms a first-grader could understand. Another thought occurred to her, and she grabbed the pen again.

Baring my soul is not my style.

There. That ought to be letting it out enough for one day.

Her head shot up as the car engine drew closer, evidently bypassing the scowling witch. Stupid bastard. What was she supposed to do, dump a load of pig turds on him to get the message across? That might work if they were driving a convertible.

They usually were.

She despised the arrogant, self-confident yuppie asses who thought the whole world was their oyster. Didn't "Private Property" mean anything to them?

Apparently not. The car engine zoomed right past the pop-up sign she'd rigged in the middle of the lane. Forgetting to turn off the system before she'd left for work, she'd driven around the sign one too many times herself, and the dirt bypass was clearly visible. She'd plant a palmetto there tomorrow.

Slamming the notebook into her desk drawer, she picked up her purse and donned her sunglasses. She hadn't quite perfected the mechanism to shut the swinging post barrier on the access road. She hated the idea of erecting a fence across there. The moron would simply have to drown if he insisted on using her beach. A bad undertow past the jetty made this a dangerous strip for swimming, but she supposed the No Swimming signs wouldn't stop the nematode either.

Maybe she could rig a siren to a motion detector. There wasn't any law out here for it to summon, but tourists wouldn't know that.

Pulling out her truck keys, she almost didn't hear the purr of the engine turning into her drive, but the shriek of a hidden peacock warned of the intrusion.

Damn. Did the jerk think the house deserted? Admittedly, she hadn't bothered painting the weathered gray boards and the sagging shutters, but she kind of thought them picturesque. And it wasn't as if she'd not littered the place with warning signs. If the town council insisted on encouraging film crews to work here, she'd be prepared to keep them out. She hadn't traveled an entire continent to have that California lifestyle follow her.

She waited as the barking guard dog yapped through its entire routine. A real dog would scare the peacocks, but the tape recording was usually effective. Amazing how many people were frightened of barking dogs. The mailman had quit delivering to the door after he'd heard it.

Cleo sighed as the driver shut off the car engine instead of turning around. Determined suckers. Only Maya and Axell ever got this far past her guardians. She could slip out the back way, but curiosity riveted her to the window. Standing far enough back not to be seen, she couldn't wait to see how her intrepid guest reacted to her burglar alert system.

A pair of long-legged, crisply ironed khakis appeared beneath the porch overhang. A man. She should have known. Men had to prove themselves by showing no fear. It didn't seem to matter if they showed no intelligence while they were at it.

The lean torso decked in a tight black polo appeared next. She was sick of looking at fat slugs with pooching white bellies and hairy, sunken chests cluttering the view from the beach. At least this ape strode tall and straight and . . .

My, my. She stopped chewing a hangnail to relish the loose-limbed swing of wide shoulders and a corded throat topped by an angular face with more character than prettiness. He was all length—arms, legs, nose, neck—but they all fit together in a casual sort of package. His hands were in his pockets as he gazed up at her mildly eccentric porch, so she couldn't see his fingers, but she'd bet they were a piano teacher's dream.

Tousled sable hair fell across a tanned brow, and she was almost sorry she'd left the security system on. If he was selling insurance, she wouldn't mind listening to his pitch just to hear what came out of a package like that.

The aviator sunglasses were a downright sexy trim for this parcel.

"*You are under alert!*" the loudspeaker blared as soon as the intruder hit the first porch step. She'd used an army drill sergeant for that recording. It would scare the pants off any normal person. This one halted, and removed his sunglasses now that he was in shade, but his gaze traced the bellowing voice with curiosity, not fear.

"*Turn back now. This is your only warning!*"

Cleo bit back a sigh of exasperation as the jerk bent over to examine the step for wires. Did he think her an idiot to put wires where someone could cut them?

"*Your location has been verified, and you are now under surveillance. Put up your hands, or we'll shoot.*"

The man straightened and seemed to be whistling as

he craned his neck and surveyed the underside of the covered porch from the step.

Shaking her head, Cleo reached for the "off" switch, but she waited for his reaction to the final performance. Sure enough, her visitor disregarded the warning and fearlessly breached the porch gate. Sirens screamed, strobe lights flared, and a fedora-hatted skeleton dropped down between him and the front door.

Jared McCloud came eyeball to eye socket with a six-foot bag of bones baring a smirk through a cigar clamped between its teeth. He'd been given enough warning to expect it, but he couldn't help grinning in appreciation of the coup de grâce. At night, with the shrieking siren and strobes, it would have any potential thief shitting his pants.

"Pleased to meecha, Burt," he murmured, inspecting the wires that must have held the freak to the porch roof. He didn't know anything about mechanics, but he knew an overactive imagination when he saw one. "Guess this means the old witch isn't at home."

"Guess it means the old witch is on her way out."

Jared blinked at the apparition in the doorway. He hadn't heard the door open. Shouldn't the hinges of a place like this creak eerily?

He smiled in satisfaction at the full impact of the skeleton's creator as she emerged from shadows. Far from being an old witch, she was his newest dream of perfection. Not too tall or too short, but sturdy, she packed a lot of punch into a compact, sexy bundle. Her knee-length man's checked flannel shirt effectively disguised the best of her curves, but he loved exploration and discovery even more than having it all laid out for him.

Generally, women didn't appreciate being ogled, so he

respectfully raised his gaze to absorb the rest of the glorious sight. Rumpled short hair revealed roots of auburn beneath a mousy brown dye job. Tinted half glasses attempted to hide eyes of a spectacular green—not contacts, either. He could see specks of brown in them.

He thought he was in love.

Of course, he'd been in love last week and the week before, and mostly it was a major distraction he didn't need right now. If he didn't finish the piece of idiocy they called a screenplay by December first, he'd be in breach of contract. Another failure and his name would be mud, even if the last failure was more the fault of death-by-committee than anything he'd done.

His agent was already antsy over the cancellation of the comic strip by some backwoods string of newsrags claiming his teenage nerds had become "tiresome." It had been quite a few years since he'd been a teenager, but from his current outlook, that's what teenagers were—tiresome.

None of that seemed relevant to the moment. "Name's Jared McCloud." He smiled with as much charm as he could summon. Maybe this was a young relative of the old witch the kids had warned him about. "I'm looking for Cleo Alyssum."

"She's not here."

She said that so promptly, Jared figured this had to be her. Well, well. Curiouser and curiouser.

He produced a business card from his pocket with his hotel phone number scratched on the back. "I've been told Miss Alyssum is owner of the beach property back of here, and I'm interested in leasing it. I'm prepared to make a generous offer." From the look of this run-down sprawling plantation-era farmhouse, she could use the cash.

She took the card and dropped it into her shirt pocket.

"She doesn't like neighbors." Turning around, she shut and locked the peeling white door, and did something that reeled the skeleton upward like a collapsing party favor.

"Your car's blocking my drive," she said curtly as he moved aside to let her pass. "And you're trespassing, in case you didn't notice."

Not a smile, not a dimple, not a look of interest crossed her stoic features. Jared shrugged and ambled back toward his Jag. Women usually liked him, and he couldn't see that he'd done anything to tick this one off. No Trespassing signs applied to salesmen, not legitimate visitors, as far as he could see. Surely she hadn't really thought to scare him off?

"Do you have some idea when Miss Alyssum might return?" He played along with her gag and cast her a sideways look to see if anything registered in her expression. She had a short, finely honed aquiline nose with a sprinkle of freckles across it, and a mouth drawn too tight to reveal any trace of humor. He wouldn't call it a friendly face by any means. He could cut timbers with the sharp edge of her voice.

"She won't be interested. As I said, you're trespassing. I'd advise you to turn around before the police arrive." She headed for a beat-up black Chevy pickup, opened the door, then waited for him to move his car.

She didn't even show an interest in his antique Jag. Damn. That car drew more comments than honeysuckle drew bees. Was she blind?

There had to be some way around her. He'd never accepted no as an answer in his life. Not that many people told him no in the first place. He wasn't an unreasonable man. She had a run-down beach shack going to waste. He wanted to put it to good use. He couldn't see the problem.

"I can afford whatever price Miss Alyssum thinks the property is worth. I'll buy it if she'd rather not lease it. Just pass the message along, will you?" He leaned against his car door and watched her climb into her truck without replying. Well, damn.

Maybe she *was* a witch, but she had all his incorrigible pheromones humming. He sighed as she cranked the truck to life without looking back. He'd better move the Jag or she'd drive over it.

Spinning his tires in the soft sand, he edged out of her way and let her fly off down the lane. He wondered if signs would pop out of the road and witches fly from the trees as she left, or if they were rigged only to greet incoming visitors.

He sure did like the way her mind worked. Wonder if she could rig up some of those spooks for him once he figured out how to obtain the beach house?

Bumping the Jag over a timber barrier, he drove down toward the beach to inspect the house he'd only seen from a distance. The real-estate agents had said there was nothing available out here in the middle of nowhere, but a friend of a friend in L.A. had told him about this island. The film business was a small world.

This place should be ideal. He could feel it in his bones. None of his friends or family would go out of their way to reach this remote spot. Surely, once he cleared his head, he would be able to think again. Surrounded by all this peace and quiet, he'd cruise right past the roadblock in his mind that had prevented his coming up with any fresh ideas lately.

A witchy landlady would be a distraction, but one distraction against the many his places in New York and Miami offered seemed a fair trade. His fingers itched for the computer keys already, just thinking about the sand and the waves and the peace.

Driving with one hand, he idly swatted at something tickling his ankle. He'd have to remember insect repellant. Beaches were notorious for bugs.

The house ought to be just beyond that curve in the road ahead, if he'd calculated correctly. He didn't know the name of the scrub brush blocking his view, but it grew in heavy thickets neither man nor beast would dare enter. He'd have plenty of privacy.

Before he could grin at the thought, an eerie high-pitched shriek shattered his eardrums, and an object the size of his mother's frozen Thanksgiving turkeys smashed into his windshield, scattering brilliant blue-green plumage across the glass, obstructing his view with an iridescent psychedelic hallucination.

Frantically swiping at the irritating tickle crawling up his leg, cursing the Technicolor windshield, he slammed the brakes. The car's rear end resisted and the tires swerved wildly in the soft sand.

Crawling. Up his leg.

Clinging desperately to the wheel for control, Jared glanced downward.

A shiny black snake's tail whipped his leather moccasins. The head had disappeared up the leg of his khakis.

Clutching the spinning steering wheel while cursing frantically, Jared lost control as the car veered sideways on the soft shoulder.

The low-slung chassis hit the ditch at the side of the road, sailed upward, and landed, roof down, in the wax myrtle thicket.

❧ **TWO** ❧

"Cleo, you can't stand in the path of progress," Marta exclaimed in exasperation. "Just look at the money a Hollywood film crew could pour into this town."

"And the drugs and alcohol that would flow from that generous pitcher," Cleo scoffed, scribbling up an invoice. "I lived in L.A., remember. Film crews are people, just like everyone else. They bring their problems with them." She ran an adding machine tape on the total and stapled it to the top sheet.

"And their *money*." Marta stalked off toward the storeroom. "And glamour," she threw over her shoulder.

"You've been listening to Katy," Cleo shouted back. "This town was a sandbar, not a pirate hideout!"

Marta didn't answer. Cleo blamed the owner of the local B&B for the pirate hideout theory that had attracted the director of the pirate film. She didn't place much faith in anything coming of his interest. Once these Hollywood people realized the town's claim to fame was one B&B and a Holiday Inn, they'd skedaddle fast enough.

She heard the bell ring over the door but didn't look up. Customers knew where to find her if they needed her.

"Cleo!" a small voice interrupted her thought processes.

"Gene?" Cleo angled her head to see down the aisle between the shelves of hammers and the bins of nails to verify the identity of the whisperer. She recognized the tight brown curls instantly. "Why aren't you in school?"

They'd been around this subject a few times, so Eugene generally didn't put in an appearance during the school day. She'd argued with him and berated him for his truancy, but she wasn't his mother and had no authority to do more. And she had no intention of turning the kid in. He had enough trouble in his life, and she had long since lost respect for officialdom of any sort. Eight months behind bars had solidified her dim view of the tight asses and narrow minds of authority.

With a little more confidence now that she hadn't yelled at him, Gene eased closer to the counter, keeping a sharp eye on the front door. Short for his thirteen years but sturdy enough to predict muscles for his future, he hid easily behind the hardware store's tall racks. "There's somethin' bad happened."

Cleo's stomach froze. She could think of a dozen bad things involving Gene alone. Her own life was such a disaster that she'd quit worrying about any pending catastrophe there as long as Matty was safe. Gene could have no knowledge of her son's problems. "Are you going to tell me what it is or just stand there looking like a whipped dog?"

He scowled at her blunt tone, but he knew better than to come to her for pampering. She provided a listening post and a helping hand, and on the whole, he respected that.

"That Jag was at your house?" he asked diffidently, drawing out the drama while looking for a means of diminishing his involvement.

Cleo leaned her shoulders against the shelves, crossed her arms, and waited.

The boy scuffled a torn tennis shoe. "It turned over out on the beach road."

Uh-oh. Years of disaster had taught her to hide fear well, but Cleo had a bad feeling about this one. Gene wasn't looking at her. The boy was playing truant and didn't want to get caught. He usually hung out down by the deserted beach house . . .

Which the guy in the Jag wanted to rent. "How bad?" she asked gruffly. She wasn't responsible for Gene or the yuppie in the Jag, but that was her property out there. Visions of liability suits rose right along with specters of smashed aviator glasses and blood marring a long nose. That's how her life usually happened.

"It turned upside down." Gene grimaced and used the flapping toe of his shoe to scratch his ankle. "He's out cold. I had to use your phone to call 911."

Cleo uttered a few mental curse words. She was trying to break the habit of saying them aloud, for Matty's sake. How the devil had the jerk managed to flip a car on a road where the highest possible speed was fifteen miles per hour? "Where'd they take him? The clinic?" Should she call and see if he was all right? Or would that be acknowledging responsibility? For all that mattered— "How did you get back here? Hitch a ride?"

Gene shrugged off the last question. She'd warned him enough times not to take rides with strangers, but the beach was a long bike ride from town. "He's over at the clinic. I heard the sheriff gripin' 'cause he warn't carryin' no ID. And the plates were out of state."

"He *wasn't* carrying any ID," she corrected absently. She had the stranger's card in her pocket. She hadn't even looked at it. Why would he not carry ID or a car registration? Because he was a lamebrained yuppie who thought he was above the rules.

"He's still out cold," Gene said worriedly. "Reckon he'll die?"

She narrowed her eyes and pinned him in place. "What did you do to him?"

Gene shrugged nervously. His T-shirt had a tear in the armhole seam where he'd stretched too far and burst open the worn threads. "I didn' do *nothin'*," he said belligerently.

"Eugene Watkins, there's no sense lying to me, because I'll find out anyway." She had Gene and his sister half convinced she *was* a witch, but only because she knew how to find out things and their mother had too many problems to try.

"Well, Blackie mighta got into the car with him." He hung his head. "And the peacocks, well, they got kinda stirred."

Blackie, the black snake—one of Gene's and Matty's many exotic pets. Cleo rolled her eyes and tried not to imagine what the friendly snake would have done in a Jag. There weren't many places a snake could wrap around in a car. And the peacocks! She winced and nailed Gene with a glare. "If you hurt those birds, I'll pull every kinky curl out of your head, do you understand?"

"Yes'm. But they ain't hurt. Just riled a little."

Shootfire, heck, and darn. She'd taken anger management classes. She knew better than to take the boy's head off. She even understood why the brat had done what he had done—had she been thirteen, she would have protected her privacy the same way.

"The guy's unconscious and the sheriff doesn't know who he is?" she asked to distract herself from Gene's depredations. How would anyone notify the yuppie's next of kin? What if he needed surgery? A man driving a Jag was bound to have anxious, wealthy family somewhere. *Damn.*

"Yes'm. I'm real sorry, Cleo. I won't do it again. I didn't mean for nothin' bad to happen. I was just playin'."

"I know, kid, but you're getting too old to play those kinds of games. You know better. He would have gone away and left us alone when he got bored. Go get Marta out of the back. I'd better go over to the clinic."

She sure the heck wasn't going to the sheriff, but the clinic, she might handle. As Gene took his guilty expression to the storeroom to fetch her clerk, Cleo removed her carpenter's apron and stashed it beneath the counter. She hated getting involved. Maybe the guy had regained consciousness by now and could tell them who he was. Or the sheriff had traced his license tag.

Her visitor had been an arrogant jerk, but he hadn't deserved Gene's dirty trick. The counselor had said she had to learn to accept responsibility. The counselor was a dipshit, but she knew he was right about this one.

Cleo checked her pocket to make certain the card was still there, told Marta where she was going, and headed down the bucolic town street shaded from the September sun by live oaks and Spanish moss. Glancing up at the antique four-sided clock in the courthouse steeple, she saw she'd missed lunch again. The clock chimes hadn't rung since World War II, from all reports. The town citizens weren't particularly concerned, but the clock's gradual slowing of time had caused a number of jokes. Maybe now that the weather was cooler, she and Ed could climb back up there and take another look, provided he wasn't down at the bar talking about the German U-boat he'd seen from the tower during the war. Ed had a little drinking problem.

She adored this town. It was as far from the filthy city apartments of her childhood as she could get. L.A. to rural South Carolina, quite a leap, but the right one for her. She was comfortable here.

All she had to do was stay clean and responsible, keep the feds off her case until her parole expired, and she would become a model citizen. Sort of. She had learned the hard way that the local hardware store was the heartbeat of the community, and high visibility made her twitchy. For Matty to grow up here, she had to fit in, and that wouldn't happen if anyone learned of her background. Keeping a low profile and avoiding gossip was a tough act to maintain in a small town. She didn't go near the Chamber of Commerce's chatty little get-togethers, but she dealt with customers, paid her dues, contributed to charity, and did whatever else money could do. She figured that ought to be enough to encourage a business that had no competition.

She had her store and her house and her life and Matty, and she'd learned to survive very nicely here.

Except Matty was hardly ever home. And Gene and his sister needed a sober adult in their lives, and she had apparently been nominated. Life certainly took ironic twists.

What if the stranger wanted to file a complaint? How would she keep him away from Gene? The thought of taking the blame on herself caused a brief spurt of panic. The sheriff would trace her prior record, call the feds, and before she knew what hit her, Social Services would be carting Matty off, and everyone would shun the store in horror, and she'd be out on the street again. No way.

There had to be a more reasonable method of settling this, although trying to imagine settling a wrecked antique Jag was a large hurdle to handle. And if the yuppie moron really was seriously injured . . . She wouldn't consider that. Maybe she could bribe him with the rental of the beach house.

Like she really needed that turkey cluttering up her life.

But better than being sued for everything she owned, or both her and Gene going to jail.

Cursing over impossible choices, she shoved open the

clinic door. A blast of air-conditioning smacked her in the face. The nearest hospital was over an hour away, so the town furnished this hole in the wall with a few beds, a nurse, and some paramedics as a stopgap. The place was scrupulously clean, but small. The instant she walked in, she could hear voices rising from the back.

"I tell you, a *snake*! The monster could have swallowed Texas, and it was crawling up my leg! And then, feathers—*splash*—everywhere! After the witch and the skeleton, I swear to you . . ."

Uh-oh. Sounds as if the yuppie moron was recovering. They didn't need her. She'd just mosey along out of here—

"Hallucinating," a stage whisper carried over the descriptive yelling. "We'd better send him on to Charleston."

"Well, we've had reports of other pranks out there. If he ain't been drinking, might orter look into it. His car was pretty much totaled."

The sheriff. Shit. Shoot. Double-d bad word, as Maya always said. She didn't need the sheriff snooping around. There was no telling what kind of ordinances or laws or who knows what she'd broken, and if he found out how Gene and his sister were living . . . She wouldn't let that happen, upon penalty of death. Those kids did not deserve the fate the sheriff would unthinkingly assign them.

Straightening her shoulders beneath the checked flannel shirt, fighting an unreasonable panic bubbling up from the murky depths of her past, Cleo shoved her half glasses up her nose and tried to look respectable as she invaded the back room.

She didn't know why all Southern sheriffs seemed to be massive men with big bellies, but the town's man with a badge didn't disappoint. He sported a bristly straight mustache to make up for his receding hairline, and turned an unfriendly gaze to Cleo. But then, she'd never seen a law official with a friendly gaze.

The dark-haired, dark-eyed man lying in the bed with a bandage taped to his high brow was still yammering about witches and skeletons and feathers, but the instant he spotted her, his long-lashed eyes narrowed. "There she is. Tell him I'm not crazy," he demanded.

He was even cuter in one of those horrid blue hospital gowns. Cleo had a weakness for the lean, hungry Cassius types, although this one didn't look as if he'd starved anytime in the near past. His shoulders bulged interestingly as he lifted his nearly six-foot frame up on one elbow. She didn't want to do this. She really didn't. Her only hope was that he'd take one look at the run-down shack and flee in the opposite direction. She'd concentrate on the power of positive thinking.

She quit looking at sin and turned to the nurse instead. Recognizing the petite redhead as a customer, Cleo marginally relaxed and pulled the business card from her pocket. "He is crazy," she said with all solemnity, "but that's his natural disposition and not a result of the accident. He's considering renting my beach house, which proves my point. If he's all right, I can take him there." Maybe that would keep The Jerk from getting ideas about lawsuits.

The patient in the bed cast her a disbelieving glance. Well, at least she'd shut him up.

The nurse passed the card to the sheriff. "There's some possibility of concussion, and he's been raving since he woke. I don't know . . ."

"I'm not raving! I tell you, there was a snake three feet long—" he shouted furiously.

"Jared McCloud?" The sheriff read the card aloud. "Cartoonist?" He lifted his balding head and stared. "*The* Jared McCloud? The guy who does *Scapegrace*?"

The man in the bed waved his hand impatiently and

glared at Cleo. "Tell him. Tell him there was a witch and a skeleton. Then maybe he'll believe the snake."

"A witch, a skeleton, three clowns, and a Prince Charming," she agreed soberly. "It was a very grand affair." *Scapegrace?* This jerk wrote the comic strip about the teenage nerd? She couldn't believe he'd ever been a nerd in his life. She crossed her arms and raised her eyebrows at his glower.

"Hell, I'd be honored to take you wherever you like, Mr. McCloud." The sheriff intruded on their staring match. "My kids fight to see who gets to your strip first. He ready to travel, Dixie?"

Cleo cursed a mental blue streak. Now look what the rat had done. He'd have the sheriff out there inspecting her premises, and she sure as hell didn't need that. She'd just sacrificed her privacy to spring him out of here—for nothing.

Eyes widening as if he'd read her mind, *The* Jared McCloud suddenly grinned like a devil about to claim a soul. His eyes practically danced as he inspected her as if she were some kind of alien from outer space. She ought to walk out of here and burn the beach house before he got anywhere near it. Any man in his right senses would be so mad at her right now, he could spit.

Boy, she was going to make Gene pay for this.

The Jerk wrapped the bedsheet around him and swung his legs over the side of the cot. His thick sable hair fell forward over the bandage, and his bare toes stuck out from beneath the sheet. He had strong, slender feet and toes, adorned with a dusting of silky hair.

Cleo couldn't believe she was staring at his feet. Had it been that long since she'd seen a man's feet? She jerked her head up again.

"I need to check out of my hotel, Sheriff. Miss Alyssum and I haven't had time to make the final arrangements on the house, so maybe I'd best go with her."

Cleo tried not to exhale too sharply or look too closely to see how the law officer took that. Experience had taught her to keep a large canyon between herself and the authorities.

"Well, if I can be of any assistance while you're here, son, you just call on me. Maybe you can come out to the school sometime, talk to the kids. They'd get a real kick out of that." The sheriff turned and nodded politely to Cleo. "Miss Alyssum, it's a pleasure to see you. Take good care of the boy."

"The boy" winked at her behind the sheriff's back, then returned to the immediate subject. "What about my car, Sheriff?"

"Looks like it's a goner, son. When you get your billfold from your hotel room, stop by the office so I can file a report for your insurance. Shame, a car like that."

An antique Jag. Cleo shuddered. The thing probably cost seven fortunes. And Gene had destroyed it, nearly taking its owner out with it. She supposed she owed The Jerk, but she didn't have to like it. Gene was in for a lot of window washing.

The Jared McCloud grimaced, then looked at the nurse expectantly. "May I have my clothes, please? It looks as if I'll be relying on Miss Alyssum's hospitality a great deal more than I expected."

Like her car, her house, her life . . . Cleo understood blackmail when she heard it. Not deigning to acknowledge his implied threat, she backed toward the door. "Sheriff, why don't you take him to the hotel while I check in at the store. Drop him off there when you're done with him." The very best defense was a strong offense, her daddy had told her long ago.

And she could be amazingly offensive when the notion took her.

⊰ THREE ⊱

Jared glanced at the stone-faced example of the fairer sex in the driver's seat. Every once in a while, when he was exceptionally lucky, he ran across a truly clever, creative female mind like this one, a puzzle meant for solving, and his anticipation soared. His new landlady's small, pointed chin practically strained to clamp her teeth tight on her anger. He didn't know what she was angry about, but she'd get over it. In his business, it never paid to take life seriously, and the anger of women was a fleeting thing, he'd learned.

It wasn't as if he considered himself exceedingly clever or handsome or any of those things he assumed women wanted. His two brothers had pointed out often enough that he was the runt of the litter, the shallow ne'er-do-well with no driving ambition to improve the world. They'd left him with few illusions of ego. But even his brothers admitted that women liked him. Even as the class freak, he'd escorted the valedictorian to the prom, because he was persistent, and he listened to her.

That's *all* he'd ever done, listen, because he had been, after all, a skinny freak who drew cartoon characters for amusement. Besides, Regina had been a stuck-up bit of rudeness most of the time. He'd just liked the way her mind worked, and they'd agreed that going to the prom together made sense. He must have shined up pretty good because he'd ended up taking both Regina and the football captain's date home that night, and what Regina hadn't offered, the cheerleader had.

Not that any of that had any relevance to the fascinating creature sitting next to him, doing her best to pretend he didn't exist. He'd put on his cowboy boots for her, and she didn't even notice when he propped them on the dashboard. But she was aware of him, all right, and she was madder than a wet cat about it. Hell of a reaction to the electricity bouncing around in here.

"I never got a chance to look at the place. Is it in good repair?" he asked idly, trying to divert her attention from her mad-on. He loved Spanish moss, and admired the way it drooped over the crushed shell highway they roared down. He trusted the truck had four-wheel drive, or they'd be headed for a skid shortly. He wasn't too eager for a repeat of the day's earlier catastrophe. Broken hands or head would not bode well for his currently flagging career. Good thing he'd sent in that last batch of strips before setting out on this adventure. One more black mark against his name and his agent was likely to can him. A cartoonist without a career was a pretty sad affair.

"It needs a new roof," she answered curtly. "No one lives there, so I don't pay much attention to what shape it's in."

"Why haven't you sold it, then? Beachfront property has to be worth a mint."

"This isn't California, and I like my privacy. Keep that in mind, and we'll get along fine."

Jared hummed a country song he'd heard on the drive down and tried to imagine why a creative woman like this would be hiding in the outback of a swamp, but his mind wouldn't settle on any one reason. Maybe she was an inventor afraid of someone stealing her ideas before she patented them. If she wasn't, she ought to be. That cackling witch sweeping across the road on her broom was enough to cause heart failure. He particularly liked the witch's stringy hair and red shoes.

"Fine with me," he agreed easily. "I was feeling burned out and needed to get away from distraction to finish this project." *Finish*, his foot and eye. All he'd written so far was cow manure. He had to raise it to bullshit, at the very least. He'd manage. He always had.

Except for that last project. He hid his grimace at the unfamiliar sensation of the ground cracking under him. "Failure" wasn't in the McCloud family credo.

He'd rather think about the current object of his interest. "I've always found the pounding of surf relaxing."

"Swell for you," she mocked. "It's hurricane season. Maybe you'll hear some *real* surf."

"I live in Miami. I know hurricanes," he said comfortably, not about to be scared off, if that was her intention.

"Surf is about all you'll hear out there. I don't think the place is wired for much more than a light and a stove and the well pump."

"Mind if I upgrade the wiring if I need it? Computers are finicky about electricity." He hadn't counted on rewiring, but if there was electricity, it shouldn't take much to run in a line or two for his stuff.

She shrugged. "Your money."

She didn't even ask him how long he would stay. Entertaining.

In the interest of seeing just how far she could ignore him, he hunted for a more telling question. That didn't take much thought. "Why'd you change your mind?"

For a moment, he thought she wouldn't answer, she stared out the windshield so fiercely.

"I like my privacy," she repeated.

"That doesn't answer the question." Jared tried not to smile as she struggled to find an answer that wasn't an answer. His older brother, Tim, had once warned him that he would someday run into a nutcase who would blow him away for his annoying persistence, but Jared figured he'd take his chances. Risk nothing, gain nothing, was his motto.

He wondered if she'd forgotten the question or simply refused to answer further, but she finally gritted her teeth and shot him a glare.

"I prefer you to the sheriff."

Remembering the paunchy, balding man of the law, Jared crossed his arms and lifted his eyebrows. "Gee, gosh. I'm overwhelmed."

He wanted to cackle like her witch as she threw him another glare, but then her lip twitched, and she almost smiled.

"Well, Vern is a pretty impressive sight, you have to admit."

"I'm honored. Now, if I could just figure out what hit my windshield and why a snake crawled up my leg . . ."

The dawning smile slipped away. "You were trespassing."

She didn't admit guilt or look guilty. Maybe his freaking imagination had finally fried his brain. "I thought these beaches were public property," he insisted.

"Not when you cross private property to get to them." No witch sailed across the road on her mechanical broom as she shifted gears, popped the clutch, and took the beach road at an illegal rate of speed. "There's a bad undertow out here. I suppose you ignore No Swimming signs, too."

Jared was too absorbed in the sight of a peacock

feather caught in a prickly shrub to comment. Peacock feather. Did peacocks fly?

Snakes didn't. He couldn't imagine one crawling over the Jag's shiny hood either. He grimaced as the Southern sun caught on the glitter of red and chrome as they roared past the place he'd gone off the road. He couldn't see enough of the car to verify the full extent of the damage, but Jags were temperamental creatures at the best of times. Sand and palmettos wouldn't improve its condition. If the evil genie beside him hadn't wrecked the car, he'd damned sure find out who had. The Jag had been a childhood dream that had cost him the cash advance on a script he hadn't written yet.

His head began to throb in earnest. "Guess I'd better find some transportation next." He figured he was talking to himself, but to his surprise, she actually responded.

"You'd better have one of those expensive varieties of Triple A. I doubt you'll find a Jag dealer closer than Charleston to tow you. The dealer might have something to rent."

He slumped back to rest his pounding head against the seat. "Nah. A Jeep's probably best out here. I can see right now that Jags shouldn't leave Miami." He winced as the truck hit a rut.

She eased up on the accelerator. "Sorry. Head hurt?"

He hadn't expected sympathy. Maybe she was just testing the extent of damage for liability purposes, as his younger brother, Doubting Thomas, would say.

His life was too cluttered and disorganized for Tom's cynicism. Maybe he'd adopt brother Tim's narrow focus and pretend the world didn't exist outside his head. Painful thought. He grimaced and rubbed the ache. "Nothing a few aspirin won't cure. Am I taking you from your job to drag you out here?"

"I've got someone covering for me. I figure you'll take one look at the shack and back off."

Even with his head pounding and his Jag no more than a gasoline spot in the sand, he knew the answer to that one. He was staying. She'd have to deal with it.

Cleo watched in growing agony as *The* Jared McCloud wandered aimlessly from the tattered screened porch, past the worn vinyl, down the squeaking-board hall, and up to the overheated half attic. Standing below, she held her breath as he leaned his lanky frame against the splintered wood rail of the balcony overlooking the beach and stared in absorption at the rising tide. That was her favorite spot up there. From that vantage point, the uncontrollable freedom of the waves both terrified and elated her.

Right now, she feared he'd fall through the rail.

She knew what he would say before he returned to the porch to say it. The leaky old house should have fallen to pieces long ago, but it exuded love and warmth and the tenacity of lifetimes of vacationing families. More likely, it just symbolized the childhood she'd never had. Whatever, she hadn't had the heart to tear it down, or the stupidity to restore something that the next strong wind or tide could rip away.

"How much?" he asked the instant he hit the sagging front step.

Cleo could read the gleam in his eye through the pain etched on his forehead, and she set her jaw stubbornly. "I'm not selling." Why couldn't the dork just see the place was a catastrophe and leave? She really hadn't believed a rich yuppie could tolerate such primitive conditions. She definitely didn't need his restless, sexy carcass in her backyard.

He shrugged and shoved his hands in his pockets as he

studied the bird nests in the eaves. "Fine. I'm not much good at fixing things. What's it worth to you to put it into habitable condition?"

Damn him. Well, she'd give him credit for not being an airhead. He knew it was unlivable. "It would cost three fortunes, and the insurance out here is astronomical. Beach houses come with a high price for a reason."

"Pare it down to one fortune, and I'll do it. You hire the help, I'll pay for it."

Cleo gaped at the inverted triangle presented by Jared McCloud's back as he walked away. She shouldn't be seeing muscular shoulders narrowing to trim waist. She ought to be seeing dollar signs, or an invasion of privacy. She ought to be screaming bloody murder and heaving obstacles in his way. Or at his inviting back. She never looked at men that way. *Never*.

She hurried after him as he captured a sand dune. She knew his sort—patrician good looks, easy life, and wealth to throw around. He'd rub her the wrong way one too many times, and she'd have to kill him. Or maim him badly. Either way, she'd be back in prison and Matty would be lost to her forever. No way. She knew her limits.

Of course, her usual reactions to stress were self-destructive rather than violent, and she couldn't afford that any better.

"That's ridiculous," she practically spluttered upon reaching the top of the dune. She hadn't thought spluttering a possibility until she did it. Drat the man. Drawing up straight and forming her words carefully, she continued in her more forthright manner. "The place is falling apart. I won't sell. What's the point of your repairing it for the few months or however long you want to use it?"

The ocean wind blew his hair back, revealing a long,

straight nose and firm jaw that could have been carved out of marble and placed in a museum of Roman artifacts. He shrugged with much more fluidity than marble. "What's the point of having money if you can't spend it on what you want?"

Sighing, Cleo stared at the sun sparkling off the water. Maybe it wouldn't be too terribly bad to have one lone guy living back here, pounding on his computer. Her store was on the mainland anyway, so she wasn't here all day. What would she see of him at night?

And it would be kind of nice to have the beach house fixed up—at someone else's expense—when family visited.

"How long you staying?" she demanded, not giving in immediately.

"Until the project is finished. A few months, probably. I can't see staying in this place at Christmas. You'll have a great beach house and I'll have my privacy. Fair trade, don't you think?"

He wanted privacy, too. That could work. Maybe she wouldn't even see him. Other than letting Maya and her family visit more often, she had no idea what she would do with a beach house, but she could think of something.

"Who pays for the insurance?" She'd learned to be practical. It took a lot of scrabbling to get where she was today, and she wasn't letting loose of a penny without earning two pennies in return.

He slanted her a satisfied look. "I'll pay for six months' worth of insurance and all the repairs in lieu of rent. How's that?"

"You have no idea how much that's going to cost," she warned. "The roof alone will set you back thousands." And she'd have to pay the insurance after he was gone. She'd have to rent the place at least part of the year to cover the cost. If the town persuaded the film director to use the harbor, they might even list her as having available housing. Curses. It would be much simpler if he'd just go away.

"A place like this in Miami would rent for thousands a month. It's no big deal, provided you know who to call." He shot her a challenging look. "You do know someone who can get right on it, don't you?"

She owned the only hardware store within fifty miles. She knew everyone. "You want the best, or the most cost-effective?" she countered with a hint of defiance. She didn't like people underestimating her.

"The best and most efficient. If I'm working out here, I don't want to waste time chatting with carpenters while they drink their coffee."

Had he been anyone else, she might have smiled at the recognition that he'd had some experience with Southern construction crews. She still didn't like the light in his eyes when he looked at her. She bit off the smile, nodded curtly, and started sliding down the dune in the direction of the truck. "I'll take you into town, call my attorney to draw up an agreement, and call a few workmen. One of the car lots should have some kind of four-wheel-drive vehicle available. You can call around."

She didn't even know if the clown was who he said he was, although the Jag and the way he carried himself surely showed he could afford to put his money where his mouth was. Still, she wanted this right and tight. She disliked officialdom, but she knew attorneys. Lots of attorneys.

The idea of this desk jockey occupying her personal space for months still ticked her bomb. She'd have to remember Gene and the sheriff. The boy didn't deserve a rougher life than he already had, and if The Jerk ever figured out who put the snake in his car . . .

Window washing wasn't enough. She'd have Gene

scrubbing floors—with his nose—for getting them both into this.

⊰ FOUR ⊱

"Hug your mommy, and we'll be off, sugar," Maya called from the driveway.

Sitting cross-legged on the porch, Cleo opened her arms to hug her seven-year-old son. Weekends simply weren't long enough. For Matty's sake, she was getting better at hiding her tears with each of these departures. One of these days, she might even figure out how to hide them and still be as sloppy sentimental as her sister. Then she could whisper foolish love words in Matty's ear as he slobbered sloppy kisses across her cheek.

Probably not, though. Squeezing the boy tight, she kissed his forehead, then set him away from her as she always did. She despised tears and sentimentality. They were a weakness she couldn't afford. Matty had enough problems without learning of her weaknesses. He needed to be happy and comfortable going off with his aunt.

"Iggy really liked that lettuce you brought him, so grow some more, okay?" She brushed the hair out of his eyes and smiled at his earnest expression. Matty loved taking care of animals, and he was good at it. Maya had taught her to encourage him in the things he excelled at instead of dwelling on the things he couldn't do well— like reading and writing. She supposed his father must have had dyslexia as well, and maybe if someone had taken the time to teach her late ex-husband, the bastard wouldn't be dead right now. But that was an old story beyond her control. Matty was the important part.

"I'll draw a picture of Petey, too," her son declared stoutly.

Matty wasn't quite so good at drawing, especially peacocks, but Cleo grinned in appreciation of his offer. "You do that, kiddo. Now hurry and get in the car before Alexa crawls out of her seat."

She bit her lip as Matty ran to entertain his baby cousin, then finally faced her sister, who stood waiting for her turn.

"Come December, he'll be all yours again," Maya reminded her, as she always did.

"I don't want anything less than the best for Matty, and you're the best." Cleo had been over this a dozen times a day and always reached the same conclusion. She could have had Matty placed closer to home, but she wanted him where he was happy, even if the distance made *her* miserable. If she kept her head on straight, she could suffer a few more months for his sake.

Maya looked skeptical, but Maya never argued. "What happened to the new tenant you told me about? Is he really the guy who does *Scapegrace*?"

"Says he is. As long as he's paying the bills, I'll take his word for it." Cleo read the look of interest on her sister's face, but she sure as hell wasn't supplying her with more ammunition. Now that she was happily married and settled, Maya meddled.

"I read about him. The article said he's a real playboy. What's a playboy doing out here?"

Cleo shrugged. "Working on some project, if you can call drawing cartoons working."

"Those animated things he does for TV have to be

work, but they're a bit too childishly snide for me. I bet he was a sociopathic teenager." Maya gathered up Matty's collection of backpacks and sneakers. "Maybe you could introduce us next time I'm down."

Cleo couldn't picture the happy-go-lucky idiot currently occupying her beach house as a sociopathic anything, but Maya's assessments tended to be right on when it came to people. She hadn't even realized he worked in TV. If she had time to be suspicious . . . She didn't. She stood and helped with the assortment of kid litter. "Bring Axell and the kids, have a cookout, and introduce yourselves."

"That sounds like a great idea." Blithely ignoring the sarcasm behind Cleo's suggestion, Maya heaved the baggage into the back of the SUV. "Now that Axell has a manager who's on top of things, we can get about more. If you don't mind all the kids invading your territory . . ."

Cleo threw in Matty's jacket, hamster cage, and bag of books. Maya knew every one of Cleo's buttons, but she never pressed them. She just discreetly buzzed around them. "The kids are fine. Bring sleeping bags and they can camp in Matty's room. I just don't think Axell will appreciate roughing it."

"It'll be good for him, and he'd love to meet Jared McCloud. Call and give us a date."

With a blizzard of last-minute admonitions, questions, and reminders, Maya had the car loaded, the children settled, and the engine running. Cleo hated to see them go and wished her sister would just get on with it, before the tears stinging her eyes started to leak.

"I love you, sis!" Maya called out the window as she eased the car down the drive.

Cleo waved and smiled until she thought her face would crack. It was nice that her otherworldly sister had found happiness and love and the good life. Cleo didn't think she possessed what it took to even define happiness.

As the car disappeared past the pines, she swiped at an errant trace of moisture on her cheek, kicked a clamshell, and wandered in the direction of the brush on the other side of the drive. Matty's tiny menagerie had grown to a regular zoo with Gene's aid. Feeding and watering the critters would give her time to pull herself together. Then she'd check the freezer to see what she could defrost for dinner. She hated eating alone, without Matty's cheerful chatter.

"Hey, Cleo," Gene greeted her as she pushed through the shrubbery. "I've got 'em fed. What did Matty think of the baby bird?"

"You could have asked him yourself." Cleo checked the water in the bird's box and fed it a mealworm. Gene tended to disappear when Matty was home, but she figured thirteen-year-olds and seven-year-olds didn't mix.

"He's just a kid." Gene shrugged it off. "That new guy sure is building a palace down there, ain't he? Reckon he's rich?"

"Reckon he's got more money than brains anyway." She didn't want to talk about Jared. She'd rather pretend her tenant didn't exist than admit she was curious about what he was doing. He'd had a phone installed before he'd bought a Jeep, and all she ever heard of him was from the end of the telephone wire.

"I'm gonna be rich someday," Gene declared. "I'm gonna have me a fancy car and house."

"You gonna let me come visit?" Sitting on a rotten log, Cleo fed Matty's pet iguana while Petey the Peacock screamed a complaint behind her. She'd never been much of a dreamer, but she could remember her fierce determination to escape the horrors of her life at Gene's age. She knew where he was coming from and all the pitfalls ahead. She wouldn't tell him how difficult it was to climb out of the hole. She didn't think Gene had a respectable grandfather who would pop off and leave him old buildings as hers had—for what little good the man had done her growing up.

"Sure," he said confidently. "You and Matty can come live with me, if you want."

"And how are you planning on earning these riches?" At least they didn't live in a slum, or his first choice would probably be dealing drugs, given his mother's predilections. She shouldn't be so cynical. Linda had been doing well lately. She'd held on to her typist's job for almost six months this time.

"I'm gonna be a wrestler," Gene said with satisfaction. "I don't have to be tall to be a wrestler."

It would probably help, but she wouldn't burst his bubble. "Then you'd better go to school more often and learn how to invest all that money you'll be making. You don't want them thinking you're a dumb jock."

"I'll hire people," he declared airily. "That's what Jared does, I bet. I don't see him studying no books."

"You've met Jared?"

"Nah, I just watched him. He's on the phone or the 'puter all the time. I didn't see him moving in no books, no way."

"That's spying. You ought to go down and introduce yourself. That's the neighborly thing to do."

He gave her that teenager-to-adult look of incredulity. "Right, like he's got time for *me*," he scoffed. "Maybe he'd want me to shine his shoes."

"Boots," she corrected. "He was wearing cowboy boots last time I saw him." She wouldn't correct Gene's cynicism any more than she'd burst his fantasies. The kid could very well be right. Neither white nor black, Gene inhabited none of the local racial microcosms. Mother a crack addict, father AWOL, he and his sister lived in a run-down house his mother had inherited, usurped, or stolen from some relative. Some people wouldn't trust him to shine their shoes.

"Cowboy boots!" He rolled his eyes and fed the iguana a lettuce leaf. "Man, all that money, and he's a redneck."

"Don't think so. Sounded Yankee to me. Go on down and say hi sometime when he's not working. Can't hurt."

"Maybe I will. Maybe I can get his autograph. Kids at school would get all bent if they knew I got his autograph."

Cleo wished she had the power to help him with the kids at school, but it was all she could manage to help herself. Maybe she'd go talk to his mother. Again.

"Forty-nine, fifty." Jared dropped to the floor and contemplated another round of push-ups, but the laptop under his desk shot baleful explosions from its screen protector. He figured he'd either have to move the laptop or attempt something productive. He wanted that screen credit and all the success it represented, but the idea of dealing with those Hollywood production committees freaked him out after the TV ordeal. The moguls were already making suggestions that had nothing to do with his characters.

His family would tell him to grow up. It would have been more useful if they'd shown him how. With a professor father who lived inside his books and a socialite mother bent on reforming the world to her taste, he didn't have much of a clue.

Figuring the hammers pounding on the floor above didn't help his thought processes, Jared switched off the laptop. Maybe he could get some business done if he couldn't do anything creative. Vaulting to his feet, he grabbed the cordless and jogged from the house, out to the sand dune and the limit of his phone reception. He'd already discovered his cellular was next to useless on the island.

The sand slipped and slid beneath his sandals as he climbed upward. Maybe his agent could get another extension on the contract. He'd never get the script done on time, and he could no longer give the movie people their option money back as he'd threatened before. The insurance company was giving him grief about the damned Jag.

Besides, his family would rail him out of town if he gave up. Bad enough that he was a useless cartoonist whose last TV show had flopped. To give up on a lucrative film career would brand him forever as a loser, even if he had enough to live on for life.

He just needed to get his head past that last failure. He'd never failed in his life, and he damned well didn't want it happening again. He had to come up with the perfect script, the perfect characters, ones that would stand up to the test of time and audience.

Broom-riding witches and laughing skeletons were cute, but they didn't have muscle. He needed depth, layers the audience could sink their teeth into.

Why in hell did he think he could do layers? He wasn't Dostoevsky. He was a *cartoonist*. He thrived on shallow, as his siblings lost no chance in pointing out.

The phone rang, relieving him of that particular introspective agony. Life was too short to waste worrying. Hitting the "talk" button, he grimaced at his brother's announcement on the other end that he intended to drop in for a visit.

"Look, Tim, the house is a wreck," Jared protested. "Take the Miami place if you're looking for a cheap vacation." He rolled his eyes at Tim's response, then let his gaze rest on the peaceful lap of surf below. "I did Mom's charity bachelor auction last year. It's your turn. You know what kind of women will pay to date cartoonists? Crazy ones. But if you're going to shirk your responsibility, take Miami."

He knew better than to bother arguing with Tim. His brothers always walked all over him, but Tim had a way of doing it that made it seem Jared's fault for lying down in front of him in the first place. Hell, maybe it was.

"You'll be sorry," he warned. "They've driven me out of the house with the hammering. I'll make certain they bring in a buzz saw before you arrive."

As he hit the "off" button, Jared grinned at the thought of studious, socially handicapped Tim driving through the maze of witches and warning signs. Maybe he could persuade his landlady to rig a skeleton at the beach house door.

The thought of his entertaining landlady sent him sliding back down the dune. As long as he wasn't getting any work done, he might as well shake the envelope a little. Miss Cleo hadn't bothered to check the progress of the repairs or to offer a neighborly hello. He'd particularly hoped she'd resort to that charming feminine custom of stopping by with a pie or cake to welcome him to the neighborhood.

Well, he didn't write comedy without reason.

Maybe she'd rigged up something new and even more entertaining just for him. He didn't like being ignored. He wasn't used to it.

Okay, take that back. If he was truly honest with himself, he grew up used to being ignored, and somewhere along the line had decided he wouldn't put up with it. As a teenager, he'd been damned obnoxious in his pursuit of attention. He'd learned a little finesse since then.

He stopped at the house to sketch a hasty line drawing. He did everything on computer these days, but he still had a quick hand with a pen. An original drawing spoke more eloquently than computer printouts.

He rolled up the sketch, tucking it into a cardboard tube for protection, and slipped on a shirt, before jogging up the sandy path toward his landlady's house. He'd been meaning to explore more of his surroundings anyway. Anything was better than staring blankly at a computer screen while listening to the roof being torn off above his head. His eccentric landlady qualified as far better than just "anything."

A flash of red caught the corner of his eye, and Jared turned to investigate the thicket of scrub brush to his left. He didn't figure snakes came in red, but he was being extra cautious these days. He'd had the notion that Cleo Alyssum lived alone on this swampy end of the island, but if there were others about, he'd be interested in knowing it. He had a sneaking suspicion that snakes didn't fly any better than frozen turkeys, but he couldn't see any way to blame his landlady for them.

The bushes moved in a wave proceeding in the general direction of the pines farther inland. He wasn't much interested in exploring jungle, but he could skirt around the thicket and look for a higher, dryer path.

He hoped he wasn't tracking a wild animal. He didn't want to end up like his pal Freddy, dead of a heart attack at thirty-two. Of course, Freddy had been at his desk, not stalking panthers.

Every time he thought of Freddy, Jared's heart raced as if *he* were having an attack. They'd been buddies since the age of ten, freaks together, him and Freddy and Dirk, the Three Musketeers. Freddy had been the chubby boy everyone laughed at, but he had the drive and ambition Jared had never possessed. Freddy had sworn he'd be a millionaire by thirty, and he'd done it. He'd also sworn he'd be married to a supermodel, but he'd died single and childless, and his wealth had gone to charity.

Maybe Freddy's death was the reason he couldn't concentrate these days, something about staring into the face of eternity caused one to reevaluate priorities.

He didn't want to reevaluate anything but his reason for signing that damned contract.

Call it denial, but to his way of thinking, living in the moment made more sense than regretting what was past or worrying over what lay ahead. If he had a heart attack chasing a wild animal in a red shirt, so be it. He spotted the flash of red again, darting between the pines.

Wild animals didn't wear red shirts. From the small bare footprints in the loose soil, he calculated it had to be a child.

He let the kid run ahead and feel safe. Did his landlady have children? She hadn't looked the motherly sort. He could imagine her as a sculptor wielding torch and metal, but not a mother.

Brushing past another of those damned prickly bushes, he stumbled on something in his path. Righting himself by grabbing a pine trunk, Jared jumped, startled, as a heavy rope fell in front of his face.

Before he could react, a net dropped from the tree and engulfed him in folds of rotting cords.

Well, hell, he might stick his head in the sand to avoid impending disaster, but he couldn't deny this predicament.

⚜ FIVE ⚜

"I don't think you're supposed to say those words," a girl's whispery voice commented thoughtfully from the depths of shrubbery.

Jared shut up and glanced around. He had a bad habit of not filling his pockets before leaving the house, so he didn't have his penknife on him. He could sever the rotten cords of the net with some effort, but he preferred using brain instead of brawn to untangle it. So far, he hadn't succeeded, and resentment simmered at being caught in such a foolish situation.

"Help me out of here, and I won't say them," he promised in a voice gruffer than usual. He'd embarrassed himself plenty of times before, but not in recent memory. He preferred his suave, urbane image to that of class clown these days.

"Gene keeps hoping he'll catch a panther." An awkwardly tall, skinny girl drifted through the shrubbery, eyeing the tangle of cords and ropes hanging from the tree limb. "I can't imagine what he'd do with one if he caught it."

Jared would guess her to be about fourteen or fifteen, although garbed as she was in a loose dress several sizes too large, it was hard to tell. She looked at the tree and rope and anything but him. Her wiry brownish-blond curls fell in her face and stuck out all over her head

41

without any indication that brush or comb had ever touched them. Her dusky complexion and frail features possessed an ethereal quality that—had he been a fanciful man—would have given him pause to wonder if fairies inhabited the island.

He did happen to possess an unfortunate penchant for fantasy, but he preferred superheroes to fairies.

"If you'll just grab that rope over there, I think the whole thing will lift up." Fairies and red-shirted wild animals and witches and skeletons—this island was turning into a real menagerie of cartoon characters. If he couldn't get something out of this, no one could.

She looked doubtfully at the heavy rope but gravitated toward it, giving it a slight pull that produced little effect.

"Tug harder," he urged, searching around his feet for the opening. He saw movement with her next tug and pounced on it. Whoever had rigged this trap hadn't intended it for people, at least. "A little harder, and I think I've got it."

The cords rippled, and he gathered as many as he could, locating the edge of the net and lifting until he had a space large enough to duck under. "Who is this Gene and where do I find him?" he called over his shoulder as he disentangled himself.

No reply.

Free at last, he let the net fall to the ground, and swung around to see what the girl was doing.

She was gone.

What in hell kind of rabbit hole had he fallen into, anyway?

Sweat pouring down his back, his cardboard tube battered and torn from swatting flies, mosquitoes, and hanging vines of indeterminate nature, Jared emerged from the thicket path into a clearing littered with make-shift stick cages and wooden crates.

Well, at least he knew he and his landlady weren't entirely alone out here. The paths wandering through swamp and scrub brush couldn't have been made by wild horses or whatever creatures inhabited the place. He hadn't seen a sign of animal life since setting out, but he *had* seen the girl and a red shirt. He thought.

A baby bird cheeped from a cardboard box filled with grasses and matchbox feeders. An iguana lay sleepily in a cage beneath a spreading live oak. A variety of colorful lizards scattered into hiding beneath a loosely stacked pile of rocks. And a potbellied pig snorted through rubbish inside a wire fence. Quite an assortment. As a kid, he would have loved this.

With interest, he peered into an elongated crate big enough to hold a refrigerator, and stepped back instantly. Snakes. *Black* ones.

He didn't get angry often. He couldn't remember the last time he'd been angry. But this was the outside of enough, and he'd been pushed as far as his temper would permit. It hadn't been his imagination that had ruined his antique Jag and nearly killed him. It had been a genuine live snake. Just like these.

An unearthly squawk nearly startled him out of his shoes, and Jared swung around in time to confront the beady eyes of a malicious-looking peacock. A snake, and a peacock, then. They'd been real enough. He definitely hadn't been hallucinating.

And they'd been put in or thrown at his car deliberately.

He still couldn't figure out how to blame his landlady for the trick, since she'd been in front of him the whole time his car had been parked and out of sight. So it had to be the fairy girl or the red shirt. A woman like Cleo

Alyssum might possess a couple of delinquent brats, although she didn't look old enough to have teenagers. Hell, what did he know about women and kids anyway? Although he liked sleeping with women, he couldn't claim to understand them, and his comic strip was more about himself than real kids.

Grabbing an abandoned box and snatching one of the smaller snakes from its wooden pit, Jared set off down still another path. He had a sneaking suspicion he knew the direction.

The guard peacock strutted after him, screeching its fool head off.

Watching warily for any more traps, Jared stalked through the underbrush until he heard the sounds of shouting. Well, she was definitely at home, then. It was time he had a little confrontation with one Cleo Alyssum.

"You can't keep skipping school, Eugene Watkins! You'll have the truant officer out here hunting you down. If I remember rightly, they lock kids up for not going to school around here." Dressed for work, truck keys in hand, Cleo had spotted the splash of red behind the palmettos and tracked him down before leaving. She held him by the back of the shirt now and wished she could shake him until his teeth rattled.

"They ain't never gonna find me!" Gene shouted defiantly. "They don' care if I'm there or not. They can't teach me nothin' I don' know already."

"I don't care if you never learn anything, but you have to have that piece of paper saying you're educated, or you'll not get anywhere in this world! Otherwise people will think you're a lazy bum and they'll never hire you." Cleo supposed that wasn't the world's most effective argument, but she couldn't think of any other right offhand. She knew whereof she spoke, though. If only kids could be inoculated with experience along with their vaccine shots.

"I don' need nobody—" Gene's eyes widened as he looked past her shoulder.

The back of her neck prickled. The screeching peacock should have warned her. Dropping Gene's collar, Cleo swung around, and her insides did a little kick dance she hadn't experienced in a long time.

Her nuisance of a tenant emerged from the wax myrtle bearing a cardboard box and a battered tube. Disregarding the cardboard, she gazed in wonder at the sweat-dripping, scratched, and furious man smashing his way through the shrubs. Dirt, leaves, and perspiration coated his tanned face. If he'd ever buttoned his shirt, he'd lost the buttons, because it hung open now to reveal a vastly appealing bronzed and sculpted chest. If she didn't drag her gaze away, she'd be drooling any minute. Who'd have thought the comic hero would look like that?

"Is this the brat responsible for these?" He shoved the box in Cleo's direction.

She gazed dispassionately at one of Blackie's relatives and snatched Gene's collar again before he could flee. "I never tried to figure if snakes laid eggs or not," she answered thoughtfully, "but I'm fairly certain kids don't lay snakes."

Frozen in fear, Gene didn't laugh at her little joke, but she thought the comic hero quirked his lip upward for a fraction of a second. So, it wasn't a good joke. She hadn't much practice.

"Your snake?" he asked, shoving the box under Gene's nose.

"A man admits it when he's done wrong," Cleo said quietly. "Only kids lie and pretend they can get away with it."

Gene's shoulders sagged, and Cleo released his collar,

putting her arm around him instead. He'd angered his hero, and probably lost any chance at an autograph to impress the bullies at school. She understood. But she'd had to learn the hard way to accept responsibility for her actions. She'd teach Gene the right way.

"I'm sorry," he muttered. "I didn't mean to hurt nothing."

"I might have killed the snake," Jared admonished. "And what happened to the damned peacock?"

"He got riled and lost some feathers, but he ain't hurt," Gene said defensively. "He wasn't supposed to be roosting that time of day, no how."

Jared quirked a questioning eyebrow at Cleo. "He yours?"

She should punch him for that, just for the age factor, but she supposed lots of people still had kids at sixteen or seventeen. She'd at least had the smarts to avoid that pitfall. She dug her fingers into Gene's knotty brown hair and tugged. Maybe she ought to claim him. It would save a lot of grief.

Gene settled the matter before she could. "Nah, she's a mean old witch who don't like strangers bothering her. I take care of her zoo."

"Shouldn't he be in school?" Jared asked in suspicion.

Cleo caught Gene's hair tighter before he could make a break for it. "We were in the process of discussing that." She didn't hold out a lot of hope that a snooty Yankee would help with a kid who'd ruined his car, but she wasn't shy about asking. "You want to explain to him the value of a good education?"

Jared narrowed his eyes as his gaze swept over the boy's dirty T-shirt, baggy pants, and ripped athletic shoes. "I don't remember talk being relevant at his age. Nikes mattered." He scrutinized the boy a little closer.

"Beating up bullies mattered, so size was a factor. He could always go back to school after he grows into his shoulders."

"Fat help you are." She shoved Gene in the direction of her truck. "C'mon. I'll take you in."

Gene's hangdog look tugged at her heart, but she didn't have experience in these things. She just knew the kid needed an education, and he couldn't get it playing truant.

"If they're a pair, there's another one floating around out there." Jared nodded his head in the direction of the woods.

Cleo bit back a curse and glared at Gene. "Kismet? You have your sister skipping now?"

"I don't tell her what to do," Gene protested. "We got up late, is all. Don't make a federal case of it, all right?"

"Do you have a gym coach?" Jared asked unexpectedly.

"Yeah, they got one. What of it?"

"What teams are you on?"

Gene's expression puckered into discontent. "I'm too short for any teams."

"For the wrestling team?"

"Ain't got no wrestling team." Scorn laced with bitterness in a combination only a thirteen-year-old could produce.

Cleo didn't know where Jared was going with this. The schools here didn't have a lot of money, and sports of any sort cost money. She knew Gene's mother couldn't afford athletic shoes, much less fees.

She'd like to know why her tenant had taken this sudden interest. It sure as hell couldn't be to impress her.

"I was on a wrestling team." Jared answered her question before she asked it. "Kids your age need a physical outlet. Besides, a good coach could beat some sense into you." Jared turned purposeful brown eyes in Cleo's direction, eyes that warmed parts of her she hadn't realized had gone cold. "Can you round up the other one while I get the Jeep? I want to talk to the principal, and I'd rather not squeeze all of us into your truck."

Somehow, she'd lost track of the scene. She glanced at his sweat-soaked, open shirt, and cursing her unimaginative hormones, raised a skeptical eyebrow. "If you're planning on going in there and arguing with the establishment like that, I'll hide in the woods with Kismet."

He shrugged. "I'll clean up. C'mon kid. I've got a pair of Nikes that will probably fit you. If I'm gonna knock your block off, you ought to be properly equipped for the coffin." He reached for Gene, remembered the box in his hand, and handed it to Cleo, along with the tube. "Merry Christmas."

Cleo gaped in astonishment as the two of them ambled off, Gene chattering excitedly as if they were long-lost friends. She was losing her freaking mind. How had *The* Jared McCloud turned from fury to pal over a wrestling coach? If she were the type who cared, she'd surmise he'd been in trouble with his teachers once too often and knew the solution from experience. That was *his* problem. *She* wasn't getting involved.

She set the snake box on a stump for later removal to the zoo and examined the cardboard tube with curiosity. With her luck, it would contain another snake.

Gently, she eased out the paper rolled inside, unfurled it, and studied the hastily penned cartoon. The man could say a lot with few strokes of his pen. No wonder he was famous. She wished her drafting work could be as accomplished.

He'd drawn two skeleton figures. The male one was politely bowing, hat in hand, cigar clamped between his teeth. The female one—although how he'd succeeded in denoting sex in a skeleton, she couldn't ascertain—wielded a knife in one hand and a snake in the other. She couldn't tell whether the knife was meant for the man or the snake, but she assumed this was his idea of their introduction. Very apt, if she said so herself, even if there were days she felt less female than this curvy skeleton.

She didn't want to feel gratitude toward the man invading her privacy and complicating her relationship with the kids. She resented the intrusion of dozens of work trucks roaring up and down her road all day, along with the constant pound of hammers and buzz of saws. She didn't want to look out her window and see Jared McCloud standing there with a snake in hand. Or a cartoon. Or whatever. She wanted to be left alone to put her life together again, to find some sense of security in her surroundings.

And she'd been doing just that until he intruded with his fancy cars, and teasing smile, and the boyish hank of hair she wanted to jerk out of his face. Men shouldn't be that happy. The men she knew were miserable, bitter creatures unfit for polite society. She'd like to keep it that way.

Muttering, she rolled up the cartoon and stalked off in search of Kismet. Maybe she ought to sic Jared McCloud on the kids' mother. That would bring Peter Pan back to reality.

❧ SIX ❧

"Look, you're not the kids' father. You don't even live here. I don't know what you think you can do, but I'm not going with you. I have to go to work."

Cleo stood outside the Jeep, glaring at the interfering wretch who had just increased her load of guilt. He assumed entirely too much. She'd sought the privacy of this island for a reason. She didn't need crusading heroes dragging her into something that wasn't any of her business, interfering with the lives of others, and pushing her into the kind of stress that always got her into trouble. No way, no sirree, uh-uh.

Kismet drifted uncertainly between Cleo and the oversized vehicle with her brother and Jared inside. Seizing the opportunity, Cleo opened the rear door and gestured for the girl to climb in. "He'll take you to school. It's okay. He draws cartoons for a living." She ought to thank the man for his gift, if that's what it had been, but she wasn't in a humor for it right this minute.

"I wield a mean pen, but I don't bite. Get in, Cleo. You know the situation and I don't." Jared stepped out and leaned on the car roof to argue with her.

"You've got that right. You don't know anything about the situation. Just take the kids in to school and drop them off. They know what to do." Cleo backed away, jiggling her truck keys nervously. Getting into the face of the school administration to demand a wrestling coach wasn't on her agenda. Icing down her overheating engine might be on her to-do list if he didn't leave soon. He looked just as good in dress shirt as none at all.

Jared glared at her. "Chicken. You think I'll make an ass of myself."

Well, no, the thought hadn't occurred to her. Cleo eyed him skeptically. "And that affects me how?"

He looked a bit taken aback at her reply, then shrugged and gave her the toothy grin that proved he came from a family with enough money to buy the best of dental care. "You're right. You'd probably enjoy seeing me make an ass of myself. If I promise to try, will you come with us?"

"Look, I've got *issues*, okay? Just leave it alone. Kismet, get in the car and go to school. I'll see you later, and you can tell me all about it." She shoved the girl into the car and slammed the door after her. She lightly swatted Gene in the front seat, and he grinned at her, still naive enough to believe his hero could fight dragons and win. That was all right. Kids needed heroes. She'd be here to listen to the complaints when it all fell to pieces after Jared returned to his world.

"All right, you'll be sorry you missed the show. I've always wanted to tell school officials what I thought of them." Jared swung back into the car and revved the engine.

Oh, yeah, she'd always wanted to tell them a thing or three as well. But she'd never had the money to put where her mouth was. People didn't take her kind of mouth on credit.

She watched them roll off, Gene cheering and Kismet dreamily wrapping her finger in her curls while staring into space. Cleo's heart ached at the hopelessness of their situation, but she, better than anyone, knew not to interfere between parent and child. Jared didn't have a clue as to what he was getting into.

"Cleo, there's a man out here asking for you. If you don't want him, can I have him?" Marta patted her graying hair and grinned.

On a ladder counting boxes of #10 nails, Cleo jotted down the count, and glanced at her clerk. "Why me? You know enough about this stuff to answer questions." She hadn't intended for the hardware store to become an all-female enterprise, but it had worked out that way. Men in this area weren't thrilled at the idea of working for a female, especially a bossy one like Cleo. Marta had worked construction jobs for years before a knee injury had made climbing difficult, so she'd grabbed at Cleo's offer of employment. Marta had a wide circle of girlfriends in the industry they could call on whenever they needed extra help. It had worked out far better than anyone had anticipated.

"I figured it was personal business. You mean you don't always go out with dreamboats?"

"I don't go out at all." Climbing down, Cleo shoved straying strands of hair back from her face. The storeroom didn't get the benefit of air-conditioning, and the strands stuck to her perspiring brow, but she didn't have to look good for anyone she knew.

"I can fix that for you," Marta said genially, following her toward the front of the store. "I know at least—"

Shrugging on her flannel shirt over her T-shirt, Cleo waved her hand dismissively. "You know better. Men are an evil influence." At least, the ones she picked always were. Life had become much more pleasant since she'd given up the fantasy of a mommy-and-daddy family. She had Matty and a good job and money in the bank. She'd like to keep it that way.

Using a clean rag to wipe her face, she emerged from the storeroom and almost stopped dead in her tracks. The man at the counter stood tall and broad enough to be an NBA star, but something in his taut stance and suspicious eyes spoke of dangerous intelligence. Why the devil would a man like that know her name? And then it struck her—Jared. This man had Jared's long nose and face and bones, just in a larger, better-proportioned, more hazardous package. Shootfire.

"I'm Cleo Alyssum," she said warily.

The man nodded gravely, without a hint of Jared's easy smile. "I'm Timothy John McCloud, Jared's brother. People usually call me TJ. He said you could give me directions to his place."

She considered peeking around him to see what kind of expensive machine waited at the curb, but thought better of it. Peeking around this man wouldn't be easy. Half a head taller than she, Jared was a comfortable height. This man was downright intimidating. She didn't think it wise to let him loose in her private war zone without a warning. "I can tell you how to get there, but he probably isn't home right now. He's over at the school making trouble."

Gray eyes lit with a knowing beam. "That's all Jared ever did at school was make trouble. You must be the creative inventor he told me about. I'm eager to encounter your 'lane of horrors.' "

Inventor? Well, that was a five-star word for mechanic. "I noticed he has a need to exaggerate," she said dryly. "There's a construction crew out there now, so you can't miss the place. Just take the highway out to the causeway and once you're on the island, watch for the drive on the left with the construction sign. Unless you have a four-wheel drive, go slow and be careful. I'm not set up for visitors."

"Imposed on you, did he? Jared never did learn the meaning of 'no.' He only has another two months to complete that script, so he shouldn't run over you for too long. It was good meeting you, Cleo."

With a polite nod, he strode out. Cleo caught sight of a sedate white sedan at the curb and figured it was a rental. No fun at all.

Two months? Jared was going to all this trouble for a two-month project? The man was utterly insane. And not working hard at finishing the project if he had time to chase kids through the woods and stalk school principals. But then, he hadn't struck her as the ambitious workaholic type. His brother had that look about him, though.

"My, my." Marta wiped her hands on her carpenter's apron and watched approvingly as TJ McCloud folded himself into his car and drove away. "Isn't it time you had a dinner party and invited your new neighbors and me?"

"I've got peanut butter in the cabinet. You're welcome to it." Picking up her inventory pad, Cleo returned to the storeroom. When tall dark strangers entered her life, they were usually feds. With luck, this one would disappear before she encountered him again.

Jared cursed and hit the brakes of his Jeep upon spotting Tim standing in the drive, inspecting the swinging witch. His brother would have the straggle-haired figure flat on its back and dissected if left alone long enough.

"What is the meaning of the red shoes?" TJ asked, still eyeing the witch while Jared climbed out of the car.

"Didn't you ever watch *Wizard of Oz*?" Jared shook

his head in disgust at his very literal, science-oriented brother. "I don't think we come from the same family."

"You may wish otherwise, but the relationship is rather unavoidable." Giving up on the witch, TJ turned to his younger brother. "You're not looking stressed and burned out."

"When was the last time you believed Mom? If she doesn't have anything to worry over, she makes things up. Didn't she get chosen for the Charity Ball committee this year?"

Tim shrugged. "That, and the bachelor auction. But despite your assertions otherwise, she does know we exist."

Jared snorted. "Benign neglect coupled with guilt leads to an overactive worry gland, then. If Mom's the only reason you're down here, you can leave now without a qualm." He walked back to the Jeep.

Tim ambled after him. "Your landlady said you were at the school making trouble. Does this mean you've finished the screenplay and don't have anything better to do?"

Since there was no sign of Tim's car, Jared figured his brother had walked up from the beach. There'd be no getting rid of him and his nagging now. "The project is done when I say it is. Now, if you want to reform somebody, you don't need to look further than Cleo—hard-boiled, antagonistic, and just plain mean—she ought to be a prime candidate."

TJ quirked an eyebrow as he climbed into the Jeep. "You mean you've found a woman who doesn't swoon at your feet? That doesn't bode well for making deadlines."

Shifting gears and spinning tires in the sand, Jared scowled. "Cut it out, Tim. I came down here to get away from you and all the other nattering curmudgeons of the world. Inspiration isn't something one calls up on the phone or types on the keyboard. It comes from living, and that's what I'm doing—*living*. Now, what the hell are you doing down here instead of in Africa or China or whatever?" His brother's expertise in forensic anthropology had taken him down many strange paths, all of them successful and important, many of them dangerous. Jared didn't need to be told that drawing cartoon strips wasn't anywhere in the same category. Creating TV flops didn't even rate a place on the chart.

"I'm only making polite conversation," Tim said stiffly. "I'm interested in your work. If it's a sensitive topic, I'll stay off it."

"Stay off it." Jared didn't like talking about his work even when it was going well, which it wasn't. "What happened to your lady scientist?"

"Physicist. She was a physicist, and our relationship was purely intellectual. I believe she's marrying some two-bit actor from the theater department in the spring."

Jared politely stifled his laughter. He might be a failure in the career department, but Tim had a long track record of failures with the female gender. "She went for passion, did she? Women are weird like that."

"I thought a physicist would be logical." Tim leaned forward to better view the brief flash of peacock strutting away from the road. "I didn't think peacocks native to the low country."

"Iguanas and potbellied pigs probably aren't either, but there's one of each. For all I know, there's wild boar and panthers. I don't think you'll find my landlady is strong in the logic department either."

"Interesting." Tim sat back and regarded the approaching ocean view with apparent pleasure. "I thought her quite helpful and forthright."

Jared felt a twinge of the old competitive urge, and fought valiantly to quell it. Tim had no interest in a

hardware-store clerk who wore tinted glasses and an attitude. He was just being deliberately provoking. "Can-
did to the point of brutality," he agreed.

Tim almost grinned. "Yeah. The two of you in one
place ought to spark spontaneous combustion. Invite her
for dinner."

"If you're that bored and in need of entertainment, invite her yourself." Steering into the weed patch he called
a driveway, Jared halted the Jeep. "There's beer in the
fridge. Make yourself at home."

"Jared."

He turned to his brother questioningly.

"Thank you. I needed a bit of time away."

Ah, hell. Tim must have really fallen for the fickle
physicist. He punched his brother's arm and threw open
the door. "This is away, all right. No one will find us
here."

Petey shrilled his warning scream, and getting up from
the desk where she'd spread her drawings of the courthouse clock gears, Cleo leaned against her bedroom
window frame to see who was invading her territory
now. The construction crews usually didn't slow down
enough for the peacock to scream at them.

She'd had to rip out the rotten sill in here before she
could glaze the windows, and she'd replaced it with a
wide polished pine board for piling up pillows and sitting on. Maybe she shouldn't call what she did "repairing" houses so much as improving them.

A lone bicyclist, blond hair streaming from beneath
her cap, pedaled past the pop-up warning sign, probably
because it didn't pop up. A flaw in the design required
the weight of a car to trigger the action. Crossing her
arms in irritation, Cleo waited to see which way the intruder went. She really needed to finish that barrier, but

without a fence it wouldn't stop a bicyclist. Maybe a swamp on either side of the road . . .

The woman pedaled past the drive and on down the lane toward the beach. Did everyone in the world believe No Trespassing signs weren't for them? Maybe she needed to erect a Panther Crossing sign. That should give people something to think about.

Especially if she could play a recording of one roaring. Hmmm.

Wandering back into the cool shadows of the house, Cleo checked the refrigerator for some evidence of dinner. The days were getting shorter. She hoped the bicyclist had a way back that didn't involve pedaling. This end of the island didn't have streetlights.

The phone rang, and she ignored it. Answering machines existed for the sole purpose of answering phones. She scavenged a bottle of Coke and a Styrofoam box of leftovers from yesterday's lunch at Porky's. Soggy fries and barbecue should nuke well.

Jared's mechanical voice spoke over the machine. "Cleo, I know you're there. I've got the kids' teacher here. Come over and we'll talk."

The kids' teacher. The blond bicyclist. She remembered the woman from the hardware store, buying pink paint for her toddler's room. Not a teacher, but the school counselor. Just what the world needed, another counselor. She hit the microwave setting and sipped her drink while leaning against the terra-cotta tile counter, admiring the satiny finish she'd given to the kitchen's old pine flooring. The place had been a pigsty before she'd bought it, but she was turning it around.

"Cleo, pick up the damned phone or I'm coming up there!"

Well, hell. Giving up on positive thinking, Cleo

grabbed the receiver. "Come on over, lover boy," she cooed, "and I'll feed you to the alligators."

He laughed. The wretch had the nerve to laugh! How in hell did one get rid of idiots?

"I'll bring Tim sometime and you can let them feast on him. We'll be up in a minute."

Cleo stared at the phone in disbelief as he disconnected. No one came over here but Maya and the kids. She didn't invite people here. Was the man deaf, dumb, and blind? Or impervious to verbal bullets?

She slammed the phone back on the hook and gazed frantically around her humble abode. She hadn't graduated to the decorating level of home improvement. She had a kitchen table and two chairs, one for her, one for Matty. The living room had a couch she'd rescued from the roadside and re-covered so she'd have a place to flop down and stare at the TV at night. The rest of the place was more or less inundated in electrical components, gears, cogs, bits of wood and sheet metal, and whatever else she happened to be working on. They'd walk in here and know she was every bit as dysfunctional as she appeared.

Muttering curses, Cleo contemplated turning on her security system and scaring the bejeebers out of the blond Nosy Parker.

School authority figures communicated with legal ones. The blonde would probably report Cleo to the sheriff as a dangerous psychopath. He'd look her up, and before she knew it, her supervisor would be down here snooping.

She'd known better than to let anyone out here. Hell.

With resignation, Cleo took her Coke outside, slammed the door shut, and wandered out to wait for them in the drive. No one said she had to be polite.

❧ SEVEN ❧

Body language said it all, and Cleo had a hell of a loud body, Jared thought admiringly, watching her T-shirt pull tight as she crossed her arms at their approach. Trim tanned legs that could have matched the best in Vegas emerged from a pair of cutoffs. He'd have to catch her by surprise more often so she didn't have time for her usual disguise.

"Hey, Cleo, do you know Liz Brooks?" He gestured toward the guidance counselor. If they'd had teachers who'd looked like Liz back when he was in school, he might have paid more attention in class. To the teacher, anyway. But he'd outgrown the need for sweet blondes since those days. He liked sassy redheads now.

Cleo nodded curtly and waited for an explanation. Had he a sensitive nerve in his body, he would have backed away from the icy waves rolling off her, but sensitivity wasn't one of his strong points.

"Liz says Kismet may be developmentally handicapped and should be in some special program. Do you know Kismet's mother? Can you introduce Liz to her? In a special program Kismet can—"

"I know all about special programs," Cleo said coldly. "When square pegs don't fit in round holes, schools find a special program for them."

"Square pegs need special attention," Liz said, with

60

her best guidance counselor's smile. "Teachers can't devote enough time to the ones who don't fit in with the rest."

"So you stick them in a special class where they don't have a chance of ever fitting in, instead of trying to figure out some way of making square holes for them. Kismet isn't developmentally handicapped." Cleo laced the words with heavy sarcasm. "She's *socially* handicapped."

Liz stepped backward at the hostility. "Well, that's possible, I suppose, although her tests say—"

"The mother, Mrs. Watkins?" Jared intruded with this reminder to turn down the heat. Or the cold. Freezers had nothing on Cleo. "Is she around here?"

"She works nights," Cleo responded sweetly.

Jared knew to be suspicious of that tone, but the counselor was oblivious.

"Perhaps I could see her some afternoon," Liz bubbled eagerly. "Kismet is a wonderful little girl with lots of potential if we could get her the right help."

"And Gene?" Ice edged Cleo's voice again. "Do you have a special program for truants?"

"Actually, we do—"

"But that won't be necessary," Jared interrupted. "Gene and I had a talk. If I can find sponsors to start a wrestling team, he'll stay in school. Now that he has a decent pair of shoes, he's willing to give it a try. Do you think his mother would mind if I took the kids shopping? Kids his age are clothes conscious. That could be part of their problem."

For a moment, Jared thought he might have almost caught a look of approval in Cleo's eyes. Her fleeting admiration fired his ego sufficiently to work for it again.

"I'm sure they'll appreciate the attention," she said with polite scorn. "If you'll excuse me, Miss Brooks, my dinner is on the table. The children's phone number should be in your records. Call Mrs. Watkins after noon and before six, and you might catch her."

"Thank you, Cleo, and it's 'Mrs.' I'm a widow."

Jared thought that might be for his benefit, and from Cleo's uplifted eyebrow, she did, too. She smiled silkily, made her farewells, and escaped behind the closed walls of her fortress.

"Well, I think that went well, didn't it?" Liz said perkily. "Cleo is what is known as one of our eccentric Southern characters. Every town must have one." She frowned as much as her smooth brow would allow. "She earned the reputation rather quickly, but I suppose befriending the town drunk has something to do with that."

"Come along, Mrs. Brooks, I'll put your bike in the Jeep and drive you home. It will be dark soon." Eccentricity didn't offend him. Ignorance did.

"Why, that's so thoughtful of you! And offering to help sponsor the wrestling team . . . Why, I . . ."

Jared listened to Liz's prattle with half an ear as they strode back to the beach. He'd much rather hear Cleo's opinion—not on his sponsorship of the team, but on the subject of the children's mother. He had a feeling she knew a lot more about the mysterious Mrs. Watkins than she was willing to relate for a guidance counselor.

Did Cleo only befriend drunks and truants? What did he need to do so she'd befriend *him*?

Her burglar alert system bellowed its impressive cop routine, and lying on the sprawling sofa, Cleo sighed as she threw a banana peel at the waste can. The siren on the drive had gone off when Jared took the counselor home, and again, half an hour ago, when he returned. She'd have to shut the whole damned rigmarole down just so she didn't establish his routine with the local spinsters and widows.

The door knocker sounded even though she'd heard the skeleton chain whir into place. "Go away, McCloud," she shouted, turning up the television so she didn't have to hear his reply.

He opened the door as if she'd invited him in. "You really ought to get a bolt for this thing," he commented, shutting it behind him.

She didn't want to look at him, but his energy charged the air, drawing her eye to the sexy sight of a long, lean, good-looking hunk standing inside her doorway, hands in pockets, absorbing her idea of interior decoration with an air of interest. The bottom dropped out of her stomach—not just because he was good-looking, but because he expressed interest where all else showed scorn or wariness. The damned man had so much self-confidence that he didn't need to be wary, and enough intelligence to keep an open mind when he stumbled into something—or someone—different.

He ought to have Danger—Alert signs flashing above his head.

"Early teen male, I'd say. Where are the oily car parts?" He dropped into the ratty wicker chair, waited for it to steady beneath his weight, then draped a leg over the chair arm. He grinned at her scowl, and the electricity in the room shot to megakilowatts.

"In the bathroom, soaking. What do you want, McCloud?" Maybe she could install a lightning rod and ground them both. She might be out of practice, but she knew a look of male appreciation when she saw one.

"Don't I get the standard lecture on trespassing? Or are we past that now?"

She could say something about his lack of maturity,

but she figured she didn't shine in that department herself. Giving up the routine, she clicked off the television and regarded him with as much hostility as she could summon for a man who grinned like a kid and looked like a stud. "Have you found nice neat holes to stuff the kids in?"

His grin disappeared. "They're a pair, no doubt. What's the mother's story?"

"What do you care? Aren't you supposed to be working on some project?"

"Been talking to Brother Tim, have we? Don't listen to him. He's so uptight, he actually thinks deadlines are supposed to be met. And his girl is getting married in the spring, so he's a bit on the hostile side these days. Do you have a beer? After all that sweetness and light, I need something bitter."

"Keep that up, and I just might learn to like you." Cleo swung her legs off the couch and ran her hand over her flattened hair. "I don't keep beer." Or drink it. Not anymore. One of the many reasons she limited her socializing. But she needed to be doing something before she succumbed to the intense vibrations in here. "How about a Dr Pepper?"

"How about strychnine? Same difference. Never mind. Just tell me about the Watkins woman."

Clenching her teeth in frustration, Cleo crossed her legs on the couch cushion, and watched Jared's mobile expression. He had the kind of rubber face that could be stretched into great grimaces. She could almost bet he'd been the class clown. "Just the usual. Poor, no education, no upbringing. She has a job right now, but when she doesn't, she goes into Charleston and brings back whatever she finds—money, drugs, men, anything that turns up." She watched carefully as he registered what she didn't say.

He just didn't know that she was also saying, There but for the grace of God, goes me.

"So Liz isn't likely to find her between noon and six unless she wants to be found, right?"

"With luck, she won't. Linda doesn't handle stress well. If Liz pushes her, she's likely to push back, or just drop off the deep end and drown her sorrows."

"It's a form of suicide, isn't it?" he said thoughtfully, sinking deeper into the chair. "How can she abandon those great kids for the depths of despair?"

"That's easy for you to say. You've never been there. You've got what you came for; you can go back home now. The school will do what it wants with the kids, and we don't have any say in the matter."

Jared lowered his eyebrows and glared at her. "The hell we don't. Where did you get that attitude, anyway? We've got advantages they don't. We should use them."

Cleo was momentarily taken aback by being included in his "we" with the "haves" instead of the "have nots." Why did he just automatically assume she was on his side of the money and education table? Because she owned property? Was that all it took to cross the cultural divide?

"How?" she demanded. "Buying the kids clothes is like slapping the mother in the face and telling her she's too dumb to provide. Even poor people have pride."

"Don't give me that 'poor people' crap. People are people. Some have pride, some don't. What matters are those kids. Don't you think they have pride? They don't want to look as if their mother doesn't care for them."

"What the hell do you care?" Offended that he was right when he had no business knowing anything about it, Cleo stretched one leg out and studied her wiggling toes rather than look at him. She hadn't had a man in her life in so long, she'd thought all her working parts had dried up and shut down. She didn't need his brand of electricity jump-starting her dead batteries.

Then she'd damned well better cover up her legs because he was staring a hole in them. A hot thrill shot up her spine, but she refused to acknowledge it. She was real good at ignoring what she didn't want to see. She tucked her leg back under her.

"Right. I'm just an airhead cartoonist who doesn't know beans from shit. That's what my family tells me. I'll go paddle in my lily pond and leave you alone." He unfolded himself from the wobbly chair and stood. "Sorry if I mistook you for someone who cared. That pretty well proves I have dip for brains."

He stalked to the door, threw it open, and walked straight into the unfurled skeleton. Cleo giggled. She couldn't help it. He looked so startled and aggrieved and chagrined, he could have been the cartoon instead of the cartoonist. "Burt wants to say good night," she called after him.

His grin was almost sheepish. "I almost had it going there, didn't I? I never was good at grand exits."

"You're doing fine, cowboy. Just don't invite me to your rodeo. I'm allergic to beefsteak."

His grin disappeared as he studied her. "One of these days, you gonna tell me your story?"

"Nope. Now get gone. I need my beauty sleep." She wanted him out of here, immediately, if not sooner. He made her edgy and itchy and anxious for things she wouldn't name and wouldn't think about. She needed him out of her life—*right now.*

"You're a beauty, sleeping or not. Why don't I take you to dinner tomorrow?"

"Why don't you take Liz to dinner?" Why didn't he go away? If he lingered any longer, she'd be inviting him in again just to bask in one of those admiring looks of his.

"She'll be properly appreciative. Now go before I power Burt up, and he wraps his bony fingers around your neck."

He rubbed his nape as if anticipating the encounter. "All right, I'll bring Porky's barbecue over around six, and we can picnic. See you then."

He bowed at the skeleton, and walked out whistling, reminding Cleo she still hadn't thanked him for the cartoon gift, if that was what it was. Torn between irritation at his presumption and guilt at her neglect, she merely threw a couch pillow at the door as it closed behind him.

She could do inventory at the shop tomorrow night.

"Liz is just what you need, big brother. Take her to dinner instead of moping out here, let her fluff your mind, and other body parts south. I've got a date." Jared held up his bag of mouthwatering grease. Outside, the carpenters were packing up for the day. It was almost six and he'd pretty much wasted the day doing push-ups and running the beach instead of working on his script, but he figured Cleo would rake him over a few hot coals and stir his creative juices. He'd certainly accomplished little more than think about her all day. He had a drawing pad full of cartoon sketches of evil pixies to attest to that.

"Does Cleo know she has a date?" Tim asked gravely, sipping from a beer on the newly repaired porch.

"She'll pretend she doesn't. I've never met anyone so determined to be antisocial."

"Caught by the old hard-to-get routine, are we?" Tim raised an eyebrow inquiringly. "Have you talked to any of your carpenters lately?"

Jared juggled his bag impatiently. "Why would I want to do that?"

"Because Cleo hired them. At least half of them are recovering alcoholics or deadbeat dads who are trying to

get their acts together. She apparently knows every construction worker on the Carolina coast and all their
stories. I get the feeling she's not your usual easygoing
love-'em-and-leave-'em type."

Jared shrugged. "I want to get to know her better, not
seduce her. Unlike you, I just let things happen. You
gonna be all right here alone?"

TJ swirled his beer. "I'm fine. You're the one who
seems to have a problem with solitude. Give my regards
to Cleo."

So he normally liked to party, and solitude was wearing thin. He didn't see the problem, but he wasn't the introspective sort and didn't have time or patience to work
it out. "Fine. Maybe I'll call a few girlfriends and have
one come down and keep you company if you're planning on staying long. Be good for you."

He strode off before Tim could throw the bottle
at him.

Cleo apparently hadn't had time to erect any road-
blocks preventing access from the beach, or she probably
would have thrown them in his face as he walked up the
road to her place. He didn't know what his obsession
was with the prickly pixie, but he needed to know her
better. Maybe he just needed his questions answered.

Maybe he just needed to scratch this itch.

He hid his frown as he walked down her drive and noticed the kids sitting on the front step with a loaf of bread
and a jar of peanut butter between them. They smiled at
his approach instead of running, which was probably a
good sign, but he'd hoped to have Cleo to himself for a
change. "What's up, gang? Cleo won't let you sit at her
table and eat?"

Gene shrugged. "She ain't home. We're waiting for
her."

Well, he should have known it wouldn't be easy. He

dropped the bag of greasy barbecue on the step. "Your supper is probably healthier than mine. Wanna trade?"

Obviously, shyness didn't apply to food. They tore into the sack and contentedly munched their way into the picnic he'd intended for Cleo. "You guys waiting for Cleo to give you a ride home? I can get the Jeep."

Kismet merely smiled and bit contentedly into her sandwich. Gene diligently chewed his way through a mouthful before answering. "Nah. Mom's gone into town and we're staying here. Want a Dr Pepper? I can get you one."

Jared looked skeptically at the house that usually spat nails and dropped skeletons on him. "You can get in?"

"Sure. It ain't locked. We don't have no thieves out here." Without hesitation, Gene jumped on the step that normally set off the alarm and blithely entered the front door that dropped skeletons.

Damn perverse woman. She only set alarms to ward off intruders when she was home!

❧ EIGHT ❧

Jared wasn't speaking to her.

Which was fine with Cleo. She hadn't invited him to her house or accepted his offer for supper. He'd just presumed he was welcome. Well, he wasn't. She had better things to do than amuse itinerant comics.

Sitting on her roof in the hot sun, she whammed a nail

into a shingle. She'd chosen the expensive architectural shingles, figuring she didn't have much roof to cover, and they would last longer, even if they were more work. Besides, she liked the cottage look of the light wood and shadows it created. She might not be much on decorating, but she knew good material. With some dark Charleston green on the shutters, the place would look comfortable and welcoming someday. Pity a good coat of paint wouldn't do the same for her.

From up here, she could watch the steady stream of cars and trucks and motorcycles roaring down her private drive to Jared's place on the beach. He must have invited the whole effing town for a party, except her. She would figure he'd done it to get even, but she didn't think she rated that high on a celebrity's priority list.

Maybe she ought to build a widow's walk on the roof, a tower that loomed over the trees so she could have a view of the ocean. Sitting up and rubbing her aching back, Cleo contemplated the view from here. She couldn't see the beach house or the couples frolicking on the sand, only the distant lapping of waves toward shore. It was all the view she needed.

She wondered how Jared managed to know so many people after being here only a couple of weeks, but it wasn't any of her business. Country club sorts learned to socialize from birth. Despite his weird occupation, she pegged him for the country club type. He'd probably already been golfing over at Hilton Head. He should have stayed there instead of invading her primitive jungle.

Wistfully, she glanced up the road in the direction from which Matty should be arriving—except he wouldn't be here this weekend. Maya and Axell had promised the kids a trip to the zoo in Columbia, and Matty had wanted to go with them. They'd invited Cleo. She probably should have gone. It wasn't as if Maya and her upright pillar-of-the-community husband would lead her astray. She just hadn't been up to watching a happy family at play, knowing she was deficient in whatever it took to create that same ambience for Matty.

She probably ought to go down and write something revealing in her journal right now, like: "I know I'm good and getting better, but I'm still a work in progress." Yeah, like that was real helpful.

From this viewpoint, she could see Kismet sitting on a log in the menagerie, scribbling in her sketchbook. Gene had the pig out, playing with it. Normal people had cats and dogs. She had pigs and iguanas. If the counselor wanted proof of her weirdness, he'd find it right there. People didn't give her unwanted cats and dogs. They gave her unwanted *creatures*. That was bound to say something about her personality.

Wiping her forehead with the back of her wrist, Cleo decided it was time for a break. She'd take the kids some lemonade. Their mother had lost her job last week and disappeared into the city. Again. She didn't have the heart to tell them that one of these days, their mother might not come home at all. She'd hate to see those kids lost in the vast wilderness of an underpaid, overworked Social Services department. She knew firsthand how children got lost in the system.

Maybe she'd talk to Linda again, when and if she returned. The AA program in town wasn't much help for crack addicts, but it was better than nothing. She could take her to one of the meetings, maybe make her feel comfortable by introducing her to a few of the others. As if she'd ever made anyone feel comfortable in her life.

Snorting at the idea, Cleo climbed down. Stick with lemonade. That was at least something she knew how to do.

The kids started chattering the instant she carried the

tray of glasses into their hideaway. They blossomed with a little attention, and for a brief moment she felt as if she'd finally learned to do something right. Then she noticed how proudly they showed off their new clothes, and she knew she had only done it half right. Jared had gone all the way by interfering where she never would.

And she'd been wrong. Linda hadn't come after him with a hatchet for buying the kids what she couldn't afford. If it had been Cleo, she would have taken his head off with hedge clippers, but she had a hard time remembering other people weren't like her. One of her less intelligent traits.

She sat on a log, sipped her iced drink from a plastic cup, and listened to Gene chatter about the new wrestling coach they'd have next week. It had never occurred to her that she could simply walk into the school, give them money, and they'd buy equipment to start a team. There had to be more to it than that, but Jared had pulled it off. Maybe his famous name had helped, but she had to admire the guts and sense it took to go for it. So maybe she shouldn't be so hard on him. Just because he was handsome and rich and a jerk didn't mean he didn't have any redeeming qualities.

She was going to have to break down and thank him.

She postponed the inevitable by gesturing at Kismet's sketchpad. "What do the teachers at school say about your work?"

She didn't know a thing about drawing, as her pitiful mechanical sketches proved, but maybe she ought to show Kismet's book to Jared, see if he could encourage the girl. Unfortunately, Kismet was dismally shy. She'd disappear into the ground if Cleo tried pushing her too far.

Kismet shook her head, and smiled quietly as her fingers fluttered over the array of stubby pencils she'd collected over the years. Cleo had bought her an expensive art set for Christmas, but she'd never seen it again after Kismet took it home with her. Cleo didn't think Linda could pawn an art set, but she might have sold it to a friend desperate for a last-minute Christmas gift.

There had been a time when she'd sold her own wedding ring and a birthday necklace from her sister to get a quick fix.

She didn't like looking back at those times. She was getting better. She'd never be cured, but even if she couldn't change her nature, every step she took away from the stress and horror of her prior life took her further from the evil temptations of her past. She had to believe that or kill herself.

"You know Jared draws, don't you?" she asked, uncertain how much Kismet actually observed or understood.

The girl nodded, and Gene wandered over to claim his share of the attention. "I showed her the cartoon in the newspaper," he boasted. "He does them on the computer, not on any silly piece of paper."

"He does them on paper, too," Cleo said quietly. "I have one at the house. Remind me to show you when we go back."

She didn't have time to register their reaction. The rustling of leaves warned someone approached, even if the peacock hadn't screamed an alarm. She hoped Jared's guests hadn't taken to straying this far inland.

Knocking back a hanging honeysuckle vine, Linda emerged into the clearing. Beneath the brassy blond of her thick hair, her dark roots showed, but Cleo assumed she must have been a natural blond once for the children to have the coloring they did. Succumbing to heaviness in the waist and hips as full-bosomed women often did, the kids' mother still maintained a figure that would stop men in their tracks, particularly in the tight capri pants and belly-revealing knit tops she favored.

"I've been looking all over for you brats. Get on home now and quit pestering the neighbors."

Cleo could smell the bourbon from here. Linda wasn't a polite drunk or a druggie who sprawled comatose in doorways. She could be belligerent and nasty-mouthed when under the influence.

The children didn't immediately leap to their mother's command but looked to Cleo for a reassurance she didn't possess. "They're not bothering me, Linda," she said cautiously. "Want me to send them home in time for dinner?"

Cleo didn't like thinking about how she had looked and behaved when strung out on whatever drug her ex had brought home, but she did have some memory of being steered by a careful choice of words. She figured she had a fifty-fifty chance of that succeeding with Linda now.

Linda looked convincingly bewildered and disarmed enough to give in, but easily distracted she glanced up at the shriek of a peacock and the sound of someone trampling the path on the other side of the clearing.

Cleo uttered a litany of mental curses as Jared navigated the shrubbery. Damn, the man not only had bad timing, he had to look gorgeous while he was at it. With his white linen shirt half unbuttoned to reveal a bronzed chest and a hint of pectorals no nerdy cartoonist should have, his yuppie khaki shorts creased and exposing long, strong legs that would have done a runner proud, he looked the epitome of wealthy manhood. Linda would either run, screaming, in the opposite direction, or suck up big-time.

Cleo intervened before either could happen. "Linda, this is Jared McCloud. He's living down at the beach for a few months. Jared, the children's mother, Linda Watkins. Kids, why don't you take the cups and pitcher back to the house, okay?" She'd be a real wheeler-dealer one of these days if she managed to keep all these balls rolling in the right direction without colliding.

"I want you brats home by supper, you hear!" Linda shouted after them as they hastened to obey Cleo. "I don't want you living over here no more."

"You'll be staying home, then?" Cleo had to ask once the children were out of hearing. She noticed Jared kept his mouth shut, for a change.

"I'll have welfare out here nosing around if they don't stay where they belong. I don't want them cutting off my money." She eyed Jared skeptically. "What you staring at, city boy?"

Cleo gritted her teeth and watched an ant crawl across a rock at her feet. It was so much easier not to get involved when she didn't have neighbors.

"Your children have been quite helpful," Jared said with careful politeness. "I hope you don't mind if they visit once in a while."

Cleo could just imagine the kinds of things Mr. America would be thinking about Linda—most of them accurate, if she was to be honest. Still, it rubbed the pain of self-knowledge deeper. She'd been Linda in a former life. Maybe she'd had the sense and the family to rescue her, but she'd been there and seen that bottom and rubbed her nose in the slime.

"Just keep your hands off my kids." Swaying only slightly, Linda shoved her way back through the shrubbery in the direction of the shack she called home.

Cleo listened to Jared's soft curses for a minute before she settled the roiling in her stomach and managed to stand. She didn't want to look at him. Some days, she didn't want to look at herself. She started off after the kids without speaking to him.

"Are you going to let those kids go back home to her?" he called after her in a tone of incredulity.

There it was, the challenge she confronted every day of her life. It came in different forms, perhaps, taking a different face each time, but always there. What if someone had said that about Matty and her? What if Maya had given up on her and taken Matty away, or let Social Services take him away? She'd be dead right now.

She snapped a twig from a wax myrtle and didn't face him. "She's their mother. They need her. She needs them. I'm not God."

She left him to his shock and disbelief and strode away. Someone from his world would never understand. She didn't expect him to.

Let *him* plan for a sunny future and paint rosy pictures of throwing his coins around to make things better. She did well to put one foot in front of the other and survive from one day to the next. She had money now. She knew where the next meal was coming from. It didn't change the mind-set. She lived for the moment, and in that moment, she was leaving Linda to her drunken tirades.

Jared crashed through the bushes after her and grabbed her arm with a strength she couldn't fight. "That's a damned selfish attitude."

Fighting fury, Cleo looked him full in the eyes. "She's their *mother*. She's the one who rocked their cradles and changed their diapers and gave them names. Do you think there is anyone on the face of this planet who will care for them any more than she does?"

"She's *incapable* of caring for them!" he shouted. "Good grief, woman, can't you see what she is?"

Cleo jerked her arm away. "Yeah, she's lost. She's the mother of two half-black bastards, ostracized by her family and most of society, a victim of drugs and alcohol and probably abuse and possibly incest and heaven knows what else. Everyone she knows thinks she's worthless. *She* thinks she's worthless. Hell, for all I know, maybe she *is* worthless. I'm just not the one to lay that judgment on her. All right? The kids know where to find me when they need me. That's all I can do, all I'm gonna do. Now go play with your pretty toys and leave us alone."

Shocked by her attitude, Jared let her go. Cleo didn't look any bigger than the children as she shoved through the shrubbery away from him, but he had the feeling that every fragile inch of that woman's body was packed with dynamite so volatile, it could blow him away. He knew better than to play with dynamite.

Still, the faint fresh smell of her soap stayed with him, mixed with a hint of tar. She'd probably been booby-trapping the road again. He knew she wasn't any sweetness and light socialite like his mother, pouring money on troubled waters. It shouldn't shock him when Cleo threw all his carefully cultivated beliefs back in his face with her callous attitude.

Or maybe shocking him was another one of her methods of scaring him off.

The logical next question was—why did she *want* to scare him off?

He ought to get back to the schoolteachers, but curiosity—probably driven by careening hormones—carried his feet along the path his mysterious landlady had taken.

⚜ NINE ⚜

Jared rolled his eyes in dismay as he reached the lane to the bellow of Cleo's burglar system threatening to shoot intruders, the flapping of her No Trespassing sign up and down in the road, and the sight of the high school vocational education teacher dismantling her nonworking swinging gate. Liz had draped herself over the gate to watch, and Tim leaned against a tree, arms crossed, absorbing the chaos. Having arrived in the forlorn hope of seeing some form of the overdue script, Jared's agent had wandered away from the party, probably looking for him. He now sat on the front step, searching under the porch eaves for the source of the bellows.

Jared saw nary a sight of Cleo and the kids, which was probably a good thing. A *real good thing*.

"I think your party may be getting out of hand," Tim called from his tree trunk, lifting a beer bottle and gesturing. "They're talking about skinny-dipping down at the beach. I never saw so many teachers get loaded so fast."

"Great party, Jared," the vo-ed teacher called as he examined the mechanical gizmo from the gate. "I think I found the problem on this here gate."

He hadn't found half the problem if he hadn't met Cleo yet. Maybe throwing a little get-together for the teachers to stifle some of the resentment he'd stirred by finding sponsors for a wrestling team and not funding textbooks hadn't been such a hot idea. So, who knew teachers could cut loose on a few beers? He'd thought he was helping the kids.

"I'm not certain Cleo wants the gate fixed," he said tentatively, gazing over the vo-ed teacher's shoulder at the broken gizmo.

"Miss Alyssum did this?" The teacher whistled in appreciation and began putting the mechanism back together again. "I need to get her into my mechanics class. Maybe she could persuade the little shits to build something besides bombs."

"Hey, Jared," his agent shouted from the porch steps. "How do you turn this thing off? It's creeping me out."

"Stand up, Georgie," Jared said wearily, wandering from the gate down the shell walk toward the house. He might as well give up any hope of Cleo speaking to him ever again in this lifetime. In this galaxy.

Bemused, his portly, balding agent shoved up from the step. The bellowing cop shut up instantly. George scratched his neck and inspected the step for wires.

"It's a motion detector, George. Why don't we go back to the house and discuss the extension clause on the contract and leave Miss Alyssum alone." Jared shoved his hands in the oversize pockets of his khaki cargo shorts and watched the Idea Bulb go off in his agent's head. "Uh-uh, George. She doesn't write books or comics, and if it's a how-to manual you're after, the world isn't ready for it yet."

"She's got something here, though," the agent muttered, studying the flapping sign and the nonflapping gate as he wandered back toward the lane. "If I could just—"

"Nope, you can't. Believe it or not, all this stuff is here because Cleo wants *privacy*. Kinda hard to believe, isn't it? No Trespassing signs meaning privacy? What will the world think of next?" Jared could almost hear Cleo's snicker at that. "Tim, make that damned sign stop flapping and round up your pals and get them out of here, or she'll be letting the snakes loose."

"Snakes?" Liz squealed, leaping from the gate. "No one told me she has snakes. You mean those poor children could be stumbling over snakes every time they get off the bus? That's dreadful. Someone ought to do something!"

"Someone already has," Jared assured her, catching her arm and steering her toward the beach. "They picked up the snakes and put them in boxes and only get them out when people trespass on their territory. And something tells me they consider Cleo's house their territory. Let's go get some yummy Dr Pepper. Or didn't someone bring that syrup they call sweet tea? Just what I need, a big cold glass of syrup."

"It's tea, silly, with sugar in it." Liz gaily walked off at Jared's side, chattering about the intricacies of fixing sun tea versus the way her mama always made it.

If she could see him now, Cleo would be rolling in the grass, laughing her head off. The woman had no idea what he had to put up with in the interest of getting in her good graces.

He still wasn't entirely certain why he wanted to be in the good graces of a firebomb like Cleo, except that it would be nice to have just one person in the world think he had more substance than Bugs Bunny. Why he'd picked Cleo probably had Freudian connotations far beyond his ability to analyze.

From her unfinished attic window seat, Cleo watched the tribe of intruders straggle back toward the beach. She'd made a wildly insane mistake by opening the beach house to Jared. He'd said he wanted *privacy*.

What in heaven's name did he consider privacy? First, a battalion of construction workers, and now . . .

Oh, hell, why worry about it? Leaning her head against the two-by-four behind her, Cleo let the jungle surrounding her home soothe her aching head. They were just people. Well-meaning and chowderheaded, perhaps, but just people. She was the one who didn't fit, the one who didn't dare come within a mile of a beer keg and Jared's partying lifestyle.

She'd learned she was happier climbing to the courthouse roof with the town drunk and fixing a clock that hadn't worked right since World War II than talking to anyone sane.

A normal person would have joined the party to find out what they'd done wrong with the gate mechanics. A normal person would have learned from the experience, not hidden from it.

It looked as if she had still another step to make in her progress toward sanity. Well, another day, perhaps. The kids were hiding out in the cool shadows of the front room, watching television and munching sandwiches before they went home to their nonexistent dinner. The kids understood her aversion to crowds.

Matty wouldn't. Matty adored people as well as animals, as he should. There were days when it terrified Cleo to think her son might be better off with Maya. She *wanted* to be as good with him as Maya. She'd never be as good as Maya.

But maybe someday she could be good *enough*. That was her goal—to be good enough to be Matty's mother. She figured if she hadn't killed Jared McCloud by December, she will have proved herself sane enough to have her son back.

She climbed down the attic stairs contemplating the amount of time it would take to convert the upper story to a large playroom for Matty when he moved home. She could put the walls up this winter. She'd need to install heat and air ducts, though.

The phone rang as she reached the bottom. The kids looked up at her expectantly as she passed by the front room. They probably thought people actually answered working phones.

Oh, heck, why not? She picked up the receiver with a curt "Alyssum here."

"I apologize." Jared's voice didn't sound particularly apologetic over the background noise of music. "I should have known they'd be curious. You know, if you could just come down here and meet a few of these people, they'd quit wondering and probably leave you alone."

Cleo laughed out loud. She couldn't help it. It had been an impossible day, and she was hot, sweaty, and in desperate need of a drink she couldn't have. And he thought once people met her, they'd leave her alone. How right he was!

"You can control yourself now," he said dryly through the receiver. "Maybe I didn't phrase that right, but you know what I mean."

"Strangely enough, I do." She didn't laugh often enough. It eased the depressing need for a drink. Taking the cordless to the counter, she poured a lemonade. "But I'm not about to gussy myself up to speak nonsense to strangers. This is my day off, and I don't have to speak to anyone, if I don't want to."

"All right, I won't twist your arm, but these are decent people. They don't bite. Drink too much maybe," he admitted with a hint of humor, "but not unreasonably much. It's a far cry better than one of my Miami parties."

If she needed a reminder of the distance between them, that was it. He moved in a social world that included the entire East Coast. She couldn't even manage a tiny South Carolina town. "Just don't let them go swimming in the undertow," she warned.

"They've been sufficiently cautioned. Besides, the coach is a swimming instructor and lifeguard. Look, let me make it up to you, okay? I'll take you to dinner and the movies, or bring you pizza, or whatever you like. You name it."

She wandered to the doorway of the front room, where the kids were totally engrossed in some cable cartoon. "I don't need anything. Just lay off the kids and their mother. You don't understand the situation, and you won't be here long enough to follow up on any mistakes you make. I'm tired of picking up pieces."

"They shouldn't have to live like that," he said angrily. "They deserve better."

"We all deserve better, but the chances of us getting it are up to us, not the government. Got it?"

"No, but I'll take your word for it, for now. The government has programs for just this kind of—"

"Yeah, and I'll tell you all about them sometime. Now go back and play and leave us alone, deal?"

"No deal. I'll bring a pizza by later and we can discuss the deal then. If you can keep the kids that long, I'll bring some for them."

"I send them home before dark, and you'll never get rid of that crowd before then." She didn't want to discuss anything with Jared McCloud. She wanted her life back where it had been before he started poking around in it. She didn't like being reminded of her shortcomings, and she particularly didn't like his knuckleheaded interference into things he knew nothing about. "Just forget we're here, and we'll be fine."

"Forget you're there," he scoffed. "That's like asking

me to forget the moon exists. It's time we had a talk, lady. I'll be there."

He hung up before she could argue. Cleo stared at the receiver in puzzlement. Like forgetting the moon existed? What the hell did that mean? That she was big and round and white? That she threw light on a dark night?

The man definitely did not have a way with words.

She let the kids hang around until almost dark, not telling them about potential pizza for fear they'd be disappointed one more time in their short lives. She heard the party breaking up with the roar of car engines and chatter of voices as they eased past her barriers. Once upon a time she'd been the sort of person who could mosey over to a party, down a few beers, and chatter and laugh mindlessly with others. She didn't want to dive down that hole again. Loneliness haunted her, but not enough to burn down her safety barriers.

She walked the kids through the shortcut to their house before the sun set. She saw no sign of Linda except a light burning in the front window. At least the electricity was on. The bare-board siding covered logs older than her own home, but the place had withstood a century or more of heat and hurricanes, so it wasn't in danger of falling on anyone's head just yet. When she was sober, Linda kept the place up. A couple of plastic chairs adorned the sagging porch, and a pot of unwatered geraniums withered on the railing. Somewhere beneath the brassy hair and venomous attitude was a mother who longed to make a nice home for her children, if she only knew how.

"I'll wait here until you're inside," Cleo told them. She didn't have the energy for a confrontation with Linda tonight. Nighttimes were always the worst for intelligent conversation if Linda had hit the bottle at noon.

She watched them drag into the house, knew they expected to find their mother passed out, and wished she could change things for them. But no Social Services worker in the world would let someone with her past have care of kids, and she doubted if the system could find foster parents willing to take in biracial teenagers who'd grown up wild.

Kismet waved at her from a window, and Cleo waved back. All was well, then. She could return home with an easy conscience.

She didn't know when she'd developed a conscience. It was a damned nuisance and nagged at her far more than she liked. There had been a time back when she and Maya had been shuttled from one foster home to another that she'd relentlessly tried to protect her naive younger sister. So she supposed their parents had taught her to be conscientious.

She'd lost that as soon as the system spit her out, though.

Not wanting to think of those dark years, Cleo stripped a few kudzu vines of their leaves and dropped them in the menagerie for the animals as she passed through. She hadn't heard a car drive by in a while, so she supposed Jared's guests had all departed. If she hid out here long enough, he might go away. Or maybe he'd already forgotten.

She'd showered off the tar and sweat earlier, and put on clean clothes, not for him, but for her own self-respect. She'd never actually slept in doorways, but she'd been without water and electricity and had lived in filth at one time. She took pride in knowing that was far behind her. She hoped.

She'd been lucky, but she wasn't counting on luck to help her out a second time. Instead of blowing it on a big house and car, she had invested her grandfather's unexpected legacy with the help of a friend of Maya's. She wasn't rich, but she had assets and an income, and they were growing steadily. Matty would never know the poverty she'd climbed out of. He'd forget those few early years with time.

All she had to do was stay the course, avoid situations that would bring her in contact with the wrong sorts of people, avoid the emotional chaos that could send her into a tailspin, walk the straight and narrow with the help of counseling, until she reached some semblance of steadiness. She'd been sober and drug-free for over two years now.

She didn't know how she'd know when she was steady and walking on firm ground, but emerging from the shadows of the trees to see Jared's long, sinfully appealing frame lounging on her front step with a pizza box beside him, she knew an obstacle to her steadiness when she saw one.

She should have turned the burglar alert system back on.

❧ TEN ❧

Jared watched uncertainly as Cleo emerged from the jungle of trees. A sliver of moonlight caught on the pale apricot of her cheek, accenting the fragility of her cheekbones and shadowing the depths of her oversized eyes. Maybe that's why she wore those darned glasses—to hide the emotion easily exposed by those depths.

Or maybe his imagination had run away with him again. Usually it didn't take much to live on the surface, accept women as he found them, and go with the flow. Recent events had jarred him more than he liked, and now he was seeing shadows behind every tree. Or skeletons in front of every door. Whatever.

He really didn't want to be blasted by Cleo's scathing tongue tonight. He knew he'd set himself up for it, let his confidence carry him away with a woman he knew nothing about. Any other time, he might have figured out how to shrug off rejection. Not tonight.

He hated it when a party ended and everyone went home. Usually, he had one of the women lingering behind for company. Tonight, he hadn't been in the mood for anyone but Cleo, and that bothered him. The sight of her striding toward him shot straight to his groin.

He lifted the pizza from the porch to cover his lap and tried for casualness as he rose to greet her. "Peace offering."

For a brief moment, her eyes widened, and he felt a connection, sensed a resonating loneliness and uncertainty from the woman staring back at him. Neither of them were teenagers any longer. They'd both been around and knew the score. But it was as if the years fell away, leaving them exposed and vulnerable like young kids. Or live wires.

Then she carelessly shrugged her shoulders beneath her loose cotton shirt, donned her brittle who-cares expression, and nodded curtly at the door. "It's open. I'll get us a Dr Pepper."

He'd known better than to expect beer, but he'd hoped she'd stocked something else by now. Wrinkling his nose in resignation, he opened the screen door and let her throw open the weathered wooden one. "Remind me to carry up the leftover soft drinks."

"Suit yourself. Kids will drink anything." She shoved the door open with her hip and hit the light switch. "If you don't mind eating in the kitchen, there's room on the table back there."

The lamp glowed on gleaming, newly refinished pine floors, throwing her shabby furniture into shadow. He admired the stripped and stained crown molding of the high ceiling and the thick panel doors. Most houses didn't have solid structure like this anymore. This house was meant to shelter generations.

Feeling as if she'd just thrown open the doors to the inner sanctum, Jared followed her with a mixture of amusement and anticipation. Maybe he never knew what to expect out of Cleo Alyssum, but he sure was never bored in her company.

That realization shed a light on his life that he didn't like to examine. He had a lucrative career, one he enjoyed, and everything money could buy. He had no reason to ever be bored.

He'd been bored out of his skull for months.

Okay, enough of that insight for the evening. He'd rather pry into Cleo's entertaining head.

As she flipped on the overhead light of her recently refurbished kitchen, he almost experienced disappointment. At first glance, it seemed perfectly normal. Modern stove, refrigerator, trestle table, chairs, no suffocatingly frilly curtains on the windows. Then his glance swung upward, and in the darkness near the ceiling, he discovered a grimacing gargoyle leaning over a cherry cabinet. Jared grinned in relief and inspected the rest of the shadowed gloom above his head—gargoyles and imps and devils and maybe a leprechaun or two beamed down at him from various perches.

"I really like the way you think, lady." He tossed the pizza box on the table and wandered over to inspect a cookie jar in the form of a gingerbread house, complete with witch at the door.

"Doesn't say much for your maturity," she said dryly, reaching into the refrigerator for drinks. "Maya tells me I'm expressing the inner child I was denied when young."

"Maya?" Everything about Cleo suddenly seemed fascinating. Swinging around, Jared leaned against her terra-cotta counter and watched in amazement as she reached into her cabinet and removed antique peanut butter and jelly glasses decorated with cartoon characters. An old girlfriend had bought him an identical set years ago, and he kept them on a shelf above his computer in his New York apartment.

Cleo plopped them down on the table and filled them with ice as if they were no more than Wal-Mart cheapware. "Tea, Dr Pepper, or lemonade?"

He lifted the Bugs Bunny glass and filled it with tap water. The paint colors were fading, but the Bugs Bunny toothy grin still smiled back at him. He liked the idea of using the collectibles instead of dusting them. His mother had taught her sons to value antiques and not play with her cut glass, and he'd blindly followed in her path, dusting his treasures rather than living with them. There was freedom in forgetting the strictures.

"This will do." He held up the glass, testing her. "Do you have any idea what these glasses are worth today?"

She shrugged. "Don't care. Matty likes them."

She'd already ignored his question about the Maya person. He wasn't backing down so easily this time. "Matty?" He'd seen no evidence of a man in her life. He glanced at her bare ring finger for reassurance.

"My son." Her tone held a touch of defiance as she threw paper napkins and plates on the painted tiles of the tabletop. He could almost bet she'd taken a junk table and tiled it herself. She'd spent a fortune scrupulously restoring the house, but scarcely a penny on decorating it. Gazing at her company logo T-shirt, he thought he saw a metaphor in that.

She almost stepped away from him when he pulled a chair out for her. Touchy female. But the news of her son fascinated him as much as everything else. "You have a son? Is he with his father?"

"Lord, I should hope he never will be." She took the chair and opened the pizza box, ignoring him as he took the chair opposite. "His father is dead, and with any luck at all, frying in hell."

Okay, that might be a little deeper than he wanted to dig just now. "How old is he? Your son, I mean."

She grinned wickedly over her pizza slice. "Do people age in hell? What's the matter, McCloud? You're walking around me like an elephant on eggshells."

He tried glaring at her, but that wasn't who he was. He grinned and reached for a slice. "Okay, you bring out the adolescent in me. I feel like an anxious schoolboy, afraid to say the wrong thing."

"Afraid you'll get pop dumped in your lap or afraid you won't get a make-out session when the night ends?"

"Damn, you're blunt. Didn't anyone teach you to be polite?" Since he couldn't readily answer her question, he opted for the offensive. That probably wouldn't gain him the make-out session that appealed to him. Now that she'd mentioned it, kissing those sulky lips would go a long way toward easing some of his anxiety.

"Nope. They tried to beat it into me a time or two, but I've got a hard head. Thanks for the pizza, by the way. And for the cartoon. Kismet has almost worn it out."

Jared caught the way she'd diverted the subject from the more painful admission and let her get away with it, for now. He'd ponder the thought of someone trying to beat anything into Cleo another time. "You really think she's socially challenged and not developmentally challenged? She doesn't seem too connected to reality."

Cleo emitted a little moan of appreciation as she finished chewing her last bite. "I don't get pizza often. This is good."

That little moan raised other parts of him besides his expectations, and Jared squirmed uncomfortably. He didn't hold out much hope of winning her with pizza. "I ordered extra everything. Back to Kismet."

She wrinkled her nose at him. "Men have such one-track minds. Kismet is pathologically shy; I'll give you that. Counseling might be helpful. Chances are good she's been abused in the past. Teachers really need to look for that in troubled kids. They also need to look for hidden talents. No one has ever praised Kismet, told her she was good at anything, encouraged her to come out of her shell and show the world what she is. Maybe she will never be a literary or mathematical genius. Who cares? She just needs to learn to function, and then she can find what she can do on her own."

Amazed that he'd drawn that much of a speech out of the taciturn creature across from him, Jared figured he'd hit on a hot spot and he'd best stay with it. "It's kind of hard to expect the school system to teach some kids to function while teaching others what it takes to get into college, don't you think?"

"So, what would you do with a whole lost layer of kids who've lived in mud from birth? I don't know the answers. I just know Kismet and Gene are basically good kids in a sad situation."

"Letting them stay with their mother isn't helping them." He knew better than to argue when he wanted to taste her kisses instead of pizza, but he hadn't grown up with his mother's speeches on charity and social reform without learning some social responsibility.

Cleo stabbed the pointed end of her pizza at him as if it were a knife. "You'd rather give them to a system that thinks food and clothing will solve the problem? Kids need love, encouragement, and attention, and there isn't a government in existence that can provide that. Their mother's efforts may be pitiful, but they're better than none at all."

He lifted a skeptical eyebrow. "From what I see, their mother can't provide for her own needs. I don't know how you expect her to provide for the kids'."

She ran her hands through her short hair, making it stand on end. "Not easily, but she's never been this bad before. Still, they can hope things will turn around. But if Social Services takes them away from their mother, they take away their only hope. Social workers wouldn't even have a clue if the kids belonged in a white home or a black one."

Time to derail this topic and move on to something easier. He liked knowing she could be passionate about something—it gave him hope. But he really didn't want to anger her when they were finally talking like sensible adults instead of exchanging insults. "What are you, a burned-out social worker, that you know so much about it?"

She snorted so hard the soft drink almost came out her nose. Wiping her mouth with a napkin, she shook her head in amusement. "You don't even want to go there. Let's just agree to disagree, all right? You'll go away in a few months and forget all about it. I've got to live here. Accept that it's none of your business, and we'll do fine."

He wasn't accepting anything of the sort, but he didn't have to tell her that. He liked her in a mellow mood. He'd have to bring pizza more often. "All right, then, tell me about Matty and Maya."

"Why? You're not likely to be around long enough to get to know them. You want blunt?"

She didn't give him time to tell her he'd rather forgo the pleasure.

She plunged on. "You have about as much interest in my family as I have in yours. We come from different planets. I don't know why you had to pick my beach house out of all the expensive condos you could have had all up and down the coast, but proximity doesn't make us anything but temporary neighbors. If I try, I might learn to deal with that. Don't think I'm available for anything more just because you're bored and avoiding whatever brought you here in the first place. Got it?"

The words stung, but he'd learned a thing or two about Cleo Alyssum over these past days. Her scary barriers were all for show. She would never have said what she just did if she hadn't been thinking along the same lines as he was. He had a craving for an intelligent, challenging woman for a change—or maybe to prove he wasn't as shallow as his family thought.

His family had always said he'd never learned to take no for an answer, too. About that, they were right. "Persistence" was his middle name.

Jared pushed back his chair and stood, and she did the same. He liked having women around, always had, so he'd spent a lot of time learning how to achieve what he wanted. Anger wouldn't do it.

"I got it," he said with a smile. "I don't happen to agree. Only time will decide who is right or wrong." He could see the suspicion creasing her forehead. He'd known she wasn't unintelligent.

He waited until she came around the table to ease him out the door. Then he caught her stubborn little chin and lifted it until she all but spat into his eyes. "If you try, could you learn to deal with me and not just my proximity?"

Jared didn't give her the opportunity to answer. He'd spent days imagining what it would feel like to soften her sassy mouth beneath his. Now he intended to find out.

She tasted of pizza and tartness. Exploringly, he licked the salt from her lips, and knew the triumph of conquest when she shivered and her mouth relaxed and accepted the pressure of his.

His libido screamed to grab her waist and haul her against him while he had the chance. His conscience gave her more space than that.

Sliding his fingers to frame her jaw, Jared deepened the contact, asking for the next step, the gentleness before the lust, permission before the taking.

She returned his kiss with more than interest, with a hungry need that shook him and pushed him faster than he'd anticipated. When she parted her lips on an exhalation of pleasure, he rejoiced and took possession of her mouth.

Cleo bit his tongue. Hard.

⊰ ELEVEN ⊱

"Dammit, Cleo! What the hell did you do that for?" Nursing his sore tongue, Jared stepped away from the table.

Cleo calmly began reboxing the pizza. Jared McCloud had rattled her bones. If she thought too hard, she'd realize she was shaking. "You might want to take the rest of this back to your brother." She closed the cardboard lid and shoved the box at him.

Men never touched her unless she let them. Why had she let him? She'd better figure it out quick, because she wanted his hands on her again. They'd been strong, competent, reassuring hands, and she could easily deceive herself into believing they were caring ones.

No man had ever kissed her like that. Or maybe she'd never been kissed by a real man. The possibility that Jared was the kind of man she'd never known shivered her down to her toes. She didn't need this.

His eyes narrowed as he studied the box, studied her, then focused his gaze on a part of her anatomy she'd rather not reveal. If her flannel shirt had been nearby, she'd have put it on. He was entirely too good at seeing beyond the obvious.

"If you wanted me to leave, you could have just said so," he said angrily, ignoring the offered box. "If you're still mad at me for letting my party get out of hand, you could have said that, too. You damned well didn't have to maim me."

Yeah, she did, but she wasn't saying that either. Talking had never got her anywhere. How in hell did he expect her to explain that she had the hots for him, but no way in this universe was she acting on her insane, self-destructive impulses?

"You wouldn't have taken no for an answer." She shoved the box at him again. "I'm not mad at you. It's good pizza. Go away."

He snatched the box, and for a hair-raising minute, Cleo feared he would set it aside and come after her. She couldn't half blame him. They'd really been getting into that kiss, and if he didn't leave soon, she'd be gravitating right back into his arms again. Why in hell hadn't he stomped out and left her alone as he was supposed to do?

She hadn't anticipated her reaction to his kiss, but she was prepared this time. She crossed her arms over her aroused breasts, activating all her defenses.

He must have read her body language. He kept the box in his hands.

"All right, I'm going. Hide out here all you like; it's no difference to me. I'll be gone in a couple of months. You're the one who has to stay in this prison you've built."

He stalked into the front room, but Cleo didn't follow. She wiped the pizza crumbs from the table with a cloth and listened to the front door slamming. Bone-deep loneliness seeped through her, but she was used to lonely. Anybody who could call the privacy she'd found here a prison had never been in one.

That didn't mean he wasn't right. People like her just couldn't function normally in society. She'd chosen the life that suited her best. Until Jared McCloud had come along, she'd done just fine.

When he left, it would suit her fine again.

Until then, she'd have to live with the memory of that kiss and avoid the bastard at all costs. Her fragile equilibrium couldn't handle a two-month affair, and building a secure environment for Matty was more important to her than sex. For Matty, she could survive loneliness.

"I see your sweet-talking charm didn't get you into the lady's bed." Sitting in the shadows of the deep, unlighted porch, Tim tipped his chair back, propped his feet on the rail, and took another swig from his beer.

Jared remembered now why he'd run away from home at the first opportunity. Flinging the cardboard pizza box at his brother so TJ had to drop his feet and grab with one hand, he continued up the porch stairs and toward the door. His tongue didn't hurt much anymore, but his ego would never be the same. The lady in question threw a tough right jab, and she hadn't had to lift a hand to do it.

"She's not your usual sort," TJ continued casually, balancing the box on his knee and opening it to fish out a slice of pizza.

With a sigh, Jared gave up any hope of going to his room and sulking. Helping himself to another slice and a bottle from the cooler, he settled on the newly installed planks with his back against the rail. He hadn't bothered with much in the way of furniture. After all, once the project was done, he'd be out of here. Cleo could have her snakes and peacocks and mosquitoes. He swatted at one of the bloodthirsty critters.

"Maybe I like a challenge," he retorted through a mouthful of cheese.

Jared didn't count the number of empty beer bottles his brother had lined up on the railing. A man as large as Tim could swill a case and not feel the effects until he stood up. His serious-minded brother seldom indulged, but when he did, he pulled out all the stops. Jared didn't see any point in interfering. Tim had half a foot and more than a few pounds over him, and he inclined toward cantankerous when sloshed.

"Well, you were never satisfied unless you were butting your head against a wall," Tim agreed.

"Cleo isn't a wall. Cleo is Alcatraz." He grimaced and corrected that. "She's like a wounded fox caught in a trap who snaps at anyone who comes close."

Tim chugged a swallow of beer before replying. "Call the Humane Society."

Jared popped a beer cap and thought about that. "Maybe someone already has. And maybe they hurt her worse." He'd never spent much time examining motivations before. Maybe it was time he slowed down and

took a look around, for a change. Cleo compelled him to
stop and think.

"Maybe baby brother has the hots for a chick who
told him no," Tim growled.

For all he knew, Tim was right. He didn't have much
experience at serious thought. "I think I'll call Susan and
have her come down for a few days. Should I have her invite a friend?" That was something he could do without
thinking.

Tim snorted. "Not for me. I'm supposed to be in
Mexico City on Monday. I don't think I could seduce one
of Susan's friends in two days, and I'm not about to
spend the weekend staring at her breasts and listening to
her chatter about what kind of car her last boyfriend
had."

Jared tried to chuckle, but Tim was hitting too close to
home. Susan and her friends did just that. She had a good
pair of breasts, though.

They didn't look half as intriguing as Cleo's pert,
aroused ones. Cleo had wanted him. That kiss hadn't
been fake. And there were much deeper depths to Cleo
than to material worshipers like Susan.

He didn't know why the hell he'd suddenly taken a
dislike to material worship.

"Cleo has a kid and the father's dead, but the kid apparently doesn't live with her. Wonder if he's with the in-
laws?" He'd never even asked if she'd married the kid's
father.

"I don't know a hell of a lot about women," Tim
mused, "but even I can tell your landlady hides deep waters with a rough undertow. She's out of your league,
lightweight."

Jared scowled at his bottle. "Cleo and I connect in
ways you'll never understand, big brother," he said with a
self-confidence he didn't feel. "It doesn't always have to

be about sex." Of course, this was probably the first time he'd ever said such an insane thing, but it sounded good.

Tim laughed. "Tell me you took her pizza so you could discuss mechanical witches."

Disgruntled, Jared threw his pizza bones into the box and stood up. "I'm capable of intellectual relationships. You're the one with a problem in the sex department. Good night, big brother, I've got a strip due for next week."

He maneuvered this dramatic exit with a little more finesse, slamming the screen door and leaving Tim scowling.

The day's encounters had generated a super idea for the daily comic that his fingers itched to produce. Now if only he had an idea to pull together the film project, he could forget Cleo and Tim and the rest of the world for a while. That's why he'd come here in the first place, wasn't it? Not to salivate over tongue-biting vipers.

He groaned at the image. Now he'd dream all night about Cleo as a snake wrapping around him and licking his face. His libido had careened totally out of control.

Sunday morning, Jared jogged down the eroding beach, kicking at washed-up strands of seaweed and rotten tree limbs, absorbing the roar of the surf. Tim had driven off to the airport, Susan had refused to visit a town without a designer boutique, and even the workmen had taken a construction day of rest. Only the squalls of the seagulls intruded on his solitude. Surely he could get some work done now.

Which was why he was running the beach without pencil in hand or idea one in his head. He wished he knew why he'd agreed to do the film in the first place. Probably because he thought it would look good on his résumé. If he had any character at all, he'd pay back the advance and give up his delusions of grandeur, but the Jag accident had eaten his cash, and his stocks were margined to the max. He couldn't go that route.

Besides, his agent would pitch a fit if he tried to back out. Films meant lucrative spin-offs and commercial franchises and could up the ante for books and who-the-hell-knew what all. If he could just pull together a decent draft, he would be in Hollywood by the first of the year, proving he was more than a bad artist with a warped sense of humor. He was sitting on a gold mine, if he could just dig down to it.

He'd never had to dig before. It had all rolled from his fingertips, and he wanted that creative energy back. Even his cash cow of a comic strip was losing momentum, probably because he was losing interest. That's the reason he'd jumped at the TV opportunity that flopped.

He had a nasty feeling he needed to be an angst-ridden teen again to re-create his earlier successes. He was getting old, and the passion wasn't there anymore.

What in hell would he do with his life if he couldn't draw?

Breathing hard, he stopped to do a few push-ups to unwind. He was only thirty-two. He couldn't quit now. He just needed to get his teeth into something and shake it around a bit, something that really turned him on.

Cleo really turned him on, but he didn't think digging his teeth into her a good idea. Or maybe it was, but it wouldn't be productive. She'd apparently packed up and taken off for the weekend after their little contretemps on Friday night. She hadn't even bothered activating her trespasser alert system.

Returning upright and jamming his hands into his pockets, Jared gazed around to orient himself. He couldn't see the beach house behind him. He figured the condo resort at the end of the island was just beyond the bend ahead. The wide sandy path into the jungle at the beach's edge beckoned. He ought to know better than to take any more paths, but they had a certain amount of entertainment value. Maybe he'd discover more imps and fairies.

He jogged into the dappled shade of tall, nearly branchless pines cutting off the intensity of the Carolina blue sky and sunshine. He hadn't realized what a fog Miami and New York lived under until he came here.

Maybe he could do something with that—go into some issue-oriented fairy tale that intellectuals would eat up while their children thought it was all just good fun. Who the hell watched cartoons anyway? Teenagers? Like they'd be real interested in issues.

Maybe he needed to define his market. He could give Georgie a call . . .

He stopped at the edge of a clearing leading to a crumbling clapboard shack with bits of logs visible where the boards had rotted off. A log cabin. Well, this was one of the reasons people lived in New York and Miami instead of in rural decrepitude.

A scraggly vine bearing occasional splotches of yellow flowers crawled up the chimney, and wisteria had taken root in the corner of the porch he could see from this angle. The thick woody vine had already torn through the porch roof and probably supported it more than the column it wrapped around.

The jungle reclaiming its own, he figured—another angle he might use. How would that apply to teenagers?

He ambled closer, wondering if the place was safe for exploration. Someone must have once lived and farmed out here in rural isolation and poverty. What did one raise on an island? Pigs? Goats?

The flutter of a piece of cloth to his left distracted him. He was wary of any movement around here. Gene might not intentionally mean to kill him, but a kid who raised snakes and scared peacocks into windshields could cause all manner of agony.

On the far side of a lean-to he assumed had once been the privy, a frail scarf blew in a bit of breeze. He'd always thought oceans windy places until he'd come here. Apparently the island sheltered them from the wind and the result was intense humidity. The scarf fluttered flat again.

The stench of the privy almost prevented him from investigating, but curiosity propelled him past the shed. Had this place been abandoned, a scarf would have weathered and worn into threads. This one looked new.

Just past the privy, sheltered from the house by a thicket of shrubs, he traced the source of the scarf to Kismet's slender throat. She stood backed against a pine, her face turned away from him, her baggy dress open to the waist. A white man twice Jared's size stood in front of her, blocking Jared's view.

Shock froze him in place. It didn't take much imagination to figure out what the man's hands were doing.

Kismet didn't utter a sound. For all Jared knew, she welcomed her molester's attentions. He ought to politely back out of here and amble away. This wasn't any of his business. He didn't belong here, didn't know the locals, had no idea of what was really happening. Hell, that could be the kid's husband. This was the South. They did things differently here.

The kid was fifteen years old and not quite right in the head. Jared's stomach churned and bile rose in his throat. He'd never been forced to face the facts of life in this manner before.

He took a step backward, trying to rationalize the situation, until the man started hiking Kismet's skirt up and reached for his zipper.

Rage snapped in Jared's head. Shoving away from the

bushes, he stalked toward the couple. He wasn't in the pervert's heavyweight league and didn't have much chance of bringing him down with fists if it came to that. But he couldn't let the kid do this to herself, or let the creep do it to her. Stupid of him. Obviously, he'd admired one too many comic book heroes in his youth.

"Hey, Kismet, your teacher is out here looking for you. Didn't Cleo say you have some drawings you wanted to show her?" Maybe he wasn't much with his fists, but he still had a few wits about him. Unless this pervert was the girl's husband, any mention of school officialdom should send him scampering into the woods.

The man dropped his hands and swung around. Mean brute, Jared assessed rapidly, not bright but randy. A good kick in the right place would cripple him. He yearned for an excuse to kick. Grinning at the perv, Jared dared to intervene. "She's kinda young for you, isn't she?"

Kismet darted away from the tree, away from the house, away from both of them. Bushes crackled as she disappeared into the swampy jungle, leaving Jared to face an angry behemoth.

Well, hell, maybe a good brawl would give him something to write about.

❧ TWELVE ❧

Jared staggered through the wax myrtle hedge just as Cleo pulled her pickup into the drive. Her first thought was that he was drunk or high, but he hadn't struck her as the type for either.

He stopped in his tracks at the sight of her, and swayed slightly while she parked the truck. His aviator sunglasses hung broken and useless from one hand. He wore jogging shorts and no shirt. She would have gasped at the vast expanse of nicely molded chest revealed, except it appeared to be splattered in blood. Panic mode nearly stopped her heart, but she got a grip and steadied herself. He wasn't anything to her. She would just take a neighborly interest in the situation.

It would be a hell of a lot easier if he didn't look like a gladiator who'd just ripped off a lion's head.

"Went a little round with the boys?" she inquired with disinterest. Approaching him, she noticed the bruise forming along his patrician cheekbone. She checked the urge to caress the swelling. The man practically exuded male musk and testosterone, and she halted far enough away not to be drawn into the trap.

"Look and see if Kismet is here," he commanded gruffly, swiping at a trickle of blood from his nose.

Panic immediately descended. Shooting him a look of anger and fear, Cleo swung on her heel and raced to the house. She didn't know what Jared McCloud had to do with Kismet, but from the state of his face, it hadn't been pretty.

It wouldn't help to run through the house, screaming. Forcing herself to slow down, Cleo called a greeting as she entered. Kismet was like a dog who'd been beaten one too many times. If she was here, she'd appear, tail wagging in hopes of kindness, but cringing in fear at a sharp tone.

No one answered.

Jared followed her into the house, aiming for the

kitchen faucet. "She ran into the woods. I thought she might have made her way here."

"What happened?" Cleo demanded, not waiting for an answer as she raced up the stairs to the attic. Kismet liked being alone and sometimes sketched there on rainy days. The empty attic offered no hiding place, and she saw no sign of her.

Running back down, she stopped in the bathroom for clean towels and washcloths and carried them into the kitchen. If this bastard had hurt Kismet . . .

He wouldn't. She'd learned a few things about people over the years, and she couldn't see a man like this laying a finger on a child. Dropping his glasses in the trash, Jared accepted her offering and soaked the cloth while she opened the freezer and found a package of frozen peas. "Here, put this on your cheek. Hold your head back to stop the bleeding."

She had an unreasonable urge to stroke his poor, bruised jaw, to comfort him. Like that was going to happen.

He sank into a kitchen chair and did as told. Cleo figured that was a miracle in itself. Men never did what she told them. A man who occasionally listened to her was good for her battered ego. "What happened?" she demanded again, while she was on a roll.

"Don't entirely know. I had a little encounter at a shack down the road. My kick isn't as high as it used to be."

"You kicked Kismet?" She couldn't hide the incredulity. Nothing people did should surprise her, but this didn't even make sense.

He scowled past the frozen peas and washcloth. "I kicked some big hairy brute who was molesting her. What in hell kind of perverts do you raise around here?"

Cleo sank into a chair and ran her fingers up her face and into her hair. Shit. Damn. Bloody motherf—

She halted that train of thought. Life happened. One dealt with it, one step at a time. "Where is he?" A kitchen knife. She had a blade big enough to castrate the—

Stop it, Cleo. She dug her fingers into her hair and tugged harder. Count to ten. Think rationally. Don't go over the bloody edge. Kismet needed a sane person, not a madwoman.

"Probably still groaning in the dirt. I finally connected," he said with satisfaction, although it sounded as if he had a severe cold. He tilted his head back farther.

Warily, Cleo raised her head to study him. She hadn't taken the wealthy yuppie for a street fighter, but she couldn't deny evidence of an altercation. Even with frozen peas applied to it, Jared possessed a tough, stubborn jaw she really hadn't appreciated enough. It was clenched now, whether in pain or fury, she didn't know him well enough to tell. She hoped he really had kicked the pervert in the *cojones*. Her insides did a double backflip and a triple axle in admiration. It made it hell to fight physical attraction when she had to admire his character, too.

"I'll go look for Kismet." She scraped back the chair and stood up.

"He didn't rape her," Jared warned. "She didn't seem to be protesting what he was doing before I interrupted."

Cleo nodded, and the sinking sensation in her stomach sank lower. She hadn't been here to help, and she was helpless to prevent the situation from happening again. "She's already learned she's not strong enough to fight," she murmured, more to herself than to him. She'd suspected as much all along, but Kismet wouldn't talk about it.

She ignored Jared's sharp intake of breath. He was still

capable of shock. She wasn't. She wished she had a hound dog. Kismet could be hiding anywhere.

"I'll call the sheriff and help you hunt." He started to rise from the chair.

"Sit down. Kismet won't come out if you're anywhere near. And leave the sheriff alone," Cleo warned. "She won't press charges so there's no point in causing trouble." She grabbed a cold bottle of soft drink from the refrigerator and opened the back door.

Jared stood and snatched the door away from her. He towered over her by some inches, but Cleo didn't fear him as she might have another man. He scowled and yelled, but if he was going to hit, he would have done so the other night. She hadn't realized that had been a test, but apparently it had.

"Those kids aren't safe out here. The authorities need to be notified," he insisted.

"Those kids aren't safe anywhere. Go lie down on the couch and don't say a word to Gene if he shows up. Kismet may slip in the back door, but leave her alone. Don't say a word, got it?"

"Are you out of your ever-lovin' mind?" he shouted.

Cleo walked out and let him shout.

She eventually located Kismet sketching in her favorite tree. The girl had taken to keeping her sketchpad and pencils in an old plastic storage box she'd found or stolen somewhere, so they were always available, no matter the circumstances. Cleo was half afraid to look at the pictures the child might be drawing.

"Hey, kid," she called softly. Kismet didn't even look down. "Want a pop?" She offered up the soft drink.

Kismet scrunched up tighter and didn't respond.

Cleo leaned against the tree trunk and sipped the drink. "You ought to see Jared with a bloody nose.

You'd think he was a redneck just like us instead of a stuffy Yankee."

She sensed a slowing down of Kismet's frantic scribbling but didn't look up. "I think he got in a good kick that ought to put the creep out of commission for a while, but he wants to call the sheriff. What do you think?"

Kismet uttered a muffled noise of protest, and Cleo dared to look up long enough to watch frizzy curls shaking negatively. The girl clenched her pencil like a weapon and stared through the willow oak leaves at nothing.

"I can talk him out of it, but give me a good reason," she said gruffly. She wished she was warm and motherly like Maya, but she wasn't. She didn't even know how to hug the kid should she climb from the tree. All she could do was offer to be there. It didn't seem enough anymore.

"Mama likes him." The voice sighed through the trees much as the nonexistent wind. "He buys her things."

That's what Cleo had figured. Her fingers dug into the soft drink can and her stomach heaved, but she'd experienced all these symptoms before. She'd tried fighting back once upon a time, but it had nearly got her killed. She'd tried escaping, and her chosen method of escape had dragged her through hell. She didn't see many acceptable alternatives.

"She wouldn't like him as much if you told her what he did." Logic seldom worked with a terrified kid, but she figured she ought to try.

Kismet shrugged and returned to sketching.

Dead end. Cleo guessed Kismet had endured worse at some earlier time, had probably seen worse. The kids tried to protect their mother, understanding instinctively that she was more brittle than they were. The human mind was capable of accepting and bending things with a weird rationality.

"Maybe you ought to stay with me when your mama's boyfriend visits," she suggested. That was the only practical solution she could see.

Cleo had turned enough to watch the girl and catch her shy smile. All right, if that worked, she could deal with the kid's mother. Maybe she could kick some sense into her. Or let Jared kick some sense into her.

She kind of liked that Jared had come to Kismet's defense, even though he knew nothing about her. In her experience, people who left their own comfortable circle to help others were rare and priceless treasures. To risk being beaten to a pulp for a child he didn't know put Jared several notches above the rest of mankind, in her book.

"When you're done there, why don't you come back to the house with me, and we'll fix some popcorn? Where's Gene?"

"Fishing." Kismet examined her sketch critically, closed the book, and stuck her pencil into her thick hair.

Gene would get himself killed fishing out on that abandoned rock jetty, but Cleo knew without his fish, the kids would go hungry. On bad days, Linda forgot to feed them.

"Well, if he catches anything, we'll grill out. I have to see if Jared is all right. Come on down when you're ready."

She heard Kismet scrambling from the tree as she walked back the way she came. If she didn't find some way of saving the girl from her current situation, she'd end up raped, pregnant, and lost in the same trap as Linda. But no courtroom in the world would give the kids to an ex-con drug addict.

If she turned the kids into Social Services, the social workers would never be able to place them together, even if they could find someone who would take in teenagers for a few bucks. And even if a miracle should

occur, and they found places for the kids, there was no
guarantee that they would be any safer in the homes of
strangers. Cleo knew that from bad experience. The only
remaining alternative was a group home. Kismet couldn't
survive in that environment. She was more helpless than
dreamy Maya had been.

She didn't like the idea that Kismet hadn't run or
fought when attacked. She wasn't a psychologist, but she
knew that didn't bode well for her future. What would it
take to get the kid to fight back?

She found Jared pacing the front room, shouting into
her telephone, his bare chest still wet from washing off
the blood. She'd give the Yankee credit for shouting with
ardent volume, but she'd rather not look at his naked
chest while he did it. Dark curls between muscled pectorals did things to her libido that she preferred not to
examine.

If he was talking to the sheriff, she'd kick *him* in the
cojones.

"She hasn't returned," he shouted frantically as she
walked in. "I'm calling the sheriff."

"I'll scalp you if you do. I found her. She'll be here
shortly. Calm down and go home and we'll all cope."
She continued walking, through the front room, past
Jared, and into the kitchen. She wanted to fall to pieces
in private.

Telling whoever it was on the other end that he'd call
back, Jared followed her. Maybe she *should* kick him.
He didn't seem to get the message in any other way.

"I called a counselor for troubled teens I know. She
says we need to get Kismet out of there and into a safe
home and into counseling," he announced, as if safe
homes and counseling could be purchased at the local
grocery for the price of eggs.

"Go away, McCloud." Leaning wearily over the sink,

Cleo wished for a huge cold tankard of beer. She'd never been much of a beer fan, but she thought one might go down smooth, and ease some of this pounding behind her eyes. She knew the bliss of a crack high would work even better by making the world go away, but she didn't go there anymore. Still, there ought to be some escape she could use every once in a while.

Jared came up behind her and put his arms around her waist. Not stopping to think, Cleo simply reacted. She spun around and plowed her fist into his rock-hard abdomen. She hurt her hand more than she hurt him, but he backed off with an *oomph* of released breath, and watched her warily.

"What is it with you?" he asked in angry confusion. "I'm trying to help."

She supposed he'd intended to comfort her. Wasn't that just like a man? Did she look the vaporish sort of female who responded to quick hugs and soothing words?

She couldn't remember a time when anyone had offered her gentleness.

She wrapped her arms around her waist and fought her churning insides. Blinking an eye stinging with moisture, she tried not to ache with the need for comfort. Vulnerability didn't become her.

"Don't mistake me for someone else," she said curtly. "Kismet will be here soon. Make yourself scarce. I don't think she's in any shape to walk in on a half-naked man."

He glanced down at himself and grimaced. "Sorry, I wasn't thinking. Give me one of those flannel shirts of yours. They're big enough. I don't want Kismet afraid of me."

She really didn't know what to make of him. Other people left when she told them to leave. Other people got angry and walked out when she belted them. This man simply ignored her temper and proceeded to follow his own path. "Look, you can make nicey-nice some other time. Right now, it's girl time, okay?"

He crossed his arms over his admirable chest, and Cleo's attention immediately focused on the bulge of his biceps. Shit, this was no time for her dormant hormones to go into overdrive. She needed to remember he was male and stronger than her and ignoring everything she said because she couldn't force him do anything she wanted.

"I've seen you with the kids," he said calmly. "You'll just mother hen them. They need to know they've got someone who will stand up for them so they won't be afraid. Short of carving him into fish bait, that creep needs to be reported to the police."

She knew better than to belt him another one, but she sure would have liked to haul off and bury her fist in his gut. Unfortunately, that taut abdomen she'd been so stupid as to admire was a little tough on her knuckles. She rubbed them absently as she considered a small mole peeking through the dusting of dark curls on his bronzed chest. How did a comic strip artist get to look like that? And why did she have the insane urge to fling herself into those strong arms and let him handle the whole thing?

"I've already asked her if I could call the sheriff." Cleo swung away from temptation and reached for another soft drink. "She says her mama likes the man, that he buys her things. Kismet will not do anything to hurt her mama. You don't have to understand. Just accept that's how it is." Maybe she'd better get him that shirt. She couldn't see any immediate means of flinging him out of the house.

"You're right, I don't understand. Why should we let a kid decide what's best for her? They don't, usually."

"How do you know?" She cruised out of the kitchen

and down the hall in search of a suitable shirt. When she'd left her ex, she'd taken his entire wardrobe of shirts with her, figuring he didn't own anything else, and he owed her. She was ambivalent about Jared McCloud wearing one.

He followed right on her heels, drat the man.

"That's what I was always told while growing up, that I didn't know anything and adults had more experience. Makes sense to me."

"Yeah, some adults have more experience. You don't. Go back to Never Never Land and take my word for it on this one." She reached in the closet, grabbed a gray rayon, and shoved it at him. Having Jared McCloud in her bedroom did not sit well on her already disturbed psyche. She didn't look at him as he took the shirt.

"You think I'm some kind of Peter Pan?" Insulted, he shrugged on her offering.

Just her luck, the shoulders of the shirt were too narrow, and she had to admire the way it stretched snugly across his upper body. Well, David had been younger when he'd worn that. So had she.

The back door slammed, and she forgot the argument. "That's Kismet. I'm fixing popcorn. Say one thing to scare her, and I'll have your hide."

Jared shoved his hand through his hair and watched her walk away from him—again. One of these days, he'd figure what made her tick. For now, he had to figure out how to confront a child who had just been molested.

He was way out of his league and ought to be running as fast as his feet could carry him.

Cleo's perspective forced him to stay and reexamine his methods. He'd thought handing out money would help the kids, but he'd only clipped the tip of the iceberg. Maybe money was just another form of shallow. Damn.

⊰ THIRTEEN ⊱

He didn't have to hang around where he wasn't wanted, Jared told himself as he avoided the kitchen and Kismet, under Cleo's orders. He had Hollywood and success at his fingertips. His name would be in lights so high his family and old school critics would have to slink away with their tails between their legs or recognize his genius.

Provided he could ever draw again.

Fighting that irritating worm gnawing at his guts, Jared leaned against the door frame between the kitchen and front room, watching Cleo popping popcorn for the fey child curled in the kitchen window seat, ignoring his presence. He ought to leave. He needed to get back to work if he ever hoped to achieve success. Or at least meet his deadline.

He swung away from the family scene, planning on getting the hell out of a place where he so obviously didn't belong, when his glance fell on the sketchpad on the sofa. Kismet was always sketching in that thing. He might not belong anywhere, but drawing was something he understood. Heaven only knew, he'd spent half his teenage years with pencil in hand, or at a computer keyboard playing with graphics programs, probably because drawing was the only thing that got him noticed.

Fine. Let Cleo ignore him. He knew how to handle that.

Dropping down on the wide, comfortable sofa, Jared flipped open the sketchbook. A fire-breathing dragon practically flew off the page.

Okay, dragons were common stuff, although the angle on this one was close to brilliant. She'd probably have a white knight on the next page. Symbolic, after all.

Pumpkins, coaches—she ought to do well at Disney. Nice, relaxed hand, a little instruction needed in perspective—

An entire page crayoned in black with only a pinpoint of color in a corner. Not in the center, but almost cringing in the corner. He held the page closer to better discern the figure, but it looked like a worm or caterpillar. He couldn't grasp the significance.

He flipped another page. An upright fire-breathing dragon with rather distinctive genitalia threatened the cringing worm. Jared squirmed beneath the power of the vision. He could almost feel the dragon's breath on his neck and could crawl into the worm's skin. He didn't need a degree in psychology to read this one.

Almost afraid to turn the page again, Jared lifted his head and listened to Cleo's voice in the kitchen. She spoke in a sane, sensible tone, reassuring the child with pleasantries, food, and attention. How many women knew how to do that? The ones he knew would be hysterical, frantic, phoning the police, and screaming helplessly had they come upon the situation he'd presented to Cleo. He'd seen her panic, then quell her distress and set about finding Kismet in a rational manner. It gave him cause to wonder about Cleo's background.

Had Cleo been molested as a child? Is that why she reacted as she did?

The thought made him feel dirty inside. He knew nothing about the woman, but he'd been salivating over her like a randy teenager. No wonder she'd hit him.

After this episode, he'd have to quit looking at women as ripe oranges begging to be squeezed.

All right, so he'd spent the better part of his lifetime wrapped in his own cocoon, without any thought to others. He could learn to look around him. Cleo was a damned rough place to start, but he thought she might be worth the effort.

Either that, or she was a better distraction than the script he couldn't finish. His shallowness knew no depths.

Okay, bad joke.

Taking a breath, Jared flipped to the next page of Kismet's sketchbook. To his startlement, Cleo jumped out at him, but it wasn't through any face she'd ever presented to him. He studied the drawing, trying to see how Kismet had done what she'd done.

It was Cleo as a hawk, or possibly a phoenix, since fire danced about her feet as she spread broad wings and protected the worm from the encroaching dragon. He didn't know how he knew it was Cleo. The eyes, maybe? The attitude? The hawk certainly had plenty of attitude. Only a teenager could imagine a pose like that. The hawk ought to be wearing a backward baseball cap and baggy pants. So maybe it wasn't all Cleo, but some brash combination of people that Kismet admired. But Cleo was definitely part of the saving grace in this scenario.

He was afraid to look further. Kismet's pen wielded passionate skill, whereas his teenage years had drawn on cynical wit. If he wasn't mistaken, she drew from a well of despair and anguish he'd never tapped. Teenagers had thin skin. He remembered that part of adolescence entirely too well. What must it be like not only to be scorned by one's peers, but mistreated by the adults who were supposed to protect you? Maybe his parents had been absentmindedly negligent, but they'd never caused harm.

He had to talk to Cleo.

Carefully closing the book, Jared stood and roamed restlessly about the room. He ought to leave and come back after Kismet was settled. He didn't know anything about kids, girls especially. He'd only scare her.

He didn't belong in this situation any way he looked at it. He was the outsider here. He couldn't do anything to help.

Clenching his fingers into fists, he ached to cream the bastard who'd touched her.

He glanced out the big windows and watched as a pair of blue-jean-clad legs approached. Fine view Cleo had here. Was that how she'd watched him walk up that first day? Legs first?

Gene climbed the porch steps and, whistling, merrily flung open the front door as if he belonged here. Well, they'd said Cleo left the place open for them. Now he understood why.

Gene looked surprised and a little wary at finding Jared here, but he produced his cool-dude smile and improvised. "You camping out here, too? You and Cleo got a thing goin' on?"

He ought to pin the little turd against the wall for disrespect, but it was obvious these kids hadn't grown up in his world, and wouldn't know the meaning of respect. He'd have to teach them.

He was out of his ever-lovin' mind. Shrugging, Jared shoved his hands in his pockets. "I like Cleo, and I won't insult her with that kind of talk. She has class."

Gene looked disbelieving, but Jared couldn't tell if he doubted him or Cleo. Then the boy nodded and jerked his head diffidently at the front door. "Want to see what I taught Porky to do?"

Why was he doing this? He needed to get back to

work. He didn't need to see what tricks a potbellied pig could do.

He followed Gene out to his zoo.

Sitting on her back porch as the sun sank behind the pines, Cleo watched Jared climbing up the path from the beach. He'd kept Gene occupied for the evening while she tried talking with Kismet. She hadn't had much success, but at least the kids were squirreled away in the bunk beds in Matty's room for the night, safe and well fed. She could count that as some form of success, she supposed.

She didn't know where Jared had gone after Gene came in to eat. In the twilight, she couldn't tell how badly the bruise had spread across his cheek, but she could see a definite discoloration. He'd cleaned up and put on one of his own shirts, so that must be hers he was carrying over his arm. If he was just returning the shirt, she might handle it. Anything more, and she was likely to curl up in a ball and cry until her heart wore out.

She'd thought running up to Columbia and meeting Matty and Maya at the zoo might take her mind off things, but it had only weakened every resolve she'd ever made. Matty had been thrilled to see her and had danced around and chattered incessantly the whole time. She'd felt loved and wonderful and wished she could take him home right then.

Then he'd happily run into Maya's house with his cousins at the end of the day as if she didn't exist at all.

Kids were versatile, she told herself. He'd love it here, too, once he moved back. She didn't dare believe anything else.

Gene and Kismet didn't exactly make likely playmates.

"Hi." Jared dropped onto the step below her without asking permission.

"Did no one ever teach you the rules of civilized behavior?" she asked with more curiosity than acidity. She was too wiped to be sarcastic.

"Nope. My father always had his nose in a book, and my mother always had her nose in someone else's business. I went by unnoticed," he said with disarming charm, handing her the shirt. "What rule have I fractured?"

"Normal people wait for an invitation before making themselves at home." She folded the shirt on her lap, and crossing her arms over her knees, returned to staring at the trees. He was all sexy-smelling male and ought to make her nervous, but apparently she was too tired even for that. Somehow, she almost felt comfortable with him sitting below her.

"Way I see it, I'd never be invited anywhere at that rate. It's easier to drop in and make people laugh until they let me stay."

"So, make me laugh." Wondering how anyone as good-looking and famous as Jared McCloud could feel unwanted anywhere, Cleo refused to fall for his charm. Men like him could make themselves comfortable anywhere they went.

"I'm fresh out of laughs," he said in a disgruntled tone, stretching his legs across the sandy walkway. "You'll just have to take me as I am."

"A guardian angel for fifteen-year-old girls? Okay." She owed him for that. He looked more like a sulky boy than a dangerous man right now, so she saw no need to fear him. And she was too wrung out to respond to her rampant hormones. She simply wouldn't look at him.

She'd probably spend the whole damned night dreaming about him.

He wrapped his hand around her bare ankle and stroked it without any apparent thought. Energizing heat instantly flowed through her, striking a place better ignored. Cleo tried to wriggle her foot free.

He caught her ankle firmly. "I won't remove your foot, I promise. I just can't talk unless I'm touching, all right?"

She settled down and contemplated means of scalping that beautiful head of thick hair. "You'd better have something good to say."

"Wish I did." Tensely, he stroked her ankle, and at her irritated attempt to retrieve it, he glanced at her. "Did I mention I'm usually good at distractions? I lack focus."

He said that in such an aggrieved manner, Cleo figured he'd been told that by his browbeating family a few times as well. She almost chuckled. "You must be a trial and a nuisance," she agreed.

"I am." He fell silent a minute longer while he rubbed her. "Hell, I'm no good at this. It's not any of my business, I know, but what are you going to do about Kismet?"

She'd kind of figured that was what this was about. She shifted her trapped foot sideways, but he wouldn't budge, just ran his hand higher up her calf. How did he expect her to think when he touched her like that? "She's inside, safe and sound. Just butt out. It's none of your concern."

"I looked at her sketchpad."

Cleo caught her breath. She'd never dared invade Kismet's privacy by prying, but Jared had strange ideas of personal space. She waited.

He shot her a wry glance when she didn't speak. "No curiosity? Or is that disapproving silence I hear?"

"Along with all your other faults, you're an annoying bastard; you know that, don't you?" Too bad her voice lacked conviction.

He chuckled, and in the warm September night, it sounded healthy, familiar, and somehow reassuring. Cleo couldn't remember the last time she'd spent more than a few minutes talking with a man. With anyone. People usually backed off at her prickly attitude. She liked it that Jared got beyond her surface.

"So I've been told," he replied without rancor, his thumb rubbing at her ankle. "But this isn't about me. Kismet has enormous talent and potential, and it's being crushed by the hell she's living in. We can't let that happen."

"I think it's about time you recognize that all the money in the world can't fix some things," she answered wearily. "People have to *want* to change. I can buy Kismet's mother a new house, put her through school, find her a job, but until she's ready to accept that she's worth saving, she won't give up drugs or booze. Believe me, I know. And those kids need their mother."

He sifted through her words and came up with the wrong part. "How do you know? How can you say a new house and job won't give the woman her self-respect back?"

Her stupid statement could have raised any of two dozen questions, and he had to pick on the personal one. Well, fine. Let him know up front what he was dealing with here. No point in getting too comfortable. "Because I've been there, done that, and I know. Got it?"

He sat silent for a while longer, his thumb tracing a steady circle around her ankle. His touch drove her crazy, but she wouldn't let him know he was getting under her skin. People didn't touch her. She didn't like being touched. But he hadn't run the instant the words were out of her mouth, and she couldn't break the tentative bond forming between them. He was listening. Really listening. She longed for someone to actually hear what she was saying, for a change—someone who wouldn't condemn or pity her for what she said.

"You're a recovering alcoholic? What brought you

around? Is there some way we can apply it to their mother?"

He was listening, but he wasn't hearing. She ought to be content with half a glass, but she couldn't leave well enough alone. For the first time in centuries, she'd forged a human contact, and she wanted all or none.

"Forget alcohol. I'm an addict, period. My brain chemistry is screwed, my life is screwed, and my self-esteem rates right around minus ten. I dried out in a jail cell, and came out still possessing enough intelligence to figure out if I touch another illegal substance, my life is over and Matty will end up like me. Linda hasn't got that much intelligence, and no family for support. Just exactly what do you think her chances are?" That ought to sever any illusion of bonding.

His fingers circled her ankle again. "If she wants her kids back, wouldn't she be willing to straighten out?"

Cleo listened, amazed. She'd just told him she was an addict and an ex-con, and he still wasn't letting go. Didn't he have any understanding of what was happening between them? He should be running for his life.

"No. I just told you," she said with irritation, momentarily surrendering to his insanity so she could get her point across. "She has to want to dry out for herself, and that isn't going to happen if she loses the kids. That will just give her one more excuse to kick herself. And the kids will be shoved into situations they can't handle, which is even worse."

"Worse than rape?" he asked quietly.

❧ FOURTEEN ❧

There, he'd said it—the word that scared him shitless—
"rape." Jared wasn't at all certain he had the right inter-
pretation. He wasn't a child psychologist, after all, just a
cartoonist. He was still struggling with Cleo's revelation
that she was an addict who had been in jail.

His mother would call his current companions trailer-
park trash. She would be appalled at his association with
any woman who'd admitted to addiction, much less jail
time. He was pretty appalled, as well, but whether with
himself or Cleo, he didn't know yet. He had ten dozen
questions and no lessening of interest in the woman who
was barely tolerating his stroking. Electricity and tension
vibrated through his fingertips, and he didn't think it was
all his. He'd done shallow attraction before, but what he
felt right now shot off the altimeter.

But first things first. They had to save Kismet. Like he
was capable of that.

Cleo dug her fingers into his hair. Jared merely glanced
up at her.

"You saw that in her sketchbook?" she demanded,
hastily releasing his hair at his heated look.

"The sketch is ambivalent, but I'd say it reflects op-
pressive fear and an unhealthy knowledge of male physi-
ology, okay? I don't know how a psychologist would say
it." He released her ankle before she yanked his hair.

Tension throbbed between them, and he figured he'd better concentrate on matters of importance. Avoiding Kismet's situation wasn't an option.

Cleo practically breathed a sigh of relief as he inched to a safer distance. Jared was tempted to reach over and stroke her, just to feel her tense up again. His ego shot several notches higher knowing she wasn't as impervious as she pretended. Better yet, he liked that she was focusing on his concerns and not scoffing at his overactive imagination.

"I can't believe Linda would let her men out of her sight long enough to cause harm, but if today was any evidence . . ."

He waited while she struggled with the consequences. He didn't understand her passion to protect the children on her own. As far as he was concerned, that was the job of the police and social workers and whatnot. But he didn't live here and she did. He'd have to rely on her judgment, respect her opinion as she apparently did his. He could get into being appreciated for his intelligence instead of his money or warped humor.

She unconsciously ran her fingers through his hair as if he were no more than one of her weird animals. Well, he could handle that, he supposed. For now.

"I'll keep Kismet here, talk to Linda again," she muttered aloud. "She may take a knife to her current boyfriend if she suspects it's him, or she may not believe me. It's a no-win situation. I wish I could teach Kismet how to protect herself, but she doesn't know the meaning of fighting back. I could teach Gene . . ."

He wanted to shake her. That was not the reply he wanted. This respecting each other's opinion business only went so far. Yanking his head away from her invading fingers, he glared up at her. "There are *laws*, Cleo! This has gone beyond negligence to child abuse.

They need to throw Linda's screwed-up head into jail and get those kids some help. Why the *hell* do you think you're the only one who can protect them?"

She stood up and walked away, toward the woods. Not a word. Not a sound. Just walked away. Damn, but he'd thought *he* was good at avoidance. Cleo could win awards for it.

He didn't know why the hell he cared. Maybe some of his mother's do-gooder training had surfaced. He despised the patronizing ignorance of his mother and her cronies, but he simply couldn't ignore this situation. That kid needed help. And Cleo knew it. Something else was wrong.

He jumped up and stalked after her. Against the backdrop of the pine woods, she appeared more wraith than human. The cheap dye job was fading from her cropped hair, and he could catch an occasional glimmer of red. He didn't want to examine why she hid herself behind men's clothes and bad haircuts, but a whole new world was opening before him. Or he'd just opened his eyes for the first time.

Grabbing her shoulder, he sucked in his abs in case she wanted to bruise her fists using him as a punching bag again. She didn't. She simply stared at him blankly. "You've got a kid," he said accusingly. "Would you want his plight disregarded if someone was abusing him?"

For half a moment, Jared thought her eyes swam with tears, but then she reached for the nearest tree branch and hauled herself up where he could barely see her. He leaned against a nearby tree trunk and waited.

"What do you want, McCloud?" she demanded from the safety of her branch. "My life story? My credentials to prove I know where I'm coming from? Why should I smear it all out for your perusal? Why can't you just believe I know what I'm doing and go away and leave us alone?"

"Don't you think I've been asking myself that?" He crossed his arms and glowered at her unsuspecting tree. "Damned if I have an answer. What did they do, take your kid away from you? Is that why he's not here?"

An enormous pinecone bounced off the tree over his head, but it fell apart. Apparently, he'd hit too close to home. He almost chuckled. He had her treed like a trapped raccoon. This time, he'd get some answers. He shot her a smirk she probably couldn't see in the rapidly descending shadows. "Pretend I'm Superman and trust me."

"I should trust a guy in blue tights and a cape? I'd trust your *Scapegrace* character sooner." She wrapped her hands around the branch above, not looking down at him. "Matty is with my sister. If I'm a real good girl, I can bring him home in December."

"Then what are you afraid of? You afraid you'll take up Linda's occupation and neglect him?" He was probably risking his life by antagonizing her like this, but it seemed safer than what he really wanted to do. Maybe if she put him off enough, he'd get the message. Generally, he fell out of love as easily as he fell into it.

He just had a sneaking suspicion that this time he'd been snagged by something far more complicated than a few weeks of lust and illusion. Usually by now he'd be hitting the party circuit, not watching angry pinecones flying over his head.

"I won't," she said fiercely. "I'd never hurt Matty. Never."

"You just admitted you were an addict. That's what addicts do, don't they? Hurt everyone, including themselves?"

She uttered a foul curse, flung another pinecone, and climbed to a higher branch. Jared feared she meant to spend the night up there. Maybe he ought to go away so she'd come down before she broke her neck.

"I was clean when I had Matty," she asserted out of the darkness. "David and I both were. We were in counseling, had jobs, and a decent place to live for a change. I thought we'd finally climbed out of the gutter and found a normal life, and I wanted a family so badly I could taste it. David didn't want the responsibility of me or a kid or anything else, but he said he wanted to make it work. I should have known better. We limped along for a year, until I came home one night to find him higher than the Mars mission. He'd somehow forgotten to tell me he'd lost his job and had taken up pushing to meet expenses."

She didn't say more, but Jared's insides clenched as tightly as his fists at the lost-child pitch of her voice. He didn't dare speak.

"You might have noticed I don't have a polite mouth on me," she finally said. "That night, David decided to shut it up by slamming me against the wall. I was nine months pregnant and started hemorrhaging. My screams brought the neighbors running. When I woke up in the hospital, Matty was healthy and David was gone."

Jared could hear the anger and tears in her voice. He thought he ought to stop her, that he didn't deserve her trust, that he wasn't worth this pain, but she plowed onward as if once under full steam, she had no brakes.

"I knew where David was, of course, knew who he was with and what he was doing, but I'd lived that horror for years and wasn't going back to it. I was scared out of my mind, but I packed everything up, sold anything I could lay hands on, and moved back to the town where I was born, on the opposite coast. I figured running away would keep me safe from who I am inside, but I was kidding myself."

Tears slid down Cleo's cheeks, but she clung to the

branch above her for support and couldn't wipe them. "I never neglected Matty," she asserted firmly. That much she knew, no matter what anyone accused her of. "I didn't have a lot of education and didn't know a lot about running a shop, but I set up business and we got by. I got a break on the rent and a loan, and I could work and keep Matty with me. He was the most beautiful baby, and he never gave me trouble. He was perfect, and I'd never hurt him."

Tears dripped off her cheeks and onto her shirt, because she knew she was lying now. She hadn't wanted to hurt him, but she had, and that was the whole problem, in a nutshell. "But sales were lousy, and I couldn't make the rent, and if I couldn't keep the shop running, I'd lose the apartment, and I knew they'd take Matty away from me. So when I found out the guy who owned the building was dealing with pushers, I demanded a piece of the take. Stupid, but I was desperate.

"I would have slit my *wrists* to keep Matty with me," she cried. "I knew what it was like to be neglected, and I'd not let any child of mine suffer what I had. Never."

"You don't have to tell me more," Jared said quietly from below. "It's not any of my business."

"If you tell anyone about this, you'll have to die." Viciously, she swiped at her tears with one hand. "I'm stupid, okay? I'm not like Maya. I didn't go to college, didn't have the sense to stay away from danger, and thought I was tough enough to take on the world by myself. When the bastard offered me a joint, I took it. Big deal, a little pot. I'd been doing pot since I was a kid. I only used it when Matty was asleep, to help me relax. I wasn't hurting anybody. It didn't cost me. It was *free*."

She choked on a bark of laughter. "Nothing in life is free. I had to buy a gun because the thought of dealers in the back room scared me shitless. Then one week the bastard told me he was a little short of cash and offered me some crack as collateral. I wasn't into selling, no way. The stuff sat in my cash register for weeks.

"I'd been trying to teach Matty reading and writing so he wouldn't start school behind the other kids, but he didn't catch on real well. I'd get frustrated with him, and he'd cry when he couldn't please me. And then I'd cry, and he'd try to make me feel better, and I'd cry worse. I was a basket case. The store was still going downhill, I had crack dealers in my back room, I couldn't afford good clothes for my kid, and I had a stash of crack sitting in my cash drawer instead of money."

She sobbed and hated herself for doing so. She was past that stage now. She was strong. She'd had counseling. She understood the destructive forces that had made her do what she'd done. None of it helped. She wept and rubbed her eyes with the back of her sleeve.

And then Jared pulled onto the branch beside her, scaring her half to death. With one arm wrapped around her, one-hundred-eighty pounds of solid male crushed her into the tree.

"Stop it," he hissed. "Quit beating up on yourself for my sake. I don't care what happened." With his free hand, he brushed a tear from her cheek, then he pressed a kiss to her forehead.

She shivered all over, craving a healing touch, knowing she didn't deserve it. She simply needed to gather sufficient strength to push away. He pressed her tighter, as if reading her thoughts.

Oh, God, he smelled of male musk and aftershave and all those masculine things she hadn't known she'd missed so much. She wanted to collapse into his strong arms like some weepy teenager and simply let him handle it all. He held her as if she mattered, as if she were actually valuable instead of a piece of shit. She so desperately wanted to believe she was worth something.

"Come on, let's get down." His arm closed firmly around her waist, forcing her into close contact with his shirt. Cleo dug her fingers into male warmth and muscle, took a deep breath, shoved against his shoulders, and jumped.

She knew how to land like a cat, bending her knees and letting her hands and the balls of her feet break the impact. She could hear Jared cursing above her as he grabbed a branch and climbed down in more traditional fashion. She had a chance to run, to hide, to slam the door and lock herself in, but she didn't take it.

She didn't know why, precisely. It had something to do with his strength when he held her, the way he'd come up after her when she certainly hadn't encouraged him, the way he'd stood up for Gene and Kismet and took all the damage thrown in his direction. She couldn't brush him off as a polished yuppie any longer. Somewhere behind that smiling demeanor was a tough streak of incorrigible.

"I thought you'd be halfway home by now," he admitted as he swung down.

He didn't attempt to hold her again, and Cleo relaxed. She couldn't have tolerated a touch right now. She needed her distance. "You didn't let me finish," she said accusingly.

"I got it. You're not Linda. You got straight and protected your kid and then you strayed. What happened, cops find the crack in the register?"

He said it dismissively, as if it didn't matter. Even her own sister was horrified that she'd let it happen, but this man stood there all loose-limbed and accepting and ready to move forward. *She* couldn't get beyond what she had done, and he acted as if it were something that had happened to some other person and had no relevance to here and now.

"On Matty's first day of school, I got high, that's what I did." Dammit, she'd rub his face in what she was, make him *see* her. "Matty always adored animals, and I wanted to buy him a teddy bear to show how proud I was of him. Just a simple teddy bear. He'd never had one." Hands on hips, she tried to glare at him, but a single tear strayed down her cheek.

Jared crossed his arms and watched her warily.

Satisfied, she continued. "People on drugs are *stupid*. Instead of going to Goodwill, I floated out with all the cash in the register and went to a toy store in a grandiose gesture to prove my love. I didn't have enough to buy even a baby bear. But I was high and brave and alternatives aren't what it's about with all that muck shooting out brain cells. I simply walked out with the biggest, most beautiful bear I could find."

He snorted, but didn't say a word.

Turning her back on him, Cleo started toward the house. "The cops caught me a block from the store, of course. They knew I was high. They got a search warrant and searched the store, and I was busted for shoplifting and possession and illegal weapons. It's a wonder they didn't hit me with dealing after they pulled my California record. I didn't even get to meet Matty when he came home that day. Social Services did."

She wouldn't cry. Not anymore. She'd cried until her lungs dried up and her soul shriveled, and she'd become an inhuman monster. She didn't go there anymore—only this once would she open that snakepit, for the sake of the kids. To make him understand.

He came up beside her. "They took your kid away from you?"

"Maya ran to the rescue." She still sounded bitter, although she'd been eternally grateful and simply didn't know how to express it. She'd give her soul for Maya, if she had one. "She knew what it meant to be left to the state, and she wouldn't let it happen to Matty. She took care of him for nine months while I dried out again. If I hadn't been busted, I would have been doing crack within another day or two, and dealing soon after, so don't feel any sympathy for me. I can't control the compulsion any more than Linda can when she's under the influence. It's physical as well as psychological, and it never goes away."

"But you *tried*," he insisted. "You took your son away from dangerous forces, and Linda doesn't even recognize them. Don't make her into your image."

Cleo laughed shortly. "Like my image is so great. Get real, McCloud. Linda tries. She gets jobs and keeps them and she stays sober for a while. She fixes the house up, cooks a great meal, and loves her kids, even though the kids' father got her disowned by her family and most of the town despises her for them. You don't know half the names they call those kids around here. Then one of them comes home crying over some insult, or the teachers finally get through to her and report their failings, and she goes off the deep end and loses her job and it's another snowball downhill."

He walked silently beside her for a minute, considering, but he still shook his head. "That's Linda's problem. The kids shouldn't have to pay for it. They need to be placed in a safe home."

Cleo climbed to the top step, and hands on hips, glared down at him. "Are you saying that I'm such a pitiful excuse for a human being that they're not safe with me?"

He didn't answer fast enough.

Biting off another curse, Cleo swung around and

stalked into the house, slamming the door in his face and fastening the lock.

⚜ FIFTEEN ⚜

"Hey, Cleo. Look at *Scapegrace*!" Gene shouted from the kitchen, where he'd spread the morning paper across the table to read the comics.

Well, at least Jared's comic strip had the kid reading a newspaper, Cleo thought as she tried to balance her checkbook at the desk in her bedroom. Shoving aside the calculator, she followed the sound of Gene's voice to investigate. She'd originally thought the strip funny, but for the last few months or more, the strip's teenage boys had become irritatingly whiny, and obsessed with girls. Still, it did have a wry wit she could appreciate, and the man definitely had a talent for depicting teenagers.

Gene grinned and pointed as she entered. "Think that's your skeleton?"

The cartoon skeleton bore a striking familiarity to the one Jared had sketched earlier. She scanned the strip and grimaced at the characters' mischievous prank to scare off their science teacher. Jared had probably gotten away with those kind of pranks as a kid. She'd have been expelled.

She hoped and prayed he didn't intend to use his experiences here to fill his strip. She'd have to maim and murder him, for certain.

"He even calls this one Burt," she said. There wasn't any point in worrying the kid with her concerns. He thought Jared hung the moon, and he needed that kind of male role model.

"Yeah," Gene breathed in satisfaction. "Can I take this to school?"

"Sure. But you'd better hurry or you'll miss the bus. Where's Kismet?"

"Dawdling," he said scornfully as he ripped the page out. "I'll go get her."

Kismet seemed her normal, vague self as she drifted out the door with her brother a little while later, her arms full of books. Cleo watched from the porch as they climbed on the bus, then meandered back into the house with her insides in an uproar.

She'd moved here to achieve peace of mind as well as soul. She'd thought she'd accomplished that. Yesterday had proved how wrong she could be.

Why the hell had she dumped all that garbage on a comic strip artist? An itinerant skirt-chaser who knew how to get under her skin? She should have shut him out like she shut out everyone else. The world was so much simpler that way, with everyone going about their own business.

But Jared McCloud didn't know how to mind his own business, and for that, she had to be grateful. It grated, but she owed him for saving Kismet. That didn't mean she had to hand him her life story.

He'd found Gene a wrestling team. Maybe he could find counseling for Kismet.

What the devil was she thinking? She couldn't ask the man for anything. She'd chased him off, and he could stay chased off.

But Kismet needed counseling. His psychologist friend was right about that. She'd never placed a lot of faith in shrinks herself, but it sure helped to talk things out when one didn't have anyone else to talk to. Kismet needed someone who could keep a confidence. Not that the kid would ever speak. Maybe shrinks knew tricks to make a kid talk.

Of course, if Kismet really told her tale, the counselor would probably report Linda to the police and have the kids jerked out of their home. Double-edged sword, that one.

She was waffling. Still, it was hard making decisions for someone else. She didn't have a lot of experience at it.

She could call and ask her counselor, but he'd want to know why she asked, and not knowing if he could report her confidences, she couldn't tell him.

Could Jared tell her if a counselor would report Kismet's mother to the authorities? She knew she was paranoid about the system, for good reason, but she had to get past her own fears and suspicions for the sake of the kids. Authorities had to abide by all sorts of rules and regulations that didn't make sense in terms of real-life situations—like tearing kids from a shaky parent but providing no substitute to take her place.

A balanced mind would attempt to see both sides and not think too irrationally about do-gooders who did more harm than good, so she ought to at least consider alternatives.

That would mean tackling Jared in his den, after she'd slammed the door in his face last night. She was an adult now. She should be able to overcome her childish neuroses and deal with uncomfortable situations.

She didn't want to. The whole point of living out here was to not get involved in stressful situations, so she could straighten herself out and get Matty back.

Kismet desperately needed help.

Shit.

The phone rang, and grateful for the reprieve, she actually answered it. She regretted it immediately as Jared's chocolate-warm voice poured through the receiver.

"Got a problem," he stated immediately, before she could hang up.

Wrinkling her nose and leaning her elbow against the counter, Cleo poked at her cookie jar witch. "And that concerns me, because . . . ?"

"It's your damned toilet and I'm no plumber. What do I have to do to make it stop running?"

"It's on a well. You could let it keep running," she suggested helpfully. "You stole my skeleton," she added, for good measure.

"You saw that?" He sounded more pleased than irritated at her comment. "I figured not too many kids could come up with skeletons, so I was safe using that prank."

"It was a stupid prank. You've got an intelligent teenager with lots of potential, and you let him do stupid, superficial things." So, maybe she was tired of people picking on her and felt like turning the tables.

"It's a *comic*, Cleo, not serious literature."

"Yeah, like you're a comic, not scholar material. Excuses," she scoffed. She wondered if the silence at the other end of the line meant she'd scored a point.

"All right," he answered begrudgingly, "maybe the kid needs to think once in a while. He's not inclined toward pithy conversation."

"He can learn." She had a very odd sense that they weren't talking about the *Scapegrace* character any longer. Uneasy with the observation, she returned to the original topic. "I've got to get to work by ten. Did you jiggle the handle?"

"Give me a break," he said scornfully. "I knew to try that much."

"Well, if you want me to fix it, I'll have to come by

now." She didn't know why the devil she'd said any such thing, but she just couldn't seem to shut Jared out. Probably because he ignored closed doors, and she admired his confidence entirely too much.

"That's fine. I've been working since six. And before you say anything, I *do* work occasionally. A daily strip isn't a flat-out cinch."

"Right. I'll take your word for it. I'll be down in a minute." She hung up before he could make her like him any more. The man had a real flair for that.

He'd held her when she'd cried.

Don't make anything of it, Alyssum, she warned herself as she jabbed a hair pick through her mop, then looked for her wrench. She found it in the kitchen drawer with her steak knives. Men like him probably had women weeping on their shoulders all the time. That didn't mean he wasn't a bastard out looking for sex any way he could get it.

Fixing a toilet did not equate sex, and crying didn't have anything to do with Jared. Kismet's situation had upset her, and she'd let it out on him rather than falling apart in front of the kids. Her counselor might even think that an improvement over her usual self-destructive tactics.

This was not a setback. Other people cried all the time.

Setting her jaw, she marched out of the house, wrench in hand. She'd fix his damned toilet, find out more about counseling—provided Macho Man knew anything about it—and be on her way.

He met her on the porch wearing a Hawaiian-print shirt, a straw fedora pulled down over his forehead, and chomping on a huge cigar. She'd never seen anything so sexy or so comical in her life, and the female part of her lurched happily. Damn, but he was good.

He grinned around the cigar as she approached. "Super Cleo, come to save the day! I really like that wrench as an accessory."

"Where'd you get the cigar?" She knew she sounded rude, but it was the only line of defense left to her.

"Carpenter's assistant just had a kid. He's handing them out. Want one?"

Cleo rolled her eyes and walked past him, into the house. He followed right on her heels. He'd just shaved. She could smell the lotion, and she had an irrational impulse to rub his jaw so her hand would smell like him. She desperately wanted any excuse at all to touch him. How insane could she be?

Pretty insane, if past evidence could be believed.

"Downstairs toilet?" she asked, ignoring his cheerful expression.

"Yup. Do you always wear flannel in this heat?"

"I freeze in air-conditioning." She took the back off the toilet tank and tried concentrating on its mechanics while he leaned against the vanity and watched her. She didn't like that he noticed what she wore. It made her self-conscious.

"I heard there's a fifteen percent chance of that hurricane in the Caribbean turning this way. Does this humidity up the odds?" he asked.

"Haven't the foggiest. This time of year, expect rain from now on." Maybe that would chase him off. Buckets of rain had a way of putting a damper on beach lovers.

"How do they warn people to evacuate the island in the event of a hurricane?"

"Don't know. I've been here less than a year, and they didn't have one last fall." She unhooked the chain, lowered it several notches, and hooked it up again. If it was something that simple, she could be out of here in minutes. The long length of lean man focusing all his charm and attention on her was more than her defenses could handle. Her hands would start shaking any minute now.

"How's Kismet?" he asked idly, but Cleo sensed the tension behind the question.

So, maybe this wasn't entirely about his toilet. She flushed the tank and watched the water level. "She seems fine. Could your friend the psychologist recommend someone around here? I figure I'll have to take her into Charleston."

Jared crossed his arms and watched Cleo's bent head warily. She'd made some damned telling points about his lack of character earlier, so he couldn't believe she was asking for his help now. He couldn't miss the opportunity to show he possessed some competence. "I'll call and ask her. Do you think Kismet would go?"

"I don't know. And if she goes, I don't know if she'll talk." She finally turned in his direction, and the defensive barrier was so blatant as to be almost visible. "She won't, if she thinks it will hurt her mother. Do counselors have to report abuse?"

"I don't know. I'll have to ask."

She nodded curtly. "Do that. She definitely won't talk otherwise."

A word from the wise, he figured. He attempted to look at her sturdy, flannel-clad figure as nothing more than his mechanically inclined landlady, an ex-addict, ex-con, hard-talking piece of Southern culture, but he failed dismally. He saw her tears and caring and lonely defensiveness and had to fight the urge to cuddle and comfort her. She'd probably rap his skull with the wrench for his efforts.

He didn't have time to get involved. The deadline loomed closer, and all he had was a bunch of rough sketches and even rougher ideas. And he still had next week's strips to put together. He was getting further and further behind. He couldn't afford to lose his syndication on top of everything else. He'd been insane to offer his last few thousand for the wrestling team.

He saw her off with no more than a casual wave. He needed to plant his ass in a chair and get some work done. No wandering beaches, watching waves, waiting for life to happen. He'd had about enough life for the moment.

The phone rang a little after noon and Jared knew he should ignore it. He hated writing, but he'd managed to cram together enough words to present half an idea to George. If he could pull together the rest—

He grabbed the phone off the hook. He deserved a break.

"What?" he demanded rudely. He'd purposely given only immediate family and his agent this number so he'd have peace and quiet. Normally, they never bothered him.

"Obviously, island life isn't suiting you," a lazy drawl declared.

"Doubting Thomas," Jared mocked, while internally groaning. What had he been thinking? His family always bothered him. "What can I do you for?"

"Not a thing, bro, but our mutual broker is frantically trying to track you down. I don't suppose you've been paying any attention to the market today, have you?"

Oh, shit. He didn't have cable internet out here. He couldn't even go online until he got his brother off the phone. He never followed the market, didn't understand any of it. He just knew he had a lot of money in it, and right now, he couldn't get online to see what was happening. "Get off the phone, and I'll check," he growled, refusing to ask.

"Well, all I can say is, I told you not to buy on margin. How's the work coming?"

He loved his brothers when they were a thousand

miles away, and he couldn't break their heads through a brick wall. "Swimmingly," he replied. Thomas would never catch the sarcasm.

What in hell was "margin," exactly? He vaguely remembered the broker mentioning the term in the same relation with "leveraging" and "risk." The only part he'd really grasped was "more money."

"We going to see your name in Hollywood lights?" Tom asked with interest. "Is that program I wrote helping with the graphics?"

Oh, hell, the kid meant well. Just because he should have been strangled at birth . . . "Yeah, it works far better than Microshit. I'll endorse it when you're ready to market it."

" 'Hollywood screenwriter Jared McCloud swears by his brother's graphic software.' Yeah, that works. So, what's the script about?"

As if he knew. "Look, I gotta finish this. I'll tell you all about it later, okay? Thanks for passing on the message." Jared pried his younger brother off the phone and punched in the buttons for his broker. He had a feeling he didn't want to hear this, but he'd lost his train of thought anyway, and he didn't need the question nagging him.

"Hey, Caleb, Tom says you're looking for me. What's happening?"

Caleb was one of those old high school comrades who'd once ragged on Jared for his artistic inclinations. Caleb had followed his stuffed-shirt father into the brokerage and now lived in a mansion in Schenectady, of all places. He sounded tired and anxious as he answered. "Market's down three hundred already this morning, and plunging fast. I've got to cover your margins on the tech stocks. If you wire me a hundred right now, maybe things will turn around before the day ends, and we won't have to sell. I've been making calls all morning and people are going crazy on me, but I figure you're good for it, at least."

He might have been good for it before Jag, beach house, and the loss of royalties on hick newspapers, not to mention the end of the TV money. Jared winced as his house of cards slowly but surely tumbled. "A hundred?" he inquired cautiously. He could manage a hundred dollars without a problem. He had a nasty feeling Caleb wasn't talking a hundred dollars.

"A hundred thou," Caleb confirmed. "That covers the outstanding debt and should keep you in the market until it turns around."

"Sell," Jared ordered wearily, sinking his head against his computer and wishing he dared bang it a few times.

He couldn't afford a new computer if he smashed this one.

⚜ SIXTEEN ⚜

Jared swung his mouse, and red fire breathed from the dragon's nostrils. Kismet's dragon, to be exact. What in hell was he doing drawing dragons?

Maybe he could use it in the Sunday strip. Could stealing from unpublished work be plagiarism? So, okay, he'd pay her.

With what, might be the next question.

Caleb had suggested selling the New York apartment instead of his stocks. It would only take a phone call, and he'd have a bank loan on it. He supposed he wouldn't need the place if he was going to L.A. Money was easy.

Failure wasn't.

We won't go there, McCloud. Easing back in his chair, Jared stared at the screen. It was a pretty darned good dragon if he did say so himself. It could work. If Cleo wanted depth, he could have the characters delve into the monsters in their souls—although the main monster in an adolescent soul was usually hormones. Minor matter.

He certainly couldn't put Kismet's *real* dragons in a comic strip.

Shit. He stared at the fire-breathing screen, then glanced at the telephone. The kid needed help. Cleo had asked him to get it for her. Cleo never asked for anything.

He didn't have time for Cleo's problems. She very obviously considered him a nuisance who stood in the way of her taking care of the kids. *Her* way of taking care of the kids. Not that he agreed with it. Not that it was any of his business.

His business was drawing next week's strips and producing a screenplay. And salvaging his investments—what was left of them.

Saving the computer dragon with a button stroke, he reached for his planner. It wouldn't take a minute to call Holly. She could find out about privacy laws and give him some names of local counselors. Then he could write off any further responsibility to the mixed-up mess of his neighbors.

He made a face at that thought. Maybe Cleo and the kids were mixed-up, but they felt things he didn't. They were real. Some days, he thought he belonged in the comic strip with his characters.

That kind of stupid psychobabble was what he got

from hanging around women. He preferred action. He hit the telephone buttons.

Ten minutes later he had the information he needed and that Cleo wouldn't like. He also had the germ of a real idea for the film script, and not that mindless trash he'd been scribbling.

He glanced guiltily at the computer screen, then at the phone numbers in his hand. Cleo was at work. He couldn't just run over to the house and give these to her. He could call her, but he wanted to *see* her. Maybe Tim was right and he needed a challenge and Cleo was it. He just needed to see her, to hear her commonsensical approach, to have her put his world into perspective.

Getting her into his bed would certainly do that. Talk about your marginal chances . . . He'd have better luck in the stock market.

He needed a break, and there wasn't anything worth eating in the house. He could run into town, see if she wanted lunch. He didn't think even his best smile could persuade Cleo to do what needed doing with the kids, but he could try. Then he could go back to work with a clear conscience and a clearer head.

He'd call the apartment manager in New York first. They usually had a waiting list of eager buyers. And the bank, for a quick equity loan until he had it sold. He'd worry about moving all his stuff some other time.

He wouldn't even think about what he would do if the script he had in mind didn't fly. Bankruptcy didn't become him.

"No. No, I'm not talking about Matty, but a friend. Good grief, what kind of monster do you think I am?" Cleo glared at the phone, wishing she hadn't got daring and called her stupid counselor. Counselors always thought the worst of everyone, especially ones with criminal records.

She lifted her gaze and grimaced as Marta rolled her eyes in sympathy, then grinned as her clerk spun her index finger at her temple to give her opinion of all counselors everywhere. Marta understood. Marta didn't have a clue, however.

"Look, all I wanted was some advice, all right? If you can't tell me what I need to know, that's fine. I have other sources. Give the feds my love when you snitch to them." Cleo very carefully, very politely, lowered the receiver to its cradle. Then she slammed her fist into the counter.

"Effing morons! Blunderheads! Bean-brained bastards of bloated banality—"

"You're beginning to sound like your sister," Marta said calmly, dusting off a line of paint cans. "Call the shitheads what they are. They don't live in our world. They've got desks and cubicles and brick walls and layers of regulations insulating them. They'd hyperventilate and asphyxiate if they ever wandered out and saw the real world."

Cleo snorted at the idea of sounding like Maya, but Marta was right about the rest. "You been taking vocabulary lessons or dating a teacher?" she asked to divert the discussion. Marta had the reassuring habit of not asking questions, but she knew her clerk was curious.

"Taking courses in first aid over at the clinic. Lots of times I saw accidents on the job I could have helped if I'd known how. Fat lot of good it does me now, but I feel better learning. You're never too old, you know." She watched Cleo with curiosity and a good dose of compassion. "Anything I can help with?"

No one in town knew Cleo's past, and she wanted to keep it that way. Marta knew she saw a counselor,

because someone had to cover for her when she drove
into the city. Lots of people got counseling. She just
didn't have to explain why.

As much as she would have liked to talk about her
problems and as much as she trusted Marta, she simply
couldn't risk her store and Matty's happiness by letting
anyone know she was an ex-con. She'd seen firsthand
how small-town gossip could affect business and personal lives. All the good people would drift away, and
her store would turn to dust. Nope, keeping to herself
was the only way to survive.

"Nah, just a problem with the neighbor's kids." She
returned to filling out her hardware order.

Short, fiftyish, and as well muscled as any man, Marta
used her fireplug body as expressively as a ballet dancer.
Cleo read curiosity and concern in the way she leaned
forward across the counter, and saw understanding in
her flip arm gesture.

"You know I'm here if you need me," was all she said
before the bell over the door rang, and she turned a smile
of greeting on their next customer.

"Got any witches or skeletons in stock?" a husky male
voice inquired—Jared.

Just his voice warmed places that had been shivering a
second ago. She resented his effect on her. She contemplated retreating to the stockroom for her inventory
sheets, except she refused to let him drive her out of her
own shop. "What do you want, McCloud? We're fresh
out of cartoon characters today."

"McCloud?" Marta kicked in cheerfully, diluting Cleo's
acidity with eagerness. "The comic artist everyone's talking about? My niece adores your stuff. I'm Marta."

Jared stuck out his hand. "Happy to meet you, Marta.
Do you think you could push old Gloomy Gus over there

out the door for some lunch? I had in mind feeding her in hopes of sweetening her disposition."

Marta giggled like a teenager and Cleo scowled harder. "Every Peter Pan needs a Captain Hook," Cleo reminded him.

"Well, Wendy was always a little saccharine for my tastes." He shrugged, shoved his hands into the spacious pockets of his camp shorts, and gave her an admiring once-over. "I prefer Tinkerbell's attitude, although I figure someone will end up swatting her one day."

Cleo bit her cheek to fight back a smile. The man simply didn't take no in any fashion, and his humor softened his perversity. "I'm not hungry," she lied, just to assert her independence.

"Neither am I, but we have to eat for our health. I heard there was a great place down on the bay where they serve their grease fried. Maybe you can kill me with cholesterol."

How could she refuse an offer like that? She was starving, the restaurant in question packed maximum calories into scrumptious mouthfuls, and she could make the Yankee eat the old-fashioned traditional Southern dish of lamb fries. Worked for her.

Throwing her apron on the counter, she turned the store over to Marta, and stalked into the back room to wash. She refused to call it primping. This wasn't a date. She didn't date. This was tricking sheep testicles down a Yankee's throat and watching him gag after she told him what he was eating. A day at the amusement park.

But she didn't want to look like a complete redneck in a fancy place with linen tablecloths. So she scrubbed the dirt smudge from her cheek, stabbed a lipstick tube at her mouth, and ran her fingers through her hair to give it some life. Squinting in the semi-lit mirror, she decided maybe she'd let the rest of the brown dye fade out. It was a nuisance to mess with and didn't disguise the red enough to matter.

Grabbing the knitted sack she called a purse, she sauntered back to the front as if she "did lunch" every day with rich New York artists. She wouldn't even ask if they were going dutch. For the first time in her life she had a credit card and knew how to use it.

"Ready, lover boy," she stated boldly. "Can I choose your last meal?"

Jared winked over Cleo's head at her clerk. "That's what I love about her—always ready, willing, and able."

"Don't let her feed you lamb fries!" Marta called as they headed out the door.

Damn interfering woman. Cleo smiled sweetly at Jared's questioning look. "Don't ask."

"Okay, but if they're anything like prairie oysters, I like 'em." He blithely steered her down the street with a firm grip on her elbow.

Cleo gave up and went along for the ride. No matter how hard she tried, she couldn't despise this obtuse, genial idiot. His possessive hand on her arm was another matter entirely. He had to quit touching her, or she had to quit shaking when he did.

"Hey, Cleo, where you goin'?" As they turned the corner to the harbor, a waitress sneaking a smoke in the garden of the local B&B waved them over.

Katy, the proprietor of Blackbeard's B&B, was one of the major promoters of the pirate film idea. Cleo supposed if she ever bothered attending a Jaycees' meeting, she might point out all the pitfalls of bringing L.A. types in here, but she was more comfortable with waitresses than high-falutin' *proprietors* seeking yuppiedom.

"Hey, Stella, seen Ed lately? We need to get back to work on that clock." Jerking her elbow free of Jared's grasp, Cleo crossed in the middle of the shady street.

"Imagine he's down at the Blue Monkey as always, lifting his elbow and seeing German spies on every corner."

Cleo sighed in exasperation at Ed's habits. If the old man was back on his spy kick, then he'd be up on the courthouse roof with his binoculars, looking for U-boats again. The sheriff hated it when he did that. "If any spies ever landed here, they'd probably be down at the Monkey with the other old fogies."

Stella shrugged. "Then Katy would want a World War II movie and we'd be called the Third Reich Inn. Keeps me employed." She batted her eyelashes in Jared's direction. "Thought you'd keep that one from us, did you?"

"He said he'd feed me, so he gets to choose his own poison." As Jared came up and rested his hand on her shoulder, Cleo gestured at the tall, henna-haired waitress. "Stella, Jared McCloud. If I talk him into feeding me here, you could dump soup in his lap."

"I think my mama lied about Southern hospitality," he murmured near her ear before shaking Stella's hand.

All right, maybe she liked his touches, but they were a damned irritation, sort of like being taught to appreciate caviar, then told it cost too much.

"That's a cute TV show you had," Stella all but simpered. "What brings you to these parts?"

"The lovely ladies, of course." Jared made no effort to retrieve his hand from hers. "Has anyone told you that you ought to be in movies?"

Stella's eyes widened, and she grinned in appreciation. "Damn, you're good. Don't suppose you know that film director Katy's so hot to get here, do you?"

Cleo'd had just about enough of this. Before she could break up their Mutual Admiration Society, Jared startled her with his reply.

"Shelton? Nah, he's the top muckety-muck. But one of

his writers on the pirate script worked with me on the show, and he recommended this place."

Cleo's jaw dropped too far to close before Stella jumped on his revelation.

"You know the writers? Did they tell you they're filming here?"

Jared shrugged. "Nobody in the business knows what they're doing from one minute to the next. Sorry. I just know they've scouted here."

"Oh, fine!" Cleo finally exploded. "I'm harboring a damned Hollywood spy. That's just what I needed to hear. You get your privacy, then leave us overrun with Hollywood prima donnas. How swell of you."

"I don't have a thing to do with what Shelton does," Jared protested. "Give the town credit. This place has atmosphere." He gestured at the moss-draped trees in front of faded mansions and the sailing yachts bobbing in the harbor. "It's perfect for a pirate movie. And Shelton's crew would add to the town's economy, help fix up the schools, maybe."

"Swell, *now* I'm aiding and abetting the corruption of the last untouched piece of the coast. You get your privacy for two months, then pass on the information to your Hollywood friends so we're flooded with gawkers into eternity. I really need that." Cleo started off down the street without him. "Come along, McCloud," she shouted back. "The tables fill up fast and you promised to feed me. Stella, let him go and I won't tell him what color you painted your boyfriend's car."

Stella waved them off as Jared hurried in Cleo's wake. "I get off at two, Jared," she called after him. "You just stop on by!"

"What color?" he asked in a whisper as he caught up with her.

"Pink. With purple polka dots. It was a 'Vette," she

said with satisfaction, still steaming over his betrayal. "I helped her choose the enamel."

Jared drew a few succinct words from his extensive vocabulary before eyeing her warily. "Okay, I'll bite. What did her boyfriend do to deserve that fate?"

"Now, *that* I won't tell. Suffice it to say that he'd had it coming and I would have painted his appropriate body parts to match. He got off easy."

"I think you're finally scaring me," he mused while pushing her up the stairs of the antebellum-mansion-converted-to-local-restaurant.

"Took you long enough. Mention me to your director friends, tell them I don't welcome their L.A. crap down here."

"What in hell did L.A. ever do to you?" he asked, opening the door for her.

Cleo tried not to be intimidated as a gracious silver-haired matron greeted them, but she held her tongue while the hostess led them to a table in the bay window overlooking the harbor. More silver and glassware than she owned decorated the linen. One thing they didn't teach you in jail was proper table etiquette.

Somewhere in her wasted youth someone had attempted to teach her manners. She knew enough not to tuck her napkin into her shirt. And this was a sailing town. All the boats at the dock weren't yachts. Out of the corner of her eye she could see tourists in plaid shorts and bronzed crew members in cutoffs. No matter how the blue-haired ladies tried, this wasn't the Old South any longer. She could manage. She shrugged out of her flannel shirt, stripping down to a tank top. Air-conditioning didn't come with antebellum mansions.

"L.A. is where I grew up," she whispered back as the hostess left them with the menus.

"L.A. is a big city," he muttered in return, eyeing her

vivid pink top with appreciation. "You can't write off the whole town." She raised her eyebrows and he grimaced. "Okay, *Hollywood* isn't big, but they could bring in big bucks, and they'd be gone in a few months."

"Right." Rather than argue over the dubious possibility of a nonexistent film, she examined her menu.

"Fried okra, fried tomatoes, batter-fried broccoli and cauliflower—is there any vegetable they don't fry?" he asked in fascination, apparently sensing when her attention strayed.

"Corn?" Cleo scanned the menu, noting prices and debating whether to stiff him with the expensive check. A lifetime of pinching pennies didn't allow the freedom of considering food first and cost later. "If you're not in the mood for lamb fries, you can always have fried fish, fried chicken, fried pork, or chicken-fried steak."

She thought he laughed softly. She shouldn't be trying to make him laugh, or getting pleasure out of it. She ought to be finding out what he wanted. She didn't have any illusions that he'd come all the way into town to treat her to lunch or argue over L.A. She couldn't believe he had connections to that damned film.

"I think I love this place already." With a sigh of happiness, Jared slid back in his seat and sprawled his long legs under the table until his foot brushed hers. "Did anyone ever tell you how cute you are when you scowl?"

She didn't know whether to laugh out loud or bean him with the fresh flower arrangement. A grin curled unwillingly at one corner of her mouth. "What's the male word for slut?"

His mouth stretched into an even wider smile. "Am not. I just like women. And food. Can't get enough of either, although if you're willing . . ." He wiggled his eyebrows suggestively.

He was too outrageous to take seriously, and Cleo

relaxed a fraction. Overgrown schoolboys were well within her capacity to handle. Sophisticated city men might make her wary, and Jared possessed all the outward attributes of sophistication—expensive sunglasses, blow-dried hairstyling, manicured nails, and designer shirts. But she knew a thing or two about outer appearances and inner realities.

"In your dreams, McCloud. What brings you to town? Gene plant snakes in your filing cabinet?"

The waitress arrived to take their drink order and present a wine list. Jared waved it away and ordered bottled water.

"Not on my account," Cleo objected. "Get beer, if you want. I happen to *like* sweet tea."

He shook his head and dismissed the waitress. "And I happen to like water. Believe it or not, I have a few friends in AA. It's not a problem, so knock the chip off."

Cleo sank back in her chair and considered sulking, but Jared's dismissive attitude made it impossible. One of the reasons she avoided social situations was the awkwardness others felt around her if they knew she couldn't drink.

Another reason was the temptation to test her willpower against a glass of chilled Chardonnay or a finger of Jack Daniels.

As if he had no sensitivity whatsoever, Jared flipped the menu to the back page and pointed out the list of nonalcoholic concoctions. "Or we could indulge in Merry Mary Margaritas or some of these Yummy Tummy Strawberry Dairy-kiris. Makes the mouth water, doesn't it?"

No, actually, it revolted her as she remembered the sickeningly sweet drinks she'd first started out on as a teenager. Wrinkling her nose in distaste, she gave up any interest in sulking. "I never even liked beer. I just drank it to be sociable."

"Yeah. Friend of mine did the same. In college, he was hospitalized after a binge drinking episode to be sociable. Graduated to wine and became a connoisseur to impress us after college and stuck with that for a while, then sampled martinis to impress his colleagues over business lunches. By the time he was thirty, I never saw him without a glass in his hand like a crutch."

"Does this story have a happy ending?" she asked dryly.

He lifted a careless shoulder. "He's dry, for now. His wife agreed to give him a second chance. But he could have taken out an entire busload of innocent teenagers when he drove home drunk on the wrong side of the turnpike one night. Fortunately for everyone, he swerved at the last minute and only lost a kidney in the wreck."

"That *was* lucky. The drunk is usually the only one who walks away unharmed. I might start believing in the Almighty if the drunk got creamed more often." Uncomfortable again, Cleo stared at her menu. Wasn't he supposed to *avoid* these kinds of subjects?

"I'm not totally shallow," he said, out of the blue.

Cleo made the mistake of looking up and really *seeing* him. Eyes so dark they almost appeared black stared back at her, and for a moment, she could almost feel him reaching out to her, for the connection that shimmered in the air between them—a connection that whispered temptingly of trust and understanding and something far more elusive.

She wasn't that big a jerk. She slapped the menu closed. "That's what I'm afraid of."

❧ SEVENTEEN ❧

Jared tried not to feel disappointment at her reply. For a moment there, he'd thought they'd really linked, that she'd understood what he was trying to tell her and how much it meant. He'd almost felt a chord humming between them, but then, he had an active imagination.

Maybe there was something wrong with him. It didn't take much to know when a woman simply wanted his influence, his prestige, his name on her bedpost, or just the jollies of good sex or laughter or even a shoulder to cry on, and he'd never exerted the effort to understand more—until Cleo. He'd thought with Cleo he could really connect on a deeper level. Stupid of him.

She thought all he wanted was sex.

Until now, she'd probably been right.

Whoa, one step back, boy. Maybe he really was starting to lose it. First the TV flop, then the writer's block, and now he was looking at an ex-con addict as a soul mate? Worse yet, a narrow-minded zealot who hated Hollywood and probably screenwriters as well. Had he turned into Tim when he wasn't looking?

The waitress arriving to take their orders relieved him of any responsibility to respond. Cleo ordered a salad with fried chicken nuggets on top for her cholesterol of the day. With his eye on the enormous dessert menu,

Jared stuck to the basic food groups of fried chicken and mashed sweet potatoes.

Once the waitress took their menus away, Cleo nailed him with that steely glare of hers. "All right, McCloud, tell me what this is really about. You didn't come all the way into town to tell me you're not a jerk."

"I might have been looking for a little positive reinforcement," he said in a tone of aggrievement. "But then, I really would have to be a jerk to look for it from you."

She burst out laughing, turning all heads in the dining room to the delicious sound. Jared grinned in approval at how her whole appearance changed in a moment of unself-conscious enjoyment. The sunlight from the window caught the red highlights of her hair, her hauntingly beautiful eyes lost their shadowed cynicism to crinkle in wide-eyed pleasure, and her mouth . . .

That mouth was straight out of heaven's pleasure book. He could watch the way it curved seductively or scowled ferociously or trembled uncertainly for the rest of his life, but parted in laughter, it was a joy to behold. All right, he was truly smitten. He could handle that for a couple of months.

"You won this round," she agreed, visibly smothering her laughter into a smile as the waitress brought her tea. "You're not shallow."

The sparkling water could have been champagne bouncing effervescent bubbles through his brain as Cleo actually relaxed in his presence. He'd always resented his family's opinion of his character and occupation, but he'd never really cared what women thought of him—until now. For some reason he wanted this wacky, hard-nosed female to see him as something besides a free ride. "Convince my family of that."

She lifted a lovely tanned shoulder in a shrug. "Why

bother? You're the one who has to live inside your skin, not them."

"How simple you make that sound," he said dryly. "My father is an eminent authority on pre-Elizabethan literature. My mother is on the board of half a dozen well-endowed charitable trusts. My older brother has degrees in more obscure sciences than I can remember, and even my baby brother has copyrighted enough software to make Bill Gates green. I took folklore and basket-weaving in college and was too busy drawing cartoons for syndication by my senior year to remember to graduate."

Instead of shaking her head in disapproval, Cleo grinned in appreciation. "Making people laugh at their own foibles is not something everyone can do. Science degrees and software come a dime a dozen."

"Yeah, well you try being court jester in a castle of knights sometime," he grumbled testily. "And I'll really have them rolling on the floor when they learn I probably lost everything in the market today. They told me to put it into bonds."

She shook her head with no sympathy. "Easy come, easy go. Are you trying to tell me you can't pay for lunch? Want my credit card?"

Something tight in Jared's chest suddenly loosened, and he regarded her with more than his usual admiration. "Damn, you're tough. You don't flinch an inch. If I could bottle your attitude, we could make a fortune."

It was her turn to squirm. "I am not tough. You saw plenty of evidence of that the other day, and I'll thank you not to mention it. Now quit diverting the subject. What is it you want, McCloud?"

"I talked to my friend the psychologist. She says if Kismet tells a counselor of anything that smacks of criminal abuse, the counselor is legally responsible to report it or they can get sued." There, he'd said it. He still thought reporting the abuse the best for everyone concerned.

Cleo grimaced. "Yeah, I got the same answer. If I'd had a crystal ball years ago so I could see the result of my stupidity . . . There isn't any way I can persuade the court to let me take them. I am officially labeled a poor risk, the next best thing to incompetent."

Jared breathed easier. He'd thought she might storm out in fury over the bad news. "All right, so you're incompetent and I'm a failure. That doesn't help the kids."

A large group of laughing, office-dressed women entered and headed for a meeting room in the rear. The noise effectively cut off her reply, and the familiar figure swerving from the group at the sight of them shut Cleo's expression into its usual closed mask.

"Jared! Cleo! Just the people I need to see." As the laughing group proceeded on without her, Liz Brooks stopped by the table. "I've been trying for days to reach Kismet's mother, but no one ever answers. I'm concerned. One of the teachers reported Kismet slapped another student today. The child is troubled and is desperately crying out for help."

Cleo sank deeper into her chair and didn't say a thing. Jared kicked her shoe but she only scowled at him.

"Gene told me his mother is out of town this week," he lied. "But we've talked to Linda. She says she can't afford counseling." There, that ought to start a discussion.

"The county provides services for those who can't pay," Liz said primly. "That's no excuse. We'll be fortunate if a parent doesn't call the sheriff and complain. I don't want to see the child expelled, but we are responsible for the well-being of *all* our students."

That was guaranteed to put Cleo in a receptive mood. Jared didn't even have to look at her to feel the steam rising. "I really don't think Kismet could hurt a fly, so you might investigate the allegation a little more thoroughly, Liz. But we're on this. We'll keep trying."

He could see the struggle between disapproving teacher and feminine flirt as Liz sought a reply. Flirt won. She beamed at him. "I'm sure you'll do what's best, Jared. Are you ready for a hurricane? We just heard the forecasters say it turned away from Florida and our likelihood of being hit is up to thirty percent."

"I live in Miami. I know how to run." He considered reaching over and squeezing Cleo's hand to prevent her from scratching Liz's eyes out, but she'd just tell him that assuming she was jealous smacked of male ego. She'd be right.

"Good seeing you again, Cleo," Liz said cheerily. "Gotta go."

"I bet she knits baby booties," Cleo growled as the counselor walked away, blond hair swaying gently across the pink silk of her round collar.

"And sticks pins in pincushions," he agreed solemnly, enjoying the flash of ire in eyes he could swear suddenly turned pure green.

"Shut up, McCloud." She stabbed her fork into a chicken nugget on the salad that had just been delivered. "Your superficial tendencies are showing."

"So, shallow is easier. We can't all hold grudges against civilization." He sampled his mashed sweet potatoes, considered the levels of butter and sugar that rendered them palatable, and wondered if he should save them for dessert. "I assume you have a weather radio so we can know if the storm does turn this way?"

"You assume wrongly. Weather radios cost about a hundred bucks so no, I don't have one."

"Primitive. With the way my luck is running, the

whole island will blow away." He considered the likelihood pretty high. Maybe he ought to pack up his computer and move inland.

"My truck is available if you're thinking of leaving," she said sweetly, reading his mind.

He shot her a dark look. "You'd like that, wouldn't you? Then you could pretend I didn't exist and whatever this is between us is a product of your imagination."

She sucked in a breath and stared at him in disbelief over a forkful of lettuce. "And you said *I* was blunt. Do you ever listen to yourself?"

Not if he could help it. He was already down for the count, he might as well lie here and let her walk over him. Maybe it was this damned tendency to lay himself open that got him trampled so often by his family. "You're gonna deny it?" he demanded. "I'm scaring you silly, and you're trying to close your eyes and make believe I'll go away."

Cleo shoved her lettuce aside and forked a cherry tomato. "This is not a productive topic," she said stiffly. "If you want to discuss how to help Kismet—"

"Counseling will help her. Arresting that pervert will help. Getting her out of hell will be a major step forward. But I'm not calling the sheriff until you give the okay, so this isn't a productive topic either."

Cleo gritted her teeth and tried to stay calm. This was the reason she didn't socialize. People prodded her private space, battering old bruises. Instinct required she strike out, but she didn't want to strike this man anymore. It wasn't any more effective than slamming her fist into his iron gut.

"Then maybe we should discuss hurricanes," she agreed gloomily.

"The weather as a conversational icebreaker, how

original. Look, Cleo, I'm trying to help. I *want* to help. You're just not giving me any options."

"What difference does it make to you?" she demanded. "You'll be gone in a couple of months. Go back and draw your pretty pictures and let us scrabble along like we have been."

The lines around his mouth tightened but he calmly finished chewing his chicken while his dark, understanding gaze penetrated her soul. She *hated* it when he did that. It made her feel things she had no right feeling, want things she couldn't have.

"Ever heard of cars, Cleo?" he finally asked. "Telephones? Airplanes? The world is a very small place these days."

"Definitely not big enough," she agreed. "But I can promise when you finish whatever it is you're working on, you won't look back here. Just drop it, all right? This isn't a date, we have nothing in common but deprived hormones, and we'll never agree on anything."

He grinned as if she'd handed him the moon. "It isn't just me, then. You're feeling the tug, too. Admit it, and make the one bright spot in my really lousy day."

"I'd have to be a loon to admit any such thing." She was already kicking herself as it was. He made it too easy to reveal things she never even said to herself. "You'd never leave me alone. The lunch was nice, McCloud. Let's not do it again."

Cleo left the store early to be home when the school bus arrived. She wanted to make certain the kids got off at her stop. She hadn't had time to confront Linda and her new boyfriend. In actuality, she hoped they'd both go away and make things easy on her.

Instead of the school bus, Jared's bright red Jeep roared into the drive, bearing both Gene and Kismet.

Apparently not seeing anything strange in this development, both teenagers ran for the kitchen and food while Cleo remained on the porch, arms crossed, waiting for an explanation.

"I didn't want them going home," he said gruffly. "This haphazard arrangement of yours needs to be ironed out."

Another time, another person, and she'd have smacked him for the insult. Instead, she admired his directness and his concern. He'd finally succeeded in turning her brains to mush. "They're not stupid," she reminded him. "They know they can come here when Linda is orbiting another moon."

"That's a nice way of putting it." He climbed up the porch stairs and met her nose to nose even though he stood on a lower step. "I've got to get some work done. Will you let me kiss you before I go?"

He'd actually asked. She stupidly wanted to reward him for his thoughtfulness. Her heart thumped hard enough to be a reply as he lingered too close for comfort and met her gaze with a hot look that could smolder stone. She wanted his kiss more than she'd ever wanted a drink or a toke. The result would most likely be just as destructive.

"I'm an addict, remember?" she said softly, willing him to understand.

She watched her announcement hit him and course rapidly through his overactive brain. She thought the heat between them escalated another ten degrees as he grasped how her admission affected him.

"I think I like the idea of someone being addicted to me," he said slowly, testing to see if he'd taken her words correctly.

"That's swell of you." She stayed where she was, waiting for him to grasp the rest of it. She trembled beneath the intensity of his stare. She really, really wanted him, she finally acknowledged. She wanted the insanity of first love, the overwhelming loss of self in sensation, the bliss of that first meeting of minds and souls, and the surrender into someone else's care. She longed for it with all her lonely stupid heart.

Been there, done that. She didn't need to be that naive kid all over again. She had matured enough to know she couldn't blame her late husband for her chemical dependencies, but she'd seen the disaster of relying on anyone else for happiness.

Jared's dark gaze dipped to her mouth, and arousal coursed through her veins like a drug more powerful than any created by man. She tried not to look at the competent hands that had held and comforted her, the strong arms that had made her feel secure when she needed them, but Jared was all man and every cell in her body was aware of him. It finally occurred to her that he hid his brains and talent and courage behind a mask of humor just as she hid behind her cynicism. Just that knowledge breached her defenses far more than anyone else had in a long, long time.

"I don't know how to handle this," he finally admitted, studying her expression. "I'm usually pretty good at talking women into bed, and I never say stupid things like that to anyone else." His smile was rueful. "You force me to be honest when I don't want to be."

"If you're really honest with yourself, you'll realize this won't work, and you'll go back to your drawing board and leave us alone. This is where mature adults recognize the impossibility and part ways." She crossed her arms protectively across her chest.

"Maybe that's why I'm resisting growing up." He rubbed a finger over her bottom lip, nearly bringing her to her knees. She couldn't respond even had she wanted to.

"But I've grown up enough to know how to wait. I'm not one of the nightmares you try to scare away with your mechanical monsters, Cleo. I won't hurt you. I'll give you time to realize that."

He walked away, leaving her weeping inside for what she could never have.

❧ EIGHTEEN ❧

Jared tossed in his rumpled sheets, threw back the top one, and cursed the sweat-soaked pillow. It was nearly the end of September. It shouldn't be so danged hot.

The rhythmic pounding of waves against the shore should have soothed his restlessness. He'd left the windows open for just that purpose. He could hear the wind rising, but no air blew through the screens.

He'd been dreaming again. What his imagination denied him during the day was appearing in Technicolor and surround sound in his sleep. Images of Cleo's emerald eyes weeping crystal tears etched the drawing pad of his mind so thoroughly, he wanted to reach out and comfort her. He could even imagine those firm curves and small bones pressed into him, his leg wrapped around hers, his hand stroking the soft strands of her hair. He could imagine a damned lot more than that, and he threw his feet over the side of the bed, sitting up, rather than go there.

He slept naked, but his arousal didn't respond to the cooler air from the window as he peered out. He wished he could at least see the lights of Cleo's house through the trees, but it was late, and even if he could see the house, there wouldn't be lights. He wondered if she wore something silky and sexy to bed, but figured it was more likely a T-shirt.

He didn't know why he had this irritating caveman urge to stand as a bulwark between her and the world in place of her ridiculous skeleton. Cleo would probably roll him up as if he were Burt if he tried.

Maybe her defiant attempt to hold off the world was what was so endearing about a cynical case like Cleo. He could see right through her camouflage into her lonely soul. They had a lot in common in the masquerade department.

Well, stewing over their similarities wouldn't put him back to sleep, or get him into her bed. As long as he was wide awake, he might as well put his brain to work. That script wouldn't write itself, more's the pity.

Thinking of Cleo fed his urge, and he sat down at the keyboard with an eagerness he hadn't known in a long time.

"They called her a whore," Gene related matter-of-factly over breakfast the next morning. "They said Mama's a whore who sleeps with niggers, and Kismet is one, too. So Kis snapped them with rubber bands. Served 'em right."

Cleo ran her hands through her uncombed hair and tried thinking of a reply to the unthinkable. Her brain was too dead to process this. Jared had messed with her mind until she'd tossed the night away. Why were kids so blamed cruel to each other?

"What do you say to the kids when they tease you like that?" she asked sleepily, dragging out the coffee and filling up the filter.

"They don't say things like that to my face because they know I'll beat the snot out of 'em." Gene spread what appeared to be half a jar of peanut butter on his toast. "If I'da been there, I'da whupped them good."

"Fighting isn't the answer." She didn't know what was, but she'd learned that much. "You'll only give them an excuse to kick you out of school, and then you won't get to take wrestling class."

"Don't care," he said defiantly, shoving the toast in his mouth and speaking through it.

Yeah, she knew that attitude as well. She rubbed her face and thought about it. "All right, first off, you know those morons are simply trying to get you into trouble, don't you? They want you to strike first so they can go whimpering to the teacher. That's their way of getting rid of things they're too stupid to understand. Got that?"

He narrowed his eyes suspiciously but nodded as he chewed.

Well, at least he was listening. "So, what you need to do is put them in a place where you can whup them without being thrown out of school. The only place you can do that is in wrestling class. I'll have Jared talk to your teacher, and let him help you out with this. Can you do that? Tell them to take their insults to the gym and then the better man wins?"

Gene screwed up his face in disapproval, but he nodded again. "It ain't gonna work, but I'll try. Can I do that for those shits who ragged Kismet?"

Cleo shrugged and stuck her coffee mug under the flow from the machine. "Give it a try." As she sipped the hot black brew, her mind woke to another thought. "What you both need is some friends who'll back you up. Are there any of them you like? People we could ask over and maybe have a beach party or something?"

Gene's eyes lit with all the joy of a child meeting Santa Claus. "You mean that? Really? We can have people over?"

Cleo thought she'd probably lost her mind, but she blamed Jared for that. "Sure, kid. Why not? What's one more reptile or two around the place?"

"All right! Wait till I tell Kismet." He took off like cannon shot, shouting through the back of the house.

Now she'd done it. She'd have half the delinquents in town rioting on her beach. She'd have to remind herself sometime why she wasn't supposed to do self-destructive things like that.

Maybe Jared was right. Maybe the kids did need to be jerked out of Linda's negligent care. She just couldn't see Social Services or a group home providing a beach party to make them happy either.

One of these days, she'd learn to mind her own business.

Sipping her coffee and staring out the window at the wind-tossed trees separating her house from Jared's, she no longer believed her own lies.

"The radio reports a fifty percent chance of it hitting land near here," Cleo said briskly into the telephone to her clerk. "I'm not feeling lucky today, so I'm putting up the shutters. Have your son come in and nail up the plywood over the storefront, will you?"

She answered Marta's quick questions with only half her attention. Her gaze kept straying to the rising wind whipping the palms outside her window. She had only two of the tall trees, but she figured they served as some kind of signal she ought to obey. Besides, she was feeling antsy and outside of herself, and didn't think she'd be any good at the store.

If the hurricane hit here, it wouldn't be until tonight. Could she persuade the kids into a shelter on the mainland if their mother wasn't home? The town was protected by the island and wouldn't see the waves that would smash out here.

She probably ought to check on Linda, but she needed to nail this place together first. She'd spent months of work and effort on this house, and she didn't want it destroyed by a storm that blew in one day and left the next. Maybe she could persuade Linda to go into town to ride it out.

She'd tried calling Jared, but his answering machine was picking up. He could have heard the radio and taken off for dry land already. He'd said he was used to evacuations and knew enough to leave when a hurricane threatened.

As she wrestled with the last of the shutters, cursing their rusty recalcitrance and wondering why she hadn't had the sense to look at them sooner, a strong gust of wind almost blew her off the ladder. Well, if that wasn't a hurricane moving in, she didn't want to see the real thing.

Black clouds boiling overhead warned she'd better decide whether to hit the road or ride it out. Hurrying down the rungs, she started for the house and the radio. Maybe it had hit the coast south of here and this was just the rough edge. She knew absolutely nothing about hurricanes.

Switching the radio on, she dialed Jared's number again. She ought to go down there and make certain he'd left. He could be working and just not answering.

A pounding on the door interrupted the newscaster

announcing evacuation routes. Well, so much for hoping it had hit elsewhere. She'd better add Linda to her list of to-dos. That rolling wreck of hers didn't start half the time.

She hung up the receiver and jerked open the front door.

Linda stood there looking so strung out, she swayed. Cleo started to haul her in and sit her down, but the woman's eyes lit like the fires of hell as soon as Cleo tried to speak.

"I told you to leave them kids alone!" she screamed. "I've got case workers all over me now, sayin' my kids ain't living with me and threatening to cut off my checks, and it's your damned fault!"

"Linda, calm down. We can talk—" As Linda grabbed the door frame, Cleo recognized the fresh needle tracks on her visitor's bare forearm, and with horror, she cut off whatever she'd been about to say. If Linda was mainlining, there wasn't a chance of getting sense out of her.

"My kids ain't comin' here no more!" Disregarding Cleo's incomplete sentence, Linda belligerently slammed the door frame. "I'm calling the police the next time you kidnap them. Let the sheriff find out what kind of criminal you are! I sent Lonnie in to make sure they come home, so you stay out of this, if you know what's good for you."

Bits and pieces of Cleo's soul tore loose at Linda's threats. The kids could run and hide from their mother, but she couldn't. In offering to take Linda to AA with her, she'd revealed her innermost secrets to a woman who now sported track marks on her arm. The safe, sane world she'd been carefully constructing cracked as they spoke.

"Linda, you have to listen to reason—"

"Stay away from them! Don't you dare come to my

place no more. I've got a man looking out for us now."
With that irrational warning, Linda staggered down the
porch stairs, nearly tripping on the last step before tottering away on her high heels.

Clenching her teeth to prevent their chattering in fear,
Cleo didn't watch her go. She could call the police. She
turned and contemplated the phone with as much horror
as Linda had generated. The sheriff would ask questions.
She couldn't afford to have Linda spilling what little she
knew. All it would take was for the sheriff to notify the
feds that she'd been hanging out with a woman who did
drugs. She'd never see Matty again.

She couldn't let that pervert have Kismet.

Oh, God, what could she do? Matty came first. Matty
was her number one priority. The counselor had said she
had to list priorities, and Matty was at the top of every
single list. He had to have a sane mother, one with a
steady job. She wanted him home with her, but Linda's
lies could bring the feds to her door, and she might never
see Matty again.

If she did nothing, Linda and her bully would go away.
If she did nothing, Kismet could be destroyed.

The wind screamed overhead as she frantically grabbed
her purse and car keys and headed out. If she was lucky,
the school wouldn't release the kids to a stranger like
Lonnie. Would they release them to her? What would she
do with them after she picked them up?

The roar of Jared's Jeep rocking up the beach drive followed almost immediately on the hiccups of Linda's car
bumping in the other direction, to the main road. Relief
so overwhelming Cleo almost cried swept through her.
Jared. Jared would help. The teachers liked him. They'd
listen. Maybe he could call the police, and she wouldn't
have to get involved.

In near hysteria, she ran outside to flag down his car. There had to be something they could do to save Kismet.

Jared threw the gear into park and switched off the ignition, leaping out before the engine stopped running. "Why aren't you out of here?"

She nearly threw herself into his arms but stopped just in time. "The kids!" she shouted, wanting to shake him into understanding. "Linda was just here. We've got to get the kids." The first splatters of rain hit her arms, but Cleo was beyond worrying about the storm as she jerked open his car door and pointed him into it. "She's sent her boyfriend after them. She's shooting up, Jared! She's beyond reason. You've got to go in and save those kids."

Jared cursed vividly. "Come on, we need to get to the mainland before the storm hits anyway." He grabbed her arm and tried to shove her into the Jeep.

Cleo balked as the wheels in her mind finally began to click. "What if he already has them? What if he brings the kids back here? They'll try to come here. I can't leave them out in the storm. I can't go with you."

"Are you out of your freaking mind? There's a hurricane coming! If they're picking the kids up, they aren't coming back here. Come on."

She dug her heels in. "You're not hearing me. Linda's mainlining. That creep probably put her on the hard stuff. They're not listening to weather reports. They're hearing the shit running through their veins. Stop them, if you can, but I'm staying here in case you can't."

She jerked free of his arm and headed back to the house. "I'll try calling the school. Hurry!"

"The line is down. I already tried calling you." Jared ran after her, trying to tug her toward the car. "You can't stay here in a hurricane! This damned island will catch the brunt of it."

She didn't care. She could ride out a storm. The house

had stood here for decades of hurricanes; it could stand one more. She was terrified of Linda and her threats, but she was more terrified for the kids. "I'll explain it to you in dirty details sometime, McCloud. Just not now. Go see if you can find those kids. I'm staying right here."

Jared glanced at his watch, looked up at the boiling clouds and dancing palms, then back at Cleo, shivering with her arms wrapped around herself. "I'll be back," he warned. "I'll take the kids to shelter and be back for you."

She watched as he roared off, and wished she knew how to pray.

❧ NINETEEN ❧

Curling black waves capped by ominous white froth smashed against the causeway as Jared floored the Jeep down the two-lane. Apparently the few tourists in the condos farther out on the island had already evacuated, and the hardy souls who lived here year-round planned on digging in for the duration. There was hardly a car in sight.

In town, traffic lined the streets bumper-to-bumper, heading for the interstate and safety. He switched on the radio for the latest report. There might still be a chance the storm would pass them by. He hadn't lived in Miami more than a few years, but he'd already learned the high fallibility of hurricane forecasting.

Zigzagging through cross streets where he could, he poured his energy into reaching the school. Surely they had dismissed classes. If the kids had sense to hide when Billy-Bob Pervert showed up, he might find them.

The sick feeling in the pit of his stomach said he should have done something about this problem sooner. He should never have listened to Cleo. That's what he got for thinking with the parts below his belt. The kids would be in some safe home by now.

Not according to Cleo. Shit.

He preferred delegating the responsibility to the state. Cleo preferred accepting it as her own. He didn't know who was right.

Orderly chaos surrounded the school. The last of the big yellow buses bounced from the drive as Jared slowed to a crawl in the line of traffic created by parents preferring to pick up their little darlings in person. He listened to the radio report of school closings and hurricane paths while tapping his hand on the steering wheel and scanning the line of cars. What would Billy-Bob be driving?

Maybe the kids were on the bus. He couldn't see them in the milling mob in the yard. They were sensible kids, but even kids would be torn between going home to their mother during a crisis or hiding somewhere safe onshore.

Not that hurricane winds were ever safe. They really needed to go inland with the rest of the traffic. The weather reports still weren't exact enough to give him a time schedule for picking up the kids, racing back to Cleo, and finding safety. He had his computer and clothes in the back, ready for anything, but he doubted if the kids had anything with them except schoolbooks. Should he take them to a shelter like that? How much stuff did they keep with Cleo? If the island flooded, it could be days before they returned home.

Restlessly, he scanned the crowd of teenagers, the line of trucks and cars, and the street ahead. Why had he thought life would be simpler out here in the middle of nowhere? He was supposed to be working on that screenplay, not hunting down abused children and running from hurricanes. He might as well have stayed in Miami. At least there, he didn't have to worry about anything more critical than where to eat and with whom.

He spotted a frizzy brownish-blond mop of curls behind a hedge at the same time as he noticed a burly man in a John Deere cap arguing with someone Jared assumed to be a teacher. The mop of curls dropped below the hedge as the cap turned in that direction, and he knew instantly what was happening.

Jerking the Jeep out of the line of cars and parking it in the grass, he sauntered casually toward the hedge. If he could act as cover, the kids could jump into the Jeep before Pervert could stop them. It might be a little tricky if Billy-Bob saw them and followed, but he'd kicked the guy in the balls once, he could do it again. Maybe.

Fistfighting in front of the school—gee, that brought back old memories.

"Jared!" a familiar voice called from somewhere past the Pervert's cap. "You're just the one we need. Have you seen Gene and Kismet? They've disappeared."

Liz. Jared grimaced as Billy-Bob and the teacher turned in his direction. Liz was the queen of bad timing. He was afraid to look toward the kids and reveal their hiding place. What the hell did he do now? With everyone looking in this direction, the kids wouldn't dare run for the Jeep behind him.

"Haven't seen 'em," he called back. "Cleo was worried, so I came to see that they got home safely."

"You keep your hands off them kids!" the capped bully shouted, fisting his fingers as he turned toward Jared and away from the teacher. "I'm their father, and you ain't got no right to do nothin' with them."

"Yeah, right." Jared rocked back on his heels and grinned, praying the kids could find some way of backtracking to the car. "And my old man is Ray Charles." He nodded at the worried teacher, then waited for Liz to reach them. "This jerk is an impostor. The kids are terrified of him. That's why you can't find them."

"He has a note from their mother," she said worriedly. "He's authorized to pick them up and you're not."

Shit and other more explicit epithets. How did he get around that one? Tell her their mother was a crackhead? That would go over swell. Well, he'd learned casual and unconcerned at his mother's knee. Stick with what he did best.

Stall. He shrugged and gave the creep the old once-over. "Well, you do what you think's best, but he's already lied to you. Anyone would have to be blind to believe he's their father. Their mother is the blond one in the family, if you haven't noticed. You might want to ask why he would want to lie about something like that."

"Look, you shit-lickin' asshole . . ." Pervert took a step toward Jared. "Butt out. Them's my kids and none of yours. Want that nose of yours broke again?"

"Didn't break it last time, Perv. How are the family jewels doing today? Blue?"

Billy-Bob swung. His kind always did. Jared dodged neatly, but the teachers screamed anyway. From the direction of their gazes, though, they weren't concerned with his welfare but had seen the kids. Multiple exclamation points and asterisks, as the comics always said. He jerked around in time to see Kismet running for his Jeep.

"Guess we know who she's with, old boy. Good hitting at you." Avoiding another swinging fist, Jared dodged the crowd on the sidewalk while keeping an eye open for Gene, but Liz screamed, and he couldn't stay focused. He spun around again.

He almost didn't see that one coming. He ducked, and Billy-Bob swung off balance trying to connect. Jared really wanted to plow his fist into the soft belly now at eye level, but maybe he had grown up a year or two. Fighting in front of the kids didn't seem like a wise choice.

Out of the corner of his eye he saw a policeman hurrying in their direction. Double swell. Cleo would really light into him if he involved the law in this. She'd already read him that lecture. He stepped back out of the arc of the pervert's fighting arm, tried to catch a glimpse of Kismet, but the teachers and the policeman all flocked in at once.

"Them's my kids!" Pervert shouted, as if repetition would make it so. "Kismet, you get your hind end back in the truck where it belongs," he bellowed over everyone's heads.

"Can you have someone hauled in on assault and battery if they don't connect?" Jared asked thoughtfully as the policeman pulled out a notebook and looked confused.

Both teachers spoke at once, then diverted their topics as Gene reluctantly appeared from behind the hedge. The policeman now looked grim.

"Maybe I'd best haul all of you downtown until we get this straightened out," he decided, with the air of a man prepared to pass on all responsibility to a higher authority.

"I ain't goin' downtown." Gene stood belligerently at a distance from all of them.

Jared could see stalemate from a mile away. Catching the kid's eye, he nodded at Kismet, who stood uncertainly beside his Jeep. "I'm going back to Cleo's. I'll be right behind you, all the way, okay?"

Gene shot the policeman a scowl, glanced halfheartedly at his mother's latest boyfriend, and nodded once. "I hear you. Cleo staying if there's a hurricane?"

"Looks like it." Jared had no idea what she'd planned, but if those kids were out there, he knew she would be there for them. He really had rocks in his head for becoming involved with another do-gooder. His mother made him crazy enough. "And you and Kismet know you can come to me. Just be careful."

Billy-Bob was too dense or too stoned to comprehend their cryptic conversation. He merely reached out to collar Gene and haul him toward a battered pickup parked haphazardly half on the sidewalk. His curt gesture at Kismet indicated he thought he had the upper hand.

Both teachers watched worriedly as Kismet trailed after her brother.

"I think we better call Social Services," Liz murmured. "That man's not their father. Should we have detained them? He's endangering their lives taking them out there in this."

The policeman shrugged. "If the mother sent a note, you ain't got the right to stop him. It's a domestic problem. If you want to report abuse, then I can call in the department."

No one could report abuse but Jared, and he'd sworn to leave them alone. He lifted his hands helplessly. "I'm out of here, folks. I'm following them home. You do what you have to do."

He cursed Cleo, himself, and the heavens above all the way through town as he tracked the ramshackle truck through the intense traffic going in the opposite direction. He didn't want to be on an island in a hurricane. He didn't want to feel responsible for two kids he hadn't known existed a few weeks ago. Most of all, he didn't want to feel compelled to see Cleo again, to ask her what they should do, as if they were a couple who decided things together. He'd quit letting other people guide his life long, long ago. But he desperately needed Cleo's clear-eyed outlook right now. Those kids were headed for trouble.

As they reached the island, the truck shot ahead in the direction of the shack farther inland. Jared slowed and turned down the lane toward Cleo's.

Cleo hadn't bothered turning on her early warning system. No witch flashed across his windshield. No strobe light shot through the growing gloom of heavy clouds and spattering rain. With any other woman, he'd figure she'd had the sense to pack her valuables and be halfway across the state by now. Not Cleo.

He found her heaving a squawking peacock into the shed and slamming the door after it. The truck sat in the drive unprotected, displaced by the menagerie.

Cleo wasn't wearing her tinted glasses as she swung in his direction, and he could see the storm clouding her eyes as he drove in without the kids.

"You couldn't find them," she said flatly as he climbed out.

"I found them, but the Perv was there first, with a note from their mother."

Cleo scanned Jared's face, trying to read the message behind his strained tones and tense jaw. He radiated angry energy and a masculine charge that electrified every cell, drawing her like a paper clip to a powerful magnet. She stopped just short of reaching out to touch his shirt, and only then because she didn't know if she was offering comfort or seeking it.

"What happened?" she demanded.

"A cop showed up, their teachers didn't know what to do, and I told Gene we'd be here. I think the kids will find some way of running. Maybe we can drive them inland once they show. Even if the hurricane strikes south of here, we're in for a bad blow."

All right, Cleo, don't panic, think straight, don't go after Linda with a hammer. Cleo wrapped her arms around herself and tried to nod calmly. "Okay, that's the best we can do for now. Thank you for trying. You'd better take off before the storm hits. If you don't have a place to go, I can give you directions to my sister's place near Charlotte. They have loads of room."

Jared emitted a string of expletives she'd never heard him use. Before she knew what he intended, he caught her arm and all but hauled her toward the house.

"You dragged me into this; I'm staying. I still think we ought to call the cops, but they've got their hands full right now. So we wait. Unless you have a better idea of how we can go in there and pull them out."

Cleo attempted to shake free, but his anger had focused on her. Watching this easygoing, always laughing man turn into a grim savior of kids was fascinating and had her insides doing flip-flops, but she couldn't afford fascination. She wanted him out of here, now, if not sooner.

"There's no sense in both of us hanging around," she told him. "None of this is your concern. Get your computer and your work to someplace safe. I can look out for the kids." She jerked her arm from his grip as he reached for the door.

Brown eyes were supposed to be soft, but his hardened

like lodestone. "I'm not leaving unless you call the cops."

No way was she involving the authorities, and the damned man knew it.

❧ TWENTY ❧

Cleo stalked into the shuttered front room as Jared opened the door. A gust of wind nearly hurled the door after them. "This isn't your fight, McCloud. Linda is beyond reasoning. Social Services is apparently threatening her welfare check, and she's blaming it on me. I'm the one standing to get hurt here. If you just mosey on out, we won't miss you."

Jared caught her wrist, turned her around, and hauled her against his chest so that her knees nearly buckled. She wanted to slide down and melt on the floor. She didn't like being manhandled like this. She didn't even like people touching her. She needed support so badly she wanted to wrap her fingers in his shirt and hang on for dear life.

"Don't lie to me, Cleo. You can be as honest as you like, and I won't run, but don't ever lie." Dark eyes bored holes right through her. "Tell me you know how to handle this. Tell me you really wish I was dead and gone, if that's the truth. But don't say it if you don't mean it."

Now was a fine time for the comic to turn into Stallone and get tough. She wanted to scream at him in rage, pound him with her fists, drive him out of her life so she could go back to her steady, plodding method of picking out one step at a time. But who could fight Stallone? Instead, she twisted free, dropped on the couch, and buried her face in her hands. Where was the black rage when she needed it? Only fear and worry and total uncertainty boiled up inside her.

"I can't think," she whispered. "I want to hit somebody. I want a smoke. I want oblivion. I want to tear Linda apart. But I can't *think*."

Jared stood uncertainly in front of her for half a minute, then dropping down on the couch, he pulled her hands from her face and held them. Cleo looked anywhere except at him, but the strength pouring from his tough, hard palms warmed her.

"You *can* think. That's your whole problem," he said steadily as she glared at the shuttered window. "You can think of too many things, and none of them are good. Stop thinking for a minute. Just sit there and wipe the slate clean. I'll hold you, if that will help."

The strength for fighting was gone. Kismet had gone home with a rapist, and she was here dithering in fear. She needed a knife, not cosseting.

"All right, hit me," Jared said with a sigh, pulling her into his arms. "Get it out of your system. *Then* we'll talk."

She didn't hit him. She collapsed into his arms instead. Burrowed there like some small terrified animal. Heat and strength enveloped her. Hard muscles held her up so she didn't curl into a ball and cry. She just let his stability seep into her and tried not to think about the electric flashes jolting every nerve, screaming a more primal need than fear.

"The system stinks," she muttered incoherently into a linen-covered shoulder that smelled faintly of male musk. His muscles tightened as he crushed her closer, probably hoping to squeeze her brains out her ears so she would quit thinking. He was right—she couldn't quit thinking. Her brain whirled like a crazed dervish, and she couldn't stop it. "People stink," she added for good measure.

"I'll buy a stronger deodorant," he said dryly.

She liked it that he could joke and not go all sloppy sentimental or freeze up at the first sign of her meltdown. She liked it even better that he didn't take advantage of her temporary insanity. "This isn't working, McCloud. I've got to kill Linda."

"Try calling me Jared, would you?" he asked in exasperation. "I feel like I'm back in school, and I hated school, I might add."

She eased a palm between them, opening a space before she spasmed out. "I want to go get them—*Jared*. I don't want them running around out there in the storm."

"You planning on taking a shotgun?" he asked, unlocking his arms slowly, as if reluctant to do so. She didn't know if that was because he didn't trust her not to run for a gun or because he liked holding her. There was a thought she wouldn't ponder.

"I won't go up to their door. I'll park somewhere off to the side where the kids can see me from their bedroom. Linda will be too stoned to notice." She stood up, shaking herself off as if he'd planted pheromone magnets all over her. She had a plan. Now she needed him out of here.

Jared stood, too. He loomed larger than Superman.

"*We'll* go get them," he corrected. "You're good, but I don't want you punching Billy-Bob in the balls. That's my job."

"None of this is your business," she restated wildly. "There's a hurricane coming. Get out of here while you can."

"Look, Cleo." He grasped her arm and tugged her out the door. A bitter line cut across the bridge of his nose as he headed for the Jeep. "I'm not an incompetent ass, a lazy coward, or any of those other things you think I ought to be. Got that? This is *me*, not your ex or your father or whoever else did you wrong before. I'm doing what I think is right, and you have no say in it. Period. I'm willing to listen to your advice when I think you know more than I do, but right now, you're running on fear and you're not thinking straight, so I'm taking over."

Well, guess that told her. Cleo stared at him in incredulity, unable to think of a single thing she could say to cut him down from whatever tree limb he'd climbed out on. Well, hell, it was his life. Who was she to tell him what to do with it?

She shrugged and strode toward the Jeep. "Whatever you say, cowboy. Let's get out of here."

The gusty rain burst into a steady downpour as the Jeep navigated the narrow treacherous road to Linda's. Cleo dug her nails into her palms and tried not to let her teeth chatter. She wished she believed Linda and friend had the sense to run for shelter, but she knew they wouldn't. They were floating on clouds by now, secluded in their own little world and not seeing anything but the empty insides of their skulls. She wished she could wipe out her memory of living the same jackass existence.

Jared parked the Jeep behind a thicket of wax myrtle and palmettos. They could see the back corner of Linda's shack through a small hole in the hedge, but Cleo had no idea if the kids could see them. They would just have to watch for activity.

Rain blurred the windows, and the palms out by the beach whipped back and forth in the wind. She thought they were both insane to believe this would work, but desperation caused people to do insane things. She knew that much for a fact.

The heat permeating the car wasn't entirely the result of humidity. Cleo didn't dare look in Jared's direction. She could no longer dismiss him as a cartoon character or another nameless, faceless entity passing through her life. Something very real pulsed between them that she'd rather not admit, but she'd stopped trying to fool herself some time ago. She didn't have to act on hormones like the misguided teenager she'd once been.

Jared turned the radio on low. "I don't think the causeway will take too much of this weather," he commented cautiously. "If they don't come out soon, we'll not make it back to the mainland. Are you prepared for that?"

"I don't have a generator, if that's what you're asking. And the well operates on an electric pump. We'll have to put out pots and barrels to catch rainwater when the electric blows. I have a freezer full of food we'll have to eat before it goes bad. It's better than a snowstorm. At least we won't freeze."

He sat silent after that, and the image of the two of them trapped in her small house without any other human contact for days rose unbidden between them. He couldn't go back to the beach. It would be inundated.

A slender figure shot out the back door, fleeing toward the cover of trees behind the shed. Kismet.

Cleo reached for the door. Jared touched her arm, halting her as another figure stumbled down the back steps.

"Billy-Bob," Jared muttered under his breath. "I'm gonna break that man of a bad habit." He turned the key in the ignition and shifted the Jeep into gear.

"Billy-Bob?" She hadn't inquired the last time he'd called Lonnie that.

Jared didn't answer but gunned the Jeep on an intersecting path between Lonnie and his prey. Since they followed no road, this required a certain rearranging of shrubbery. Cleo held on to the dash and her breath.

Until she saw a third figure leaping from inside the shed, a hefty stick of kindling in his hands. "Gene," she shouted. "Stop, Jared. That's Gene, and he'll kill him!"

She didn't specify who would kill whom, but Jared hit the brake just as Gene swung his weapon at the back of Lonnie's head.

They both jumped from the car as the stick connected. Lonnie staggered and Gene looked ready to swing again, until he caught sight of Jared and Cleo breaking through the bushes, shouting. The boy's hesitation gave his target sufficient time to right himself and come after him with a roar.

Gene took off like buckshot into the bushes, racing after Kismet.

Cleo heard Jared's curses through the cacophony of wind and rain, but she had only one goal in mind—preventing Lonnie from hurting anyone else, ever again.

She'd almost reached the stick Gene had dropped before Jared caught her by the waist and hauled her from the ground, kicking and screaming. She clawed at Jared's imprisoning arms as Lonnie glared blearily at them. Maybe she could connect with the bastard's balls if she kicked high enough.

Apparently a primitive instinct for self-preservation still functioned inside Lonnie's thick head. Avoiding Cleo's flailing feet and Jared's threatening demeanor, he lumbered back toward the relative safety of the dry house, leaving Kismet and Gene to fend for themselves in the threatening weather.

"Calm down," Jared ordered, slowly lowering Cleo to the ground as the object of her rage disappeared from view. "Will the kids run for your place, or will they double back here?"

Without rage to motivate her, she couldn't think again. Soaked to the skin, she tried without effect to pull from his grasp, but Jared seemed intent on keeping her from sinking into the mud. She scanned the bushes but could see no sign of either teenager through the driving rain.

"We won't find them unless they want to be found," she said wearily, giving up her fight against his hold.

A roar of wind akin to the sound of a tornado rushed through the trees, and Jared simply nodded and steered her back to the car. Stumbling through the mud and debris, dripping wet and miserable, Cleo let him help her inside without any regard to the upholstery. Just the break from the wind relieved some of the misery, and she could turn her thoughts to the kids caught out in this. They'd be terrified.

Jared climbed in and shoved a soaking hank of hair from his forehead. The thunder of rain against the roof prohibited conversation.

He drove slowly, apparently hoping to see the kids through the waterfall of rain and leaves slashing across the windshield. Gene could find the road if he wanted. Kismet was probably hunting for her drawing box. If Cleo knew how to pray, she'd pray they'd be all right. She had to stop thinking.

"I should have called Maya," she said irrelevantly, in a futile attempt not to think.

"Phone's out," he replied, bending over the wheel to see out the window better. "And what would you say anyway? 'I'm staying out here in a hurricane'? Maybe she'll think you're safely trapped in traffic on the highway back to her."

He turned the car down the drive. A palmetto lay across the path, and he steered the Jeep around it. The wheels sucked mud but successfully pulled back to the shell drive again.

Cleo stifled her natural inclination to laugh derisively at his assumption. "Maya knows me better. My self-destructive tendencies have been evident since childhood."

A transformer exploded somewhere in the distance, and the automatic security light over the house flickered. Cleo drew in a breath and willed herself not to search too obviously for some trace of the kids.

"Flashlights and battery radio?" Jared asked.

"I own a hardware store. What do you think?"

He looked grim as he steered the Jeep as close to the house as he could. Maybe the kids were already inside. Their path through the woods was shorter than the road. "I think you ought to stock weather radios, is what I think."

A blast of blustery air rushed in when Cleo opened the car door. She cupped her hand around her ear as if listening to her own private radio. "The forecast is for rain and wind throughout the night. Evacuate all outlying areas."

He slammed out of the Jeep and came around to get her before she blew away. "Smart-ass. I'm the comedian around here."

Her ten-ton burden lightened perceptibly when Jared wrapped his arm around her, sheltering her from the wind. Surrendering to the inevitable, Cleo allowed him to guide her toward the house. The tall palms bent to the ground, the wind threatened to whip their wet clothes from their backs, but Jared's strength pinned her firmly to the uncertain ground they trod.

A shout from the distance brought them both to a halt. They swung in unison and scoured the woods for the source.

"We've got company." Jared's comment was the only

dry spot on the island as two bedraggled figures raced from the cover of trees.

❧ TWENTY-ONE ❧

The electric lines blew out not long after the kids sauntered off to the back room for the change of clothing they kept there. Cleo switched on her battery-operated radio to see if they still had time to reach the mainland.

She ignored Jared as he returned to the Jeep to retrieve his suitcase so he could change. The kids were safe. He could go now. She didn't want him here. She could deal with Gene and Kismet. She couldn't deal with an active volcano—and she could tell Jared was rapidly approaching that state. She hadn't forgotten that much about the male psyche.

The radio reported the causeway as well as the main highway into town were closed. So much for that fantasy. She snapped it off and wished she'd had the sense to call Maya. Matty would worry.

Jared blew in with the wind, creating a daunting awareness of her own drenched clothing. Puddles of water soaked the floor beneath her feet, but that wasn't the reason for her self-consciousness. She thought her overheating skin ought to steam the cold damp cotton of her clothes while she watched her unwelcome guest stripping off his shirt and shoes. She was thankful the lights had blown.

"You can hang your wet things in the bathroom," she said with what she hoped was a dry tone. She thought her voice shook a little.

As Jared bent to shove off his shoe, he glanced up at her from beneath a fall of wet hair. "I'm giving you first dibs on a hot shower, unless you want to share one?"

She *knew* this wouldn't work. She wanted to wrap the tablecloth around her so he couldn't see the way her shirt was plastered to her skin, revealing the aching swell of her breasts. He was too damned observant not to have noticed, hence the shower suggestion. Wrapping her invisible dignity around her, she stalked past him, toward her room. "Wells operate on electricity, remember. No shower."

It was going to be a long night.

"Spaghetti from a kerosene stove never tasted so good." Jared lazily threw a stick of kindling onto the fire and leaned back against the cushion Cleo had thrown on the floor for him. Although anticipation hummed somewhere just below his skin, he liked the restful hominess of the warm fire, a full stomach, and a woman at his side.

Not exactly at his side. She'd relegated him to the floor. But she was within reach, and that was all that mattered. This was a far cry better than the lonely house on the beach, even with the howl of wind and crash of surf to keep him company.

"And you're a connoisseur of kerosene cooking," she said with sarcasm, dropping onto the sagging couch after checking on the kids.

"Learn to take compliments. It was delicious. Are they sleeping?"

"Like babes. Living in terror is exhausting."

Jared leaned back against the pillow and let the fire warm his socks. The old house creaked and swayed beneath the tumult of wind and rain, but other than the two tall palms, Cleo had no trees threatening the roof over their heads. He tried not to think too hard about his newly restored beach house at the mercy of the tide. He could hear the roar from here.

The chaos outside seemed somehow diminished by the disturbing vibrations bouncing around inside this small room. If he had any smarts at all, he'd bury his head in a book and pretend he didn't notice. That had always worked in high school. College and career had taught him to let problems slither off his invincible shield of laughter. He could apply that now, but he no longer wanted to.

He wanted—needed—to pierce Cleo's equally indestructible shield. He had the gut feeling if he let this opportunity slide by, he'd spend the rest of his life slip-sliding away.

"You know all about the exhaustion of fear?" he asked casually, not looking at her. Just listening was painful enough. He'd spent a lifetime complaining about his dysfunctional childhood. He knew enough already to understand Cleo's pain outdistanced his whining by miles.

"Shut up, McCloud."

He didn't have to look to know she had curled up defensively in the far corner of the couch, beside the kerosene lamp. She would fight him tooth and nail every step of the way, but he thought she was worth the battle. "Are you going to call Social Services when this is over?"

"I told you before—"

"I know, I know, but isn't fear of violence a little more destructive than the coldness of a damned group home?" This time, he turned sufficiently to watch her face.

In the flicker of the lamp, she looked pale and weary, and he thought he ought to be ashamed for driving her harder. But he wanted this battle settled and out of the way so they could move on to the good parts. If he was wrong and there were no good parts, he wouldn't die of it. Not immediately.

"They put Maya and me in group homes a couple of times." Defenses down, she responded with irritation. "Maya was always doing something weird that freaked people out, like painting walls with roses and dragons, so we got thrown out a lot. Most foster homes don't like teenagers and don't want two at a time if it can be avoided."

She sank into silence as if this much confession exhausted her. Jared waited patiently. She had reserves she didn't know she possessed, and he counted on them. His patience was rewarded.

She tilted her head back against the couch and stared at the darkness of the ceiling. "They have counselors in group homes, and security guards, and sometimes a few jerks who don't know any other way of making a living, along with the do-gooders."

He wasn't going to like this, he could tell already. "They hurt you?" he asked harshly, hoping to get it over with all at once.

She shrugged. "Most of the time, I'm my own worst enemy. I know that now. I didn't then. One creep offered me cigarettes if he could cop a feel. I figured, sure, why not?"

Jared shuddered and started to rise, but her body language blatantly warned him to back off. "We can warn Kismet," he said carefully.

She ignored him. "I liked it," she said defensively. "Nobody had touched me since I was a kid. I mixed up touching with feeling. I had no self-respect anyway. What did I know?"

He was sorry he'd started this. He had the gut-awful

feeling he knew what came next. Pushing his pillow back from the fire, he reached over the cushion to capture her foot. She swung it restlessly, but he wouldn't let her go. He pressed the curved underside reassuringly with this thumb. "What you did then isn't who you are now."

"Don't be a dolt, McCloud. We're made up of all these bits of our past. Block on block, we build ourselves. Cop a feel for cigarettes one time, neck a little for a car ride and a movie, what's one step more? By the time I graduated from group homes, I could get drugs or alcohol or cash anytime I wanted. That's how I learned to deal with life."

He leaned his back against the couch and circled her foot with both hands, massaging. He knew what she was saying. He hadn't figured her for a virgin. "So group homes taught you a trade. Are you still practicing?"

"Screw you, McCloud," she said wearily. "And this is about Kismet, not me. I'm telling you I know what it's like. Trying to determine if she's better off with one pervert within the familiar boundaries of home or exposed to different ones on unfamiliar grounds is not a decision I want to make."

He idly rubbed the slender tendon above her heel. "All right, that's a tough call, and you don't feel qualified to make it. I buy that. What if I make the call? I'm telling you frankly, I'm not letting them go back there." Lay it all out on the table. If she was going to cream him, he might as well have it over now.

"Fine. You make that call. Give me time to list the house and store and move out, because Linda will make my life a living hell after you do."

"Maybe I can prevent that." Sliding his palm up her firm calf under her khakis, he couldn't fight the pressure building beneath the unforgiving denim of his jeans. But wanting Cleo and having her were two entirely different equations, and he didn't know how to solve either.

"Too many superhero comics, boy genius," she taunted.

"Yeah, I know. I've got this complex that makes me think I can save the world. No wonder everyone laughs at me." He didn't entirely know what he was doing here. He wasn't a man who got involved—with women or kids or politics or anything else. He scribbled his irritation with the world's foibles into his comic strip upon occasion, and he sometimes wished for a stronger platform from which to launch his opinions, but he'd never actually got off his butt to make a difference. He'd never had to work hard at anything.

He dearly wanted to do something now. He craved Cleo's respect, and his own, when it came down to it. He wanted to save those kids.

He wanted Cleo, in more than just the usual way.

So he stayed where he was, massaging the tension from her muscles, letting her become used to his touch much as a horse whisperer calmed a nervous mount. *Bad choice of words, McCloud,* he corrected. His chances of mounting Cleo were pretty close to nil, he figured. Seduction wasn't his department. Women generally came on to him, not vice versa.

He was trying now, but he thought his chances hopeless.

"I'm not laughing," she said tensely. "Let me go."

He glanced up with interest at her tone, his thumb pressing into the muscle of the one leg she allowed to hang over the edge of the couch. She looked pretty grim and wild-eyed with her auburn hair practically standing on end, but from the way she crossed her arms over her breasts, he judged she was holding herself back with a thin thread.

"You know we could work things out much better if

you'd quit fighting me," he said thoughtfully. "Together, I think we'd be a formidable force."

"Yeah, together we could destroy each other instead of just ourselves," she mocked. "We'd make a great pair."

"You plan on spending the rest of your life behind walls, never risking anything?"

Ire flashed briefly across her expression, her nostrils flared, and she regarded him with all the intensity of her passionate soul. Here was the depth he didn't possess, and he just might drown in it.

"You figuring we've got a few days to kill and we ought to do it in bed? That the kind of risk you have in mind?" she demanded.

Well, he'd certainly never have to read Cleo's mind. That might make life more difficult, but he was ready to take her on any level she preferred.

"I had a physical not too long ago," he answered with equal bluntness. "I'm clean. I've got condoms. That the kind of safe risk you want?"

The way she flinched, he thought maybe he'd hit her too hard, but she rallied quickly enough. Pure malicious devilment lit her eyes. "I quit screwing around when I walked out on my husband. My head's messed up, but the rest of me is just fine, thank you."

Excitement hit his veins like a shot of adrenaline at the possibility that they were finally operating on the same wavelength. Caveman instinct told him to grab and claim her while the opportunity beckoned, that once he breached her indestructible walls and possessed her, she was his for a lifetime. But he liked to fool himself into believing he was a little more evolved than a Neanderthal. Not much, maybe, but enough to let her reach her own conclusions.

He was taking a chance that she wouldn't conclude he was a waste of time.

"Your head works, from my viewpoint, and the rest of you is way more than fine," he agreed, not releasing her leg now that he'd made this much progress.

"You think so?" she asked with raised eyebrows that didn't indicate doubt in herself so much as doubt in his honesty. Before he could answer, she cut him off. "As long as we're distracting ourselves by discussing body parts, if you won't let it go to your head, I think you have a mighty fine ass."

"I assure you, my head is the last place that's going," he said dryly.

Without any warning signals, Cleo swung from the couch to straddle his already too alert lap. Her trouser-clad legs clamped his knees together and her flannel shirt pressed against his nose, but she smelled deliciously of woman and weighed almost nothing, despite all those rich curves just within reach. Jared contemplated drooling as his hands itched to reach for what she so temptingly offered, but he forced his palms flat against the floor.

"If this is a test, I'm about to fail it," he warned.

His eyes practically crossed as she slowly began unfastening her shirt. He'd seen her in a tight tank top. He knew what she hid under there. He wanted to touch so badly that he thought he'd explode with the need, but he damned well wouldn't be one of the creeps in her life wanting to cop a feel for a pack of cigarettes, or whatever else in hell she wanted now.

"Think we can do this just once and not again?" she asked with a definite taunt in her voice as her fingers continued down the front of the shirt.

"Nope. If that's what you want, you can stop right now." He hoped his voice wasn't as strangled as it sounded. One part of his anatomy was quite willing to take up her offer.

"What about twice?" she jeered. "Just for the duration of a hurricane, maybe?"

The shirt came undone, and she shrugged it off her shoulders, letting it fall over her arms. She wore a knit top with only thin straps to hold it up, and nothing under it. He could lean over and nibble the tight points of her breasts and have her under him within seconds. All the blood in his head rushed south, but he continued obdurately clenching the floor. Not an easy object to grab, not nearly as easy as the ones he wanted, but he possessed some hidden strengths.

"That may be all you want," he warned, "but it's not what I have in mind."

"It never is. A free ride for life is what you all want, no matter how civilized your veneer." She dropped the flannel shirt completely and flung it across the room. "I want to touch you," she declared unexpectedly. There was nothing predictable about Cleo.

She unfastened his shirt buttons as easily as her own. Jared had to hold his breath as her heated hands slid beneath the fabric to stroke his skin. She might as well have heaved a stack of kindling on the fire. His body roared with flame.

"Don't do this if you don't want it all," he cautioned. "I'm not anywhere near as civilized as you're pretending. Right at this moment, I don't give a damn about once, twice, or forever."

"Good, because I live only in the moment." She caught his nipples between her fingers and stroked, then leaned forward to press her mouth against his.

Jared broke their kiss, twisted her knit top in both hands, and ripped it over her head.

⚜ TWENTY-TWO ⚜

Cleo gasped as Jared flung her tank top to join the shirt she'd already discarded. She'd meant to push him over the edge. She hadn't planned on him taking her over with him.

Or doing it so abruptly. Her breasts gravitated toward his bare chest with a will of their own. The brand of his skin against hers sapped any will to fight. She slid her hands over his shoulders, shoved off his shirt, and raised her head for his kiss.

He still didn't grab her, but took her mouth with a possessiveness that robbed her of breath. Hard male lips covered hers with a controlled hunger she couldn't remember ever experiencing. *So, this was what it was like with a real man,* she thought vaguely, even as his hands finally circled her waist and lifted her from his lap to place her squarely on the floor beneath him.

She knew better than to do this, with this man or any other. But her self-destructive tendencies were in full control, and for once she did nothing to rein them in. She wanted his hot breath searing her lips, and she opened her mouth to take him deeper.

Bliss. Oh, the sweet bliss of capitulation to uncontrolled male animal lust. She dug her fingers into the muscles tensing in his back, took his invading tongue and entwined it with her own, wanting this more than she had imagined possible. The psychology books could call it a primal need to mate, but this was the total surrender of self no drug had ever given her.

Jared slid his kiss from her mouth, down her jaw, to nibble at her ear, jarring her back to some sense of reality. She was on the floor. In her living room. About to do something she'd sworn never to do again.

As if sensing her tension, Jared propped himself over her, then bent his head to lick at her breast.

Cleo almost came off the floor. Heat shot through every cell and pore and found its target between her legs. She would have exploded had he touched her there. He didn't.

Instead, he wrapped one arm around her waist and lifted her shoulders to the cushion he'd abandoned earlier, then returned to plundering her breasts until she quaked with need and sought to lift her hips to his, to feel his need as well as her own.

She ought to say something, offer some token protest, a sarcasm to prove this meant nothing, but words had fled her brain. She *wanted*, and he offered. Simple.

Insane.

His kiss moved upward again, giving her time to breathe, while his hand continued what his mouth had begun. Cleo tried to just feel, not to think, to accept the moment as it was and not go beyond.

But he wouldn't leave it alone, wouldn't let her pretend he didn't exist as more than a source of sexual satisfaction. Resting on one elbow, Jared teased her breast with one hand, and forced her to look up at him.

The one uncontrollable hank of hair fell across his forehead, but she hadn't the strength to lift her hand to push it back. His face had a lean toughness to it, a determined tautness of muscle over cheekbone that said he wasn't the clown he portrayed, but a man with needs and goals of his own. She wanted to be afraid of that man, but she couldn't. She waited, quivering with need yet refusing to admit it.

"I won't let you shove me out of bed when I get too close," he told her. "I've got brains enough to know when I'm holding something special, and strength enough to take whatever you throw at me."

She didn't really believe him. He was just saying what she wanted to hear, disturbing all her hardwired responses, interrupting her peaceful slide into oblivion. She always reacted to fear by going on the offensive. This time wasn't an exception.

She tore open his belt buckle and reached for his zipper. Vaguely, she knew the storm railed outside, that branches ripped at the roof, wind howled through the chimney, and torrents pounded the windows. No hurricane could compete with the tempest swirling her willpower into shattered particles of need and desire and fear. "Don't preach," she warned. "I want this now, not tomorrow."

"Now *and* tomorrow." He opened the zipper for her.

His promise inflamed her as much as the sight of him did. Jared wasn't any skinny hairless youth from her past, no potbellied lout looking for an easy lay. No wonder she'd been able to swear off sex so easily. She hadn't known its full power until now.

He rolled over and produced a packet of condoms from his back pocket, proving he'd come prepared for this. She admired his annoying tenacity as much as his responsibility, but her interest fixed on watching him tug off his jeans and underwear. She quivered a little as she delighted in the length and strength of him. My dear heaven, he was long *all over*. Long, powerful limbs emerged from the chrysalis of clothing. Long torso turned and stretched taut as he persuaded her back down on the pillow again. And for the rest . . .

Cleo reached for her trousers, but long fingers beat her to them. He unsnapped and unzipped and slid them over her hips as she arched to give him access. She kicked free of the hampering cloth, and lay stunned and naked, waiting, robbed of the ability to take the offensive again.

He kissed her cheek and waited for her to focus her gaze on his. "Did you know you have a dimple below your belly button?" he teased, delight illuminating his eyes and pulling at the corners of his mouth.

Oh, Lord in heaven, don't make her laugh now. She couldn't bear it. She didn't want to like him and want him both. She was already wet and eager and he was almost where she wanted him and she couldn't bear a minute longer . . .

"I intend to kiss it," he informed her solemnly. "And then I think I'll ravish you. Do you have any last requests?"

He may as well have said "rash requests." This whole thing was insane. She didn't know how to go about this when it included talking. She just wanted him to do it and get it over and move on. The infuriating man had other ideas.

"Speechless, hmm?" He raised his eyebrows and without waiting for agreement, dived down to her belly and began nibbling and kissing until she reached for his hair but didn't know whether to pull or shove.

He knew. He wrapped his hands around her thighs and held them firmly apart as he grazed his teeth across the sensitive underside, then soothed the nibble with his tongue until she writhed and heaved helplessly in his grasp. Only then did he move higher and attack the place that most needed attention.

Cleo bit back a scream just in time. They couldn't do

this in the middle of the living room floor. She shouldn't do this at all.

She erupted without any further effort or thought of her own. Fell apart, shattered, became one with the universe and Jared's marauding tongue. He wouldn't let her fall apart alone. He held her down and worked her until she whimpered and lost control over and over, until she was a weeping, sodden puddle of honey and tears, begging for more.

And then he didn't give it to her. Instead of filling her as he ought, he covered her with his length again, and began all over, nibbling her ear, caressing her nipples into sharp, aching points, kissing her until she groaned and kissed him back with all the stunted instinct left in her.

Only when she wrapped her arms around his shoulders, desperately followed his tongue with hers for more of the same, and voluntarily lifted her knees to offer herself to him did he act on his own impulses. With a swiftness that halted her screams, he filled her.

He hadn't left her mindless, but aware and aching for more. Determined to give as much as she'd taken, she held nothing back, allowing him full access, encouraging, and then meeting him with frantic, grinding thrusts that drove them both straight to the top. He took her nipple in his mouth and pitched her over again, but this time, she brought him with her. Jared muffled his cries in her shoulder and pounded into her with all the force of a male animal determined to stake his claim.

They woke and rolled over and began a more gentle exploration of naked bodies and trigger points until they had the sense to pick themselves off the hard floor, gather their clothes, and collapse on Cleo's bed in the darkness of the stormy night. The wind hurled rain as if in a fury for not gaining entrance, but it seemed a far distance away in comparison with the heated proximity they shared.

"How long will it take before you admit you want me?" he murmured in her ear as his fingers returned to their expert game-playing.

"I want you," she admitted without complaint, arching her hips to the evidence of his equal desire.

"Progress. Now admit that you need me."

"Never. I don't need anyone." She said it without anger, though. It felt oddly freeing to let loose her anger. Peace flowed through her, and she stretched languorously beneath him, teasing him with brushes of her body. She'd never really surrendered to the sensuality pouring through her now, but she liked it. Temporarily.

"You need me," he said with irritating confidence. "And I'm afraid I'm in danger of needing you."

"Don't. I'm not reliable. Let it go, McCloud. Just let this happen and don't fret it to death."

"Jared. Call me Jared." He stopped touching and lifted himself on bulging arms so their bodies no longer connected.

"Jared," she agreed. "I bet they called you Jarhead in school." She ran her hands down his biceps, collapsing him against her again.

"Yeah, but once they learned I could get them back with my twisted wit and caricatures in the school paper, they stopped. I was never a model student. Not in educational matters anyway." He proved his power of learning with a kiss to a strategic area that had her aching for more. "You'll learn soon enough that I can't be stopped. It's impossible to tell me no."

She was terrified that he was right, but that didn't stop her now. He refused to offer her oblivion, but he offered something far better. She gripped his biceps, lifted herself to lick his nipples, and laughed as he rolled over and pulled her on top of him. Laughed. She didn't think she could do that anymore.

"I'll wear you out and throw you away like a used carpet," she warned. "I won't have to tell you no."

"Have fun trying." He grasped her hips, lifted her over him, and pulled her down.

Cleo bit back her shriek as he reached a place she'd thought untouchable, and she surrendered all over again.

This was not going at all the way she planned it.

She rode him as if he were a wild stallion, doing her best to break him to her velvet saddle, and Jared gloried in her effort, even if he knew she couldn't accomplish it. Despite her claim to experience, she had none. She'd been bruised and battered, but she'd never been loved. He could do that for her.

As she rocked in the first throes of pleasure, Jared rolled her over and took her up again. She climbed easily, thrilling him with her responsiveness. For her, it was just the sex, he realized. She didn't know what to make of it, didn't understand the deeper connection behind it, but it was there, a starting place. It was up to him to lead her forward.

He only prayed he had sufficient wisdom to proceed slowly and not drive her screaming behind her solid defenses again.

He let his body take over for his mind, let her drive him to that state of bliss where he needn't "fret it," as she said, and surrendered to the flood of their desires with the joy of newfound love.

Later, as they lay side by side, she curled into his embrace, and he rested his chin against her hair while she slept peacefully. Wondering what it would be like to marry this woman, to plant his child within her, the first stirring of doubt and fear tormented him.

A gap so wide it would take an engineer to bridge separated them, and neither of them were engineers. He'd known that going in, but he didn't like being told he couldn't have what he wanted, and he definitely wanted Cleo. He didn't know that he wanted her lifestyle, or if she wanted his. He hadn't even met her son. She hadn't met his overeducated, highly opinionated, and intolerably obnoxious family, except for Tim. That hadn't turned out too bad. Maybe they could make it work.

Provided she wanted to make it work. That was a huge If. Provided he still had enough money to support her if he didn't meet his deadline.

Lying there letting the worries roll over him, listening to hurricane winds slam into the house, Jared wanted to wake Cleo and seek mindless bliss again.

Maybe he wasn't as ready to grow up as he'd thought. His Peter Pan existence had definite advantages he didn't foresee in the one lying ahead.

⚜ TWENTY-THREE ⚜

The calm before the storm, Cleo thought as she woke to a disquieting silence—the eye of the hurricane probably.

A man's heavy hand fell over her waist, and his naked heat against her back shot warm shivers through her. She hadn't had a man in her bed for nearly eight years. What the hell did she think she was doing?

All right. She wasn't a saint. Everyone slipped occasionally. Matty wasn't here to see the slip, and that's what mattered. Matty was fixated on his Uncle Axell, and that's the way it should be. She didn't want him depending on a man who wouldn't be around long.

Gene and Kismet really didn't need any more examples of immorality either, but they weren't naive seven-year-olds. They'd probably thought she and Jared had been sleeping together all along and would see nothing unusual in it. She didn't know how to undo their lifetime of experience.

She did know the danger of dreaming. Maya lived in a dreamworld. Cleo had learned practicality at an early age as a self-defense for both of them.

Carefully swinging her legs over the side of the bed, she crawled from beneath Jared's hampering hold. He stirred as the cold air hit him, but she'd escaped. Let him wake if he wanted.

She desperately needed a shower but she'd have to settle for the water she'd left hanging over the fire. She could heat more on the kerosene stove later. She really should have rewired, and installed a generator by now.

"Do you always wake so early?" Jared grumbled from the bed. "You can't be thinking of going in to work."

Pulling on a flannel shirt, she darted a curious glance at the bed. His styled hair now stood on end, dark whiskers marred his jaw, and his dreamboat eyes were only half open as they watched from the pillow. Her heart flipped over in her chest, and she almost smiled in pleasure at the gorgeous sight, and that was before he pushed up on his elbows and let the sheet fall to his waist. Men like that had *never* graced her bed. It was like waking inside a TV soap opera.

"I thought I'd check for storm damage while I have a chance. You just stay where you are, Sleeping Beauty."

She couldn't help the sharp edge of her words. That's who she'd been for too long to discard it after a single night of glorious sex.

He winced and flung a pillow at her, then dragged himself fully upright. "Fine. You crawl around on the roof and I'll fix breakfast, if role reversal suits you."

"Somebody wakes up grumpy in the morning," she taunted, pulling on the trousers they'd left in a heap by the door. She looked like hell, but beauty queens didn't climb on roofs.

In one graceful move he stood, reached across the gap to grab her, and hauled her next to all that breathtaking male nudity. Cleo thought she ought to run, but the flame in his eyes fascinated her. How could he look at her like that when she was such a mess?

"No, somebody wakes up hungry in the mornings, and pancakes aren't the menu he has in mind."

He nibbled the nape of her neck, ran his hands beneath her shirt to cup her breasts, and buckled her knees before she could take a breath. Then he politely stood back, still holding her upright, and grinned at her in satisfaction.

"But I'm a patient man," he declared generously. "If this is the eye of the storm, we'd better take advantage of it, although I am beginning to see the disadvantage of kids around the house."

He released her to reach for his jeans, and Cleo ran while she had the chance. She thought she heard him chuckle, but she avoided the image. Charm like that could totally waste a woman. She knew better than to fall for it, but she didn't like to overexpose her weaknesses either. He'd even have her believing he didn't mind the disadvantages of kids.

As she crawled around on the roof a little later, searching for damage to the newly installed shingles, Gene fed the animals in the shed, and Jared climbed up to join her, carrying a steaming cup of coffee.

"That's not an easy trick," she grumbled, taking the cup precariously offered and sipping while scanning the landscape below. Her witch tree had toppled. She'd have to power up the saw before a car could get out or in. Regret over losing her favorite mechanism stabbed at her, but the man surveying the scene from beside her soothed the worst of the pain. His laid-back presence had a way of taking the edge off. She sipped the scalding coffee peacefully.

"I don't want to go up to the top and see the beach, do I?" he asked.

"You can't really see anything but the surf from here. The tide is high and a lot of beach has washed out, from the looks of it." And that was only the first half of the storm. She could feel the wind rising beneath the heavy clouds already.

"I always wanted to live right on the beach." He leaned back against his elbows and scanned the drive. "But I can see where it might be a problem losing a house every few years. Can you rebuild your witch?"

He seemed so calm about it. She was up here frantically checking every shingle to be certain her home didn't blow away, and he was already accepting the possibility that his had washed to sea. Of course, he had others to take its place. That was one of the many huge gaps between them.

She shrugged at his question. "I suppose, but I don't like repeating myself. Shows a lack of imagination."

He snorted, and gave her a look that should have pierced like a laser. He knew her far too well already.

"I am not a repeat of your past mistakes," he reminded her. "We have our differences, and we might not work them out, but giving up without trying would be the mistake here."

It frightened her that she almost believed him. She handed him the cup, and slid toward the attic window. "We'd better go in before we blow away."

He'd scared her by pushing too hard. Jared drained the cup and glanced over his shoulder in the direction of the beach. He'd loved that house. He didn't want to think what would happen if it was gone. Cleo might not appreciate his moving in with her permanently just yet.

His agent would have a dire fit if he didn't turn in his strips soon. A sensible man would have stayed on the mainland and taken shelter instead of wasting time out here without the means to finish his work.

The world was full of sensible men. He wasn't one of them.

Sliding down the roof to follow Cleo, he could hear his family's admonitions already: "Wastrel. Slacker. You could have a brilliant career in films. How do you plan on getting ahead in the world if you don't apply yourself?"

He had yet to figure out what he was supposed to get ahead of, much less why.

Gene was haunting the kitchen while Cleo poured batter into a frying pan over the kerosene stove as Jared entered.

"Cleo says the strawberries are melting in the freezer and we'll have to eat them up. And there's whipped cream in the fridge we've got to finish off. I'm starved!"

"Yeah, the kid with the hollow leg. How you can eat after everything you put away last night is beyond me." Jared affectionately clipped the back of the kid's head and watched Cleo's economical movements as she flipped one pancake, poured another, and reached for a plate. When he realized he could stand here all day and watch a wild-haired woman flip pancakes, he knew he was in deep trouble.

She looked up then and their eyes met. The bolt of lightning between them should have fused them both to the floor.

Rearranging a suddenly stiff portion of his anatomy, Jared smiled ruefully and eased out from underfoot. He now understood the custom of a honeymoon. Two people in the throes of first lust should not be left in the company of others, especially not impressionable teenagers, drat it.

He discovered Kismet huddled on the floor in a far corner beside the couch, obviously doing her best to disappear into the woodwork. That cooled his ardor rapidly. He tried to imagine Cleo hiding from her molesters and couldn't. She would have defied anything and anyone and thrown their advances back in their face, then taken their beatings until they ultimately killed her. Instead, she'd stayed alive by killing a portion of her soul. He hadn't met her younger sister, but he suspected Cleo's need to protect had warred with her survival instincts until her confused psyche found an effective compromise. He wondered if it was really cigarettes she'd obtained the first time, or something the sister needed.

"Hey, kid, got any good drawings I can use?" He dropped into a chair as far from the girl as the small room would allow. On the surface, he had no clue as to what he was doing, but he remembered his own eagerness to show his work at that age. Kids at school had loved it. He'd quit showing his parents when their disinterest became too painful.

Kismet darted him an uncertain look, slowly flipped a few pages of her ever-present drawing pad, and slid it toward him.

He leaned over and picked it up. The upright dragon

had shrunk to a more proportional size, still equipped with the necessary apparatus, unfortunately. Jared supposed it was preferable to sketching a real man in that position. The dragon's victim was nowhere in sight this time. He didn't want to delve into the psychology of its disappearance.

The object she apparently wanted him to see was a knight in shining armor, he supposed. Not Cleo as phoenix this time. The guy wore one of those weird visor things so an observer couldn't see the face, but the length of the knight's legs and arms and his strange fighting stance stirred uneasy recognition. His brothers had laughed at Jared's ungainly proportions enough for him to see satire for what it was. The kid would make a damned good caricaturist.

He grinned, probably weakly, and handed the pad back to her. "Give the knight a sword, at least, so he stands a fighting chance. You've got talent. We just need to give you better subjects."

A shy smile teased the corner of her mouth, and she settled in to give her knight a sword. Jared thought his heart would break at the sight of her haunting face beneath the ebullient curls, industriously bent over a psychological horror story. The child had skill to rival his. What were her chances of ever applying it successfully? He'd had connections, education, opportunities she would never see. And he'd come from a stable home with no dragons to fight while developing his work. Someone had to rescue her.

He made a damned awkward knight, just as she'd so cleverly discerned. He didn't like being so obvious.

The wind slammed the remaining palm across the shed roof before they'd finished washing the breakfast dishes. Leaves and debris crashed against the windows in the sudden squall, and daylight dimmed to night. The kids looked worriedly at the ceiling as if expecting it to take flight, and Cleo sought for some way of reassuring them before they started worrying about their mother and the shack they called home.

"Well, at least the rain will refill the water barrel," she said brightly.

"The battery in my computer won't last long enough for a rousing game of Battleship," Jared mused aloud, drying the last dish and returning it to the cabinet. "I know how to play on paper, if anyone's interested."

Cleo doubted if they even knew about a yuppie strategy game like Battleship, but she was grateful he had accepted part of the responsibility for distracting them. A man who accepted responsibility—what a concept. She'd have to play with that notion sometime when she had nothing better to do.

"How about poker?" she asked wryly when the kids looked blank at Jared's suggestion.

That offer brought grins and definite interest, and Jared wiggled his eyebrows as Gene ran off to find the cards and Kismet ambled after him.

"A little illegal gambling as a sideline?" he inquired. "Teaching them how to strike it lucky in the slots?"

"Nobody ever called me a Baptist preacher." She hung up her dishcloth and tried to avoid the penetrating light in his eyes. This house was too small for the two of them.

"I used to make my beer money at poker," he informed her, catching her by the waist before she could escape.

His nibble on her ear paralyzed her as effectively as a cobra's stare, and her pulse escalated much as its victims' must. Once confident she wouldn't fight, Jared transferred his attention to more dangerous zones. Cleo closed her eyes and clung to his shirt while his kiss devastated her defenses as surely as the storm wreaked havoc on sand dunes. She desperately wanted to be the woman he thought she was.

To hell with saving her house. Who would save her?

By evening, the frantic flailing of wind and rain had settled into a steady downpour as the storm swept out to sea. Jared and Gene had braved the wind and water to check on the animals, and lured the peacocks from the damaged shed roof into the attic. Rivers of mud and debris flowed down the drive in the direction of the beach, but the house stood firmly on its high foundation.

Cleo clicked off the staticky radio reporting flooding in all outlying areas and tried to look casual as she glanced at Jared. He worked away obliviously on some drawing project he'd started after supper. She'd insisted the kids keep school hours and sent them to bed, if only to give her guest some peace.

She'd never seen him so intense. He even made love with a carefree nonchalance that diverted and distracted instead of scaring her. She didn't doubt his desire one bit for his lack of focus. She loved the way she could distract him from one goal by offering another he'd neglected. Men who simply wanted wham-bang-snore showed a serious lack of imagination. Jared wanted it all, and her skin tingled at just the thought of what he could do to her.

But right now, he didn't even know she was in the room. If she had to guess, from what little she'd gathered from Maya, he probably had one of those hyperactive disorders of the brain. She bet he'd driven his parents insane. He was darned lucky they hadn't drugged him as a child or he would never have learned the focus that had taken him to his successful career. She wondered if he understood how lucky he was.

She eased from the room and thought she'd escaped without notice, but she only had time to splash in a little water and soap and return to her bedroom before Jared appeared in the doorway. He'd run his hand through his hair and loosened that rebellious strand again. If he knew how young that strand made him look, he'd probably cut it off. It didn't help that his gaze darkened with the same hunger as a teenager's as it focused on her.

"You're a major distraction," he muttered, strolling in, and shrugging off his shirt.

She gulped as bronzed, muscled shoulders emerged. She should have blown out the candle. "Go back to your work," she offered. "I'm not going anywhere."

"Good, because I'm not either."

Without any further warning, he backed her up against the bed until her knees folded and she was lying sprawled across the mattress beneath him. Why had she thought his lovemaking lacked intensity? Just his gaze could incinerate her.

"Do you have any idea how damned hard it's been keeping my hands off you all day?"

She couldn't answer as her breath left her lungs and his kiss trapped her more solidly than any prison cell. She ought to feel fear, but the hand insinuating itself beneath her loose shirt was gentle and loving and melted away any panic before it formed.

He had their clothes off and the lean length of him positioned over her before she remembered to breathe. She gasped when he drove into her.

This wasn't just a physical joining of bodies. She felt him inside her, filling the empty place beneath her heart, demanding the recognition she'd rather deny. Somehow, the lost child in her responded to the one in him demanding attention, and they spiraled crazily together with a playfulness and longing and thrill of release that made absolutely no sense in the real world.

But in this dark cave protected against the elemental forces outside, they sought and found something precious, probably ephemeral, in each other.

The darkness lightened as he exploded inside her, and she rode the waves of ecstasy he created. As Jared's heavy weight collapsed on top of her, Cleo brushed the hair from his face, relishing the lingering traces of pressure in her womb. Whatever the future might bring, she could cherish this moment of complete happiness. Perhaps she'd learned a few things from years of hardship. Happiness was too rare to ignore when it happened.

Matty had taught her that.

Jared propped those splendid arms of his on either side of her head and covered her face in lingering kisses. "Once we get out of here, I'm going to find a real deserted island, where we can ravish each other until we're too starved to move. Then we'll order sumptuous feasts, and start all over again."

"You might have difficulty ordering feasts on a deserted island," she reminded him wryly. "Besides, feasts involve wine, and I'll thank you to remember not to indulge me like that." She had lots of experience at bringing dreamers back to earth and pointing out the rocky shoals ahead.

"I don't need wine to make me high. I have you."

Jared pushed off of her and stood. They hadn't made it any farther than the edge of the bed. Thrilling beneath his blatantly satisfied gaze, she stood and stripped back the covers, then lay down in as provocative a pose as she could manage. "High enough, or do you want more?" she inquired in her best imitation of a whore's invitation.

His interest flared; she could tell by the darkening of his eyes as well as rising parts south, but he remained stubbornly where he was.

"I've got to earn a living, so I'll have to learn to put aside temptation when she calls." He leered appreciatively. "Get some rest. I expect tomorrow to be a test of our endurance."

With that startling statement, he grabbed his clothes and walked out. Well, hell. He certainly wasn't shy about his nudity, she noticed as she watched his taut buttocks stride away. She wanted him all over again, and considered going after him to have her way.

She'd never chased after a man in her life. She didn't need men, any man. She'd been perfectly happy sleeping alone before he came along; she would be perfectly happy now.

The wind howled in derision as Cleo pulled the covers over her shoulders and firmly shut her eyes.

⊰ TWENTY-FOUR ⊱

"Carolina sunshine . . ." caroled off-key from a not large enough distance as Cleo rolled over and jerked the sheet over her head.

The deep male chords jarred loose all the shattered pieces of her defenses, until she could practically hear the shards tinkling to the ground and disintegrating. The damned man was *singing*. In the *morning*.

Oh, God, save her. She wrapped her arms around the pillow and squeezed, but she couldn't suffocate herself. Her body hummed with vibrations she didn't recognize as her own. She didn't even know who the hell she was anymore.

Jared had come to her bed in the early hours of the morning and made love to her with a gentleness that had her weeping. *Weeping*, for crying out loud. She'd felt beautiful and cherished and whole—she'd damned well been dreaming.

Jared didn't just come from Mars. He came from a whole 'nother galaxy, far, far away, one to which he'd return one day.

Despite all her clever warnings, she still felt—odd. She'd lived in hiding for so long, she felt as exposed as an unshelled crab. She couldn't go out there like this. She had to toughen up, find her armor, *something*.

A knock interrupted that piece of panic, and she wildly grabbed the sheet to cover herself as she turned over and swiped at her hair.

"Make yourself decent, Sunshine, you've got company."

Company, her ass. She'd kill him. She'd pound him into sawdust and scatter him to the winds. She didn't own a robe or gown. She dived for a discarded shirt on the floor and pulled it over her head. "Go away, McCloud," she shouted in muffled tones through the cotton.

"We made coffee, Cleo," Gene called happily.

Oh shit—shoot, sugar. She struggled into the T-shirt, ran her hands through her hair again, and pulled the covers around her. "I'll be right out," she grumbled, but she knew the man behind that door too well.

The door popped open as expected, revealing the glorious sight of a smiling Jared in a rumpled golf shirt straining at the shoulder seams, carrying a tray of steaming coffee, eggs, and bacon. She hoped the bacon hadn't gone rancid.

She couldn't tell him she intended to kill him, that she hated surprises, and she really needed to get up and inspect the damage now that the storm had passed. The kids smiled too proudly, and Jared looked too damned pleased with himself. She wanted to cry all over again.

"You aren't going to burst out in song, are you?" she asked suspiciously as he lowered the tray to her lap and the kids piled on to the bed to help her eat.

He grinned hugely at her predicament. "Depends on how many weapons you're hiding under the pillow."

He knew quite well what he was doing to her, and he was doing it on purpose. Embarrassment, helplessness, and other emotions she couldn't name swamped her. No one had ever done anything like this for her. No one. Ever. She had no concept of how to behave.

"You've struck her speechless. I declare this a red-letter holiday and no one has to go to school." Jared pulled up an aging chair with arms, propped his socked feet on the mattress, and reached for a burned piece of toast as the kids scoffed at his declaration. School would be closed until the roads opened.

Cleo shot him a glare and turned a wavering smile on the anxious teenagers. "You're beautiful, both of you. Thank you. I feel like it's my birthday and Christmas all rolled into one."

The kids grinned in relief, chattered, and helped themselves to the food as if this were a picnic, and the bed, their table. They were so eager to please and so easily hurt—Cleo choked on the panic welling inside and threw Jared a frantic look.

He leaned over to hold a coffee cup to her lips, and his chocolate gaze warmed and reassured. "You make me feel the same way," he murmured as she took the cup from his hands.

Tears rolled down her cheeks and splashed into the coffee.

Salty coffee, damn him.

They all climbed up on the roof from the attic window to survey the submerged landscape lapping gently around them.

"At least the soil is sandy and we have no river to flood," Cleo said with a sigh as a raft of dead palmettos drifted toward the coast on a muddy current.

Jared massaged the nape of her neck and knew he'd made progress when she didn't automatically duck away. He felt more pride in accomplishment at breaking her prickly barriers than he had at scripting the stupid TV show. Reaching out and touching a woman as proud and strong as Cleo felt right. The TV show hadn't.

"You think Mama is all right?" Gene asked anxiously.

In Jared's opinion, the bastards of the world always survived, but he wouldn't say that to the kids. They both wore worried frowns, and he let Cleo offer the reassurances they wanted to hear.

It was pretty much a given that his beach house was wrecked and the condos out at the point had to have taken a brutal beating, but these farmhouses in the island's center had been built to weather storms. Rowboats bobbed on the deeper water along the roadbed and drainage ditches. People were emerging from the security of their homes to check on neighbors and damage. Several boats lingered so their occupants could hail them, but Cleo waved them on. There were others who needed help more.

He ought to be finding a way back to phones and electricity so he could send in his strips, but he feared the intrusion of the outside world might sever the slender bonds that held Cleo to him for now. Once she returned to her usual routine, she wouldn't need him. Or wouldn't admit she did, anyway.

Jared felt as oddly floating and cut off as the house. He didn't mind the feeling, but he knew it couldn't last. The real world waited out there, ready to dig its ravenous claws into the still vulnerable connection they'd developed. He didn't know how anyone could establish a solid, steady relationship in this day and age. Maybe he was fooling himself to think he could. He didn't lead that kind of life. Neither did Cleo.

Negative thinking. He'd have to get past that if he really wanted something more substantial than his prior so-called relationships. Was that what he really wanted?

"You need one of those powerboats if you're going to keep living here," he said idly, watching one zip by, destined for a crash.

"I'll trade in my truck." Her sarcasm lacked its usual edge.

Jared smiled and ran his fingers into her stubby hair. This time, she brushed his hand away but didn't fight when he caught her waist instead. He had no idea why this bristly porcupine attracted him. Maybe he was under a spell and it would dissipate when he left here.

He didn't think so. He couldn't think of another woman in the world with whom he would be willing to share a two-bedroom farmhouse and two teenagers and still feel good about it. If he tried analyzing the whys and wherefores, he'd figure he just knew Cleo was rock-solid honest, and she valued his opinion. And he knew her well enough to know she wouldn't have gone to bed with him unless she thought he was special. Obviously, the knowledge had gone to his head. And elsewhere.

"We'll do pizza when the water goes down," he promised.

The kids cheered, and Cleo slanted him an odd look.

Damn, but he liked the way she looked like a mischievous elf and an evil genie at the same time. She had the kind of thin, aquiline nose and pointed eyebrows and delicate chin to pull it off. The short auburn hair completed the picture. His fingers were itching for the drawing board again.

"You hear that helicopter?" she asked.

Uh-oh. He watched her expression in suspicion. "Yeah. TV news, I figure. They love disasters."

"Wave when it goes over," she said complacently.

Damn. He scanned the sunny sky, finding the distant dot over the causeway. He could see it now on the Channel 6 Sky News broadcast across the country— Jared McCloud, comic artist, stranded on rooftop in nation's worst flooding since . . . yadda yadda. His mother would be in hysterics—especially when she saw who he was with.

"Maybe we should go back in before we make a spectacle of ourselves," he said doubtfully, not really believing anyone would notice or care where he was. Of course, Tim knew, but he was probably on the other side of the Pacific somewhere and hadn't a clue. His agent knew, but he'd just curse and walk the floor and fret about the missing strips and the complaints pouring in from the newspaper syndicates.

"Pity you haven't met Maya." Cleo leaned back on her palms and admired a bird flying overhead.

"I'm not about to, am I? You haven't got a helicopter pilot for a sister, as far as I can tell."

"Nope. I've got a dreamer for a sister. But she's smart, Maya is. She married a man who gets things done."

He could tell from the way she said it that he wouldn't like the kind of things the mysterious Axell got done. Visions of cruise ships mooring to the rafters rose before him. An entire army of aircraft and rescue boats, perhaps. Hadn't she said he was a bartender or some such? Impossible. Maybe the guy had a lot of drunken cronies with fishing boats.

The helicopter drifted closer, occasionally dipping to check out other roofs or entertaining sights. Definitely TV news, Jared figured. The place would be crawling with journalists. Shit.

"Think they brought Matty?" Gene inquired with interest, evidently fully believing Cleo's insinuations.

"Nah. Maya wouldn't trust him up there. And Matty would want to climb down, and she'd have a heart attack."

"So would you." Jared knew that much from her brief expression of alarm at Gene's words. She loved that kid. He needed to meet him.

Cleo shrugged. "Maya is a ditz, but she'd never let anything happen to any kid, ever, if it was within her power to help."

"Wonder where she got that from?" he asked teasingly.

She shot him a disbelieving look, but the helicopter seemed to pick up speed and roared closer, distracting her.

"Hey, they've got something hanging!" Gene shouted, starting to jump up until Cleo caught his belt and yanked him down.

"This is a roof, kid. Sit or you go back inside."

"Yes, ma'am." He didn't look daunted but continued watching the dangling crate from the helicopter as it hovered closer.

Jared read the huge television news call letters on the side and rolled his eyes. "Your sister has TV connections?" he asked in disbelief.

"Heck if I know. Maya can connect with anybody, anytime." She waved at the crew filming in the big window as the copilot carefully lowered the container into reach.

Jared held Gene down with one hand, and carefully stood to grab the rope with the other. At least no one was climbing down to join them. He unhooked the heavy crate and gingerly settled it on the shingles.

The helicopter lifted to a safer distance but hovered. He could see a camera aimed through the back window as he cut the straps with a knife from his pocket. Special delivery in a hurricane zone. He'd shake his head in disbelief but he figured his brains would fall out.

Cleo snapped the lid open with crisp efficiency, and laughed out loud at the cell phone displayed prominently on top of an assortment of other packages that the kids eagerly dug into.

Jared loved the way she smiled. He'd have to figure out how to make her do that more often. Bless her sister and the unknown Axell. Maybe the world out there wasn't as bad as he'd feared. His family might not care if he drowned, but hers did. For Cleo's sake, he was glad. That kind of support had saved her; he better understood that now.

Cleo punched in the numbers in a note attached to the phone. "Okay, which one of you is the joker?" she asked with her usual tough edge. But she laughed at the reply, and Jared relaxed. Let the news shows make of it what they would. He didn't mind as long as Cleo didn't.

"Yeah, tell Headley hi and I'll give him a kiss next time I see him. That ought to scare him into moving to California. Tell Matty I'm sunbathing up here, we're all fine, and his menagerie is safe, eating like the pigs they are."

She listened for a minute, shrugged, and smiled faintly. "Maya's a nag. Don't worry her with the details. And no, I have no intention whatsoever of verifying the occupants of my rooftop. Thanks. We have all we need for now."

She clicked off, the helicopter dipped a farewell and

slowly drifted toward the more disastrous areas along the coast.

Sitting patiently beside her, Jared waited. Cleo studiously ignored him while watching the kids dig into candy bars and explore the battery-operated computer games Maya had sent to entertain them. One package apparently contained lettuce and animal food from Matty. He figured the rest contained food and bottled water. For a dreamer, her sister had her head on straight.

"Well?" he finally demanded when she made no attempt to explain.

Cleo shrugged, but the smile still played faintly around her mouth. "Told you. Maya worried, Axell got on the phone, and *voilà*! Things happened."

"Who's the Headley you're going to kiss?" All right, so he was learning he had a jealous streak. He'd handle it.

The smile played brighter and reached her eyes as she glanced over her shoulder at him. A look like that could smite him straight through the heart and tumble him off the roof if he wasn't careful. She didn't know how dangerous she was.

"Friend of Axell's. Says he's retired, but he knows everybody in the media business. I suspect Maya told him you were out here and that inspired the news crew. They asked about you."

"Well, that ought to look just swell on the morning news," he grumbled, watching Gene shoot down an alien spaceship on his new handheld game. "Comic-strip hero stranded on rooftop in backwoods of South Carolina. My mother will be thrilled."

She giggled. Actually giggled. Jared grinned with a small amount of pride at accomplishing that. Maybe he wasn't a total loss, after all.

"Could be worse," she admonished when she'd recovered from her unusual fit, although laughter still flirted on her lips. "They could call you a cartoon character and insinuate they'd exposed your secret love hideaway. *'Bugs Bunny and Minnie Mouse, uncovered!'* Wonder how desperate the gossip rags are for news these days?"

As the outrageous image hit his funnybone, Jared burst out in laughter. He lay back against the warm shingles and just let it explode as his imagination carried it further.

" *'Rocky and Bullwinkle in flooded tryst!'* " he caroled. " *'George Jetson and Wilma Flintstone stranded in beach love nest!'* I love it. Can we call your sister and order copies of all the headlines?"

Gene and Kismet looked at him as if he were crazed as he pounded the roof with his hands and feet and roared. He wanted to plant the stories himself. He wanted to see his parents when their country club friends produced the papers and asked them about it. They'd never had the imagination to see him as his own cartoon character, or even seen themselves in the adults in his strip. His brothers had, though. He'd never dared give his cartoon character any siblings. Pity. *'The Three Little Pigs Came Home'* would make a great headline.

"It's okay," Cleo reassured the kids. "He has these fits every so often. We can call for medical treatment if he falls off." She edged her way to the attic window, dragging the crate with her.

"Cell phones don't work out here!" Jared yelled at her, controlling himself enough to halt the progress of the crate before she fell two stories to the muddy ground.

"Obviously they operate on the roof. If you've recovered from your fit, help Kismet down."

He hadn't recovered. He'd probably never recover. Freed of constraint, his mind danced across dozens of topics, all of them hilarious. Whatever spell Cleo had worked on him, it had knocked his writers' block off and smashed it to smithereens. He felt like a helium balloon.

He didn't *have* to do what his family expected of him. He could sift shells by the seashore, as long as he was happy with that. Cleo thought his characters *shallow*, and she was right! He'd been protecting himself and his family by hiding what he really wanted to do with them.

These chaotic thoughts tumbled through his head as they helped the kids inside, lowered the various packages one by one, and listened to the peacocks in the attic squall as Gene fed them.

Cleo threw him an uncertain glance as she dangled on the roof edge. "You all right?"

"Never been better, I promise. I think I love you, you know." Jared ran his hand through her silky hair, pushing the short bits from her face, watching her eyes widen in shock as she absorbed his casual comment.

Then sparkling emerald narrowed to her usual wariness. "And you love Pop-Tarts and comics, too. If Maya told those reporters you're out here, they can look up your file photo. The whole world will know you're here."

"The whole world doesn't give a damn." That discovery had set him off. What he did mattered to no one but him. His family worried about how things *looked*, and he'd thought he should care about that, too. Stupid. "My agent will love the publicity. My mother will have spasms. My brothers will laugh and go back to whatever they're doing. That's the extent of it."

She seemed to relax at that. "All right. Just as long as the place isn't flooded with worried fans or newshounds or something."

"I'm hardly a blip on their radar so long as the strip appears every day. My agent will order the syndicate to run reruns until I can reach a phone and hook up my computer. Your wise sister has done me a favor."

"Maya isn't wise," Cleo grumbled, inching her legs over the edge, toward the windowsill. "Maya is insane. The world just seems to respond better to insanity than logic."

"You have a point there. I'd just forgotten it." She was good for him. He'd forgotten a lot of things. And there were a lot more he had yet to learn. He hadn't felt excitement like this since he was a kid and had planted firecrackers in the football team's lockers. The dumb jocks had been so busy griping about the caricatures he'd posted on the board, they hadn't even noticed the fuse.

Of course, he hadn't been caught that time. One of these days . . .

Nah. He was an adult now. He wouldn't do anything illegal.

Whistling, he lowered himself through the window into the flock of outraged peacocks. Battling flying feathers and pecking bills, he heard Cleo's laughter trailing down the attic stairs.

All right, maybe he should consider something illegal.

Planning murderous tortures didn't appeal anywhere near as much as kidnap seductions. Maybe he could tie her to a merry-go-round. A roller coaster would be more apropos. A mountaintop cabin with bear rugs. And wolves outside the window.

Better yet—Jared dodged the birds and tripped jauntily down the attic stairs, a full-blown screen script of kidnapping Cleo dancing through his head.

❈ TWENTY-FIVE ❈

"It's Friday and the school won't open until Monday, Cleo, even if the road's clear. Half the county is still without electricity. Let me just mosey in and have a chat with the sheriff. You don't need to do anything. Once the pervert is behind bars, you won't have to worry about the kids." Jared read the panic and concern creasing her forehead, but he had to put his foot down at some point. He'd been the one to see what was happening to Kismet. He would take responsibility for unleashing the authorities on Linda and friend. "Linda can come after *me*, if she likes."

"That's not the way it works," Cleo whispered, turning her back on him to stare out at the muddy remains of her yard now that the waters had receded.

He might not understand all of her fears, but he could sympathize. He was living on the thin edge of panic himself these days. Uncertainty was a terrifying thing, but the only way he knew to fight it was to do something. At least by taking action he controlled some of what happened.

Of course, knowing his actions could have more than one result left more uncertainty in its wake. He'd finally persuaded Cleo into bed, but that hadn't solved a damned thing, only raised a hundred different questions.

"I'll be here, Cleo. Whatever happens, Linda can't

take you down. I won't let her. Give me that much credit." No one else ever had. He didn't know why he expected Cleo to take him at his word. She didn't trust anyone. Why should she trust a cartoon hero?

She gripped her elbows and bent her head as if summoning some inner strength. They'd spent these past three days and nights together in each other's heads as well as in bed. He knew as well as she did the arguments swirling around inside her. He had the uneasy feeling they'd just reached a crossroads.

"All right, do it," she muttered, still not turning around.

Pent-up air expelled from his lungs, and Jared circled her waist to hug her. "It's gonna be okay. We'll be with them every step of the way, doing whatever we can. It has to be better than letting them go back there. You can't keep fighting Linda on your own."

She leaned into him, letting him support her for this brief moment. He relished that small surrender, the admission that she needed him. He'd thought that her giving in would be enough, but now that they'd chosen their path, he could see catastrophe on the horizon. If anything happened to those kids, he would be the one she blamed.

The burden of that responsibility all but bowed his shoulders. No wonder she'd finally caved. How had she carried it all this time?

"We're human, Cleo," he whispered against her ear. "We can only do what seems best at the time."

"Why can't any of the choices be good ones?" she asked bitterly.

"Well, we wouldn't learn anything from easy ones, would we?" Like he had a lot of experience in this department. He supposed he had to start somewhere, especially if he meant to take on Cleo for a lifetime.

Hell, he wouldn't need a Jag for excitement then. She'd ride him over hills and hurdles faster than lightning.

The thrill shooting through him was definitely not vicarious.

As soon as the radio declared the causeway open, Jared piled them all into the Jeep and cruised in for pizza. They'd caught Gene eyeing the flooded paths through the jungle leading home and decided it wouldn't be safe to leave them alone, so he left Cleo valiantly guarding the kids in the back room of her hardware store while he drove over to the sheriff's office. He didn't know how long Cleo could prevent them from slipping away to check on their mother. The sheriff would have to act quickly.

Jared had promised to return with pizza, and a new notebook for Kismet since he'd scribbled all over hers, but he had an uncomfortable suspicion his return might be accompanied by the police or a social worker. The kids would probably hate him forever.

He could shoulder their hate if it saved their lives—if only he could feel equally comfortable with the idea of Cleo slamming the door in his face.

The sheriff frowned and sighed heavily when Jared arrived and reported his tale. Bouncing his pencil up and down on the desk blotter, he reluctantly reached for the telephone. "I've seen cases like this," he warned. "The kid won't place charges. If you're willing to sign a warrant, we might put the bastard away until he stands trial, at least. Won't promise nothin' after that."

Jared nodded. That didn't sound like enough justice to him, but it would suffice to keep Kismet safe a while longer.

As the sheriff phoned the social workers, Jared wondered how long it would take for a trial. He had a dozen

new ideas for the strip and the screenplay, but he really
had to go to L.A. to present the script and answer questions and do the rewrites after the first of the year. He
pretty well understood that Cleo wouldn't come with
him. Would she go with him to his parents' house for the
holidays at least?

That might depend on the outcome of the sheriff's
conversation.

All he'd wanted to do was write the damned script.
How had he gotten involved in all this?

The sheriff hung up the phone and nodded. "We have
it under control, son. The caseworkers are up to their
armpits with disaster relief right now, but they'll be out
to the island by Monday. I've got a man going out there
now to pick up the SOB, so he won't hurt the kid none in
the meantime. All you have to do is sign the warrant."

Jared signed with a flourish. He had no qualms at all
about removing a child molester from the streets.

Striding out into the brilliant sunshine, realizing the
month of September was gone and he had exactly two
months to turn the chaotic sketches in his mind into a
script, Jared shoved his hands into his pockets and gazed
up and down the street. Cleo had told him it could take
days before they fixed the utility lines on the island. He
needed a phone, and he didn't think it a good idea to use
the one in Cleo's office.

Not knowing how much his family knew of his where-
abouts or if the news had picked up the story, he figured
he'd better call them first. Maybe his cellular would
work here in town. He'd get the calls done, buy pizza
and a notebook, then see if Cleo had a place to plug in
his laptop at the store. If he could find a scanner, that
would help.

Driving the Jeep to the closest thing resembling a hill
in this low countryside, Jared began his round of calls.

He tracked his mother down at her office, where she wasn't too busy to yell at him for not telling her he was in the middle of a hurricane.

"Mother, there's the small matter of downed phone lines in high winds—"

"I had no idea you were in the path of a hurricane until your father showed me the clip from CNN. You made a public spectacle of yourself, Jared. On a roof like some white trash too foolish to leave—"

He didn't think he wanted to get into that argument if it progressed to the other occupants of the roof. "I'm fine, Mother, I survived, and I'll try to be home for Thanksgiving so you can see for yourself. If not Thanksgiving, then certainly by Christmas."

"Surely you'll be here when Timothy receives his award for solving that case in Singapore, you know the one, where the government asked for his help? It will be on the news."

His brothers made news with their successes. He only made the news with his failures. He got the connection.

Static finally ended the conversation, and he wearily punched in the numbers for his agent. He'd had the right instinct to run and hide on Cleo's island. Now, if only he'd overcome his compulsion to communicate with the rest of the world, he might get some work done.

His agent heartily cheered the hurricane publicity as if he'd scheduled the storm on purpose. Jared leaned the Jeep seat back and listened as Georgie extolled the virtues of the franchise deal he was packaging with the film producers for the characters Jared had already drawn.

Maybe he could take a hiatus from the daily strip if the film deal worked out. He was too out of touch with teenagers to take *Scapegrace* into any new territory, although Gene and Kismet had fed him a few ideas to drag it out a little longer. Now, if only he could do one about truly troubled teens . . .

Ha, like that was going to happen. Ann Landers had that one covered.

Bankruptcy loomed too close for comfort. He couldn't abandon *Scapegrace* until he had some assurance of income elsewhere. Maintaining three residences wasn't exactly cheap.

Or maybe just one. If the Manhattan apartment had sold, and the beach house was the disaster he figured, he'd only have the place in Miami. How would Cleo like living in Miami?

She wouldn't. He realized that with a sinking sensation just as Georgie told him he needed signatures on the franchise contracts pronto. Telling his agent he'd scout around for a fax, Jared hung up and dialed the Manhattan office to see if they'd sold the apartment yet. He'd like some good news for a change.

Good news—they had a buyer. Bad news—he needed to sign the sales contract and empty the place.

Calling his broker and ascertaining that the loan had covered his losses, but his savings had not miraculously rematerialized with a sudden stock market boom, Jared punched the cell phone off and stared gloomily at the horizon of trees.

Life didn't stop just because he decided to drop out for a while. His life wasn't here. Cleo's was. He loved parties and people and a faster lane of living than this backwater. Cleo would be destroyed by it. Just because they'd shared a few halcyon days out of the rat race didn't mean they could survive once they returned. He intended to try, to find some means of making Cleo a part of his life, but he had the black feeling Cleo wouldn't budge an inch.

He couldn't sacrifice his career to become a beach

bum. The idea had a certain childish appeal, but despite his current string of disasters, he loved drawing cartoons. He couldn't *not* draw. If *Scapegrace* had a chance of keeping him happy and in the money, he might conceivably drop all his other endeavors and stay here to draft it. But he already had one failure behind him, and he could feel another coming from a mile away. *Scapegrace* should go out in a blaze of glory, not die with a fizzle. He probably should retire the strip now and finish the film script, if for no other reason than to keep him solvent until he came up with a strip he could love again.

So, maybe Cleo would fly up to Manhattan with him, meet his family, help him clean out the place, and stay safe while the law dealt with Linda and the kids.

And maybe butter flies.

Cursing obdurate women, his own asininity in falling for an obdurate woman, and the fates for creating them, Jared keyed up the ignition and hit the gas. He had to find electricity and a scanner, get his strips out of here, then confront Cleo with the real world.

He'd rather drive a truck.

Carrying his laptop on top of a pizza box into Cleo's hardware store, Jared gazed at the crowd emptying the shelves of repair supplies, caught Cleo's eye, and nodded at the computer. She gestured toward her back room and returned to punching in sales at the register.

A girlfriend who ran a hardware store—Jared shook his head in disbelief at what he'd gotten himself into now. He couldn't remember the last woman he'd dated who'd actually had a job.

Kismet and Gene were looking bored and anxious in Cleo's office, and they hung up the phone with guilty looks as he entered. He pretended not to notice as he gave them the pizza and listened to their cries of delight.

The island wouldn't have phone service yet. He just needed to keep them occupied until Billy-Bob was gone. He was kind of relieved the social workers wouldn't show until Monday.

He produced the sack of drawing pads, pencils, and watercolors he'd bought along the way. They weren't the quality he could find in the city, but better than Kismet was used to. She screamed in excitement and pounced on them as if he'd given her gold. That so simple a gift could produce such sheer joy stirred him more deeply than he'd like to admit. And here he'd wasted thousands of dollars buying foolish jewelry and flowers for women who accepted them with boredom. Idiot!

Gene, on the other hand, watched him warily, with a more sullen expression than usual. The boy wouldn't understand what Jared had just done at the sheriff's, so he might as well enjoy these last few hours with the kid. Of course, Cleo would kill him if she discovered how much he'd spent, but he'd at least resisted buying anything bigger. He handed Gene another bag from the office supply store.

The boy removed the handheld computer from the box and looked at the miniature keyboard with puzzlement at first, then dawning wonder. "Is it for real?" he demanded, instantly finding the switch and discovering the battery worked.

"You can do e-mail on it, anyway. I bought a package with free service for a year. It has some games, and I don't even want to know what you keep in the notebook. You've got to keep it powered up, though. Read the instructions." He had some vague hope that maybe Gene would keep in touch if he wasn't here in a few months. He'd always been the optimistic sort until Cleo came along.

"Beyond rad," Gene whispered, poking the tiny keys

with a pointer. A frown suddenly creased his forehead, and he glanced at his sister, who looked up at the same time. "Maybe we orter keep this stuff at Cleo's?" he asked her.

Kismet nodded and went back to drawing. Gene looked relieved, and gave Jared a goofy grin. "Thanks, dude. Can I plug this in?"

Jared glanced around Cleo's crowded office. She had a new computer, a scanner—he noted with relief—more file drawers than any one person should ever see, a fax, one phone, and one tiny chair crammed into a space smaller than his Manhattan bathroom. And that was small. "See how many outlets she has under that desk," he ordered.

Verifying they had two phone jacks but one belonged to the phone ringing off its hook in the front of the store, they agreed Gene could use the other until Jared was ready to send in his material. Kismet wandered off to a quieter corner of the store to draw, while Gene sprawled across the remaining floor space—pizza in hand—to figure out his new toy.

Finally faced with a computer and the drawings he'd done on the island, Jared went to work. He had too many things he wanted to do with Cleo once she closed for the day, so he had to get this stuff out now.

Amazing how a little anticipation could glue his butt to the chair.

He gave the kids money to bring back drinks and a mid-afternoon snack when they complained of starvation, and stayed at it, scanning in the drawings, bringing them into Thomas's graphics program, reformatting them with his laptop's art files. His smart-ass *Scapegrace* teens were about to meet reality. About time, too.

He shot the finished strips off via e-mail attachment while the kids were scarfing down greasy hamburgers.

Cleo sent Marta back to eat while she handled the afternoon crowd. They'd called in extra workers who wandered in and out, awed by Jared's presence but careful not to intrude, especially since they'd have to crawl over Gene's sprawled figure to see what he was doing. Jared considered writing off the palm notebook as a business expense for the guard duty it provided and pretty much ignored the gawkers. He had a script to put together. Two, actually. The one he'd promised and the one he really, really wanted to do but doubted anyone would let him. He made notes on both faster than he'd worked in months. Years, probably.

By the time Cleo finally took a break, he was starving, the pizza box was empty, and his hamburger was cold. She dropped her sack of food from the corner restaurant on the desk, and Jared pulled her down on his lap and blew in her ear. She almost came up off the chair.

"Gotcha," he murmured, aware Gene scowled and scuttled out of the room.

"What did the sheriff say?" she demanded in low tones.

"Billy-Bob should be gone by the time we return. They'll be okay for now. Monday will be the day of reckoning with Linda."

She relaxed enough to bury her face in his shoulder for half a second, before steeling herself and pushing away. "Maybe I should arrange to be far, far away."

"I can do that. Want to go to New York with me? I've got an apartment to clean out."

She stiffened, and he knew his delirium had pushed him too far.

"You'd better see if you have a place to move your stuff to," she warned, before standing up and walking out again.

Oh, shit. Jared glared at the unimaginative bucky ball

rolling across Cleo's computer screen. The roads had been too dangerous for them to check on the beach house before they left for town, but chances were pretty much guaranteed it would be unsafe for habitation.

And Cleo wasn't planning on him moving in with her.

⊰ TWENTY-SIX ⊱

By the end of the day the kids grew bored with their confines. Gene wandered out to the shop, ostensibly to help Cleo, and Kismet switched to puzzling out Gene's new toy. Jared figured he'd done his baby-sitting duty for the day and let the boy go. Kismet was a much quieter companion while he finished his script notes. Another few days working like this, and he'd almost be home free. Nothing like a deadline and looming bankruptcy to push a man to his limits.

Or a romance going down the drain. Thinking about anything else was preferable.

About the time his mind started straying to his solitaire program and wondering if the palm computer had one, Gene bounced back in, beaming with mischief. "There's a big RV blocking all the parking out there."

"So, maybe they needed duct tape to refinish their plastic cabinets." Jared hit the "close" switch of the word-processing program. His brain couldn't take any more of this. He'd do push-ups, but there wasn't room.

Maybe he could jog up and down Main Street. He had to blow off this steam or explode.

"Nah, those people park them things out at the campground and bike in or something. This gotta be somebody *big*. You ain't expectin' no one?" he asked in disappointment.

"Sorry to disappoint, kid, but I don't know a soul who's even seen the inside of an RV." He shoved back Cleo's ugly little desk chair and stood, rubbing his aching back muscles. He was as bad as Gene. An RV on that tiny street outside would be an entertaining sight.

"Maybe it's them movie people they been talking 'bout," Gene whispered in awe, heading for the store again.

Kismet didn't even look up as they wandered out. Jared glanced down as he passed her and noticed she'd already figured out how to find Internet chat rooms. The girl wasn't dumb by a long shot.

The crowd in the store had dwindled to a couple at the cash register. The extra help had either gone home or were in the process of returning misplaced stock to the shelves.

Jared automatically sought Cleo in the cluster at the counter. A boy sat beside the register, holding a cat as large as he was and chattering away, to the amusement of the customers. Jared heard Gene's muttered "oh, shit" before he could see past all the heads to Cleo. The moment he saw her expression, though, he knew who the boy was—Matty. Cleo radiated happiness as surely as the sun shone in the sky.

Soaking up that image of Cleo's bliss, Jared longed to be the one who could make her that relaxed and happy and open. He could see the woman she should be—if only he could offer her the same kind of unconditional love and safety as her child.

Pushing down the pain of recognizing his deficiency, he fell victim to the pressure of someone staring at him. Scanning the store, he located the source easily.

A blond giant wearing a toddler on his shoulders watched him with amusement. At his side stood a slender woman with abundant red hair accented by a silver streak, with eyes more blue than Cleo's green. Her critical gaze warmed as he approached, and she relaxed to stroke the hair of a child about Matty's age hiding behind her exotically colored dress. The boy's dark coloring was closer to Gene's than the couple's, and Jared grinned. If this was the boy Cleo's sister had adopted, Cleo and Maya had far more in common than Cleo believed. Both women were apparently color-blind, and possessed a penchant for taking in unwanted strays.

Navigating around the high store shelves, he didn't notice the woman's pregnancy until he was almost upon her. Another pain twisted below his heart, and he tried not to glance in the direction of Matty and Cleo. Children weren't something he'd ever thought about until Cleo crashed into his life. Or he'd crashed into hers. It didn't take a genius to recognize the reason for Cleo's envy of her sister.

"You must be Maya and Axell." He stuck out his hand. "I'm Jared McCloud. My agent thanks you profusely for the helicopter."

Balancing the red-haired toddler bouncing on his shoulders, Axell shook his hand firmly. "But you're reserving judgment?" he finished what Jared left unsaid. "You'll understand it was either the news helicopter or Maya would have driven to the water's edge and highjacked a boat."

Maya dug her elbow into her husband's side, then held out her hand to take Jared's. "Matty was worried," she said with tranquillity.

Jared dared a glance back to the counter. Cleo was finishing up her sale and chucking the back of her son's head for something he said. "I've never seen her happier. You chose the right moment to bring him."

Before they could question him, a thin girl only a few years older than Matty who'd been examining the paint chips drifted over, and Axell introduced his daughter, Constance.

Maya couldn't possibly be old enough to have a daughter that age, but she hugged the child as affectionately as if she were her own. Coming from a family that never hugged, Jared suffered a few jealous pangs of his own. He wanted a woman who would hug his children like that.

His children. Panic ought to be setting in, but he was oddly comfortable with the idea of someday having a rugrat of his own.

Cleo appeared with Matty at her side before Jared could recover from the impact of that discovery.

"Marta can close up. What's with the RV?" Without missing a beat, she reached up to remove her squealing niece from Axell's shoulders and bounced her in her arms.

Jared lost what remained of his heart as the chubby tyke contentedly curled up beneath Cleo's chin and sucked her thumb, and Cleo rocked her as if she did it every day of the week. Smitten. Shipwrecked. Shattered. It had to be something in the position of the moon and stars—he wanted Cleo holding *his* child.

Maya was telling her sister something about "rolling hotels" as Axell grabbed Jared's arm and steered him toward the door. "It's a lost cause trying to get a word in edgewise until their batteries run down. Let's pretend we know something about road hogs and get out of their way."

Jared figured he couldn't have moved a foot without

Axell's impetus pushing him forward. His own family never overwhelmed him like this. Maybe it was because neither of his siblings had married, so he'd never had contact with so many short people at once. Rugrats and teenagers and everything in between. And women . . .

Feeling as if he were short-circuiting, Jared looked around for Gene. At least he understood the kid, but Gene had hidden from the full family effect. Couldn't exactly blame the boy.

Jared panicked as he walked outside the store and realized the full implication of the arrival of Cleo's family. He had no place to *stay*. He couldn't sleep in Cleo's bed with her son a room away and her sister and a tin can full of toddlers parked in the front yard. Maybe he should book a flight to New York for tonight.

"You know the helicopter pictures worried Maya more than the hurricane," Axell said casually, all but shoving Jared up the stairs and through the open RV door before the women and children caught up.

Catching himself in the door frame, Jared straightened his arm and blocked all entrance. The other man was bigger and brawnier, but he didn't fear his physical size. He scowled at Axell's placid expression. "Cleo is quite capable of taking care of herself. She won't appreciate interference, well-meaning or otherwise."

Axell grinned, and Jared had to remember the man was obviously more than a bartender, given his propensity for producing helicopters and enormous RVs at will.

"Yeah, that's what I figured," Axell replied to Jared's reproach. "But I thought I ought to warn you that Maya will rip your tongue out through your nose if you hurt her sister."

Jared shook his head in disbelief and stepped inside the semi-size vehicle. Expecting a clutter of kid-proportioned counters and beds, he gazed in approval at the wide open aisles with comfortably padded bench seats and captain's chairs. "Where did you find this thing?"

Axell shrugged and stared down the long aisle as if just discovering it. "Maya designed it. It shouldn't be bad for a day or two. Makes it easy to keep track of everybody."

They'd be staying a couple of days. Jared felt as swamped as the beach house must look.

"Leave it to you to solve everything," Cleo said dryly from behind them as the two women climbed in and the vehicle exploded with children tearing down the aisle. "The beach house might have held you if the storm hadn't taken it out."

She'd already forgotten his existence. Jared's usual childish inclination to do something irrational to catch her attention didn't materialize, though. He wasn't in the mood for humor.

"Hey, Matty, did you meet Jared?" Cleo called after her son. "He's the one who draws the cartoons I told you about."

Cleo cautiously touched his arm, and Jared read the plea in her eyes as Matty came forward and she introduced him to the son who meant more than life to her. He felt her anxiety so strongly he almost choked on it. She was trusting him, but she was terrified of doing so.

He didn't ever want her to worry. Brushing her pale cheek with his knuckle to show he understood, he crouched down to Matty's height. "Your mother says you draw wicked peacocks. Gonna show me sometime?"

Boys, he could handle. This one grinned from ear to ear, and tugging his hand from Cleo's tense grip, Matty grabbed Jared's arm and led him back to his own personal storehouse of possessions.

Cleo watched the tall man following in the wake of the small boy and tried not to panic. Jared's sable hair was only a few shades darker than Matty's. They'd almost pass for father and son.

"Impressive." Maya whistled quietly behind her. "Housebroke but as untrainable as a big cat, is my guess. My money's on Aries."

"Teenage nerd," Cleo countered sarcastically, "with Peter Pan rising."

Maya muffled a laugh. "Your inner child to his outer one. Perfect. But immature men do not turn their backs on a woman to cater to a child. He's all full-grown male, sis. Watch out."

"Will you two stow your carving up until I'm out of hearing?" Axell ordered. "I like the man, and I'm tired of being outnumbered. Keep him, Cleo." He sauntered off to remove Maya's red-haired toddler from her stubborn determination to claim Matty's box.

"I've got Kismet and Gene in the store." Ignoring her brother-in-law, Cleo retreated toward the door. "I need to go get them."

As if by magic, Jared appeared at her elbow, with Matty in tow. Cleo didn't think she could handle the juxtaposition of dangerous man and lover with the safe sane world of sister and son, but he didn't intrude. He merely provided the strength her backbone needed to deal with the inevitable collision. Jared did strong and quiet as well as gregarious and sophisticated.

"The kids are hiding in the back room," he offered as Cleo reached for Matty's hand. "I'll take them to the island, if you'd rather ride with your sister."

She heard the question in his voice, the one she couldn't answer even if she dared think about it. Maya slipped away, leaving them to discuss the problem with only Matty to hear. The boy grabbed this opportunity to climb into the driver's seat to play with the controls and wasn't listening.

"I don't want to take them back to Linda's," she whispered.

"They'll go, whether you want it or not," he said matter-of-factly. "They may come back, but with the Perv gone, they may not. Not while your family is here."

He knew them as well as Cleo did. She nodded agreement. "I almost wish Social Services had come and taken them and got it over with." It tore her gut to say it, but the sooner they were ripped out of her life, the better for all concerned. She'd been risking Matty and her stability by playing with fire—again. If only she could learn to really wall herself off . . .

Jared rubbed her cheek gently, as he had earlier, reminding her he was there for her without embarrassing her with a more affectionate display. "Tell me what you want me to do, Cleo. If the beach house is still standing, I can camp out there and keep an eye on them." The pressure of his fingers became a little stronger as he forced her to look at him. "Or I can book a flight to New York and take care of business. I can wait until your family leaves, if you will go with me."

Oh damn. Oh double damn. There it was, the decision that had to come sometime. It might as well be now, while her insides were already ripped to shreds, and she wouldn't feel it as much. Sort of like having one hand chopped off and sacrificing the other since the pain was already so bad.

"I won't go with you," she told him flatly, not meeting the look in his eyes but concentrating on holding herself together while the whole world watched. "Go take care of business. We'll be fine."

She was certain he stared at her for an eternity. His hand dropped away, and she could feel that first cold rush of air breaching the connection between them. *Go,* she urged silently, *go before I lose it right here and now.*

As if hearing her plea, Jared ran a reassuring hand up and down her arm. "I'll be back, Cleo. It's not over."

He strode down the steps and out of sight, and she was certain she would never see him again. He'd come to his senses once he was gone.

⊰ TWENTY-SEVEN ⊱

Cleo's happy family had apparently stopped the RV somewhere on the road. They hadn't reached Cleo's place by the time Jared let Kismet and Gene out in the drive. Fearing for their safety at the beach until he'd had time to inspect the damage, he couldn't take them with him.

Driving the Jeep through the muck and debris of the narrow lane, he rather missed the shrieking witch. Cleo had turned off the system when even the bouncing sign only halfheartedly lifted from the debris littering the road.

Reaching his drive only to be confronted by a mountain of driftwood, sand, and washed-up palmettos, he halted short of the beach. Cleo wouldn't need her trespasser deterrents with the road cut off like this.

Leaving his laptop in the car and locking the door, Jared climbed the treacherous barrier and slid down the other side. At least it looked as if the house had weathered the storm in one piece. Maybe he could stay here until Cleo's family left. His request for her to travel with him at a time like this had made her nervous, he realized. He understood anxiety far better than he used to. He felt as if he had electrodes attached to all his nerve endings, which shorted out every time he thought of Cleo.

Maybe she was right, and whatever this was between them wasn't worth their energy. If this was love, it was hell. He didn't like being jerked around by invisible wires. He had too many other things on his mind. He didn't have time to wheedle Cleo around to his way of thinking. And why should he cater to the obstinate woman?

All the rationalizing in the world couldn't hide the fact that he was a stubborn ass who wouldn't give up when he wanted something. And he wanted Cleo.

The damage to the beach house was more obvious as he approached. The sand dune on the shore had all but disappeared, and waves lapped a few hundred yards from the door. Half the dune had shifted to the porch. The storm had ripped shutters from windows, and shards of glass caught the last rays of twilight. The new roof had held, but one of the front dormers had crumbled under the stress of wind, leaving a gaping hole in his bedroom.

Using a stick of driftwood to remove the shattered pane from a lower window, Jared climbed over the sill. He had picked up his duffel at Cleo's, but he needed clean clothes if he intended to travel.

Now that he saw there wasn't any danger, he wished he'd brought Gene with him. He worried the kid would take off through the woods before Cleo returned. He'd promised to drive them to check on their mother after he examined the damage here, but Jared knew the kids were impatient. Maybe he wasn't handling this right.

He probably wasn't good father material anyway. L.A. wasn't a place to raise kids, and his future was in L.A. He hoped. He could only handle so much denial at a time.

He threw some clothes in the duffel, the ones that weren't a sodden lump on the bedroom floor. Maybe he'd better call Marta and have her send someone out to board up the broken windows so the kids wouldn't hurt themselves trying to get in. Cleo would be too occupied with family to think of it. To think of him.

He didn't know why her rejection hurt so much. He had expected it, after all. Cleo was Cleo. There wasn't any changing her.

Matty had changed her without even trying.

Cursing, Jared climbed out the first-floor window again, duffel in hand. He'd finish his business and come back to hack this out with Cleo once her family departed.

Returning to the Jeep, Jared discovered Axell lounging against the hood, arms crossed, waiting for him. Matty stood on the Jeep's roof, eyes wide at the sight of the surf lapping so close to the road. Grimacing, Jared heaved his duffel into the backseat. Casually, so as not to show how hard he really wanted to try, he handed a starfish to the boy, who squealed in delight at the gift. Then propping his shoulder against the back door, Jared adopted the same antagonistic stance as Axell. Axell didn't look impressed.

"Where are the kids?" the big man demanded.

"If they're not in the house, then they're just where I told Cleo they would go. Home." Jared figured that wasn't the real question here, but he'd let Axell get it out. He wasn't helping him any.

At Matty's request, Jared turned and lifted the boy down. "Don't go out of sight," he warned. "There could be sharks in the sand."

The boy turned big green eyes up to him—Cleo's eyes—and Jared nearly melted on the spot. At the boy's disbelieving giggle at the idea of sand sharks, he let him go, too stunned to do more.

"He's a great kid," Axell said as Matty scampered to investigate the dune of debris. "Cleo will worry herself into an early grave trying to shelter him from all harm."

Jared was inclined to agree, but it wasn't his place to say so. Relieved to set aside the intensity of his sudden emotion for Cleo's son, he replied laconically, "She has her reasons."

"As long as you understand that." Axell shoved his hands in his pockets and tried to look nonchalant. "Is the house reparable?"

"Probably, once a bulldozer plows through. The windows need boarding up or the kids are likely to hurt themselves climbing in." He had to book a flight to New York, drive to the airport in Charleston, and call half a dozen people. He didn't have time for this.

He'd have to make time if he was serious about Cleo.

"Cleo says you're going back to New York."

Jared almost smiled at the threat in the Viking god's tone. "For two days. And I offered to take her with me. Unless you're planning on telling me the secret to handling Cleo, butt out, okay? As Cleo says, we have issues. They take time."

Axell eyed him speculatively. "I'm amazed Cleo hasn't eaten through your tender hide. I think she chews nails for breakfast."

Knowing the other man didn't mean harm, Jared let the insult go. "I wouldn't have made it as far as I have in my career without a tough hide. That's not our problem here."

They both looked at the boy contentedly sitting in the mud, digging out some buried treasure.

Axell nodded briefly. "She'll sacrifice anything or anyone for him."

"If I ever have kids, that's the kind of mother I want for them," Jared said quietly.

"You're leaving because of us, then?" Axell relaxed his defensive posture and shoved his hands into his pockets.

"Yeah. I figure Cleo will let me know when she's ready to let me into Matty's life. Right now she has more trouble than she can handle with her neighbor. If you're here to keep an eye on things, it should be safe for me to make a quick trip. I should be back Monday night."

"Pirate bones!" Matty crowed upon discovering unexpected treasure.

Amused by the boy's imagination, relieved at the interruption, Jared turned to see what he'd found. His jaw dropped at the sight of the leg bone Matty waved at them. He'd seen enough of Tim's textbooks to recognize human remains.

Axell uttered a muffled curse. "How do I pry *that* from him?" he asked rhetorically, striding toward the boy even as he asked.

"By calling the sheriff?" Boy, Cleo would lose it for certain. Maybe he'd better stay. He was looking for excuses to stay. Pirate bones worked.

With both men praising him for his discovery, Matty willingly relinquished the gray and brittle bone for their admiration, but it took a little more persuasion to prevent him from digging for more.

"Probably an old graveyard," Axell murmured, hauling the boy away from the mound and toward the house. "Happens all the time around here. I'll have someone look into it."

Deflected by that reasoning, left holding the bone while a pleasant sea breeze lifted his hair, Jared wondered if he'd ever possess the other man's confidence that the world was a safe, sane place. For Cleo's sake, he'd have to. He grimaced at the grisly remnant in his hand. What the hell would he do with it?

As Matty waved back at him, Jared smiled and relaxed. He could do this. He wouldn't let anyone tell him otherwise.

"Jared, you must be out of your mind. You can't *do* this." Virginia McCloud stared at her son in dismay.

Ash-brown hair styled and cut for a minimum of care and a maximum of elegance, tailored suit fitted to a figure maintained by a daily exercise regimen, his mother was everything Cleo was not, Jared noted with interest. Perhaps he ought to get counseling to understand the psychology behind that.

"I already have, Mom. The apartment is sold and the movers are hauling the furniture off to storage as we speak." He dug into his seafood pasta with a healthy appetite now that he had one less worry. He'd outgrown his need for the Manhattan playboy lifestyle anyway.

"Well, this is always your home, dear," his mother said doubtfully. "I'm sure if your market losses are that severe—"

The front door slammed. "Hey, Jared, you here? Mom said you were back." Jared's computer genius younger brother ambled in, his eyes sharp and discerning as he encountered the luncheon tête-à-tête.

"Your brother has sold his apartment, dear." With an imperturbable air, Virginia gestured toward a chair. "He has some foolish notion of returning to that hovel in the South."

Instead of sitting, Thomas Clayton McCloud leaned his square shoulders against the door frame, crossed his arms, and lifted his eyebrows in the distinctive family expression. "Couldn't take the ice queens up here any longer, could you, bro? Are the Southern belles any hotter?"

Two years younger than Jared, with their mother's ash-brown hair and their father's gray eyes, Thomas was the fair-haired boy the ladies swooned over. Unfortunately, his overgrown brain had given him a cynicism Jared couldn't maintain if his life depended on it. He figured Doubting Thomas would die a confirmed bachelor before admitting the existence of love and romance.

"Hot enough for me," Jared said placidly, spearing another shrimp. "Have you patented the graphics program? I can't find a flaw in it."

Clay drew up a chair, straddled it, grabbed Jared's salad fork, and helped himself to the pasta on his brother's plate. "Patented, and if all goes well, distributed next spring. Get famous in the film industry, old boy. I can use the endorsement."

Get famous. Right. He should be so lucky.

"Thomas, stop that. Where did you learn such appalling manners?" Virginia smacked her son's hand and rang for a maid. "Pull your chair up correctly and I'll have a plate brought for you."

Jared spared his brother an understanding glance. "Congrats, kid. Even if you don't hear it elsewhere, I'm proud of you and think you're a genius. I might even admit we're related upon occasion."

Clay hooted, but Jared thought he'd scored points. It was about time someone in this family recognized their personal achievements instead of their public awards.

After seeing Cleo with her family, he wondered what she would think of his family's inability to relate to one another, but he couldn't picture Cleo even sitting down at a table that harbored his overachiever mother. They'd despise each other on sight. Well, that could result in some interesting holiday fireworks.

"Hey, bro, you're drifting away. Surely you're not dreaming of the cute chick with the kids, are you? Those kinds are just looking for an easy meal ticket."

Miraculously, Jared recognized Clay's unease for the

concern it was and didn't belt him one. He saw no good way to reassure him, especially since he couldn't discern whether Cleo or Gene and Kismet were his brother's biggest fear. If he and Cleo married, could they adopt the kids?

The phone rang in the distance and no one leapt to answer it.

"If you're talking about the news clip, those weren't Cleo's kids," Jared said absently, toying with his remaining pasta while wondering if he could persuade Cleo to marry him on the basis of adopting the kids.

"I should hope not," his mother said vehemently. "It's bad enough to have your picture broadcast across the countryside on the roof of a shack, but in the company of—"

Jared tuned out the static and listened to a maid answering the phone. He'd given his family's phone number to the kids in case they needed him. Not that he could do much from here, but he was learning responsibility carried a lot more worries than he'd anticipated. He had a flight booked for tonight. Idly, he wondered if he could catch an earlier one if he headed for the airport after lunch.

"Mother, you're a bigot," Clay was expostulating as the maid appeared in the doorway, carrying the cordless receiver. "This is the twenty-first century. In another hundred years we'll be fortunate to find gender differences much less racial ones. I read a book . . ."

The maid held out the receiver to Jared rather than interrupt one of Clay's lectures.

It could be the movers with a question. He didn't have any reason to panic. He'd meant to call Cleo this morning to make certain the kids had gone off to school all right, but in the chaos of moving, his phone had been disconnected. He'd only reached her machine all weekend. Not talking to her for over two days was about to drive him up a wall. Or maybe his family had already done that.

Pushing away from the table, Jared slipped away, taking the phone into the hallway. "Yes?"

"I have those franchise contracts revised, so stop by and initial the changes before you leave." George always spoke abruptly, as if he were doing three things at once. "Where are you on that script? Bring it with you. I have the producer coming in this afternoon and he wants to talk with you about it. Plan on being here by three."

Jared contorted his face in a grimace he once used on his teachers. Cleo and the kids had him practicing clean language. "I don't have anything in hard copy, George. I want to take this in a different direction than originally planned." There, he'd said it. Impending bankruptcy terrified him, he didn't know how he'd handle it, but he had some weird idea that it wouldn't faze Cleo one iota if he risked pauperdom for creative freedom.

He could almost see George hitting panic mode as he practically bit off the telephone. "What do you mean, a different direction? You're using the same characters, aren't you? We're signing the deal this afternoon for those characters!"

"They can't print anything until I draw them, George. Keep your ass on. This will be far better. I just may need a little more time." Jared winced at the string of epithets flying over the phone wire. So, he'd better work fast. He'd have to learn better working habits. This wasn't high school anymore. He could do it. "I'm on my way. We'll talk."

He hit the "off" button, his mind racing over all the things he needed to gather before leaving. He wanted to head for the airport as soon as he left his agent's office. He might still catch an earlier flight.

His mother called his name as the phone rang again. Mind on other things, figuring it was George again, he hit the "talk" button. "Yeah, what is it now?"

"Jared?" a timid voice inquired.

Kismet. Panic sprang full-blown. "Yeah, Kis, is everything all right?"

"Gene's in jail," she whispered.

Keep it cool, boy, he told himself, as his gut clenched in fear. *Don't scare her.* "All right. I'll see what I can do. Where are you, hon? Have you talked to Cleo?"

Silence, then a whispered, "Help her, Jared." Gently, the line disconnected.

Ohmigod. @#$%!

Something had happened to Cleo. He knew it with every terrified nerve in his body, and his mind shrieked into overload.

Career or Cleo.

His whole life—his career—lay on the line. After the TV flop, he couldn't afford to tick off his agent and the only producer willing to take a chance on him. He had this absolutely fantastic new idea that he *really* wanted to do—

Not without Cleo.

That realization whopped him backward as he dropped the phone in its cradle.

Not without Cleo, who had inspired him. Who couldn't survive in L.A. Who didn't belong anywhere but where she was.

Cleo—of the warm heart and prickly exterior, with the cynical green eyes that lit with joy when he held her. The woman who had been knocked down and shoved around and still determinedly scaled the ladder, intent on providing a better life for her son.

Cleo, who had given him more joy and life than a dozen Jags or three dozen bachelor pads.

Cleo.

Ignoring his mother's increasingly strident tones, Jared returned to the dining room and smacked his brother on the shoulder.

"Got your car? I need to get to the airport, ASAP."

Clay lifted a cynical eyebrow. "Hollywood calls?"

Jared preferred to think he acted on sound instinct and not impulse as he threw his career down the toilet in exchange for the doubtful hope of building something good with an evil genius like Cleo. It no longer mattered if he made a right or wrong decision. It was the only one.

He shrugged. "Hollywood be damned. This is *my* life."

Eyeing him with a measure of respect, ignoring their mother's cries of annoyance, Clay stood and reached for the keys in his pockets. "Maybe you've got the right idea, big brother. Who needs fortune and fame anyway?"

He walked toward the front door without further explanation, and Jared didn't demand any. He'd ask what was eating his little brother some other time.

Right now, he had Cleo on his mind.

❧ TWENTY-EIGHT ❧

"Where the hell is she?" Jared refrained from leaping over the counter to strangle a strangely taciturn Marta.

Even the store seemed silent, although a few people quietly browsed the counters, throwing him surreptitious glances.

He'd caught a departing flight by the skin of his teeth, and repeatedly called Cleo from the plane, but he'd only reached her answering machines. Terror had become permanently embedded in his back teeth. And now he was here, and no one would tell him anything.

"Haven't seen her," Marta said stiffly.

"Kismet called." He tried not to shout. He was known for his good humor and laid-back manner. He wanted to scream the roof down now. "She said Gene's in jail. What do you know about that?"

Marta nervously wadded a corner of her shop apron and stepped back. "They caught him with an ounce of crack over by the school this morning."

Inhale, Jared. He gulped air and thought frantically. "He wouldn't do that," he said in decision. But what would that do to Cleo? She'd have nightmares.

"Gene's mother says Cleo gave it to him. Word is, she's been arrested before for possession. Know anything about that?" Marta asked a little too casually.

"Dadblameit, woman!" he exploded. At least he'd managed to control his choice of words. One did not swear at women down here. He knew everyone behind him was listening intently, but panic laced his blood, and he didn't give a damn. "What do you think? You think Cleo would give those kids crack? *Are you out of your friggin' mind?*"

Perhaps he'd raised his voice a little too much. Marta took another step backward—and this was a woman who looked like she could bench press a sumo wrestler. Jared forced his voice down to a dull roar. "You'll have to ask Cleo about her past. That's not for me to say. But I can tell you this, Linda's lying through her pointy black teeth. *Think.* Would the Cleo you know do anything at all to hurt those kids?"

Marta's shoulders slumped, and she wiped her eyes with her apron. "Cleo's the one who found my brother-in-law a job after he got sober," she muttered almost incoherently. "He has three kids to support, and they would have all been evicted." Dropping the apron, she set her chin pugnaciously. "She never says anything. She just goes to work and does it. I couldn't believe the gossip, but it's all over town. There's not a soul here who'll buy from a known dealer. Not in this town. I didn't know *what* to say."

All right. He'd told Cleo he could deal with that. Give him something he could do, and he was okay. It was the helplessness that made him crazy. "Linda wants revenge." He didn't lower his voice. Let everyone hear him. "She's out to get even with Cleo for calling Social Services about the kids. You call every damned soul Cleo ever helped and you tell them that. And you tell them to get their rear ends over here and let Cleo know they're behind her, one hundred percent. That's what friends are about."

He stormed out, glaring at anyone who dared meet his eye. No more Mr. Nice Guy. People occasionally needed a good kick in the derriere to prompt them to do the right thing. SuperGoof could play Mr. Ass-kicker just fine when the occasion warranted.

His fury carried him halfway to the island, and fear took over from there. Would they have arrested her yet? Or would she be turning the house into a bonfire in a fit of self-destruction? Any normal person would be hunting Linda down with an ax, but not Cleo. She'd hack off her own hand first.

He knew her entirely too well, and that made him very afraid.

No witch or skeleton interfered with his progress. No Cleo sat on the roof, pounding out her rage. The house sat ominously silent, waiting.

He crossed the weathered soft gray of the porch. Cleo hadn't painted it, but she'd used treated lumber for repairs, making it stronger than the original. He could see Cleo reflected in this house, a sturdy gracious lady who scorned useless adornment but who would weather any storm and shelter those she loved.

She would be protecting Matty.

He strode in without knocking. All the pieces of sheet metal and cogs and gears had disappeared, but she'd done most of that earlier to give the kids room. Dropping his duffel and laptop on the armchair, he followed instinct, knowing she was here.

He found her sitting cross-legged on the bed, flipping through a scrapbook of photos and mementos. Beside her she'd heaped children's toys and collections of shells and stones, apparently in preparation for packing. The floor was littered with carefully sealed and labeled boxes.

Her eyes were dry when she looked up, but he could see tear tracks in the dust on her cheeks. She didn't look pleased to see him. She simply turned back to what she was doing.

"Have you called a lawyer?" he demanded. He had no patience left for sloppy sentimentality. Someone around here had to keep their head.

She shrugged. "What for? A public defender can handle Gene's case. He'll plead innocent. It's his first offense; they'll let him go."

"And you?" That sounded too easy. Something was wrong here.

"Gene won't testify against his mother," she said flatly. She left him to figure it out. Linda claimed the drugs came from Cleo. Gene wouldn't deny it. Cleo would return to jail.

"And you're sitting here packing up Matty's stuff and not even trying to fight it?" he asked incredulously, anger escalating.

She shot him a look of curiosity. "It's not as if I have any say in the matter. Just being involved with anyone who deals in drugs is a violation of my parole."

"You're not even going to *fight*?" he yelled. "What the hell do you think lawyers are for? You're not guilty this time, Cleo! You've got a case. You don't have to go through this." He wanted to pick her up and shake her, but she'd had enough violence in her life. He turned and slammed his fist into the wall instead.

"I trust that made you feel better," she said dryly.

Shaken by the extent of his fury, not ready to deal with the source of it, Jared nursed his bruised fist and glared at her. "Sometimes, it pays to get angry. Have you called Axell? Have you heard from Kismet?"

He thought he saw concern finally awaken in her eyes. The fool woman wouldn't fight for herself, but she'd fight for someone else. All right, so he was in a relationship with a schizoid. He damned well had no intention of sacrificing his career for a woman who would spend the next year or two in jail rather than fight for her rights.

He'd make her fight. Thinking of Cleo behind bars would unhinge him.

"I assumed she was with her mother," she answered tentatively. "The kids haven't been home all weekend. I looked everywhere. Wasn't she in school today?" Alarm danced across her features as she slowly realized how far she'd sunk into that depressed state she used as self-defense.

Jared wanted to reach out and comfort her, but Cleo had to learn things the hard way. He knew that now. He was far more relieved to see the alarm and anger building than the sad, defeated expression he'd seen when he entered. "She called me in New York. I don't think it was from school. I'll call Liz and find out."

Cleo clutched the scrapbook to her chest as Jared spun around and walked out. He'd looked harried and exhausted, with taut lines drawn about his mouth, not at all the smiling, charming man who'd left here. Had she done that to him?

Thoughts chased madly in circles in her head as she heard his low voice on the phone in the kitchen hall. She was so used to being alone that she hadn't thought of how she was hurting anyone but Matty, and she was doing her best to shield him. He would be happy with Maya. She was packing up all his beloved things so Maya could come get them. She didn't know if Maya wanted the animals, but she'd thought Gene would be returning to tend them after she was gone.

She hadn't thought about how all this would affect Kismet. Or Jared.

Of course, she hadn't thought Jared would return. She'd figured someone would tell him she'd been shipped off to prison, and he'd shrug and get on with his life. She'd tried hard not to think about it. She must have blocked out Kismet completely in some subconscious attempt for sanity. Now that Jared was here, the block dissipated, and all the emotions tumbled out: fear and anger and guilt and all those things that caused her to lose control.

She didn't want to go back to being that insane woman she'd been in the past, the woman who needed drugs and alcohol to cope. The desperate craving for oblivion sang through her veins, whispered temptingly at the back of her mind, promised freedom from the panic freezing her thoughts. She was going to jail again. The clickety-clack of the train rumbling closer while she lay tied to the track obliterated any coherent plan of action.

She would lose Matty, her house, her store . . .

Kismet could be sold into drugs and prostitution. Gene would have a record. They already had two strikes against them. The law would never give them a chance— just as it had never given her a chance.

She watched in wide-eyed terror as Jared returned looking grim.

"She wasn't at school. No one knows where she is."

The social worker must have shown up and set Linda off on this trip. Kismet must have run away. Had Lonnie hurt her?

Cleo bit her lip and desperately tried to think through the chaos in her head. "I'll go back to her house. I know a couple of her hiding places." She dropped the scrapbook and swung her feet to the floor. She couldn't go to jail until she found Kismet. She'd focus on that.

Jared caught her arms before she could go a step farther. "I'll go to Linda's. You call Axell. Get the name of a lawyer. If you won't do it for yourself, do it for me and Gene and Kismet. I'll lose my mind worrying about you behind bars. Don't put me through that."

Cleo gazed at him in wonder and disbelief. Disbelief won, but the concern in his eyes was too real to ignore. She didn't doubt that he'd worry for a while. She smoothed his creased, bronzed cheek with her palm, wishing she could wipe away the worry, knowing she wasn't worth his concern. "Axell would shout and yell. I'll call a lawyer tomorrow. I doubt I'd find one at this time of day. Go to Linda's, but be careful. I'll check Kismet's hiding places."

He didn't look happy, but there wasn't much she could do about that. "Why did you come back?" she asked out of curiosity. "You could have just called someone about Kismet."

He looked decidedly grim glaring at her like that— Superman in a tantrum. "Cleo, when this is all over, I'm going to shake you until your teeth rattle." He walked out again, as if afraid he might not wait but would do it now.

Well, that was an interesting reaction to stress. She'd have to try it sometime. Meanwhile, she had to find Kismet. Worry gnawed at her insides as her mind swept away the cobwebs of her own fears and focused on others.

As Jared roared the Jeep from the drive, Cleo set out down the mangled paths the kids had made through the overgrowth between the houses. The hurricane had ripped trees and bushes out by the roots, and in the growing dusk, it was hard to see where she was going. Mosquitoes buzzed and bit, and she had to be wary of snakes and sand traps. Kismet's favorite hideouts might be gone. She may have found new ones. Cleo had tried to keep an eye out all weekend while Maya and everyone were here, but she'd seen no sign of either Gene or Kismet. Jared had brought them to the island on Friday, so she'd figured they had to be here somewhere.

Gene had been arrested at school this morning. The sheriff had interviewed Linda in town, so she must have taken him to the mainland.

But not Kismet. That did not bode well. Had the sheriff arrested Lonnie as promised?

Kismet had called Jared. She was safe somewhere. Cleo had to believe that or lose what remained of her mind.

Not finding any sign of the girl in the tangle of brush, Cleo turned toward the beach.

*   *   *

Cleo's screams hit Jared the instant he switched off the Jeep's ignition outside her house. He couldn't tell exactly where they came from, but the logical place was the beach. He'd already exhausted all the fear in him and had reached numbness some time ago. Cleo's screams induced terror, more because they were heartrending wails than cries of pain.

Hitting the ignition again, he floored the Jeep's gas pedal and careened down the narrow lane toward the beach. He'd searched Linda's filthy shack but hadn't found Kismet or anyone else. Something told him Cleo had found what he hadn't.

The debris barrier blocked his way. Someone had been back to dig around the graveyard Matty had uncovered, but they hadn't opened the road. Leaping out of the car, he raced up the tangle of roots and limbs and sand. He used muscles he hadn't known he possessed to reach the top, and skidded all the way to the bottom on the other side.

Cleo's screams sounded closer now, and bordered on hysteria.

The sun had set, but enough light remained to see her slight figure silhouetted against the backdrop of shimmering waves. He could see no one threatening her, no ominous figures or vicious animals. She seemed to be holding something, but the shape wasn't recognizable.

Adrenaline drove him. The sand dune had shifted, but what sand remained was loose and impossible to navigate smoothly. He nearly fell once, then tripped on driftwood and went sprawling. Picking himself up, he proceeded with even less caution.

She quieted as she saw him running, but she was shaking all over by the time Jared reached her. Clasping her against him, ignoring the article of clothing she clutched in her fists, he gasped for breath and held her tight, taking her shudders into him as she sobbed and beat her head against his shoulder.

"Cleo, don't," he pleaded. "You're scaring me. What's wrong? What happened? Are you hurt?"

"Kismet," she gasped. "It's her sweater. Her things. Her drawing pad. She's . . ." She couldn't finish but wept harder.

He'd thought Cleo had drained him of all feeling, but sorrow deeper than anything he had ever known permeated his bones. Disbelief followed close behind, then rage. Never in his life had he been through something like this. He'd never lost a loved one. Cleo had lost both parents. He'd never suffered grief, and given the cold competitiveness of his family, had never recognized love. She was putting him through every emotional wringer in existence, and he simply didn't have the experience to handle it.

He held her, let her weep, and had absolutely no idea what to do except weep with her. He despised this feeling of helplessness.

Waves washed gently against the shore, and struck violently against the rocks she'd warned him about the first day he'd arrived. He watched the rising moon against the tide, expecting to see a dark head of curls emerge from the water as it would in the movies. No such image appeared.

"We'll call the police," he murmured. "They'll send out boats. We can look for her." Her body, at least. He couldn't imagine gentle Kismet battling an undertow to swim away to safety and happiness.

He mourned the loss of all that talent, of a child on the brink of life who had so much to see and do ahead of her. It didn't seem fair. Why would evil creatures like Linda survive and gentle ones die?

He rocked Cleo silently until she ran out of sobs.

Together, they gathered Kismet's favorite possessions and walked quietly back to the car.

❧ TWENTY-NINE ❧

Coast Guard cutters and yachts from the harbor turned out to sweep the water with searchlights once word spread. The sheriff called in off-duty officers, and the state police walked the storm-ravaged shore.

Cleo refused to leave the beach. Jared wrapped her in blankets, sat her down on the sand, and curled his arms around her to protect her from the cool wind off the water. Nothing stopped her shudders.

If he could rip his heart from his chest to ease her sorrow, he would, but he was helpless. He'd thought he'd grown up a little these past weeks, but nothing had taught him how to deal with tragedy. Cleo had shown him how to look outside himself, how to accept responsibility for others, even how to use all his advantages for a good cause, but what good did that do when he couldn't change the wrongs that needed righting?

So he held Cleo, and cherished her, and vowed he would turn the world upside down before he let it hurt her again.

One by one the searchers gave up, promising to return in daylight. By the time the last searchlight switched off and the sheriff stopped to offer stilted condolences, Cleo had fallen asleep in Jared's arms.

"Sometimes, life don't make no sense, boy," the burly man said, shaking his head. "It ain't gonna be any easier for her tomorrow. Take her home."

Jared wished he could. Home for him was in Miami, in his sunlit apartment overlooking the water. He'd tuck Cleo between satin sheets, lock the doors, and open the windows to the sound of surf and laughter.

He'd known Cleo would never share that with him, but the full implications were just starting to sink in. He couldn't push Cleo. He had to wait—patiently—until she was ready. He'd never possessed a large store of patience.

She stirred as he carried her to the car and tried to settle her into the seat, but she apparently didn't want to wake any more than he wanted to think. She was unconscious again by the time the Jeep purred to life.

He had a few hours before dawn to lay awake and plan his next action. He'd need more than a few hours to figure out what to do with the rest of his life now that he'd blown his career to smithereens.

Cleo woke the instant Jared climbed from the bed in the morning. Her head pounded, her eyes were too groggy to open, but she sensed his absence instantly. He'd been a part of her all night, like blood flowing through her, keeping her alive, and his absence emptied her as brutally as a cut artery.

She must have been drinking.

She squeezed her eyes tight as she listened to him dress quietly, trying to remember if she'd opened those beers she'd bought. She'd had some notion that she might as well enjoy her last few hours of freedom. What would it matter if she poured poison into her system when she would be soul-dead soon enough? But she'd wanted to pack Matty's things before she sought oblivion, and then Jared had come home.

Home. This wasn't his home. But he'd come back. And he'd held her all night, this man from another world, the gilded world she'd never known. He didn't belong in the mud wallow of her life.

She wanted to go to sleep again. She didn't have the strength to face the day. If she woke any more, she'd have to face the horrors lurking just behind her eyes.

Jared sat on the edge of the bed and ran his fingers through her hair, then kissed her cheek. She must look like death warmed over.

"Cleo, hon? I've got to go into town to take care of a few things. Why don't I just call Axell and look into a good lawyer for you? I can drive into Charleston, interview them, find you and Gene someone willing to fight for you. I'll be back as soon as I can. You just stay here and get some rest."

Like hell she would. She wasn't a baby to be coddled and cooed at.

But it was nice of him to try. She wouldn't bite his head off for that. She thought it might hurt her as much as him if she tried.

That was the damnedest part of this sharing business. She couldn't yell or snap at him any more than she could at Matty.

"My address book is in the desk," she said wearily, accepting this part of the reality awaiting her. She still couldn't face the glaring emptiness that was Kismet's place in the world. Some as yet undefeated part of her couldn't believe Kismet would take her own life.

"Lawyers are listed under 'L,' for liars," she told him, curling up in a tight ball around her pillow. "The page under 'A,' for assholes, was full. Most of them know me, but they'll not thank you for your business."

She thought he chuckled understandingly. She'd harrassed every lawyer she'd ever come across—and she'd come across plenty dealing with some of the people who came to her for jobs.

He wandered off, and she tried summoning the energy to get up. Her hair felt stiff and matted from the salt air. Jared had apparently removed her clothes before tucking her into bed, but he hadn't been brave enough to remove her T-shirt and panties. She hoped it was a sign that she still tempted him. Or maybe not. Maybe he'd be better off developing a disgust of her, and getting the hell out of here.

She'd bled enough for now. She would cut that artery some other time. Wrapping the sheet around her shoulders, she sat up and rubbed her eyes against the light from the window. They'd be out on the beach again, searching. She didn't want to know how often the bodies of drowning victims returned to shore. Matty's discovery of the old skeleton seemed somehow prophetic. The sheriff had said it had probably been some long-ago drowning casualty.

Katy from the B&B had declared the skeleton a victim of pirates, of course, and had demanded excavation. Cleo supposed rumors of buried treasure were already whispering through town, and the beach would be inundated with curiosity-seekers.

No manner of diversion could hide the fact that she'd failed Kismet. She'd enjoyed her weekend with Matty and family and hadn't looked hard enough to find her. She'd assumed the sheriff had arrested Lonnie and everything would be all right. She'd assumed too damned much. Just like Jared.

So, that's where optimism took you. To hell and back.

Or not. If Kismet had heard the sheriff's theory about the skeleton, what were the chances her active imagination had led her to plant those items on the beach so no one would look for her?

Jared returned with the address book and a pad of rough sketches. "What are these? I found them on your desk. It doesn't look like Kismet's stuff."

Sitting on the bed's edge, Cleo looked around for her jeans without glancing at what he held. "I tried to show Axell how gears work together to make motion. I've been studying the courthouse clock with Ed, and I had some stupid idea I could fix that cog. Now I know how Da Vinci must have felt when he tried to explain flying machines. Except he could draw and I can't."

"You need to learn computer drafting. It's easier." He threw the sketchpad on the bed. "I'm taking your address book with me. It's easier than copying everything down."

She nodded and pulled a cotton shirt over her tank top. She needed to shower anyway. If he didn't mention Kismet, neither would she. Talking couldn't help. Maybe time would.

She still felt the stark horror of her mother's untimely death from a ruptured appendix. But she'd been a kid then. Maybe these things got easier with age. Or maybe she didn't really believe Kismet was dead.

"Whatever," she said dismissively. He had to feel helpful, so she'd let him. She knew better than to believe a lawyer could help, but people from Jared's world evidently felt better talking to leeches, and that was fine with her. She had better things to do, and she needed to concentrate on them. *Before it was too late* rang in her mind, but she was denying the inevitable in favor of *one step at a time*.

Before Cleo realized he'd entered the room instead of leaving it, Jared jerked her from the bed, caught her face between his hands, and kissed her until her head spun.

She had to grab his arms for support or her knees would have buckled.

Only then did he release her to meet her eyes with that fiercely determined gaze she'd seen once or twice before.

"You're not going to jail, Cleo. Believe me. I'm taking care of this. You just hang on until I get back. I have things I want to do with you that I haven't dared dream of yet. Think about it."

She collapsed back on the bed, her heart thumping like a wound-up toy drum as she watched his formfitting polo shirt and khakis stride purposefully from the room. A man like that could almost make her believe in miracles.

Hope had never been part of her nature, so she wasn't certain if she could recognize it now, but something fluttered in her chest besides her pounding heart. Maybe she had gas.

Marta looked surprised as Cleo stalked in, jaw set and chin tilted in an attempt to maintain her battered pride.

She'd gone down to the beach to see if anyone needed coffee or if she could help in the search, but no one would talk to her. They simply set about their organized plans and left her to stand alone, dying inside. She'd be *damned* if she'd be treated like that before she was even convicted of anything. Let them search the ocean. She needed to search elsewhere. Kismet had brains. If she wanted to elude her mother and whatever danger she presented, she would find a way besides suicide. Maybe she was fooling herself, but it was better than waiting uselessly.

"I don't push drugs," Cleo said flat out to her startled clerk. "I stole a teddy bear, for pity's sake. If you're going to look at me as if I'm a two-headed dragon, you can get out now. I don't need you or anyone else." She stalked to the coffeemaker and poured some of the strong stuff Marta favored.

"I believe you wouldn't hurt those kids," Marta agreed. "Why don't you return the favor and trust me with the story?"

Cleo didn't like talking about herself. She didn't like her past. She didn't much like herself some days. But Jared had taught her talking could ease the pain, and she was carrying a bagload of grief right now.

She talked.

Despite the hurricane, business remained slow. Maybe they were all going to Charleston and the big warehouse stores to cut costs. Or already boycotting a drug pusher before she was found guilty. At the sound of the front door opening, Cleo caught herself from jumping up from her computer. Marta could handle a single customer. She didn't need to go out there.

Hand on the phone, ready to call Linda's house again, she couldn't resist listening to the conversation in the front of the store. She'd intended to spend the rest of her life in this town, to raise Matty to be happy and healthy with friends all around him. She'd wanted to be a pillar of the community, sort of. Yesterday had dashed all that. She knew it. She simply couldn't help hoping for a reprieve.

She ought to smack Jared for that stupid thread of optimism.

"I'm here to see Cleo Alyssum," a commanding voice announced at the counter.

She knew that voice. It had the power to strike fear in her heart. Not yet, she pleaded with unseen forces, returning the phone to the cradle and clutching her desk edge. She had to find Kismet first. And get Gene out of jail to safety. Who the hell had called the damned feds? Her supervisor ignored her as long as she attended counseling.

"She's busy," Marta said curtly. "If you'll give me your name and business . . ."

Marta could smell the law from half a mile away. With Cleo's story fresh on her mind, she'd know the visitor wouldn't be good news. Frantically, Cleo tried to think of all the things she needed to do before they carted her off to jail. She hadn't said good-bye to Matty, or called Maya with instructions about what to say to him. And she was the only one Kismet would trust. If she was alive, Cleo had to be there for her.

Jared would be frantic if she wasn't here when he returned.

That was a new and scary thought. She'd only had Matty to worry about in the past. Worrying about Jared in the same way caused her heart to stutter, but it felt right to worry about him. Jared had showered her with more love and concern than any human being on earth. Even Maya thought her a pigheaded fool. Despite their differences, Jared still managed to see through all her defenses, touch her in ways she hadn't known she could be touched. And he cared. He believed in her. He'd actually left his rich world to come back here to help her. She couldn't let him down, even if he was insane enough to believe she could be saved.

She hit frantic overload as the deep voice boomed angrily.

"She's violated the terms of her parole. The judge will hear her story when the time comes. For now, I have to take her in."

"She's done absolutely nothing wrong," Marta shouted back. "You can't believe a lying no-good druggie over a decent hardworking store owner, you pig! The whole town will rise up in arms."

Nice thought. Cleo was up and moving before she knew what she intended to do. She had no illusions of the town rising to her defense, but she didn't want to go anywhere until Jared returned, and that was final. She had to know that Gene would be all right, that Kismet lived, that Jared understood, and she didn't cause him pain.

Besides, she was damned sick and tired of being treated like a piece of garbage by the government meant to protect her. She was a human being, and she'd damned well proved she could live as decently as anyone else. She'd earned some respect here. Jared was right—it was time she learned to stand up for herself. She deserved it.

Driven by the pure fires of righteous anger instead of the chaos of panic, Cleo stalked into her storage room, grabbed the tools she needed from the shelf where she'd left them a few weeks ago, and stormed out the back door. To hell with the feds. To hell with this damned bloody town. She was making a statement here.

His cell phone rang as Jared navigated a narrow picturesque street in search of yet another Charleston lawyer. He'd learned to park in New York City. He could park anywhere. He swung the Jeep into a miniscule space between a Rolls and a Jag and only ran one tire onto the crumbled—probably historic—sidewalk.

He snatched the phone from its socket and barked his name into it. He'd left messages with half the lawyers in town, and if they were all like the one he'd just seen, he might as well handle the case on his own. Cleo had been dealing with some pretty smarmy characters.

"Jared?" Marta's voice sounded uncertain and a little scared.

All right, he'd scared her to death yesterday. Maybe she had some right. He just had the ominous feeling that it wasn't him scaring her this time. "I'm here. What's wrong?"

"It's Cleo."

Hell, he'd known that. He was getting a handle on this panic mode, though. If he bit his tongue hard enough, he didn't yell as loudly. "What's happened?" Okay, he didn't yell, but he sounded terrified.

"She's on the courthouse roof," Marta whispered.

Jared closed his eyes and leaned his head back against the seat. "The courthouse roof?" he asked carefully. He didn't even want to imagine where this was leading.

"She said she knows how to repair the clock up there. She took her tools and climbed up and moved the ladder on the steeple so no one could follow her. And she's chained herself to it so they have to take down the clock to get at her."

He damned well could see where this was leading now. Well, he'd told her to fight. He just hadn't told her how, and Cleo didn't know "appropriate" from a hole in the wall. "Why?" he asked, in brave hope that his theory was wrong.

"Because the feds came to pick her up," Marta whispered, as if fearful the officer could haul her away for just mentioning it. "The clock weighs two tons," she added, as if that helped.

He almost chuckled. If it weren't so serious and so painful, he could almost see the humor in this. He'd already drawn the entire scene in his mind. He'd have his audience rolling in the aisles. Damn, he loved her wicked mind.

"Is she safe up there?" he demanded.

Marta hesitated. "I suppose so. She's been up there before with Ed. She can't *stay* up there."

"Knowing Cleo, she'll stay up there until the gulls pick her bones clean if we don't do something. That's one stubborn woman. I'll make a few phone calls and see what I can do. I've got an idea."

He hung up, threw aside Cleo's list of sleazy lawyers, and dialed Axell. "Give me the name of the best, the most charismatic, the loudest, most publicity-hungry lawyer you know," he shouted into the phone.

Axell did.

❧ THIRTY ❧

"Hey, gull, I want you to know . . ." Cleo tried singing to the bird cocking his head and eyeing her as if she might be a dead fish. At the sound of her voice, the gull flapped its wings and sailed off. Figures. She couldn't even entertain scavengers.

Setting her wrench on the clock sill, she gulped the bottle of water she'd brought up here and waited to see who was rattling the fire engine ladder this time. As far as fits went, this was probably the finest one she'd ever thrown. Not her smartest, maybe, but a truly fine fit. She suspected half the town had wandered by the square patch of courthouse lawn sometime during the day.

She didn't think she was being purposelessly self-destructive this time, though. The pig would have locked her up, after all, and then they'd take away Matty again. So she'd just chosen her own poison in hopes of bene-fiting Gene and Kismet. Not that anyone down there quite got the connection yet. Would Kismet hear about this and contact Jared? If she knew Jared had the kids in hand, she might deal with prison better.

She couldn't see anything near the courthouse wall from this angle, but she'd been watching some guy with a full head of gleaming silver hair haranguing the crowd in the square for the past hour. She'd taken him for a preacher, except he wore his hair to his shoulders and tied in a ponytail. He'd so enraptured the crowd, they'd just about forgotten her. She hoped he was converting them to a good cause.

Maybe, if she really wanted to go out in a ball of flame, she should have brought something stronger than water up here. She gulped another swig of Evian as Marta's brother, the fireman, stuck his head over the edge of the roof below her.

"Hey, Jack," she called, "Who's the Boy Scout providing the entertainment down there?"

Jack knotted a plastic sack to the rope ladder she lowered for him.

"Marta sent supper." He glanced down at the preacher in the square. "That's your lawyer. He's good."

Cleo pulled the rope up to retrieve the sack. Had it been anyone but Jack and Marta offering food, she'd be suspicious of their motives. Actually, before Jared came along, she'd have been suspicious even of them. She was learning to trust. Scary. Probably self-destructive, too, but she might as well go all out.

"My lawyer?" she asked, examining the contents of the bag. Her chosen methods of self-destruction didn't involve starving to death. Even a Big Mac smelled good. "I know lots of lawyers, but that guy isn't one of them. Sure he isn't a preacher or country singer?"

Jack shrugged. "He's a lawyer, all right. He's filed for court injunctions and threatened to sue everyone from the janitor on up to the Supreme Court, from what I can tell. Says you're innocent of anything but trying to protect yourself, and the feds violated your rights to the Second Amendment for arresting you the first time around, and if they try to intervene in this matter, he'll haul their asses off to jail. Figure the temperature down there has risen ten degrees already. Much more pleasant up here."

"Yeah, that's how I've got it figured." Cleo popped a fry and savored the grease. Hell, if she was going to die up here, she might as well take a little cholesterol with her. "I like the sound of this lawyer. Tell him he's hired, but not to defend me. I want Gene out of jail, and his damned mother and her child-molester lover arrested. Linda has finally forfeited my sympathy. I'm gonna take her down with me."

"If I can get him to shut up long enough, I'll do that," Jack said doubtfully. "The sheriff told me to tell you he's gonna throw your ass in jail for causing a public nuisance if you don't get down from here."

Cleo grinned around her grease-covered finger as she sucked on it. "Tell him to come up and get me."

"The fed is threatening a SWAT team to do just that," he warned.

"Fine. If they want their knees whacked, I'll whack 'em." She didn't even bother indicating the crow bar dangling from the chain she'd wrapped around her waist. She about had the broken cog off. Maybe she'd drop it on somebody's head.

"Way I look at it, you'll have to whack their thick skulls." Jack dubiously eyed the steep shingles between them. "Not that they could send up more than one man at a time. You planning on staying up here all night? The boys in the department don't mind getting a little overtime."

"I figure they'll let me become a skeleton to scare the pigeons before they settle anything down there. Reckon they'll make a movie of that, or are they still on that pirate kick?" Not waiting for an answer, she sucked down another fry and frowned at the arm-swinging preacher. "Maybe I ought to talk to the lawyer guy and give him a few clues."

"A cell phone might work," Jack said cautiously. "The guy's too fat to climb up here, for sure."

"Jack, you're amazing when you apply yourself." Cleo savored the hamburger and kicked at the gull landing near her knees where she straddled the rooftop.

"Well, the fed suggested it," Jack admitted. "But the sheriff figured you'd heave it at them, and it would be a waste of good equipment."

"Good man. Tell you what, tell them I want to call my lawyer. Get the phone up here, and I'll talk to the wild man. *Then* I'll throw it at them."

Jack laughed. "They're gonna grill your ass on hot coals when you get down."

"Linda's ass fries first," she corrected.

"You got that right." Grimly, Jack backed down the ladder.

She'd thought it would be peaceful up here, but it was kind of lonely. She'd hoped she'd have space to figure out what to do next, except she wasn't much good at thinking on her own. She needed Jared to bounce ideas back at her. She'd never had anyone to argue with before and hadn't realized how useful it was for seeing all sides of a problem.

That was not a productive train of thought. She was heading back to prison as sure as God made little green worms, so none of this was relevant. Saving the kids had to be her priority now. Of course, she might be in denial about Kismet, but she'd rather cling to hope. It gave her strength to fight.

So, if she could wrangle the lawyer into looking after

Gene, and set Jared to looking for Kismet, she supposed she'd have to come down. Maybe she could persuade Jack to bring her some fireworks, and she'd wait until it was dark. She ought to have some fun out of this last fling.

With that resolve made, she glanced over the roof edge again. Some of the people in the yard were toting picket signs. Maybe the lawyer had convinced them the world was coming to an end.

For a few odd days there, she'd actually been foolish enough to think she'd turned her life around, and she might actually be allowed a little pleasure for a change. Stupid of her. Jared had inspired that false sense of hope, but she supposed he'd also given her the courage she needed to finally stand up to authority. So, she couldn't call their relationship a total loss. It had been kind of fun, while it lasted, if one wanted to call what they'd shared a relationship. She didn't expect even friendship to last beyond prison walls.

She missed him desperately.

Before she could cry over that stupidity, Jack's head popped back over the edge again.

"Got the phone. They programmed in the lawyer's number, so all you have to do is punch star nine."

"Clever." She dropped him a rope and hauled on the line to retrieve the attached package. "I wish I'd had this guy the first time around. He's good."

Jack nodded. "Yeah. He's already got half the crowd convinced you were railroaded. Of course, he's also said stupidity shouldn't be worth federal prison time."

Cleo laughed. "I definitely like this guy." She dialed star nine.

The lawyer roared her name into the receiver. She could see him gesticulating below as Jack backed down the ladder.

"Are you all right up there, young lady?"

Young lady. Only a Southern lawyer would call her that. She leaned back against the steeple and watched the last of the sun's rays reflecting off the clouds on the horizon. The ocean looked peaceful today. Pity she'd never had time to add a widow's walk to her roof. She kind of liked the scenery from this height.

"Doing fine. And yourself?" she asked politely. One did not get straight to the point with Southerners, she'd learned.

"I'm having a fine old time. I'll thank your friend for the opportunity when he arrives. Last I talked with him, he'd run into a little trouble, and had a few errands to run."

"Trouble?" she asked. He *was* talking about Jared, wasn't he? She hoped he hadn't run into any more peacocks.

Being a lawyer, he didn't reply but bellowed onward. "The judge is a tad hostile to our case, seeing as how he's had this crowd outside his courtroom all day, but my assistant is thorough. He'll have you released from custody shortly."

"I'm not in custody," Cleo reminded him. She'd hate to think of Jared turned over in some ditch again.

"Why, of course you're in custody, dear lady! They have you unjustly imprisoned on their roof as we speak. I intend to have your case overturned, your name cleared, and the federal officers out of your life before this is over."

"Yeah, and my name is Jesus Christ. Look, I just want them to go after Linda and her boyfriend before anyone else gets hurt. Has anyone arranged bail for Gene?"

"We've arranged to have the child remanded to the custody of Social Services. The arrest warrant has been served on the molester in Charleston, where he was hiding. The mother has been picked up on a variety of charges ranging from welfare fraud to persistent drug violations. You are not to worry, ma'am. I shall see justice served if I must take the law into my bare hands."

Reflecting that good Southern lawyers had seen the insides of too many Baptist churches, Cleo rubbed her sunburned nose and tried to feel triumph. Mostly, she felt an urgent need for a toilet.

"I appreciate that, Mr. . . ." She didn't even know the name of her lawyer. Where the hell had Jared found him?

"Daniels, ma'am, Amos Daniels, at your service. You just hold on tight, and we'll have you off there in no time at all."

She wasn't at all certain she wanted to climb down to the shattered remains of her life. Where would she go now? Everybody on the whole East Coast would know her name. She'd never live this down, even if the crazy lawyer could find some way of keeping her out of jail. And after embarrassing him totally like this, Jared probably wouldn't even speak to her.

That path caused too much pain to travel, so she sought a better-known one.

Would they let her keep Matty?

She'd been terrified to ask, and she didn't know how to pray. Balling up the McDonald's bag, Cleo flung it over the roof's edge to the shouting crowd below. She couldn't hear what they were saying, but they were becoming right boisterous. Propping her elbows on her knees, she rested her chin in her hands and tried not to think at all. The sky was turning a lovely pink. It would be too dark to work on the clock shortly.

The shouts continued, and Cleo glanced down again. Standing on a makeshift platform, the overweight lawyer was speaking with someone considerably better proportioned. The fading daylight prevented seeing more, and she returned to staring at the sky. She lacked the energy even to wonder if the growing crowd intended to egg or lynch her. It was past the supper hour, she calculated, and this was better entertainment than TV news.

The fire-truck ladder wobbled again. Maybe Jack had brought dessert. A good Häagen-Dazs would be nice. A bathroom would be nicer.

"I brought some fireworks."

She must be hallucinating. Cautiously turning her head, Cleo gazed at the top of the ladder. In the fading light, she could see the white of the paper sack easier than the man holding it. She didn't have to see the man holding it. She could feel his vibrations all the way up here. Jared. An unfamiliar excitement lurched in the vicinity of her heart.

Obviously hallucinating. "Got a match?" she asked laconically, returning to staring at the skyline. She used to talk to hallucinations, but she was a bit out of practice. She was starting to shake all over. The rope ladder fell from her hands, and she didn't attempt to catch it.

"Yep." The ladder instantly tensed with a heavy weight. "Although I have to admit, you've topped any prank I ever dreamed of. The jock's locker explosion pales in comparison."

"Pity we didn't attend the same school. I would have gone for the gym coach as well, but it would have involved file cabinets and not lockers." She glanced down, unable to prevent her heart from crawling up to her throat and lodging there as Jared's thick sable hair moved closer.

"You'll have to give me a hand with these things. Mine seem to be otherwise occupied." He clung to the ropes several rungs below her and shifted to hand up the sack.

"You'll break your scrawny neck." She leaned over to take the sack so he could manage the tricky task of straddling the roofline sans benefit of the rope and chains that held her. She was amazed that she could speak at all. Even if he was an apparition, he was the most beautiful sight she'd ever seen. Tears sprang to her eyes as he grinned at her. Damn, but she loved that goofy grin too well. No one ever grinned at her.

"But you gotta admit, if I've got to go, this would be the most appropriate way." He dug a pack of matches out of his pocket.

She stared at him in astonishment. "You mean it? You mean there really are fireworks?"

"Of course. Why would I make up something like that?" He leaned over and appropriated the bag. "You're not the only one who can think like a child. Most of us just don't act on it. And I have good reason for celebrating."

She looked at him dubiously. "Such as?"

A wicked grin bared gleaming white teeth through the dusk. "The phones on the island are working again. Kismet has Gene's palm computer. She e-mailed me from your place. She's fine. She faked The Perv out, big time."

Cleo choked on a sob. Tears spilled down her cheeks, and she wanted to reach over and hug him in joy and relief, but the chain at her waist prevented immediate action. She couldn't summon a suitable reply, and speechless, she merely rubbed her eyes.

He shrugged at her silence and dug a large cardboard tube with a wick from the sack, then handed her the matches. "Want to do the honors?"

Why not? It was about the only thing that made sense of this day.

With joy, relief, and fear coursing through her, Cleo struck the match, leaned over, and carefully applied it to the fuse he held.

With a throw that would have made a baseball pitcher proud, Jared flung the firework toward the bay. Together, they watched the night sky erupt in a shimmering shower of rainbow stars.

The crowd below cheered as one by one the tubes of colorful gunpowder exploded from the courthouse roof. For the first time in her life, Cleo celebrated hope in company with the rest of the world.

⚞ THIRTY-ONE ⚟

"Climbing on roofs isn't the way mature adults handle problems," Axell said wearily, wiping his eyes with the heels of his hands as he sprawled in the ramshackle wicker chair. Jared had brought Cleo home after the fireworks display, to find Axell waiting for them. He should have known Cleo's sister would insist on reinforcements.

"So sue me." Hugging her knees, Cleo nearly disappeared into the corner of the couch. A single lamp illuminated little more than her bare feet with their curled-up toes.

Jared thought he recognized a resemblance to Kismet's turtle act in her body language. After the scene she'd created, she ought to be accustomed to being a target. If he was too rattled to think clearly right now, he supposed she had to be in worse shape. Without asking permission, he lifted her off the cushion and hauled her into his lap. She didn't struggle but curled up beneath his chin, her head warm against his chest. That behavior frightened the hell out of him, but he wouldn't let her brother-in-law know that.

"Give it a rest, Axell. Does the lawyer really think he can keep Cleo out of jail? If not, I'm liable to act just as childishly."

"Why does this not surprise me?" Axell slumped in the chair and glared at both of them. "I should have let Maya come down here, except I figured she'd join Cleo on the roof and blow bubbles, and my heart couldn't stand the shock."

Jared could sympathize, but not right now. The shoulder of his shirt was growing damp where Cleo's tears soaked into it. She hated for people to see her cry, so he pretended to ignore her temporary relapse. He hadn't sat on a roof all day, defending helpless kids, so he had strength enough for both of them. "We can discuss womanly quirks some other time. First I need to know if I should be booking tickets to Venezuela."

Axell snorted. "Now there's an idea, but no, don't do it for my sake. Amos could talk the sun into exchanging places with the moon if he applied his mind to it, but since heavenly bodies don't pay his rates, he'll plead Cleo's case. It's your money. If it were me, I'd still let her cool her temper in jail a while, even if she has a respectable argument."

Cleo twitched in his arms, but Jared held her down. Fortunately, she was too emotionally drained to argue, and she just leaned her head against his shoulder instead.

"Cleo was railroaded the first time," Jared insisted. "I won't let this happen again. If she's definitely not going to jail anytime soon, then our next priority is the kids. Kismet won't come out of hiding until she knows she's safe. What do we have to do to get them into a good home?"

"Marry Cleo and adopt them," Axell offered cynically. "No one else will take in wild teenagers, one of whom has been charged with possession with intent to sell, I might add."

Cleo lifted her head and glared at her brother-in-law. "Yeah, like they'll let me adopt when I've just blown my chance to get my own kid back. That's gonna happen. Go home to Maya, Axell. Her insanity is catching, but at least it's legal."

"Teach her gratitude, will you? Respect and politeness is too much to ask." Axell hauled himself out of the tottering chair.

"I appreciate what you did today," Jared offered.

Axell smiled wearily. "It was all your idea. All I did was hire what you wanted. And I was joking earlier. I'll help with the legal fees. She's family, and if the feds gave her a raw deal, we need to call them on it."

"I'm still in the room," Cleo announced edgily. "I can pay my own damn bills. If you really want to be helpful, hire a hit man to take out Linda and friend."

"Oh, that's good, Cleo. The feds will like to hear that." Jared dropped her back on the couch and stood to see Axell out. "There's room here, if you need some sleep before driving back."

Axell shook his head. "I brought one of the kids from the bar with me. He can drive. Thanks for the offer, though. It gives me hope that at least one of you might be civilized. That fireworks display left doubts."

Jared shrugged. "It gave people something to talk about while we sneaked down. I had a great getaway planned if the lawyer hadn't said he had Cleo's bond in hand."

"I don't want to hear it." Shaking his head, Axell let himself out.

As the door closed, Cleo returned to hugging her knees. "Where is Kismet?" she demanded.

"Safe. You don't need to know more tonight." Jared pried her hand loose from her knees and dragged her upright. "Go take a shower and hop in bed. I'm too rattled to yell at you, so I'll wait until morning."

"You have no right to yell at me, McCloud." She planted her hands on her hips and glared at him. "This is my life, and I'll live it as I choose."

"Yeah, right, without any thought to those who love you. I know." Exhausted from too many rampant emotions for one day, Jared didn't give his next action a second thought. He grabbed Cleo's waist, heaved her over his shoulder, and carried her, kicking dangerously near his crotch and pounding his back with her fists, to the shower, where he proceeded to strip off her clothes.

"I won't be treated like a recalcitrant child, you lummox," she shouted as he dragged her shirt over her head and threw it on the floor.

He ignored her protest and ripped open her button-fly jeans. She grabbed his shoulders before he could tip her over trying to pull them off.

"I can get them off myself! Go away. Leave me alone."

"I'll leave you alone once you get in bed." He let her finish stepping out of her jeans while he flipped on the faucet handles. Adjusting the temperature, he lifted her into the tub as soon as she was bare. He told himself he wouldn't take advantage of her when she was dazed and vulnerable, but damn, all that naked female flesh in his arms felt good. He ought to be too tired to care.

As soon as the water hit Cleo, he began stripping off his own clothes. He could be strong and resist temptation, but only so much of it.

Cleo gasped and crossed her arms over her soapy breasts as Jared climbed into the shower with her. Her gaze instantly dropped to the evidence of his arousal, and she glared at him. "I don't go to bed with bullies."

"I'm not a bully. I'm just at a disadvantage because I'm male and can't hide what I'm feeling like you do. That doesn't mean I have to act on it." He reached for the soap and began lathering his chest. "I like your double-headed shower. Planning on holding any orgies?"

"I like water and space," she grumbled, grabbing her soap-soaked scrubby and scouring the day's horrors from her skin, if not her soul. It might be the last time she showered without a roomful of women around.

She ought to turn her back on him, but she couldn't if her life depended on it, and it wasn't just admiration for those nicely proportioned muscles. He'd not used his strength to harm, but to help. He'd come back for her, even though she'd thrown a fit and made a scene and could easily end up in jail for a few more years. If he'd smacked her around or walked out on her, she'd understand and react accordingly. As it was, she didn't know how to behave.

"Want me to wash your back?" he asked with a hint of wryness as his erection grew harder under her admiring stare.

Oh, hell. There was only so much self-denial she could manage in one day. Deciding she'd had enough thinking, she took her scrubby to his chest, creating soap sculptures in his chest hairs, massaging tense muscles, closing in on his "disadvantage."

"You scared me to death out there," he whispered, grabbing her waist and hauling her to her toes so he could kiss her.

Hungrily, she took his kiss, let his excess of energy pour into her depleted reserves, and his outpouring of passion revive her long-dead soul. She clung to his slippery shoulders, and pressed skin to skin as his mouth plundered and claimed, and she relinquished all control to his demands. Newly awakening emotions left her helpless and weak as a newborn.

She might come to like this business of trusting someone else to occasionally take command of her insane life. She gasped, then sighed in ecstasy as Jared massaged her soapy breasts with gentleness, arousing the nipples until her entire being concentrated on the need for joining. His plundering tongue wasn't enough any longer. Need drove her.

Jerking away from the captivity of drugging kisses, she followed the cascading water down his chest, nipping at his flat brown nipples until he grabbed her hair and tried to drag her up. She wasn't having any more of his commands. It was her turn.

She sank to her knees and committed her own act of possession as the shower pounded on her hair, and Jared groaned in protest above her. Satisfied she had him where she wanted, she stood up again, grabbed the shower handle behind him, and placed one foot on the seat molded into the shower wall.

He wasn't slow; she'd give him that. Grabbing her buttocks firmly in his artist's long hands, he took her invitation and lifted her into place, driving deep until she had to wrap her other leg around his hip to hold on.

"It's not about control, Cleo," he muttered through clenched teeth, abruptly stepping out of the shower with her still attached, shutting off the water with his toes. "It's about accepting and sharing." He caught up a heavy bath towel and wrapped it awkwardly around her back as he carried her across the hall to the bedroom.

She didn't care what the hell it was about as long as he satisfied the need spiraling higher with his every movement. Just holding in one place was driving her crazy, and her inner muscles frantically gripped him, trying to force the rhythm they required. She understood the physical far more than the emotion behind it.

She groaned a protest as he dropped her on the bed, but he covered her before she had time to grow cold, and entered her deep enough to draw a cry of anguish and satisfaction from somewhere in her soul.

Here was the drug she'd needed all those years ago, the peaking excitement, the thrumming of life, the rhythm of inner music she'd sought in all the wrong places. She'd thought it denied to her, but he offered everything her lonely heart desired, with no price tags attached. Heaven couldn't be sweeter, and he took her heavenward again and again, producing convulsions of joy and the elusive oblivion that made the world go away with these few moments of bliss.

As Jared finally lost control and took that same release, she hugged his shuddering shoulders and let pleasure drain the tension away.

"It has to be love, Cleo," she heard him mutter as she slipped down the path to sleep. "My heart aches."

So did hers. Another worry she would put off until tomorrow.

Lying on the rumpled sheets with the late-morning sun already high above her bedroom windows, Cleo let the delicious smell of frying bacon and fresh coffee waft around her while she stared at the ceiling, trying to absorb this odd sensation of peace. She had no right to feel peaceful. She was in danger of losing Matty, returning to jail, going broke, and never knowing what happened to the kids.

But Jared had taught her the dangerous appeal of sharing her troubles as well as her pleasure. The cliché that two heads were better than one almost made sense while lying here recalling the night's physical excesses through the various aches and soreness of her body. They'd both lost their heads, if she wanted to be realistic about this, but hunger prevented logic, she concluded.

Jared appeared in the doorway looking as rumpled as the sheets but so sexy with his day's growth of beard and his hair down in his eyes that she smiled without thinking. The tray in his hands might have had some influence as well.

His jeans rode low on his lean hips, and he hadn't bothered donning his dirty shirt, so she could admire all that tanned, muscled leanness in the light of day. "Hi," she said a trifle warily since he didn't smile back.

He rested one knee on the bed as he adjusted the tray in the middle of the mattress as if it were the most important task in his life right now.

He was supposed to be creating a screenplay, not baby-sitting her.

She sat up, pulling the sheet with her. She'd let too many fantasies dance through her head. The world had gone away last night, but it was back full force this morning. "If you start yelling, I'll hurl coffee at you," she warned.

He smiled then, a curling of one corner of his mouth and not the full white-toothed grin that could bring her to her knees. "That's the Cleo I know and love. Eat something. It improves your humor."

Satisfied the tray was stable, he sat cross-legged on the other side of it and drank deeply from his mug of coffee.

She watched the muscles of his throat work as he swallowed and wondered what it would be like to share this intimacy with a man on a daily basis. She'd never known security in her life. She longed for it, but not at the sacrifice of other lives.

She sipped her coffee and nibbled at a slice of bacon as she waited to hear whatever wonders swirled in his brain now. The way his mind worked excited her as much as the way his body felt inside hers. She thought that might be a lethal combination.

"Carbohydrates." He pointed at the toast. "Raise the blood sugar."

Obediently, she tore off a corner of buttered toast. She didn't have to be told to eat, but if it satisfied his need to command, fine by her.

"You don't have to baby me," she said, wiping the butter from her lips with the back of her hand. "I'm perfectly capable of facing the consequences on my own. You need to be working."

"I'll work when I'm ready." Stubbornly, he wrapped a fried egg and a piece of bacon into a slice of toast and bit into it.

"All right, then remind me of the order of today's events. Do I report to the sheriff's office, the courthouse, or call a real-estate agent to sell everything I own so I can slip away in the middle of the night?"

"We'll let them figure it out when they're ready. Our friend Amos is keeping the law busy for now." He sipped his coffee, then eyed her askance. "Unless you have some place to go, I wouldn't recommend the real-estate company just yet."

Her stomach tightened, and she looked away. "I'm not rich. I need to work, and I don't imagine business will be booming anytime soon. I can't think of too many places that will accept a crazy ex-felon with open arms."

"You'd be surprised." He didn't sound concerned. "I think we need to concentrate on doing something about the kids."

Well, at least that gave her something positive to think about. "Social Services has them, I assume?"

"Gene was remanded into their care, yeah. Kismet's holding out, but she can't do it for long. I didn't connect with their caseworker yesterday. Guess that's a starting place."

She nodded. His tension upped her level of anxiety. "I can handle that, if you have some way of reaching Kismet. I don't know if the caseworker will let me see them once they're in custody."

"Probably best if you don't until the law straightens out Gene's story. He's got to be pretty confused by now."

"I'm not blaming him for whatever he said. He didn't know what would happen, and he didn't want his mother going to jail."

Jared nodded and looked past her to the window. "I'm going to ask the lawyer if I can adopt them. It's a long shot, but I can't abandon them to the system you described."

If she'd doubted what she felt about this man before, she didn't any longer. She wouldn't apply fancy names to the emotion welling inside her and threatening to spill over into tears, but she didn't think she'd ever feel this way again, not with any other man. She wouldn't destroy him by telling him that, though.

"Even should their mother relinquish her rights, that's asking a lot," she said cautiously. "You don't know anything about raising kids, and you've got the kind of life that doesn't adapt well to teenagers."

"I know. I've been giving it some thought, but I figure I'll take this one step at a time."

The look he gave her curled her toes. She didn't want to know the words behind that look. She couldn't handle them right now. "So I'm supposed to sit here and wait to see if the law comes to haul me off in chains, and leave the kids up to you?"

"Yep." He finished his coffee. "You had your day in the sun. Now it's my turn."

Blithely, he unfolded from the bed and wandered off.

Cleo couldn't decide whether his attitude was worth getting angry over. He was depressingly right, and she couldn't think of any immediate solution.

Finishing her food, she heard him go out to the car to find his duffel, listened to him shower, and waited anxiously until he returned to the doorway.

"I'm going out," he said. "Don't leave. I'll call you to see what you've found out from Social Services after I leave the lawyer's office."

"All right." She'd learned a modicum of caution over the years. She used it wisely now. One temper tantrum a decade was enough for her. Until yesterday, she hadn't thrown a proper fit since the time her ex had knocked her against the wall and she'd run away across the country. She really didn't want to repeat the experience.

"I'll be back," Jared reminded her, before striding off.

She believed him this time. Picking up the newspaper he'd left beside the breakfast tray, she turned to the comics.

The teenage nerd in *Scapegrace* attending a party where marijuana was being smoked wasn't funny, even if the kid fell into a pool and drowned a teddy bear in his frantic effort to escape. The final panel showed Emergency Services arriving to rescue him while all his socialite friends fled.

If Jared was putting himself in the place of his teenage character, the symbolism was too painful to consider, even if the strip had been drawn weeks ago.

❧ **THIRTY-TWO** ❧

"They done tole me not to say nothin' to nobody."
Gene crossed his arms and stuck out a defiant lip.

With Liz's permission, Jared had cornered the boy at
school. The counselor had sacrificed her office so they
could speak privately.

"You send Cleo up the river, and I'm coming after
your scrawny hide," Jared warned. "She understands,
but I won't. You can lie to the law and lie to yourself but
you can't lie to me. Cleo didn't give you those drugs. I
figure Lonnie the Pervert for that one. What do you think
will happen if he gets out before Cleo does? Who do you
want to see out there on the streets with Kismet, Cleo or
the Perv?"

"Ain't no difference to me," Gene responded sullenly.
"They busted me, and I'm runnin' before they put me behind any bars."

Jared rubbed his hand through his hair and tried to
put this in terminology a terrified kid could understand.
"I've hired the best lawyer in the state. He says even if
you *knowingly* possessed drugs with intent to sell, they
can't put you behind bars for a first offense. They're has-
sling you if they say otherwise."

Buoyed by the first sign of interest the boy had shown,
Jared shoved the door open a little wider. "If a lawyer
can prove you didn't know you were carrying an illegal

substance, you'll walk. You'll need Cleo's cooperation as a character witness, and mine, possibly, but he thinks he can pull it off if you tell him the truth."

He waited tensely as the boy pondered the pros and cons. The truth would incriminate either his mother or his mother's boyfriend, undoubtedly. It was tough asking a kid to throw his mother in jail. Clenching his hands into fists and trying not to throttle the kid, Jared gave him time to think.

Gene looked up at him through narrowed lashes. "What happens to me and Kis if I tell the truth? Cleo ain't gonna let me stay with her anymore."

"Cleo would take you both in a minute if the case-workers would let her. But I'm going to be honest with you, it doesn't look as if they will. I'm trying my best to get you and Kismet a good place to stay, but you'll have to trust me on that one."

"Kis ain't gonna like it in that home." Gene crossed his arms so tightly his shoulders drew inward. "She gonna lose it if they make her stay."

Jared wanted to hug those sturdy shoulders and tell the kid he'd make all his troubles go away, but the lawyer had told him already that as a single man, he didn't have a chance in hell of adopting them, even if Linda signed her rights away. And marrying a convicted felon would demolish all hope. He was still furious and looking for a way out, but he couldn't do everything at once. He needed Cleo's name cleared first.

He'd already called his agent and told him to forget the screenplay. He could hear George's screams of rage and despair still, but Cleo's cries were more powerful, and these kids more important. So, if George didn't want his other idea, he'd wash dishes for a living. He had no business going to Hollywood when he'd finally found a place where he was needed, and where he needed to be.

"Kismet will like it less if Lonnie comes after her," he told Gene. "We need to put him away for a long time. Then we'll have time to figure out what to do. Cleo will help. I can promise that much. But you've got to help her first."

Gene struggled a little more, wiping anxiously at moisture in his eyes and fidgeting, looking away from Jared to the crowded bulletin board in the counselor's office. "What about Mama?"

Well, here it was, sink or swim time. "She needs to get some help. She can't fight that stuff on her own anymore, do you understand?"

"I guess." Gene continued staring at the bulletin board.

Jared knew he understood. The boy had grown up far too early. It was even worse that he had to worry about his mother and older sister when they should be looking after him. Still, with the right support, he could make it in life. Obstacles could be scaled.

"If she gets clean, they'll probably let her go in a few months. But they can send Cleo up for years. Is that fair?"

"No," the boy whispered.

He'd pushed hard enough for now. Finally giving in to the urge, Jared hugged him. "I'm trusting you to do what's right. Now, you'll have to trust me to return the favor, okay?"

The boy nodded uncertainly. He'd never been given any reason to trust anyone. Jared understood that. He could only hope the kid's innate character would surface and give him strength.

Cleo had the same problem with trust. That she had finally given in and trusted him to handle this gave him reason to hope.

"I'll tell Cleo you're looking good." Jared walked out,

leaving Gene to talk to the school counselor or not, as he wished.

Cleo had looked at him with such hero worship in her normally cynical eyes, she had him believing he could leap tall buildings. Better yet, she had him believing what he wanted to do was more important than what others wanted him to do. His family and his agent and everyone else in his former life would react in horror at his abandoning his lucrative film contract to work on an experimental project that might never sell. Cleo would simply tell him to do what he thought best. She accepted that he had enough sense and intelligence to do what was best for him—and for her, although he didn't think she realized her part in his plans yet.

Feeling two tons lighter for being rid of a screenplay that would have stunk as badly as the television show once the committee of rewriters and producers sucked the blood out of it, Jared swung the Jeep into traffic and headed out to pick up Kismet. He wouldn't try using e-mail to persuade her that a group home was safe. That would require a personal visit. She hadn't said where she was hiding, but he was fairly confident she was on the island, dividing time between unoccupied houses. He hadn't received e-mail from her since Cleo returned home, which meant she was staying somewhere without electricity or phone. That pretty much narrowed it to her mother's or the wrecked beach house.

First, though, he'd better visit Marta. Cleo's livelihood might be the only one they had if his strip syndication bellied up. Grinning at the thought of relying on someone else for support, Jared swung down the usually empty street where the hardware store was located.

To his astonishment, traffic blocked the lanes as cars maneuvered into the few parking spaces at the curb. The public parking lot was packed. Pedestrians gathered beneath the overhanging oaks to chat in the shade. Others waved to neighbors as they headed down the street—to the hardware store.

Jared sat in the traffic and stared, a growing grin of elation tugging his mouth as he realized the job Marta had done. He had to fetch Cleo for this. Every person she had ever helped and apparently every member of their families, no matter how distant the connection, had arrived to show their support. He recognized teachers from the school walking out with full sacks. A trio of firemen carried out a ladder, and even the sheriff stood talking to one of his deputies, a sack from Cleo's store in his hand.

It was going to be all right, his heart sang as he drove past the store and on toward the island. Everything would be all right. He just needed Cleo to believe it.

Cleo would believe concrete evidence. Whistling, Jared did an abrupt U-turn. No one honked in rage. Not here. This wasn't New York or Miami. This was Hometown America, a place where kids could grow up decent. His kids, he hoped.

The jewelry store didn't have a large selection, but Cleo wouldn't know the difference between a three-karat diamond or zirconia. Or care. Cleo simply needed proof that he wasn't a transient in her life.

Tucking the prettiest ring he could find into his pocket, one that included an emerald to match her eyes, Jared sauntered back to the Jeep, fully confident that life was seeing things his way for a change. A few obstacles to perfection remained, but he'd find a way to remove them now that he didn't need to worry about what anyone thought but himself. And Cleo. He prayed Cleo would understand.

Too high on life to pass by Cleo's house without stopping, Jared halted in the drive on the way to the beach. Kismet might come out more willingly if she saw Cleo.

The kid hadn't even seen the search for her. She'd been sleeping. Teenagers! If he had Gene and Kismet around, he could keep *Scapegrace* going based on their antics alone.

Cleo flung open the door as if she'd been waiting for him. Barefoot, clad in a green, silky feminine shirt that barely concealed her charms, wearing shorts so short they were probably illegal, she crossed her arms and viewed him suspiciously.

"You're grinning like you've just won the thirty-three-million-dollar lottery. What have you done?"

"I like the new you." He caught her waist and kissed her. She wore no bra beneath the piece of nothing, and he couldn't resist the opportunity it offered. She wouldn't have worn that shirt if she hadn't wanted him to touch. She looked like a water sprite with the sun glinting off the auburn of her still-damp hair, and with those glorious legs tempting him from beneath a scrap of denim. "No Burt to greet me?" he asked tauntingly when they came up for air.

"He's temporarily retired." She tugged backward and narrowed her eyes. "What have you been up to?"

She didn't leave his arms, didn't spit in his face, and her fingers were doing enticing things to his chest that he didn't have time to explore. Capturing them with his palm, he kissed her nose. "Working on the future. Is there some way we can approach the beach house without being seen?"

Her eyes lit. "Kismet? Surely not."

"I left all my drawing stuff there. Where else?"

Pulling away, she dashed inside the house, yelling behind her, "Let me get my shoes. I'll find a way."

Well, at least Cleo wasn't so stubborn as to believe Kismet would be better off in a wrecked house than a group home. Now, if he could convince her to let a man in her life again, real progress would be forthcoming.

Wearing an old pair of tennis shoes, Cleo led him out the back door and down a tangled path through her yard. The hurricane had done its work here, as everywhere. Trees torn up by the roots still littered the ground. If she would let him, he could hire landscapers. If he sold his Miami place, he'd have plenty enough to do whatever she wanted. If he could keep his strip going, he could teach her to live in luxury.

Contemplating a future with Cleo first and foremost in it, Jared followed her trail under live oaks and Spanish moss, through mosquitoes and lashing branches without a word of complaint. He was still a little dizzy at all the prospects ahead. He wasn't much for planning, so he'd never contemplated sharing his life to the extent that Cleo and her son would demand. He'd had difficulty envisioning Hollywood glamour and had considered it a joke he'd enjoy for the sake of his family. But he could easily see living here with the beach a short walk away and Cleo's crazy humor to keep him on his toes.

They approached the house stealthily from the back. Someone had boarded all of the downstairs windows, so if Kismet was here, she couldn't see them.

"You go around front," he ordered. "I figure she's been using the back door; it's not blocked. If she has an escape route in the front, you can catch her there."

Cleo nodded—without argument, he noted. He liked being thought competent for a change.

He heard Cleo ripping off one of the boards barring a front window. The front door would still be blocked by sand. He waited for the back door to fly open, but either Kismet wasn't here, or she wasn't running.

Cleo's cries of joy and delight set him jogging around

to the ocean side. Despite his confidence that he'd
guessed right, he breathed a sigh of relief.

Kismet was curled up and crying in Cleo's arms when
Jared arrived. He'd never seen her hug the kids before, and
he stood back and admired the sight. She was coming out
of her shell. She was already a different woman from the
one who'd all but met him with a shotgun that first day.

Now that he knew she could live here in confidence
with no one to scorn her, he suffered a moment's niggling
doubt about whether she would need him anymore, but
he shoved the doubt aside. What they had together went
beyond that kind of need. He simply had to make her see
his way was the right way.

The beaming smile she sent him reaffirmed his belief
that all was well.

"It's all right, Kis." Cleo hugged the crying teenager
one more time. "It's not jail. They let you use the phone.
You can call me anytime." She had difficulty fighting
back her own tears as the caseworker waited patiently
for them to part. "You scared us all to death that last
time. You don't want to put us through it again, do
you?"

Kismet shook her unruly curls against Cleo's shoulder.
"No, ma'am. Is Gene gonna be okay?"

That was something solid Cleo could grasp instead of
this welling of anguish inside. "We'll make it okay. You
don't want him having to worry about you right now, do
you?"

Kismet shook her head again and let the caseworker
lead her away. Cleo gulped back a sob. She despised as-
signing the child to the fate she and Maya had suffered.
She hated herself for not being in a position to stop it.

Hiding her moist eyes and reddening nose as they left
the government offices, Cleo stared out the window

while Jared started the car. Maybe if she asked around, she could find someone willing to take in the kids and give them a decent home. They needed encouragement and routine and support. She knew what they needed better than anyone, but she was considered unfit and Linda wasn't. The world was insane.

Jared's quiet mantle of sympathy gave her space to pull herself together. A man like that was so rare, she figured he had to be some kind of guardian angel sent from above. She so desperately wanted to love him that she choked on the need. But she wasn't whole enough yet. She still couldn't go into his world without stumbling. As recent events proved, she could barely handle the small world she'd carved for herself.

"Got something you might like to see," he said quietly, turning down the street to the store.

Cleo blinked back to the moment, rubbed her eyes, and politely looked ahead. The street seemed awfully crowded for the middle of a weekday. "Are they having a fair or something? I don't remember the Chamber mentioning it."

"Nope. Keep looking. I won't stop, but I thought you ought to see what your neighbors think of you."

Yeah, right. They thought her an insane idiot and an ex-con. Had they posted signs to that effect?

She frowned as she noted the party atmosphere of people gathering to chat. Almost everyone had a plastic sack from her store. Was Marta giving the inventory away? That almost made a sick kind of sense.

Someone looked up, saw the Jeep, and waved. Others followed suit. She sent Jared a suspicious look. "What have you done now? Bought a new school?"

He chuckled dryly. "You never give up, do you? Want me to stop so you can ask?"

She saw a reporter from the weekly newspaper scribbling notes as he talked to one of Marta's cousins, and shook her head. "No, I don't think so. My picture will be on page one as it is. I'd rather not provide the entire paper."

He shot her a look of exasperation, removed the cell phone from its holder, and handed it to her. "Call Marta."

Looking at the stern planes of his angular jaw, she gulped, and took the phone. She trusted this man not to hurt her. She dialed.

"Cleo's Hardware," a bright voice answered. Not Marta, but one of the many women who assisted during peak seasons. This wasn't Christmas. This wasn't even a weekend.

"This is Cleo. Is Marta around?" she asked warily.

"Sure, Cleo. I'll get her. Have you seen the turnout here? The registers are rocking off the counter." She set the phone aside before Cleo could respond.

Jared maneuvered around a car attempting to parallel park and slowly followed traffic past the store. Cleo could see a line of customers through her plate-glass window.

"Hey, Cleo," Marta answered cheerfully. "We've got a full house here. When you coming in? We'll need an express order to restock the shelves before the weekend."

"What the hell is going on?" Cleo demanded. "I'm out here stuck in traffic and the place is swarming."

"Jared didn't tell you? That man's a keeper, girl. Don't you worry about a thing. We have orders coming in that will keep us busy right through December."

Staring blankly out the window, Cleo nodded, said something inane, and hung up the phone. She didn't dare meet Jared's eyes but watched his long, talented fingers skillfully steering the wheel. "What did you do?" she asked very, very carefully.

She could almost hear his surprise.

"Me? Not a thing. If anyone did anything, Marta did. I just gave her a few words of encouragement, and she apparently got on the phone and called every relative in two counties. How many husbands has she had, anyway? And I lost track of the brothers and sisters somewhere after the twelfth stepbrother and thirteenth half sister on her mother's side." He turned and gave her a significant look. "And then she must have started on all the people you've helped in the year you've been here."

Cleo gulped, twined her fingers together, and let the tears pour down her face.

⁂ THIRTY-THREE ⁂

"Shall I take you out somewhere fancy to eat?" Jared asked as he helped her from the Jeep in front of the house, politely ignoring her tears. "I could take you into Charleston where no one knows us."

Cleo didn't know how to answer that. She didn't know much of anything just yet. She needed to recover her equilibrium and find the shield she used to hide intrusive emotions, the one she needed to cover up her desperate desire to be folded into comforting arms and loved.

He'd said he loved her. The panic and outright terror of that much responsibility clawed at her. She simply couldn't carry a bigger load.

She shook her head. "Maya is heading down here with Matty after school. They don't believe Axell that everything is all right." Matty. If she didn't go to jail and didn't have to move, maybe they'd let her have him home on schedule?

Despite all her efforts, hope crept through every crevice and cranny in her soul. Maybe all *could* be well, for a little while. Love never lasted, but she was stronger now. When it came time for him to go, she might survive, if she had Matty back. Cautiously, she tamped the thought down for later examination, and looked up to Jared for stability. Proved the extent of her insanity if she looked to a playboy artist for stability, but she'd learned that laughing, lanky frame of his disguised muscles and a brain and compassion.

At her look, he ran his fingers through her hair and quirked his eyebrows in a question she could read all too well. Love poured through the broken dam of her heart, and her smile shook a little.

"Don't you have work to do?" There, she was returning to normal a little bit. She'd be back in the swing of it shortly.

His gaze lingered on her face, then dropped consideringly to the highly respectable tailored shirt and khakis she'd donned for the visit to bureaucracy. "Probably a lifetime's worth," he agreed. "But I think I'll enjoy every minute of it."

Heat seeped through her breasts and up her throat. "I'm not a very profitable endeavor."

"Depends on your definition of profit." He lowered his head slowly, watching her, giving her time to run.

She didn't. With relief, she grabbed his neck, and lifted into his kiss. Sex, she understood. Or maybe not. What had passed for sex in her past was nothing like this. This was what the romance books called making love. She poured herself into the press of lips and tongue, showing him what she couldn't tell him. She prayed he understood because she couldn't sort out gratitude, joy, relief, and love in any meaningful measure. He was the life she'd never known, and what moments she could steal from his time would buoy her through a lifetime of crises.

"I think I'll buy a sailboat," he murmured against her mouth, before steering her gently toward the door, hand at the small of her back.

"Sailboat?" She halted his progress for another kiss. She needed to bank these, stack them up in her mind to be taken out and examined every time she felt lonely. He obliged willingly, cupping her breasts and stroking until she thought she'd have to have him right here on the lawn with the snakes and mosquitoes.

"I want to make love to you with the sound of surf in the background, and I have a suspicion sand and crabs would get in the way if we tried the beach." He lifted her past the steps to the porch so their lips met on an even level.

She laughed breathlessly against his mouth. "Two minds and all that. Are we getting old or just learning caution?"

"Peter Pan never grows old, but he knows better than to tangle with Captain Hook. Come along, Tink, let's tangle."

They didn't make it any farther than the wide couch cushions.

There was something to be said about the power of the male body, Cleo mused as Jared stripped off the last of his clothes, revealing the subtle musculature of long thighs supporting all that masculine studliness. She bit back a smile at her hedonism. She'd never indulged in sensuality in any form, but she thought she could learn as she reached to touch him, and he responded with an encouraging ardency.

A warm breeze drifted through the open windows. A cardinal chirruped in the branches of a wax myrtle. Sunlight stole through an opening in one of the shutters, throwing a golden path across the pine floor Cleo had lovingly polished until it shone.

Her sighs joined the cardinal's song as Jared kissed away decades of hurt and returned life where there had been none. She knew she'd have to return the favor soon, but not right this minute, with the faint scent of late honeysuckle and jasmine filtering through the air they breathed. The perfume mingled with the scents of sweat and musk as they teased each other lingeringly, neither willing to hurry.

When they could no longer deny the urgency building between them, Jared took the initiative, driving into her and taking her so high, so fast, she barely had time to catch her breath. It all burst too suddenly, in a shattering explosion of suns and stars and a deep heat within her that would keep her warm on the wintry days to come. She could hold him deep inside her in her memory for a long time. "Superman, my hero," she murmured, and he kissed her in reply. She hoped he understood.

The sun rays moved across the floor as they lay there spent and exhausted with emotion more than physical release. The world outside wasn't perfect, but it was peaceful for a change, and they let that peace seep through them.

Cleo drifted for a while, content with the heavy weight of Jared's leg across hers, his arms holding her securely. She could imagine having children with a man like this— a little girl with Jared's dark eyes and long lashes, at the very least. She didn't bother hoping, but it made a nice dream.

Eventually, they woke to the growls of their stomachs and the knowledge that Maya and Matty would arrive in a few hours. Cleo ran her hands over biceps strengthened by restless push-ups, hoping to restrain him from getting up, but Jared seemed insistent on retrieving his clothes. She let him go, and wondered how she would explain his presence in her bed tonight. She didn't think she could make him leave just because her son and sister were arriving. She didn't want to.

"This isn't the way I pictured doing this," he grumbled, pulling on his shirt, leaving it unbuttoned as he reached for his pants. "But I suppose having you naked adds an air of interest."

Propping herself on an elbow, Cleo watched him jerk his trousers over narrow hips and fumble in his pockets. Jared McCloud was one good-looking hunk of man, but she'd seen loads of handsome men. This one had something special besides the pretty-boy hair and wide shoulders and flat abdomen she adored. She'd call it intelligence, but she thought it was more than that. Understanding, perhaps. He simply understood where she'd been and accepted that without questioning. She loved him for that more than anything.

He produced a velvet jeweler's box, and she blinked in disbelief. "Payoff time?" she inquired lightly to cover her discomfiture.

He dropped onto the cushion beside her and slapped her bare rump. "I'll get even with you for that some day, but not right now. I'm too nervous to do this any other way but straight." He popped open the box.

Cleo dropped back against the pillow and stared at the shimmering ring in incredulity and shock. "You're kidding, right?"

He took a deep breath, and she watched in fascination

as his lightly furred chest swelled, probably with righteous indignation. She drew a finger down the line of hair trekking from breastbone to belt, and he exhaled.

"Believe it or not, Cleo, I'm a grown man capable of making adult decisions. I'm not kidding. I can't promise I'll be rich," he said hurriedly. "I have to pay back that Hollywood advance, my agent may dump me, and I don't know what the future has in store, but I'm confident I can make a good living if you don't require yachts and things. This may be the only time you'll see me like this, but I'm deadly serious. Marry me, please?"

She reached for her shirt and yanked it on. She didn't have the words for this. She'd never expected it. Never. Men like Jared didn't commit. They certainly didn't commit to ex-con addicts with less-than-perfect kids and a penchant for throwing really embarrassing fits, and who could still end up in jail for a few more years if the cards didn't fall her way. The future still looked far too bleak to paint a miracle into it.

Fastening a button over her breasts, Cleo eyed the ring he held as if it were a copperhead. "Jared, you don't mean this. You've just got caught up in the moment, unless you seriously think we can adopt the kids this way, and I'm not about to tie you down over those two."

She saw the anger darkening his eyes. She'd seen it once before, but he didn't frighten her. She loved him far too much to let him ruin his life. She might not have much going for her, but she was stubborn.

"I'm not an amiable idiot, dammit!" he yelled at her. "I know what I'm doing, and it's not for the kids. It's for *us.* We can see that the kids get into good foster homes until the courts decide what to do with them. I want to be here to look after them, but I don't have to marry you to do that." He didn't reach for her, but raked his spare hand through his hair and glared. "I love you, Cleo. Let down your smoke screen and admit that you love me, too."

He looked so handsome and frustrated, she was tempted to give him anything he wanted. It would be so easy to slide down that lovely road into dependency again.

But she couldn't do that to him. Blinking back the unanticipated sting of tears, Cleo stared at the window instead of the glitter of temptation.

She'd been prepared to share Jared's bed any time he asked, and to savor the memories when he left. She wasn't prepared for this, couldn't believe he'd even asked it of her.

He thought she was whole and normal. He thought she was strong enough to make him happy. Superheroes either weren't very smart, or they thought everyone as strong as they were. Or both.

Matty had always been her priority. Now it seemed she had two. Straightening her shoulders, Cleo swiped angrily at the tears rolling down her cheeks. Jared had a brilliant mind and kind soul and deserved a splendid life in the big wide world that was his for the taking. He'd sacrificed his film for her already. How many more sacrifices would it take before he realized he'd given up his soul for her? She wouldn't ask that of anybody. She certainly wouldn't ask that of the man she loved with every cell in her body.

She bit her lip as she darted one last glance at the gleaming promise of the ring. "I can't do it, Jared," she said firmly, looking away again. There, she'd been strong. For once in her life, she'd done the right thing. Steadfastly, she watched the window where she'd first seen him, while her heart shrank in misery.

Out of the corner of her eye, she saw Jared set the ring down beside her.

"You can, Cleo." Anger replaced patience in his voice.

He didn't like rejection. She'd known that. He didn't have much experience with it. He'd learn. She had confidence in him. It was herself she doubted.

"Then, I *won't*," she corrected. "I'll sleep with you. I'll rebuild the beach house for you. I won't marry you and destroy your future." She couldn't say it any plainer.

"Isn't that for me to decide?" Jared jumped restlessly to his feet and paced. "Why does everyone think I'm incapable of making my own decisions?"

"Because you don't make good ones?" she asked carefully. She hadn't wanted to hurt him, but she was treading waters she didn't know. They'd gone through a lot together, but they hadn't had time to really know each other. "Giving up success and a career you love for a loser like me doesn't show a lot of attention to detail."

Jared's arms bulged as he swung around and yanked her to her feet. For a moment, Cleo feared she'd pushed a little too far. Fury tightened the muscles over the taut planes of his cheeks, and his eyes practically danced with fire.

"Giving up money for love makes sense to me," he asserted. "Giving up stress and a committee of jerks for a woman and a real life works in my way of thinking. You just let me know when you've shed a few layers of that thick carapace of yours, Crab Cleo. I love you, and when you're ready to admit you're worth loving, you can find me. I'll wait, but I won't come looking for you this time. Understand?"

He released her, spun around, and stalked out, vibrating with male fury.

He forgot his shoes, she noted wearily as he slammed the door behind him. She figured he'd leave his shoes and all his clothes before he'd return, though.

He'd left the ring. It sparkled in a late-afternoon sunbeam.

The Jeep spun its tires in the driveway and squealed off. She just wanted to sit here and cry for a million years or so.

But she knew how to handle that feeling, too. All that glue she'd used pulling herself together over the years had some purpose.

Picking up her clothes, she went looking for a pair of jeans. She needed to start fixing up the attic if Matty was coming home.

Tears slid down her cheeks as she reached for her tool belt.

⊰ THIRTY-FOUR ⊱

December, New York

"I've been commissioned to see that you eat your supper." Tim slapped a steaming bag from a Chinese takeout in the center of a table cluttered with drawings and pages of discarded script.

"Hey, TJ." Jared glanced up from a dancing character on his computer, noted the bag, nodded, and returned to fiddling with the figure on-screen. "Didn't know you were home."

"It *is* almost Christmas," Tim said dryly. "One does what one can."

"Right. Be with you in a minute." Running his hand

through his overgrown hair, Jared growled at the unco-
operative character, hit a key, and changed the costume
to purple.

"Eat," Tim ordered, "or I'll pull the plug. I've seen your
idea of a minute, and I don't have that much patience."

"I'm working," Jared growled back. "I'll eat later.
We'll talk when I get back to the house."

"No, we won't. Mother will talk when we get back to
the house. Eat now. I brought your mail." Tim paced
back and forth across the studio floor, not restlessly, but
searching for the right cord to pull in a tangled web of
wires.

"Touch that plug and die," Jared warned, knowing his
brother's capacity for destructive action. "I don't have
this saved yet. Did the mail bring a contract for a million
dollars? Otherwise, I'm not interested."

"There's a big envelope from that podunk town in the
Carolinas."

Jared hit the "save" key. Rising from the computer,
he ignored TJ's quizzical expression as he reached for the
manila envelope instead of the food. "I sent Cleo a drafting software program," he explained, as if that meant
anything to his brother at all.

"I thought that thing with her was all over." TJ opened
the restaurant bag and poked around the cardboard
boxes, looking for his order.

Settling into an easy chair with stuffing popping from
the worn seams, Jared held the envelope warily, trying to
guess what surprise Cleo had in store for him. She never
answered his phone calls, and her taciturn replies to his
e-mail hadn't been encouraging. It took every patient cell
in his body not to pursue his earlier tactics of showing up
at her door and wearing her down. He had to have the
confidence in her that she didn't have in herself. Yet.

At least her attorney had kept in touch. The feds had

agreed to drop their case and remove all charges against Cleo in return for the lawyer dropping his suit. She was a free woman, technically. She'd sent him a cigar when Matty had been released to her. He kept it in his shirt pocket.

"Cleo has issues," he asserted, wondering if he ought to postpone opening the envelope until TJ left.

"Yeah, right, who doesn't?" TJ took one of the retro aluminum-and-vinyl dinette chairs that had collected in the studio, and using chopsticks, pried a piece of pork from the box he'd chosen. "That mean she walked instead of you?"

"She didn't *walk*." Jared grimaced as the smell of Chinese hit him. He couldn't remember when he'd last eaten. "Got any lo mein?" He grabbed the box handed to him, procrastinating over opening Cleo's envelope. "She just has this weird idea I'm some kind of superhero and too good for her, and she doesn't want to ruin my future. Like I said, she has issues."

"Yeah, she's crazy." TJ dug into his rice while organizing the chaos of papers cluttering the table. "You're thirty-two, broke, and living at home. Maybe you're the one who's crazy, and she's being polite."

Jared snickered at the idea of Cleo being polite. "I'm not broke," he protested in his own defense. "I just have all my cash invested in the future. This project will make more money than the Hollywood one ever would have. Cleo doesn't care about *money*." He knew that much. He simply wasn't certain of anything else. No one had ever called him Superman before. Finding a woman who thought him so special that she didn't deserve him had him totally flummoxed, though. How the hell did he overcome that attitude? Fail?

He had thought focusing totally on the script would help him get through these lonely months without Cleo.

It hadn't. He'd organized an entire team of animators and experienced film editors and whatnot to drive him crazy, in hopes that would drive Cleo's haunting laughter out of his head. It hadn't. He'd stayed up nights rather than sleep in his bed without her arms wrapping around him in her sleep. Remembering her tears drove him to new heights of fantasy that had his creative team believing he lived in Oz, or at the very least, La-La Land. He needed to be with her, craved the brush of her skin against his, and the taunt of her voice grounding his wilder schemes. He needed Cleo like a martini needed vodka. He couldn't be whole without her.

He kept hoping Cleo would regain her senses and let him come back.

He glanced at the envelope in his lap. He didn't think Cleo would ask him to come back in an oversized letter.

TJ was regarding him oddly, and Jared dug into his food rather than explain. Trying to explain Cleo would be akin to trying to depict the sun rising to a blind man.

"She thinks you're a superhero and doesn't care about money," TJ said solemnly, as if working through one of his theories on the origins of racial diversity. "Sounds to me like you ought to be down there on bended knee, snatching her up before someone else gets her."

Jared choked on a laugh and a mouthful of noodles. "No one *gets* Cleo," he managed to say after swallowing. He grinned again at the double entendre. "That's the whole damned problem. I can *get* any woman I want. I can *have* Cleo. That isn't the same thing as Cleo agreeing that we belong together. I'm not settling for less, and she won't settle for more. She won't be pushed, so I'm waiting for her to come around on her own."

TJ stared at him as if he'd just announced martinis were more nourishing than milk. "You're waiting for a woman to come around instead of chasing after her?"

Jared sighed and glared at the envelope. "Yeah, ironic, ain't it?" Not only ironic, but futile, he was coming to suspect. He'd hoped it would only take a week or two before Cleo realized what she'd thrown away. It had been over two damned months. Maybe he had a little higher opinion of himself than he'd realized. Maybe he ought to crawl.

Cleo would just tell him he couldn't take no for an answer and slam the door in his face.

He didn't like the sinking sensation in his stomach at that scenario. He much preferred optimism. He'd figured if he worked hard, stayed focused, and tried not to think too much about how it felt to wake up to mischievous green eyes and a lithe body that drove him insane and a wicked mind that matched his in every way . . . Kind of hard to focus thinking like that.

"You're saying you offered her *marriage*?" TJ asked in disbelief.

"Yeah. Got a problem with that?" Irritated, Jared set aside the Chinese box and tore the end off the envelope. Cleo was a stubborn brat, but she wasn't stupid. Surely she knew what they had together was special. She just needed time, that's all.

"And she *refused*?"

TJ had his own problems, Jared reflected, pulling out sheets of drawings. Maybe McClouds weren't intended for marriage. Maybe Cleo was right and he should just move in with her.

He twisted the computer-generated drawing in his hand and frowned in puzzlement, then grinned as he realized Gene had reproduced his version of a wrestling match. Not quite his sister's talent, but a warm spot burned hotter in his gut at the thought of Cleo teaching the kid how to use the program he'd sent.

The court had let Gene go, as Cleo had predicted.

They'd slapped Linda into a drug program and the kids had gone into foster care. At least Cleo's handpicked foster parents were intelligent enough to allow generous visiting privileges. Cleo had the kids as often as the foster parents did.

To hell with living together. He wanted this contrary woman to be *his*. Primitive male instinct clamored for placing his claim on her. Women simply didn't understand the concept of possession.

He'd lose what little he retained of his senses thinking she could leave him at a moment's whim. She'd taught him what he wanted was important, and he couldn't think of anything more important than hearing Cleo vow to spend her life with him. He was willing to gamble everything on the chance of winning a lifetime with her.

Forgetting TJ, he shuffled through the rest of the papers. Kismet hadn't attempted the drafting program. She'd sent colorful pencil drawings of butterflies with faces he didn't recognize—possibly her foster parents or teachers. He wished he knew. He wanted to be involved in their lives. After the vivid fullness of Cleo's cluttered world, he'd developed a loathing for the sterile shallowness of his single life.

A giant red dragon and a laughing blue clown denoted Matty's attempts at art. Cleo's son had inherited her directness, if not her complexity. Give the kid time. Jared glanced over his shoulder at the doll-sized merry-go-round of flying witches and dancing skeletons a friend had made from his sketches. He'd hoped to be down there by Christmas to give it to Matty. Perhaps he should fly down and appear on their doorstep without an invitation.

He was afraid to study the last sheet of paper in the bunch. He could tell by the intricacy of the computerized plan that Cleo had applied her stubborn brain to learning the software so she could produce it. He wondered if she filled her lonely nights with a computer, as he did. He shuffled her drawing to the top and glanced briefly at the three dimensions of her newest mechanical creature. Captain Hook.

He knew he didn't want to examine it closer, so he handed the stack to TJ and reached for his Chinese. His stomach rebelled, but he stuck the chopsticks in rather than think.

TJ chuckled at the drawing. "Looks just like you, with kind of a movie-star flair. Tom Cruise in sunglasses, I'd say."

Jared sank lower into the chair. "Tom Cruise as Captain Hook?" Maybe he'd read the message wrong.

"Nah, it's definitely you, with long curly hair and shades. Better-looking, admittedly. If that's how she sees you, then you've got her snared. All you need to do is go down and reel her in."

"You didn't happen to notice what Hook is holding, did you?" Jared covered his eyes with his palm, but nothing could make the pain disappear.

"Sure, Tinkerbell in a cage. Isn't that the story?"

"Evil Captain Hook holds Tinkerbell hostage," Jared agreed glumly. He didn't have to look closer to know whose face Tinkerbell wore.

He wondered if Captain Hook was a promotion or demotion from Peter Pan.

Either way, it wasn't an invitation to Christmas dinner.

❧ THIRTY-FIVE ❧

December, South Carolina

Waking to the sound of "Santa Claus Is Coming to Town," Cleo grumbled sleepily, curled around her pillow, and snuggled closer to a body that wasn't there.

Shit.

Two damned months, and she couldn't rid her bed of Jared's laughing presence.

Fully awake now and not wanting to be, she flipped over and glared at the ceiling. Maybe she should paint the plaster blue and ask Maya to paint rainbows. Or storm clouds. Whatever.

She'd almost finished the attic, and with winter setting in, she couldn't do much else to the house except decorate. She didn't have much experience at decorating, but she could learn, she supposed.

She'd hung a big slate board on Matty's wall so he could draw to his heart's content. He seemed happy here, although he occasionally complained of missing his cousins. Still, the school board had accepted her proposal to finance special tutors for kids who needed extra help, and Matty loved his tutor, so he was doing okay.

She'd thought that was all she needed to be happy. As usual, she was wrong.

Remembering whispered jokes and sizzling kisses in

the early dawn, and intimate breakfasts in bed, Cleo snatched off her covers and got up. Jared haunted her. She swore that man was a ghost who lurked in corners, prepared to leap out when she least expected him.

Maya had apparently shown Matty the *Scapegrace* comic in the paper and told him who drew it, so Matty demanded Cleo read it to him every morning. The nerd in the strip had taken on more heroic qualities lately, so she didn't mind, except she spent the rest of the day wondering what Jared was doing to set his leapfrogging mind down that track.

It didn't help that Gene talked about him all the time, she thought morosely, climbing into her jeans and dragging on a sweater. She and Marta had canvassed three counties looking for people willing to take in Gene and Kismet. It had been tough, but they'd found an older couple with a farm willing to give two wild kids a chance. Gene still had an attitude, but he and Jared e-mailed each other regularly, so he was cool. For now. His constant references to Jared kept the ghost alive, though.

"Mommy!" Matty burst through her bedroom door and flung his skinny arms around her legs as she put down her brush. "Is Santa comin' tomorrow?"

She ruffled his shaggy dark hair, and even that reminded her of Jared's sable locks. His impromptu hug tugged all the weak links in her heart. "Nope, not tomorrow. We don't even have a tree up yet. Want to make paper chains to go on it?"

"Yeah!" He shot back out of the room, hell-bent on doing everything at once. Not unlike a certain man she knew.

"Mommy!" Matty eagerly looked up as she strolled into the kitchen. She grimaced at the newspaper he'd spread across the table. "Jared drew Santa Claus. What does it say?"

She bent over and read the words to him. "It says, 'Gerry better get good grades at school or he'll only get lumps of coal for Christmas.' " She paraphrased the actual teenage jargon so Matty would understand better. Good thing he was too impatient to sound out the letters that jumbled so easily in his head.

Her son wrinkled his freckled nose in concern. "Santa wouldn't do that, would he?"

"It isn't really Santa, hon. Look, it's Freddie wearing a Santa suit. See, he's hiding Gerry's real present under his beard. Think maybe Jared is telling Gene he'd better study if he wants a gift this year?"

Matty lit up with excitement. "Yeah! Only here, Freddie wants the present for himself. Cool! Can we bake cookies?"

Cleo smiled mistily at the rest of the cartoon. Matty wouldn't get the joke anyway, and he'd already moved on to other things. "After we eat breakfast," she reminded him. "Get your cereal out."

She wondered if Jared's agent was pitching fits about the underlying messages in the strip lately. Responsibility, respect, and communication were a few of his favorite themes, and every prank had a consequence. In this one, Freddie ended up with the coal, and Gerry aced the test and got the present.

The strip wasn't always as funny as it had been in its early days, but it lacked the bitter edge of the past year, and she kind of liked seeing morals in comics again. Kids needed that kind of lesson.

Wondering if love made her sappy, she took down cereal bowls and let Matty pour his own. She sure as hell hoped Jared was making the best of her sacrifice, because there were nights she was so lonely even beer looked good as a method of filling these gaping wounds. If it hadn't been for Matty, she'd be a basket case by now.

Her new doorbell rang the first bars of the Hallelujah chorus, and she glanced at the kitchen clock. Ten. She'd slept late, but this was a little too early for visitors on a Saturday morning.

Of course, the steady parade of would-be archeologists, sightseers, and government officials picking at the pirate graveyard produced any number of strays lately. She'd retired Burt much too soon.

But Matty liked her giggling Tinkerbell better. It flitted past the windows in a glowing light at night, but it was pretty worthless during the day. She was almost growing used to intruders. That didn't mean she wanted that damned film company down there day and night.

"I'll get it!" Matty shouted, racing to the door ahead of her. He never walked when he could run, and he was accustomed to lots of people coming and going at his aunt's house, so he wasn't shy.

That was good. She wanted him to grow up normal and confident of his place in the world. Maya had done a fantastic job of bringing him around. Now, if she could only find a man with half Jared's kindness . . .

She stared in disbelief as Matty threw open the door, revealing the towering man filling the screen. Not completely across the room yet, she hesitated, contemplating turning and running out the back door. Then panic mode set in, and she crossed the floor in two strides.

"What is it?" she demanded, shoving the screen door open so Jared's older brother could step inside. "Is it Jared? Is he all right?"

Matty instantly retreated into anxiety as he looked up the long length of the stranger who entered. Cleo couldn't pick her son up and cuddle him anymore, but she knelt down and hugged him while TJ McCloud regarded them as if they were space aliens.

"No one's knocked him silly, or sillier, yet," TJ said

gravely, looking a little embarrassed and lifting his gaze to encompass the room instead of their huddle of fear. "I didn't mean to frighten you."

Relaxing, Cleo swept the hair off Matty's forehead and pushed him toward the kitchen. "Eat your breakfast, short stuff. This is Jared's brother Tim, and everything is fine."

Matty held his ground. He'd spent too many years protecting Cleo's broken spirits to leave her now. "Santa doesn't give coal," he told TJ adamantly, apparently naming him responsible for correcting Jared's comic strip.

Cleo smiled at her visitor's startled expression. Standing, she offered her best chair, a much sounder replacement for the old wicker. "Have a seat. Shall I bring you some coffee? It's awfully early."

"Airports keep rotten schedules." Before taking the solid rocker, he glanced out her front window. "I took a look at that skeleton bone Jared told me about. I don't think it's a pirate," he said carefully.

He'd come here to look at a skeleton? Cleo raised her eyebrows but responded in the same cautious manner as he'd used. "I keep telling them that, but the movie people think it would make great publicity."

"Movie people?" He grimaced. "That mean the beach house won't be available any longer?"

She hadn't thought about it. She had scarcely begun the repairs. If they really did film down there . . . She shook her head. "I'd rather someone convince the idiots it's a slave cemetery."

"Not unless they're white slaves," he answered gravely. Producing a videotape from his jacket pocket, he finally accepted her offer of a chair.

White slaves didn't calculate on any level. Cleo's mind slipped back to drunken Ed's stories of spies, but she couldn't cling to irrelevant thoughts while Jared's brother sat there, obviously on different business than long-lost skeletons. "Coffee?" she asked again.

"Coffee would be nice if you have some. I brought something I thought you should see."

Cleo stared at the proffered tape in bewilderment, but more than a little unnerved by his presence, she attempted her best hostess manners and didn't grab it from his hands. "Give me a minute. Cream or sugar?"

"Neither." He fell into a staring match with Matty, both exhibiting curiosity with no undercurrents of anger or fear.

Cleo could see a lot of Jared in his scientist brother, and her heart ached as she poured the coffee and returned. She thought Jared would be the kind of man who loved Christmas. Maybe his brother was the same and had decided to deliver some kind of early Christmas gift. Odd, though.

Taking a sip of the coffee, TJ nodded his appreciation, then gestured toward the video. "It didn't occur to me until I was on the plane that you might not have a VCR. Do you?"

She picked up the plastic case and slipped the tape into the machine hidden by one of Matty's towering stuffed animals. She could afford a lot more than teddy bears these days. "VCRs are a requirement for anyone with kids. Can't have them watching the garbage that passes for television." She glanced at Matty, who had settled into his favorite cross-legged position, ready to absorb any new entertainment. "It's okay for him to see?"

TJ laughed softly. "Yeah. I'm not transporting porn across state lines." He hesitated, then added carefully, "Jared doesn't know I'm here."

She'd wondered. She had a dozen questions, but it seemed easiest to punch the power button than ask.

She settled behind Matty on the floor and watched the

film flicker on. There were no opening credits. A cartoon
flared into life with a roar of trumpets and a witch rock-
eting across the screen on a purple broom tied with a big
yellow ribbon. Matty practically sighed with ecstasy,
settled his elbows on his knees, and fell into a trance.

"Jared found an animator willing to work with him,"
TJ said quietly, so as not to disturb the action on-screen.
"They've been pulling together a network of friends who
respect one another's creativity, or so he says. I don't
understand half of it."

Fascinated by the almost familiar creatures dancing
across the TV, Cleo only half listened. Jared had done this.
She recognized the style of the drawings, even though they
moved and talked instead of sitting still with word balloons
over their heads. She recognized the witch with the red
shoes, and laughed aloud as the skeleton cracked a joke.

That was definitely Jared's dry humor. A bubble of
pride swelled inside as she realized she'd done right to
send him away. He was doing splendidly without her.
This was wonderful stuff. She laughed as the knight in
shabby armor swung a wicked pizza at the wisecracking
skeleton.

"He sold his place in Miami so he could produce this
himself."

Cleo tore away from the cartoon to stare at TJ in disbelief. "I thought he *loved* living at the beach."

TJ sipped his coffee and regarded her solemnly. "He
said it was just a place and there were more important
things in life. He's living with our parents, if that tells
you anything."

Her eyes widened as she examined the horror of that
simple statement, and her bubble popped. Jared would
lose his mind living with those stifling people. What was
he, crazy?

"Mommy!" Matty shouted in excitement, bouncing

up and down and tugging at her jeans leg. "Look! That's you!"

Dazed, Cleo turned back to the action on-screen. The shabby knight had removed his visor. *Her* visor. As the character taunted the skeleton with his shallowness—a shallow skeleton, what a concept!—Cleo studied the image in puzzlement. Like all cartoon heroines, the image was young and fresh-faced and beautiful. She couldn't see anything of herself except maybe the red of her short-cropped hair. She had a mouth on her, that was certain, and Cleo smiled as the skeleton stepped back, rattling a bony hand over his nonexistent heart, complaining of being pierced to the bone. The man was good, she'd give him that.

Caught up in trying to see what Matty saw, she watched more carefully, and was transported into the story as thoroughly as her son. They both cried as a really wicked witch stole the children's magic broom so they couldn't go home. Matty shrieked at the fire-breathing dragon's appearance, and Cleo experienced a clear sense of déjà vu.

That was Kismet's dragon. That was Gene and Kismet lost in the dangerous forest.

"Porky," Matty sighed happily, pointing to the talking potbellied pig. "And Petey." Absolutely enthralled, he leaned into Cleo's embrace and let her hold him while he admired lurid imitations of his pets stalking, sauntering, and dancing across the set.

The feminine knight duly resisted involvement with a menagerie of preposterous animals, but her conscience—in the form of a nagging parrot—kept overruling her better judgment as she pulled one character after another from various disasters. The disasters tended to be stereotypical: the pig overate on magic mushrooms, the peacock let vanity lead him into a lake to better see his own image, and the children fighting over something inconsequential lost the clue that would lead them home. But they were moral tales that children could grasp while adults could laugh at the dry wit aimed at character flaws everyone recognized. It was brilliant.

The knight was a hero.

The knight was her.

Cleo could scarcely believe what she was watching, but that was her house/castle, her menagerie, her kids, her attitude. Even Matty recognized it. This was Cleo as Jared saw her.

The man was obviously demented. Grumbling, she stood and escaped to the kitchen for more coffee. TJ followed her, leaving Matty to watch the ending on his own.

"I admit, I didn't understand his infatuation," he said without prelude, offering his cup for a refill. "But when I saw that . . ." He shrugged and wandered to the table. "I saw you. I never thought of Jared as a deep thinker, but he's proved me wrong. He's not seeing you through rose-colored glasses, he's seeing your flaws as well as your strengths."

"He just has a warped view of things," she said grumpily, sitting down across from him. "I'm shabby, but I'm no knight."

"Jared talks about you constantly. Unless he's lying, you're as close to a heroine as it comes these days." TJ stretched his basketball-player legs across the pine floorboards and stared at the toes of his polished shoes. "So, why aren't the two of you together?"

She ought to be angry. He had no right to interfere.

She wanted to weep at the thought of all that brilliance trapped in the stifling environment of his parents' cold home, when he belonged on a sunny beach, chasing pelicans and laughing.

"Because he's better off without me," she mumbled. She didn't want to have to explain why.

She didn't have to. Knowing eyes bored right through her skull.

"The perpetual hero," TJ scoffed. "I always knew heroes were stupid. Jared's the one who believes in them."

"I'm not a hero." She raised her voice belligerently. "I'm an ex-con and an addict and probably worse. I can barely rescue myself."

"Tell that to Jared," he answered coldly. "The man never comes out of his studio anymore. He's so focused, he's scaring me. And I haven't heard him really laugh since he came home."

Cleo buried her face in her hands and tried not to listen. She couldn't do this. She was a nothing, a nobody. Jared was a brilliant artist with a future in lights and success written all over him. She'd ruin him.

He thought her a hero.

TJ interrupted her reverie with a nervous clearing of his throat. "A wise man once told me that acceptance must come from within. It's more important that you accept who you are than that others accept you."

The town had accepted her as she was, flaws and all. So had Jared. She hadn't. She didn't know if she could. But Jared expected her to.

Heart pounding erratically with an unknown rhythm she thought might be hope, Cleo lifted her head and met TJ's gaze.

"I've got to see him, don't I?"

Tim dipped his head in agreement. "I thought so."

❧ **THIRTY-SIX** ❧

"This is insane," TJ muttered as he nailed the last piece of paraphernalia to an ornate wooden molding near the ceiling.

"Tell me something I don't know." Climbing down from her ladder, Cleo glanced around the two-story foyer of the enormous McCloud Long Island mansion. If she'd thought she'd been right about letting Jared go before, she was firmly convinced now. This place reeked to high heaven of old money and aristocratic lineages. She could gag on the high-falutin' atmosphere in here. Even the Christmas tree had prissy white doves and angels instead of flashing colored lights. She bet they were all made by Lalique and trimmed in fourteen-karat gold. Her methods of decoration were guaranteed to drive Jared's uptight parents into hysteria.

She dropped the neck chain bearing an emerald ring beneath the neckline of her tunic. It had taken every ounce of courage she possessed to take this step out of her self-imposed isolation and face the terrifying consequences of emotional involvement. She didn't have to tattoo her heart on her sleeve while she was at it.

"You're planning on this blowing up in your face, aren't you?" TJ accused as he folded up his ladder and frowned upward at the foyer's newest embellishments.

He didn't seem particularly worried about going down as her accomplice.

Cleo crossed her arms. "Self-destruction is what I do best."

He shot her a wary look. "That's not a particularly heroic attitude."

She laughed shortly. "You're telling me that comic heroes leaping in front of speeding bullets aren't self-destructive?"

"Mommy," Matty shouted in glee from upstairs. "Look at the reindeer!"

Cleo glanced at her tormentor. Jared's brother deserved his place in hell for dragging her on an airplane and bringing her up here, but he'd been a good sport about taking along her eccentric decorations and sneaking her into the house at her request. It was a bit difficult to read past his impassive expression, but she had a nagging feeling that he wouldn't have taken no for an answer any more than Jared.

At her questioning look, TJ shrugged. "Jared rigged up some toy reindeer to make them dance. He doesn't have your flare with the mechanical, but one has a flashing red nose. Mother hyperventilated and banished them to the nursery."

The nursery. The blamed mansion had a nursery. "I'd better see what he's up to. Do I need a map to get there?"

He studied her for a moment, and Cleo nervously brushed glitter off her deep-green tunic, then ran her hand through her hair to see if it had fallen flat or something. She didn't belong here. She was so totally out of place that she was amazed the house didn't spit her out like bad meat, and Jared's brother had a way of disturbing her more than a fed could.

"Jared will be here any minute," he finally said. "Unless

you're having second thoughts and want to hide, you'd better stay put."

Terror did a step dance in her stomach, but she nodded. "Go away," she answered grimly, hearing the sound of a car purring to a halt in the drive.

Hearing the car at the same time, TJ grabbed their ladders and disappeared into the nether regions of the mansion. She'd been mad to think she could get away with this. Knowing her twisted mind, she'd probably thought she'd be caught before she carried it off. Jared's damned brother, on the other hand, seemed to be an expert on covert actions. He'd pulled off the whole thing with an inexorable timing that bordered on dangerous. She'd hate to have him for an enemy.

A car door slammed. She tugged her tunic down over her leggings and wished she'd worn something more upscale. At the time she'd bought these, she'd thought velvet was upscale.

Her gaze swung frantically to the door as someone inserted a key. She could hide— Nahh. She was here to prove a point.

The door swung open to her tape of "Silver Bells" played by the church bell choir. Garbed in leather jacket and looking taller and more handsome than ever, Jared halted in the doorway as a reindeer-racing Santa streaked past his face, flinging glitter behind him.

"Ultra-rad." He admired the Santa speculatively as it flew back across the foyer like clockwork.

Frozen, Cleo fixed her gaze on the heart-stopping sight of Jared's broad shoulders filling out a battered bomber jacket. With his face carved into interesting angles and planes, he looked more artistic and distant than she remembered. He'd let his hair grow, and rather than mess with it, he'd apparently pulled it back in a rubber band. Still, he couldn't disguise his cool competence and knowing eyes as he calculated Santa's arc in order to step past him. Wearing a hand-knitted fishermen's sweater beneath his jacket, he stuck his hand into the pocket of elegantly tailored wool slacks, and transferred his gaze from the chortling Santa to Cleo.

"Assault by glitter?" he asked impassively as Santa sparkled his hair with red and green and silver.

Terror filled her at his lack of reaction. This wasn't the man she remembered. Had TJ been wrong? Had she lost Jared with her recalcitrance? Had she really thought he'd always be there for her, even when she was behaving like a stupid cow?

Not if she knew Jared. She'd hurt him, and he was being wary. Somehow, she had to reach out and show him she had the strength to love him back—that she might be whole enough to love him as he should be loved. Heart in throat and hope pulsing, Cleo stepped backward, into the doorway she'd just finished decorating. "I don't do No Trespassing signs anymore. Consider yourself showered with welcome," she said cautiously, trying not to hold her breath.

His dark eyes lit with an unholy gleam as he regarded the spinning disco globe of mistletoe and her placement under it. "Even if it's rigged to explode, I still like your style."

"I'm the one likely to explode," she said darkly, watching him in exasperation.

His eyebrows quirked and a slow smile transformed his lean face as he got the message. "You've come to rescue me from purgatory?"

She widened her eyes at this description of his self-imposed exile, but she nodded agreement. "Yeah, maybe."

Crossing the gleaming parquet of the foyer in three strides, Jared swung her into his arms and captured her mouth with his.

She couldn't breathe, didn't dare breathe, for fear she dreamed the fantasy of Jared's welcoming arms hugging her, the bristles of his beard rubbing her cheeks, the heated hunger of desire on his tongue. She dug her fingers into the leather of his jacket, clinging for dear life as her head spun like a Christmas top.

He kissed her until both their heads spun, or the insanely flashing strobe light from the spinning mistletoe made them dizzy.

Laughing, Jared stumbled, and broke the kiss rather than fall over. Filled with the bliss of knowing she'd actually cared enough to abandon her personal prison for him, he swung her in a circle with more glee than he'd felt since he'd been six and discovered a walking, talking robot under the tree.

When he finally returned her to her feet, she nervously tugged on a gold chain at her throat, a chain bearing *his* ring, he noted smugly. Needing to touch, he ran his hand through the glimmering red of her . . . curls? He glanced down to verify this fascinating phenomenon. She glared back, and his tension melted away. All was well with his world when Cleo glared. He knew how to make her really smolder.

He sobered quickly as he read the uncertainty in her gaze. "Are you ready to admit I'm man enough to handle you and your life?" he asked quietly. Too many people had underestimated him for too long. He needed Cleo to believe in him.

"Put that way . . ." She slid her hand into his and studied him through troubled eyes. "I don't doubt your ability to leap tall buildings in a single bound. It's me that's the problem."

"Not from my viewpoint, Cleo." Jared gently clasped the ring and held it up between them. "I won't stop loving you if you throw pinecones at me or wear your porcupine shirt. Would you give up on me if I lost my job or my money?"

"I might consider it if you lost your mind. I'm kind of fond of fractured brains." She tried to tug the necklace back, but more confident now, he wouldn't let go. She quit fighting and stood there staring at him, looking lost and vulnerable. "But how would I know if you lost it? You're already crazy."

A grin tugged the corner of his mouth as he recognized her dilemma. She simply couldn't admit she was soft putty at heart. "You don't want to say it, do you?" he taunted. "It's killing you to admit you feel anything. I love you, Cleo." He backed her up against the door frame. "I'm gonna love you until the end of time." He kissed her temple and wrapped her curls around his fingers. "I'm gonna show up on your doorstep night and day if you don't admit you love me. I'll sing serenades beneath your window. I'll camp on your beach." He planted another kiss beneath her earlobe and was rewarded with a gasp.

"You have all this," she said in bewilderment, drawing reluctantly away to gesture at their elegant surroundings. "You have more talent in your little finger than I'll ever have in my whole life. Why would you want me holding you back?"

He sobered and dropped the necklace to stroke her pale cheek. "You still don't understand, do you?" No longer hidden behind tinted glasses, her eyes studied him with wariness and a prayer, waiting for the reassurances she needed, that he willingly gave.

Maybe he hadn't done it right the first time. For a moment, he feared he wouldn't do it right again.

"You freed me, Cleo," he murmured, touching her, for he couldn't not touch her, not while she was finally here, the best gift he'd ever been given. He repeated her gesture to indicate their surroundings. "All this traps me behind the iron bars of expectations. I'm not allowed to fail. I can't explore new paths, try new things, for fear that I won't live up to my success, but I can be Jared McCloud, comic artist, only so long. Then I'm expected to climb higher, become Jared McCloud, screenwriter, Jared McCloud, director, producer, superstar, whatever. I have to follow the road someone else tells me to follow." His hand slipped away, but he held her gaze. "I want to choose my own road."

The hunger flaring in her eyes showed she understood. "I'm a badly beaten path," she murmured in protest.

"A beautiful, unexplored jungle," he countered, relaxing now that they were both on the same wavelength. "But you won't expect me to be Tarzan or to mow down the jungle and create palaces. You'll let me run the beach, and inspire me to create new worlds, and you won't complain if those worlds don't suit your image of profitable."

She shot him a look of scorn. "Your talent should be for the good of all, not just the good of someone's wallet. Even I can see that. TJ showed me your film. It's *good*, Jared. Don't you dare give up that kind of work because it won't make millions."

"My damned spy of a brother must have stolen the copy, but I'll forgive him—this time." Love lightened his heart, and he smiled. "Cleo, my knight in battered armor, I don't need you to rescue me—or sacrifice yourself for my sake. Not any more than you need a superhero to sacrifice himself for you. That's not what love is about. Couldn't we just amble along the yellow brick road together and see where it takes us?"

"Only if I can be the tin man." Enhanced by the emerald of her velvet tunic, Cleo's eyes began to gleam with amusement and—he hoped—with a little more freedom from the heavy burdens love had laid on her shoulders in the past.

"You have a heart, idiot," he reminded her. "You just need to quit sitting on it." Gently, Jared unclasped her necklace, removed the ring, and taking her hand in his, slipped the emerald on her finger. "Tell me yes, Cleo. Don't make me beg."

Provocatively, she slipped a finger between her lips, tilted her head, and studied him. "I don't think I'll ever be one of the self-indulgent rich. You aren't planning on being rich, are you?"

Jared grabbed a fistful of luscious curls, wishing he could kiss her until they fell into bed and woke up married. "Depends," he answered warily. "I just sold the film for a hefty advance and a nice percentage of everything, but there's this foundation I want to fund for teenagers from dysfunctional homes . . ."

Her smile relaxed into a look of love so heartrending that he almost hauled her into his arms and carried her up the stairs right there and then.

"Like you know anything about dysfunctional," she scoffed, sliding her hands beneath his jacket collar and circling his neck.

"You could teach me," he promised. "And I'll tell you I love you before I murder you. Is that sufficiently dysfunctional?"

"Only if you remember I love you when I'm screaming at you," she agreed, kissing his cheek.

"You won't scream at me. You'll be too busy purring." Jared covered Cleo's mouth with his, and she did. Purr.

Damn, but his life had just taken a comic book turn for the better.

❧ EPILOGUE ❧

Fourth of July, South Carolina

A roar of delight resounded over the gentle lapping of tide as the flames of a bonfire ignited to sear the night sky. A straw caricature of a pirate cackled and attempted to jump the blaze, only to explode into a dozen red and gold firework stars to the sound of laughter. Unable to resist a publicly sanctioned riot, teenagers raced laughingly down the beach, setting off firecrackers to add to the tumult.

Watching two of the teens roll to the sand in a wrestling match, Jared caught Cleo's shoulder and prevented her rising from the blanket. "He's fine, Cleo. Boys let out their energies in more physical ways than girls."

"Their testosterone, you mean," she replied, curling her legs back under her again. With a sigh, she relaxed her stiff stance and rested her head against his shoulder when he wrapped his arm around her. "I suppose it's a fair trade. Kismet is so easy, Gene has to balance it out."

Jared chuckled. "If you think Kismet is easy, you can have her. That girl has a mind of her own and there's no moving her once she's made it up. Once she heard about that art school, she's been determined to get into it, even though I told her she really needs a college degree and that drawing dragons doesn't guarantee her a job."

338

Cleo shrugged. "Give her knowledge, and she'll find her own way." She glanced at a shadow emerging from the wooded path at the far end of the beach. "It would help both of them if Linda stayed clean for a while."

Jared watched Linda's uncertain gait stumble across the sand in their direction. Heels, he decided, not alcohol. "I can't believe they let her out already. I'd have kept her locked up until the kids are grown."

"You'd have kept me locked up until Matty was grown?" she countered. "That's helpful. It's a disease, McCloud, a sickness. It needs treatment and support and understanding, and yeah, I want to slap her around, too, but it's a waste of energy."

She pulled from Jared's grasp and stood up to meet Linda halfway. Unable to let her face her demons alone, Jared loped after her, hovering just beyond Cleo's shoulder as the two women met on the outskirts of the party.

"They said I could see my kids," Linda said without preamble. "I just wanta know they're okay." She glanced somewhat wistfully toward the laughing crowd around the bonfire. "But I guess they're too busy to see me right now."

"They'll know you're here. Teenagers prefer to pretend their parents don't exist in public, but they like knowing you care enough to check on them. Are you taking that job the plumbing company offered?"

Nervously opening and closing her fingers, watching the antics around the fire rather than face Cleo, Linda nodded. "They said they'd send me to computer class."

Jared waited for her to thank Cleo for talking the company into risking their time and money on an addict, but Linda didn't broach the subject. Maybe it was understood between the two of them. He'd never fathom women. He'd thought he'd understood when he was younger, but he was older and wiser now. He didn't know a damned thing.

"Did the caseworker tell you how soon you can have the kids back?"

Linda ran her hand through her newly shorn hair and nodded. "If I stay on the job and keep clean for the next six weeks, I can have them on weekends. They're not taking any chances."

Jared damned well hoped they weren't. If Billy-Bob Pervert hadn't been sent up for a dozen years, he'd have personally gone into Social Services and had the kids removed from the county. Despite her cynicism, Cleo wanted to give everyone a second and third chance. He loved Cleo's generous spirit, but he'd developed a strong need to protect the innocent since encountering her and her choice of friends. He stroked the nape of her neck now as she shifted uncomfortably, uncertain of what to say next.

"Look who's coming down the road." Jared nodded toward a stout figure striding across the bridge they'd erected over the sheriff's excavations in the dune. "Linda, you might want to find yourself something to eat over at the tables. Our legal beagle just arrived."

Linda glanced nervously at the portly lawyer and sidled away. Jared continued to massage Cleo's neck as she stiffened up again. "Easy, kid. He's on your side, remember? I can't believe you argued with him over his bill after he got the feds off your case. He made you a free woman."

"Yeah, just as I was getting kinda fond of writing insults in my journal. I'll miss that creep counselor. Now I've got to find new ways to get my jollies. Look, he's not even coming over here. He's heading right for Axell and Maya."

"I can't imagine why." Jared led her back toward the blanket. He had other plans for this evening, and talking to obnoxious lawyers wasn't one of them. "How could he resist getting his head bit off by my acid-tongued wife instead of schmoozing with a woman who laughs at his jokes, pats his arm, and floats away?"

Cleo punched his arm, and Jared caught her in a choke hold so he could plant a kiss on her forehead. She stood on tiptoe, and bending backward, gave him an upside-down kiss. This was more like it. He turned her around to do this from a better angle, but a dry voice interrupted his best intentions.

"I took a look at the bones that have been uncovered so far," TJ said in his usual no-nonsense manner, waiting until he had their attention before continuing. "I want to head an exploratory study on that site. I don't think it's a settler's grave site."

"Can you keep the damned tourists out?" Cleo demanded. "One of them will break their neck out there looking for pirate gold."

"Chain link and barbed wire," he agreed, shoving his hands in his pockets. "I'll need a place to stay."

Jared met Cleo's eyes, read her answer in her softening expression. She was a sucker for wounded souls, and TJ was more wounded than she knew. With a sigh of exasperation, he kissed her as payment for her agreement. Then he lifted his head and glared at his brother. "We're adding a wing to the main house that should be done soon. You can have the beach house then, if you like, but you'll have to find some way of protecting your gear if a hurricane comes along."

"We need to get busy protecting the site in case one comes along before then. I'll talk to a few people." He strode off without a word of thanks.

As bad as Linda, Jared decided. He glared at his beaming wife. "We're gonna start a zoo out here, aren't we? All the nutcases in the world unite."

"Reptiles are my specialty." She stuck out her tongue at him.

With Cleo, that could be interpreted as a come-on, and Jared grinned.

Matty's cries of delight echoed over the pounding surf, and they both turned to see what he was doing. A rowdy game of chicken volleyball had formed along the water's edge, and Matty was perched on Gene's shoulders, swinging his fists with all his might at the soaring ball. The ball sailed into the water, far out-of-bounds. The golden retriever Jared had bought for him dashed into the water after it. He'd thought the kid deserved one normal pet, but the dog had developed a penchant for hanging out with potbellied pigs. The pig squealed and trotted into the lapping surf after his pal.

"I don't think it can get any better than this." Cleo sighed contentedly, leaning back against his chest. "I keep waiting for the storm to break over my head."

"I'll drag you to shelter." Jared slid the hand circling her waist upward to caress her breast. Despite the distractions, he'd had only one thing on his mind all evening. Maybe now was the time to broach it. "You've got friends and family now, Cleo. You're safe. Bad things may happen, but you won't be alone to handle them. Are you ready to accept that yet?"

She reached behind her to pull his head down for a kiss. He loved the way she expressed herself. She did it with body and soul as much as language. But kisses weren't all he had in mind tonight. He pulled away, waiting for a better answer.

"I'm still trying to accept that you're willing to live

here and not L.A." As if she'd read his mind, she curled her fingers in his hair, refusing to let him go. "They're dubbing Hollywood voices to your project as we speak. How can you not want to be there?"

He shrugged. "They've paid me good money for that film. They're the best in the business. If they can't do it right, how could I make a difference? I've got my priorities straight. I'm afraid you haven't married a workaholic, love. You're stuck with a beach bum cartoonist."

"I love my beach bum cartoonist. Don't you think Maya can handle the kids for the rest of the evening? They have a nanny looking out for the baby and nothing better to do."

Jared laughed. That would be the day when her sister didn't have anything to do. She was probably the one who had started the volleyball game. Motherhood had never slowed her down. But Cleo was on the same track as he was, and he'd give her the point.

"Speaking of babies . . ." He kissed her neck and fondled her breast, feeling her arousal as keenly as his own. "Do you think we might consider making one of our own someday?"

He held his breath as she moaned softly under his ministrations and wriggled closer. He hadn't realized how much this meant to him until now. He wanted to experience all of life, and this seemed a necessary next step.

"The old biological clock ticking, McCloud?" she teased. "Afraid you won't be able to produce on schedule?"

"I want a baby with green eyes like yours and Matty's," he whispered against her ear. "A redheaded monster to scream the night away. How can I write about kids unless I have one of my own?"

He could feel laughter vibrating in her chest. She wasn't bolting from him in horror. It was a subject they should have discussed long ago, but they'd been over-whelmed by all the other problems, and he'd just wanted his ring on her finger before confronting any new ones.

"What if I can't have more?" she asked. "Maybe Matty was a fluke. Maybe I'll be a failure at this parenting business."

He released her waist and tugged her toward the beach house. "If you're a failure at parenting, then the whole world is in trouble, because there isn't a better mother on the planet. And if we can't make babies on our own, I'm sure we'll find others along the way. There seem to be plenty of kids out there. I just like the idea of *making* them."

She laughed, a crystal-clear tinkling of music over the sounds of voices and surf. Several heads turned their way, but they returned to their activities when they noted Jared's direction. The beach house was only yards away.

"*I* like the idea of *making* them," she mocked. "It's the *minding* of them that requires a superhero. Ready for that responsibility, Superman?"

Jared caught her by the waist and hauled her into his arms, carrying her up the last few steps of the porch and into the house. He nuzzled her neck through her screams of laughter, his heart pumping ferociously at the thought of the night ahead. The primitive need to procreate had conquered his imagination.

"I'm not the superhero here," he murmured, dropping her to her feet and pushing her toward the stairs to their room. "I'm not the one who can carry a ten-pound bowling ball around inside me for nine months, and I'm not the one willing to suffer the pains of childbirth in return for a screaming bundle of gas and liquids. I'm simply the lackey willing to run out for chocolate pistachio caramel ice cream in the middle of the night at the request of my superior."

Cleo raced up the stairs, laughing, and flopped backward into the nest of their wide bed. "Will you do it in the rain?" she demanded. "Will you do it in a hurricane? Will you, will you, Superman?"

Kicking off his sandals and dropping his shirt on the floor, Jared fell on top of her, catching his weight on his hands as he smothered her face in kisses. "If we're really good, maybe we can beat the hurricane season. Otherwise, I'll have to buy a yacht. I'm not trying that helicopter stunt in a hurricane."

"Supercomic," she whispered against his scratchy beard, taking his face in her hands and holding him still to kiss him. "I'd have heart failure if you took to the skies. Give me your baby, and I promise to love him with all the love in me. That's the best offer I can make."

"Her," he insisted. "I want a green-eyed witch. We already have a son to spoil."

Tears spilled from the corner of her eyes, running into the red curls at her temple as she hugged him tightly. "I don't deserve you," she murmured. "But Matty does," she finished firmly, before he could argue.

"When you're big and round and cranky with my child, you'll think differently," he answered confidently. "Until then, fine, I'm easy. I'll be Supercomic, and you can be X-Lady, capable of stomping wrongs in a single bound."

She giggled, and Jared took that as a signal to continue on the path toward his goal. As he slipped the buttons from his wife's shirt, and felt her hips surge eagerly against him, he didn't think he'd have any problem focusing on his objective this time. X-Lady's powerful magnetism held him firmly on a righteous path, but he suspected that path might include a curve or two to keep things interesting. As far as he was concerned, that made life almost perfect.

As a glowing mechanical Tinkerbell soared across the

dusk near the ceiling, Cleo reached for the elastic waist-
band of his swimsuit. March, he calculated. He'd be
SuperDaddy in March.

Laughter spilled from the direction of the bonfire, but
the occupants of the beach house had flames of their own
to entertain them.

Don't miss Patricia Rice's next historical romance

MUST BE MAGIC

Part of the "Magic Series" that began
with *Merely Magic*

Coming in August 2002

From Signet

ONE

"He's mine," Lady Leila Staines announced, studying the imposing man who stood at the entrance to the ballroom, scowling at the guests as if deciding whose head he would sever first.

Leila's sister Christina drew in a sharp breath as she followed her gaze. "*Dunstan Ives?* Don't be absurd. He's an Ives and a *murderer*."

Fascinated, Leila watched the formidable gentleman dressed entirely in black except for the immaculate white cravat at his throat. This Ives could put her world back on course. She had to have him. "He's not a murderer; Ninian says so."

"He could snap your neck with a flick of his wrist," Christina whispered, watching with fascinated horror as Dunstan's companions were announced. "Look, his aura is black as night!"

Ignoring her younger sister, Leila observed the entrance of angelic Ninian beside her handsome husband, Drogo, Earl of Ives and Wystan, but Leila's gaze followed the towering man who was now dissociating himself from his companions by lingering behind them. Both Ives men exhibited their scorn of society with their sun-darkened visages and lack of powdered wigs. The lean earl possessed an air of intellect and refinement, but his broader brother glowered with hostility as he scanned the glittering throng. In his tailored coat, with shoulders broad and strong as those of an ox, Dunstan Ives made the rest of the lace-and-silk bedecked company appear effeminate.

"I don't know about his aura, but his clothes are certainly unfashionably black," Leila observed as she studied the brooding looks and powerful physique of the man she meant to proposition. He was definitely not the usual sort of London gentleman. But then, Ives men never were.

"He must still wear black for his wife," Christina murmured. "I suppose if he did not murder her, that would be tragically romantic."

"If he ever loved her, he fell out of it," their cousin Lucinda said, joining them to hear this last. "Of course, one shouldn't assume his lack of love means he intended harm," she added.

Since Celia Ives had been murdered most violently over a year ago, Leila knew her cousin hastened to correct any impression that Dunstan might have had something to do with his wife's death. Lucinda possessed a gift for revealing true character through her paintings, and people tended to pay particular attention to even her most casual comments. She was careful, therefore, not to misstate her opinion and leave the wrong impression. Like all Malcolms, she had acquired a keen sense of responsibility along with her gifts.

Gifts that Leila still didn't possess. All her life, Leila had searched for a similar gift in herself, but she had never discovered the magic that would prove her a Malcolm. Still, even with her limited perception, she could see that the arrogant man standing in the doorway despised the parrot colors of fashion and wore black out of disdain for the society over which she prevailed. Love had nothing to do with it.

He was an Ives, after all—cold and unfeeling.

Fanning herself as she admired his stature, Leila thought of her own dark attire and smiled faintly. They were soul mates in matters of dress at least. Black gave her an authority her age did not, and it set her apart from the common herd so she might better wield that authority. She was smart, as her mother had always said. She'd focused her intelligence on understanding society, and applied what she learned to make a place for herself and her late husband in fashionable circles.

At least she'd made her husband happy.

What her intelligence couldn't master was what her family did without effort: see beyond the obvious, dabble in the supernatural, and help those around them through those gifts. All her life, Leila had been excluded from the whispered consultations of her younger siblings and cousins, simply because she could not see or hear what they could. Behind her, she could hear Christina and Lucinda whispering about their insights into Dunstan's character. Despite knowing everyone in this room, she stood alone, the solitary cuckoo in her family's nest.

Until she discovered some special ability in herself and proved she was a Malcolm, she would always feel incomplete, a failure.

She'd spent her entire life doing what her family expected of her. She'd married well, raised her husband's social and political standing, acquired wealth, made others happy if not herself. Widowed now, finally free of all expectations, she stood on the brink of opportunity, if she only possessed the courage to take the risk. With the help of an Ives, she might discover who she really was and what she could accomplish.

Leila allowed a tendril of hope to creep through her

usual restraint as she watched the commanding man in the doorway. Nervously, she waved her fan, bouncing a loose pincurl in the breeze. After a year of planning and dreaming, she'd made her choice. All she need do now was approach Dunstan Ives and state her proposal. Even if he was immune to her charm, he should succumb to her monetary largesse, and then she would have England's most learned agronomist at her disposal.

"He's an Ives," Lucinda whispered in warning, apparently noting the direction of Leila's gaze. "Don't forget what happened to cousin Ninian."

Leila was aware of the danger Ives men posed to women, and to Malcolm women in particular. The attraction between them must be as powerful as legend said if even Ninian had risked disaster to fall for one of the logical, passionless men. But Leila was prepared to take her chances with the fire of physical attraction. Although men habitually flocked around her, she had never felt passion for them in return.

Her only dilemma lay in whether she dared retire to the country in the company of a man whose adulterous wife had been found with her neck snapped. No evidence confirmed Dunstan's guilt. None confirmed his innocence, either.

Leila offered a practiced trill of laughter at her cousin's warning. "I seduce men, not the other way around. An Ives is no match for me."

"Leila, you cannot tell what he's feeling as Ninian can," Christina warned. "He looks incredibly dangerous."

"Shall I go closer and see what I can learn?" Leila snapped her fan closed, and forgetting everyone else in the room besides the Ives, left her sister and cousin.

Progressing through the crowd of London's wealthiest and most powerful, she stopped often to meet and greet her guests, never losing sight of the man she intended to trap in her net. *Mother of goddesses,* but he was built like a mountain, a smoldering one. She chattered and exchanged mindless gossip, but she couldn't look away as Dunstan Ives glared at a footman and ended up with two glasses of champagne in his huge fists.

"Isn't that the Ives who murdered his wife?" one countess whispered. "Honestly, Leila, even *you* can't expect us to acknowledge a murderer!"

"Dear, dear Betsy." Leila patted the woman's gloved hand without paying her much notice. "I invited your current lover, the father of your son, and your husband, and I'm still speaking to all four of you. Be a good girl, and don't spoil my fun."

She left the rouged and powdered countess with her mouth open.

"He looks as if he might murder someone any minute," Hermione, Marchioness of Hampton, murmured worriedly, sidling up to Leila and fiddling with the gossamer scarf about her throat. "I cannot think why you invited him."

"Because he is the best agronomist in all of England," Leila assured her mother. "Even Father says so. Since Dunstan has come to work for him, the estate has improved tremendously, is that not so?"

"Yes, but your father is a *man,* dear. It is not at all the same thing. I do wish you would reconsider offering him a position."

"But the opportunity is perfect," Leila explained. "You know Father means to put Rolly in charge of the Gloucestershire estate. Rolly loathes Dunstan, says he does not take orders well. Why should I let Rolly drive him away when *I* can have him?" Leila did not slow her progress across the drawing room. Tugging at shawls and scarves, her mother trailed in her wake.

"Leila, you know nothing of these things—"

"Ninian does, and she says he's innocent." Ninian was years younger than Leila, but she possessed a gift of empathy and a talent for healing that had saved lives and fortunes—including Drogo's. Ninian was the one her whole family turned to because she *understood* things without being told. Leila bowed to her greater gifts, even as envy devoured her.

"You know perfectly well that Ninian is not herself when she's in town with so many people around to disturb her gift," Hermione whispered. "She could be wrong about Dunstan . . ."

"I'm not changing my mind, *Maman*," Leila said. "He's mine."

A sensual shiver rippled down her spine as she repeated those words at the same moment that Dunstan turned his brooding gaze on her, and the implication of her arrogant declaration raised its serpent head.

She wanted an agricultural expert, not a lover, but Dunstan's hooded dark eyes and prominent nose stirred long-dormant feelings in her. Uneasy with the sensation, she reminded herself that no man had *ever* wielded the power to tempt her.

Safe behind a shield of indifference, Leila brushed a kiss on Ninian's cheek. "How good of you to come." Murmuring polite nonsense, she flirted with the impervious Drogo, then turned the full brunt of her attention on Dunstan, standing slightly distant from his family.

Oh, my. His presence hit her with all the force of her mother's candles scented for seduction.

"Black becomes you, sir," she murmured, drawing her black-gloved finger down Dunstan's lapel, resorting to her practiced role of flirt to hide the sensual impact of this man. Was it her imagination, or did his air of disdain conceal a slight whiff of loneliness? Perhaps his lack of artificial scent distorted her perceptions. Fascinating.

"Black's not fashionable," he replied, staring past her powdered curls.

"So flattering of you to mention that." She immediately retracted any sympathy she might have mistakenly offered. "Shall I run upstairs and slip into something more to your liking? In red, perhaps?"

Dunstan glanced down at her wide, black skirts, then focused his gaze on the expanse of bosom exposed by her low-cut gown. "Scarlet seems appropriate."

With the lady's sensual perfume of roses and jasmine wafting around him, Dunstan noticed she stood taller than most, reaching past his chin in her heeled shoes. She wore a lacy black cap over tight, powdered curls that accentuated her rouged lips and darkened lashes. Despite the starchy powder, he knew she was a Malcolm, and had silken blond hair like all the rest of her kind, along with eyes that could ensnare and bewitch. He refused to look into them.

Nodding curtly in dismissal, ignoring Ninian and Drogo, Dunstan spun on his heel and strode blindly for what he hoped was the card room.

The lady's exotic perfume clung to his senses as he departed, and raw hunger clawed at his insides—

It had been that way with Celia.

Never again. *He'd put a bullet through his ear before he became enthralled with another aristocratic, conniving female again.*

Look for these wonderful novels by Patricia Rice

Nobody's Angel

Adrian Quinn trusts no one. Four years in prison will do that to a man—especially when he's innocent. Adrian feels someone owes him the truth and not to mention a fortune he desperately needs to live on. His late partner's ex and very spoiled wife is the first person he'll look to. She ruined his life and now he'll return the favor.

Faith Nicholls escaped from her two-timing husband right after he shattered her dreams and left her with nothing. Yet, she made a fresh start in a quiet town where nobody knows her name...until Adrian Quinn shows up, dredging up dangerous secrets and awakening smoldering passions—and making her believe in love again.

Published by Ivy Books.
Available at bookstores everywhere.

IMPOSSIBLE DREAMS

Maya Alyssum's impossible dream is to open a school where kids can find unconditional love and acceptance, the very things she never had as a child. The town council of Wadeville, North Carolina, is determined to stop her until the day Axell Holm walks into her life. He's the kind of uptight authority figure she loves to hate. . .and hates to love.

Axell knows trouble when he sees it. But he needs the ethereal schoolteacher and the magic she works on his motherless daughter. He's willing to face the wrath of his hometown to get what he wants, but he's unprepared for his reaction to this strange and wonderful woman who turns his ordered life upside down, making him believe in dreams again. . . .

Published by Ivy Books.
Available at bookstores everywhere.

VOLCANO

After landing in gorgeous St. Lucia on business, Penelope Albright receives the shock of her life: She is accused of smuggling drugs. Then a sexy stranger appears, claiming to be her husband, and "kidnaps" her before trouble begins. Or so she thinks. Trouble and Charlie Smith have met. He needs a wife—temporarily—to help him keep a low profile while snooping into the mysterious disappearance of his partner. And like it or not, Penny is already involved.

Published by Fawcett Books.
Available at bookstores everywhere.

BLUE CLOUDS

Around the small California town where Pippa Cochran has fled to escape an abusive boyfriend, Seth Wyatt is called the Grim Reaper—and not just because he is a bestselling author of horror novels. He's an imposing presence, battling more inner demons than even an indefatigable woman like Pippa can handle. Yet, while in his employ, she can't resist the emotional pull of his damaged son or the chance to hide in the fortress he calls a home.

Then Pippa's amazing gifts begin to alter their world in ways none of them could have imagined. But soon something goes wrong. Dangerous "accidents" occur, threatening to destroy the tremulous new love that Pippa and Seth have dared to discover.

Published by Fawcett Books.
Available at bookstores everywhere.

GARDEN OF DREAMS

JD Marshall is a computer programming genius on the run to protect his company, his teenage son, and his life. When JD's truck flips over near the tiny backwoods town of Madrid, Kentucky, Miss Nina Toon comes to his rescue and offers him and his son shelter.

The lovely and lovelorn Nina, a high school teacher with very little experience with men, finds herself intrigued by the gorgeous, longhaired, motorcycle-riding computer nerd sleeping downstairs. Opening her home and her heart and her most precious dreams to JD, Nina decides to take a chance on love. But it will be the biggest gamble of her life. . . .

Published by Fawcett Books.
Available at bookstores everywhere.